KENT HARUF

WHERE YOU ONCE BELONGED

Kent Haruf's *The Tie That Binds* received a Whiting Foundation Award and a special citation from the PEN/Hemingway Foundation. He is also the author of *Plainsong*, a finalist for the National Book Award, and *Eventide*. He lives with his wife, Cathy, in Colorado.

ALSO BY KENT HARUF

The Tie That Binds

Plainsong

Eventide

WHERE YOU ONCE BELONGED

A Novel

KENT HARUF

VINTAGE CONTEMPORARIES

Vintage Books

A Division of Random House, Inc.

New York

FIRST VINTAGE CONTEMPORARIES EDITION, MAY 2000

Part of this book was published in different form in *Grand Street* and
Best American Short Stories 1987. It's a pleasure to acknowledge the
generous support given me by the Whiting Foundation.

Library of Congress Cataloging-in-Publication Data on file.

Vintage ISBN: 0-375-70870-7

Author photograph © Cathy Haruf

www.vintagebooks.com

Printed in the United States of America

20 19 18 17 16 15 14 13 12

For three Elizabeths:

Sorel, Whitney, and Chaney

PART ONE

· 1 ·

In the end Jack Burdette came back to Holt after all. None of us expected it anymore. He had been gone for eight years and no one in Holt had heard anything about him in that time. The police themselves had stopped looking for him. They had traced his movements to California, but after he had entered Los Angeles they had lost him and finally they had given it up. Thus in the fall of 1985, so far as anyone in Holt knew, Burdette was still there. He was still in California and we had almost forgotten him.

Then late on a Saturday afternoon at the beginning of November he appeared in Holt once more.

He was driving a red Cadillac now. It was not a new car; he had bought it soon after he left town when he still had money to spend. Nevertheless it was still flashy, the kind of automobile you might expect a Denver pimp or a just-made oil millionaire in Casper, Wyoming, would drive. There was all that red paint—the color of a raw bruise, say, or the vivid smear of a woman's lipstick on a Saturday night—and all of it was shining, gleaming under the sun, looking as though he had spent an entire day polishing it for our benefit.

He drove this car, this affront and outrage to the entire town

if we had known in the beginning who was driving it, drove it
through Holt on Highway 34 and then turned around at the city
limits and came back and drove north up Main Street past the
water tower and the bank and the post office and the Holt
Theater, and finally parked it on Main Street in the middle of town
and didn't get out. Instead, for the rest of that afternoon and on
into the evening, he sat there as if he were waiting for something:
waiting and smoking cigarettes and spitting out through the
rolled-down side window onto the pavement and only now and
then shifting in the front seat to relieve the pressure of the steering
wheel against his gut. I suppose he thought someone in town
would say something to him. But no one did. Not at first. They
did not even seem to recognize him. For at least an hour his former
townsmen merely passed along in front of him, shopping, going
in and out of the stores on Saturday afternoon as usual, without
once stopping to speak or even to pause very long to look at the
Cadillac to see who owned it.

Eventually someone did think to call the sheriff, though. This
was Ralph Bird, who owns the Men's Store.

About four-thirty that afternoon Ralph Bird looked out
through the front display window of the Men's Store and noticed
the red Cadillac across the street in front of the tavern. He did
not think much about it at first. Pheasant season had begun and
there were strange vehicles in town anyway. Thirty minutes later,
though, when he looked across the street a second time he saw
that the car was still there, with the man he had seen earlier still
sitting alone in the front seat, and that bothered him. He began
to study the car. There was nothing familiar about it. But after
a minute or two he believed he detected something recognizable
about the man inside. He turned and called to his wife at the back
of the store.

"Hey," he said. "Come out here a minute."

"What do you want?"

·

"Come out here."

Hannah Bird came out from the storeroom where she'd been working among the ranks of wooden shelves. She was a tall thin woman with hair dyed a dark shade of red. She stood in the doorway brushing the hair out of her eyes. "What do you want?" she said. "I'm trying to get these shoe boxes put away."

"Look at this," Bird said.

"At what?"

"This car. See that guy inside?"

She walked to the front of the store. "I see him."

"What do you think about him?"

"I don't think anything about him."

"Keep looking."

She looked out through the display window again. Presently while she watched, the bloated-looking man in the front seat of the shiny car turned his head to spit and now she could see the side of his face. Hannah Bird recognized him at once.

"Now don't you do anything, Ralph," she said. "You leave that man alone."

"Sure," Bird said. "I thought it was him."

"But don't you bother him. You don't have any idea what that man might do."

"He still owes me money."

"I don't care. You let the police handle this."

Ralph Bird didn't listen to her. His wife put her hand on his arm as if she meant to control him, to hold him there by force, but he brushed her hand away as though it were no more than store lint. He opened the door and stepped outside.

"Ralph," she cried. "Ralph. You come back here, Ralph."

Along the street it had begun to grow chill and raw. The mercury lights had come on at the street corners and there was a little breeze starting up along the pavement. Bird looked up and down Main Street; it was nearly empty of people; then he

stepped off the curb and crossed the street toward Burdette's
red Cadillac. When he reached it he stopped for a moment to
study the plates. The plates showed that the car had been
licensed in California. Then he moved along the side toward
the driver's door. He peered in. Burdette was staring back at
him through the open window.

But Burdette looked bad now. In the eight years since Bird
or any one of us had seen him he'd changed for the worse. He
was fat now, obese; he was sloppy and excessive; his head had
grown bald and the flesh hung on him like suet. "It was like," Bird
would say later, "like for eight years he'd been feeding on cream
pie and pork steak and lately he hadn't fed at all." Still it was Jack
Burdette.

"You son of a bitch," Bird said. "What are you doing back
here?"

"That you, Bird?"

"Yeah. It's me."

"I seen you in the mirror. Only I had about decided you
wasn't going to speak to me. I thought you just wanted to admire
this car."

"I'll speak to you," Bird said. "I'll speak to Bud Sealy too."

Burdette stared at Bird, then he laughed once, loud, harsh.
So his laugh hadn't changed at all; it was the same sudden
explosion that everyone remembered.

"That's right," Bird told him. "Go ahead. Enjoy it. You still
got a few minutes."

"Why's that? Because you already told Bud Sealy I was here?"

"No. Because I'm going to."

"Go ahead, then. I ain't going nowhere. And you can tell
Bud—" Burdette seemed to think. He spat once more out the
window into the street, this time onto the pavement at Bird's feet.
"You can tell him I'm looking forward to seeing him."

"You son of a bitch," Bird said. "You goddamn—"

Then abruptly Ralph Bird stopped talking. He moved away from the car and began to walk up the street toward the corner. He turned once and looked back, then he began to trot. By the time he reached the corner he was running. At Second Street he turned and ran east toward the courthouse a block away. He ran on, his arms pumping, a small dapper middle-aged man in suit and tie, running along the dark sidewalk past the storefronts and the brick facades, and then across Albany Street and up the court-house steps.

At the top of the steps the light in the main hallway shone out through the glass doors onto the concrete, but the doors were locked and he stood for a moment in a panic, rattling the doors and pounding on the glass. Finally it occurred to him that it was late Saturday afternoon. So he turned and stumbled back down the steps and immediately began to run again, along the high brick wall of the courthouse toward the corner of the building and then around it and along the sidewalk toward a red light above another door. This door was unlocked and he threw it open and ran down a flight of stairs to the basement. In the first office off the hallway he found Dale Willard, Holt County deputy sheriff, sitting at a desk with his feet up. Willard was clipping his fingernails.

"Where's Bud?" Bird cried. He stood panting at the counter.

Willard looked up at him.

"Where's Bud Sealy?"

"He's not here."

"I can see that. Where is he?"

"Right now? He's at home eating his supper."

"Then Jesus Christ, get him on the phone. Tell him to get over here."

Willard allowed his feet to drop from the desktop and slowly he sat up in the chair. He leaned forward and began to brush the fingernail clippings from his shirtfront onto the green blotter on the desk. He was making a neat pile. "Something bothering you, Ralph?" he said. "You sound a little excited."

"What?" Bird said.

He was still standing behind the office counter, panting and sweating, his face as red as beets and his eyes looking as though they belonged in the head of an alarmed poodle.

"Excited? Listen. By god, if you ain't going to call him, at least reach me that phone so I can. What's his number?"

"No. I imagine I can call him myself," Willard said. "Soon's I know there's a reason to call him. Soon's I have some idea what the hell you're talking about."

"What I'm talking about?" Bird said. But he was shouting now. "I'll tell you what——" Then he seemed to catch himself; he appeared to make an effort to be calm. But it didn't quite work, so that he began to speak now to Willard as though he were addressing an idiot. "What I'm talking about," he said, talking too slowly, "is how that son of a bitch is back in town. That's what I'm talking about. Now call him."

"Sure. But which son of a bitch is that, Ralph?"

"What? You mean you——"

"I mean you haven't said yet."

"Well it's Jack Burdette. Jesus Christ, you've at least heard of him, haven't you? You know who he is, don't you?"

"Yes. I know who Jack Burdette is."

"And you know what he did, don't you?"

"I know what he did. Everyone in Holt County knows what he did."

"Then call Bud Sealy. Goddamn it. Here that——" But again he was shouting. The momentary restraint he had managed to place on himself had disappeared and so he was shouting once more, his face inflamed and outraged above the loosened tie. "Here that son of a bitch is back in town again and he's driving a red Cadillac with California plates. And he's got it parked out in front of the Holt Tavern and if you don't quit asking me these goddamn questions and get up off your fat——"

"That'll do," Willard said. He stood up and leaned toward Bird. "Shut your goddamn mouth."

"—he's going to— What?" Bird said. "What'd you just say?"

"I said, 'Shut your goddamn mouth.' Now go over there and sit down. I'll let you know if I want anything more out of you. In the meantime keep your mouth shut."

Ralph Bird was astonished almost into peace by this. He was not used to being talked to in this way; it made him quiet. He sat down in a chair in the corner and folded his hands like a child. But his eyes were still wild.

Willard stood watching him. Finally he pulled the telephone toward himself across the desk. He dialed the number. While he listened to the phone ring he pushed the wastebasket with his foot until it was beneath the edge of the desk; then with his free hand he swept the neat pile of fingernail clippings into the trash.

When Sealy answered, Willard said. "Bud?"

"Yes."

"Bud. Listen. Ralph Bird is in here and he . . ." Willard went on to tell him what Bird had said.

At his home Sealy listened to Willard talking. When Willard finished telling what he knew, Sealy asked how long ago that was and Willard told him and Sealy said had he checked any of it and Willard said no, he hadn't checked any of it, he wanted to call first, and Sealy said he doubted it but after he'd finished eating he'd drive over to see for himself.

"In the meantime what do you want me to do with Bird?" Willard said.

"What's wrong with him?"

"He's still a little excited."

"Hell," Sealy said. "You figure it out. Take him home to his wife if you can't contain him. At least she can feed him his supper."

"I imagine I can contain him," Willard said.

•

*   *   *

So it was full dark now. The streetlamps shone clearly at the corners of town, making pale circles of light on the pavement under the trees. It was that brief anticipatory moment between six and seven o'clock on a November evening when the shops on Main Street have all been closed for the weekend, when the high-school kids haven't yet begun to race up and down Main Street, when even the Holt Tavern is quiet before the Saturday night rush and out along the highway there are only three or four men sitting quietly, drinking at the bar in the American Legion.

At home, after he'd talked to Deputy Willard, Bud Sealy finished his supper. Then he rose and walked outside into the dark in front of his house. The stars had come out and, looking at them, he belched once and felt better. Then he lit a cigarette and got into the sheriff's car parked in front of his house and drove north two blocks onto Highway 34, then north again onto Main Street.

Driving up Main Street he passed the water tower and the bank and the post office and the theater, just as Burdette had done two or three hours earlier, and soon, a block ahead of him, he could see the red Cadillac parked at the curb in front of the tavern. He slowed. When he reached the Cadillac he parked the sheriff's car behind it so that whoever was driving the Cadillac wouldn't escape. He released the strap over his gun and got out.

But Burdette didn't appear to have escape or anything else on his mind. He was still sitting in the front seat. He was slumped down massively in the seat and his head was thrown back against the headrest. The light from the corner lamp shone palely onto his big face and jaw.

Sealy examined him for a moment. Finally he tapped with his fingers on the roof of the car. Inside the car Burdette opened his eyes and rolled his head, looking up at Sealy as if the sheriff were of no interest to him whatsoever.

"Well," Sealy said. "So you come back, did you?"

"That's right," Burdette said. "I come back."

"Hell of a deal."

"That's what I think. I've been sitting here trying to remember what for."

"That so?" Sealy said. "I thought you was smarter than that. I thought you had it all figured out."

"I did once. But I seem to of forgot what a little piss ant place this is. I can't seem to recall now what I wanted here."

"No? Well I imagine we haven't changed so much. Not so you'd notice it anyway. We still get a little upset when somebody does something wrong to us. And afterward decides to disappear."

"That was a long time ago," Burdette said.

"Sure it was. But not long enough, don't you see? And that surprises me. Because I can't imagine what in hell you was thinking of. But I know one thing: you made a mistake coming back here. You never should of did that. Now get out of the car."

Burdette didn't move. "You can't do anything to me," he said. "It's been eight years. The statute's already run out."

"You been talking to lawyers?"

"I talked to a couple of them."

"You wasted your time. That don't mean anything. That don't mean diddly-shit."

"Sure it does. It's the same everywhere."

"No," Sealy said. "It don't mean a thing." He opened the car door. "Now listen to me. I'm through talking. I already been nice."

Burdette refused to move. He sat slumped against the steering wheel of the Cadillac, his head lolled back against the headrest.

"Okay, then," Sealy said. "I told you once. I did do that much." He withdrew the gun from its holster on his belt and suddenly he jammed the short barrel into Burdette's ear.

Burdette sat up. He tried to move his head away. But Sealy followed his head with the gun.

"Jesus Christ," Burdette said. "What in hell you think you're doing?"

"Get out," Sealy said.

Now Burdette did move. He rose up out of the Cadillac and stood onto the pavement, tall, heavy, massive, a presence above the sheriff. He was dressed in plaid shirt and dark pants; he was wearing shoes but no socks. His clothes looked as though he'd been sleeping in them.

"Turn around," Sealy said.

"Now goddamn it, Bud. What the hell?"

Sealy poked him with the gun. "Turn around."

Burdette grunted, but slowly he turned so that his back was toward the sheriff. Sealy removed a pair of handcuffs from his back pocket and locked them around Burdette's thick wrists. It took some effort to get them closed.

"Well Jesus," Burdette said. "You mean to tell me, you mean you're not even going to read me my rights?"

"What rights is that? You don't have no rights. Not no more. Now hold still while I feel you."

"You son of a bitch," Burdette said.

"That's right," Sealy said. "That's just exactly right."

He began to run his hands over Burdette, feeling up and down his pants legs and along the fat over his ribs. He turned his pockets out. When he was satisfied that Burdette was carrying nothing more dangerous than a wallet and some pocket change, he stood for a moment behind Burdette's wide back, staring at the massive and wrinkled shirt.

And yet it was still that quiet hour on Main Street, that brief elusive moment of peace and nothing was moving; there wasn't another person anywhere on the street. And so, without thought, I suppose without even knowing he was going to, while the two of them stood beside the gleaming red Cadillac in that brief tranquillity of a November evening, the sheriff smashed Jack Burdette in the back of the head with the butt of his gun. Burdette howled and fell across the hood of the car. He began to curse.

"No," Bud Sealy said, looking down at the blood trickling from the back of Burdette's head. "I thought you was smarter than that. I did think you knew better than to come back here. What in hell was you thinking of?"

· 2 ·

I had known Jack Burdette all his life. Or all of it, that is, except for the four years in the early 1960s when he was in the Army and in Holt and I was in college and then again later for those eight years after he had disappeared when no one in Holt knew him, that period when he was out in California living on his charm and that sum of money which he must have thought would last him a lifetime until one day the money gave out and he discovered he had only the charm left and not much of that. But yes: I knew him. We had grown up together. For a long time I had even liked him.

His father, whom people here still refer to as John Senior, was a well-known figure in town. He worked at Nexey's Lumberyard on Main Street near the railroad tracks and he was a big man too—like Jack was, or like Jack was to become anyway—with a considerable gut and a big loud voice that was exactly like a bull's bellow and of about that appropriateness. Still he was a likable man, I suppose. People in Holt thought so. He wore pressed overalls to work at the lumberyard, and in the evenings before he went home for supper he always drank for an hour or two in the bars out along Highway 34, in the Legion bar or at the Wagon-wheel Lounge, with some of the other men in town who were his contemporaries.

Jack's mother, on the other hand, was a very small woman, very thin and pinched-looking. She wore scrupulously clean round wire glasses on the bridge of her nose and she combed her hair in a style that would have been fashionable in the 1920s when she was young, a kind of permanent sheared-off bob. She was a very serious woman. She never drank or raised her voice much above a whisper, so we understood in Holt that she tolerated her husband's excesses because she was a good Catholic. She played the organ at St. John's Church and made confession faithfully to old Father O'Brien who wore a hearing aid. She hadn't much else in her life, so it must have been Father O'Brien and the Catholic Church which sustained her.

They lived, during the years I am talking about, over there on the north side of town on Birch Street across the tracks. It was an old yellow stucco house and behind it they had a vacant lot, overgrown with cheat weed and redroot, which ran back for fifty yards toward the fairgrounds. This was the poorer part of town then, before the new tract houses were annexed into the city in the 1970s, but people in Holt still considered the Burdettes to be an average family with adequate income and status. If nothing else, they were interesting. There was sufficient tension in the family to make them worth watching.

Jack was born in 1941. His parents were already in their mid-forties then. They had been married for more than twenty years. So I assume they had long ago stopped expecting ever to have children and had settled into that fractious kind of truce that childless couples often accept in place of real marriage. Then Jack was born. And he was quite unexpected, of course. Consequently his parents tried to patch it up for a while. His father is said to have stopped drinking in the bars for an entire year and people say his mother looked almost pretty for a time, that she appeared to have a kind of glow. But it didn't last. She never became

pregnant again. And soon the old man was drinking regularly in
the bars once more while Jack's mother went back to playing the
organ at the Catholic church on Sunday mornings, where in that
weekly hour of temporary peace she could watch Father O'Brien
from behind those clean little wire glasses of hers. It was all as if
nothing had changed—except that there was a new source of
tension now, and consequently more arguments.

Well, he was a tough kid. He had a shock of black hair and
he was always big for his age. Then when he was six they sent him
to school. With his hair combed flat on his head and dressed in
new shirt and pants, he entered for the first time that old red
three-story brick building on the west edge of town, with its wide
foot-hollowed stairs and its tall windows and that familiar smell
of swept dust, and he didn't like it. At school they expected him
to sit still, to raise his hand and be quiet. So at recess he walked
off the playground and went home. He did this about once a week.
And when he arrived at home Mrs. Burdette, that serious little
pious woman, would take him by the back hair, lean him across
the kitchen table and hit him with the spatula. Then she would
send him back. Except that he didn't always go back; instead he
often wandered about town, through the back alleys behind the
Main Street businesses and out along the railroad tracks into the
country. So in April they decided that another full year of the first
grade and another complete term with Mrs. Peach would do him
good. I don't think they believed that Jack had been fully
socialized yet.

Still I can't imagine that Mrs. Peach had any part in this
decision or that she was excited by it personally. But, in any case,
it was because of that routine first-grade truancy of his that Jack
was there again the next year when I entered school in 1948. And
since his name came after mine in the class rolls he was assigned
the desk behind me. He was already there that first morning. He
had arrived early; his wet-combed hair was stiff on his head and
he was sitting at his desk with his hands folded as if he were bored

with it all already and was merely waiting for a chance to escape. We didn't interest him at all. He was a veteran of the first grade and beyond us. Besides he was at least twenty pounds heavier and a good head taller than we were. We didn't even exist for him yet.

But later, on the second or third day of school—in the middle of the afternoon when it was hot and still in the room and when the old high windows were open to the air and there wasn't any air, and while we were sweating over the alphabet, copying out the letters onto lined sheets of paper—Jack popped me on the head. I turned around. I don't know what I expected. But on his desk there was a dead gopher. He had it stretched out over his attempts at some As and Bs. He had squeezed out a drop of gopher blood onto the paper below his name. "You want him?" he said.

"No," I said. "I don't want him."

"Well I'm done with him."

"I don't want him."

Then Mrs. Peach was standing over us. She was standing back a little too. She ordered Jack to deposit the dead gopher in the trash immediately.

Jack stood up and walked to the front of the room. In the far corner, beside the pencil sharpener where the wastebasket was, he turned and faced us. We were all watching him. He raised the gopher by the hind leg and held it there at eye level for a moment, suspended, as if he were about to make a little magic or as if the gopher itself still knew a trick or two. Then he let it go. It seemed to dive into the wastebasket. When it hit bottom it made a satisfactory bang.

"Jack," Mrs. Peach said. "You sit down."

Jack walked back slowly to his desk. At his desk he faced straight ahead and grinned. So we were not just watching him now. We were staring at him—in wonder and awe, and shocked admiration too.

Meanwhile Mrs. Peach had begun to shout at us: "Children.

Children," she shouted. "Get back to work." She began to clap
her hands at us.

But for the rest of the afternoon, at least twice each hour, one
of us would break the lead in his pencil so he could rise and walk
to the front of the room and peer down into the wastebasket and
see the gopher. It was lying on its back with its paws curled
bitterly over its fawn belly. Finally, after enough instances of this,
Mrs. Peach announced that if just one more kid broke the lead
in his pencil we would all stay after school. We were not getting
off to a good start with the alphabet at all, she said.

Thus for eight years he was passed from one grade to the next,
from one old local spinster or balding man to the next one,
passing, being promoted each spring not so much by his own
efforts with books and maps and pencils as by the absolute refusal
of our teachers to have anything more to do with him. (Because
the experiment with Mrs. Peach had failed, of course. Holding
him back hadn't improved on his deportment. And none of the
other teachers would even consider taking him twice.) No, he
wore them all out. In fact when it was their year to have him in
their classrooms our teachers, by the middle of September, were
already counting the days until the end of May. They had big
calendars fastened to the walls with heavy Xs scratched and
double-scratched through the accumulation of finished days, and
one of them, Miss Ermalline Johnson, actually resigned during
Christmas break rather than return for another half year. "I
won't," she told the school board. "I couldn't be responsible if
I did."

Then we entered high school. At Holt County Union High
School—it was redbrick too and three stories high as the grade
school had been, but it stood at the south end of Main Street and
it was more ambitious architecturally; it had square turrets at both
ends and the roof was red tile so that it looked a cross between

a prison and somebody's notion of a Mediterranean palace; you could see it from a distance, risen up above the stunted elm trees and hackberries, standing alone at the end of Main as if blocking passage out of town, the practical and symbolic notion of what Holt County thought about higher education, standing there for fifty years and more until in the middle 1960s it was condemned and they tore it down and sold off the old redbrick for backyard patios and borders for zinnia beds and replaced it with a new low one-story pedestrian affair that had a scarcity of windows—it was there, at Holt County Union High School, that Jack Burdette was even more of a presence. And I don't mean just in our lives, but in the life of the entire town.

Because he was bigger now. He was taller and stronger— taller and stronger than anybody else in school. By the time we graduated in the spring of 1960 he was six feet four and weighed two hundred and forty pounds. But he wasn't fat then. He was still heavily muscled, broad-shouldered and thick-boned. So at least physically he was more than just that one year ahead of us. He was like a full-grown man among mere children, a colossus among pigmies. He had already begun to shave the bristle on his chin in the eighth grade—at a time when the rest of us hadn't even begun to contemplate peach fuzz yet—and in high school he had a thick mat of black hair on his chest. It stuck out through his white tee shirts like little black pins. He was a kind of high-school boy's high-school boy: the supreme example of what was possible in the absolute.

The most obvious evidence of this, though—to us and to all of Holt County—was the fact that he was an excellent athlete. He started every high-school football game for four years. He played fullback and linebacker and almost single-handedly made us worth a damn. The rest of us weren't much good. I wasn't. (I played end. I was skinny, slow-footed, nearsighted, ignorant of technique and reluctant to cross the middle; I might manage to catch a pass if nobody was breathing down my neck, but only if the ball hit me square in the hairless chest.) But Jack was. Jack was something. He was a superb athlete. He was the hotshot that made it all go. When we were juniors he won the northeast conference for us. And when we were seniors he took us to the state championship, through the conference and then the playoffs and finally to the last game—which in the end we managed to lose anyway. We were playing a team from the Western Slope and they had us at a disadvantage: they were able to field more than one real player.

But in high school our teachers had that at least as leverage. Like the rest of us, he was required by state rules to pass at least three-fourths of his classes if he expected to play football. And Jack managed that in his own fashion too. He feigned attentiveness during math and history and English classes—that is, he didn't actually go to sleep—and when he was called on to recite he rose up and made jokes. Then there were shouts of laughter from the boys in the back rows and tittering among the girls up front. In short time our teachers learned not to call on him at all.

Still he had to take tests and turn in papers as we all did. And that's where Wanda Jo Evans came in.

Wanda Jo Evans loved him. I believe, if such a thing is possible, that she even loved him more than he did himself. She adored him, idolized him, worshiped him, hung on him. All of that and no exaggeration either. She wasn't even the only one; she was merely the most obvious and conspicuous about it. Well, she was a nice girl, really pretty and creamy, and still a little plump then too in a high-school-girlish sort of way, a little given to baby fat yet, with strawberry blonde hair and soft gray eyes the color of clouds. She had full breasts too and round white arms. So if she was in love with Jack—and she emphatically was—the rest of us were more than a little in love with her and would gladly have sacrificed that proverbial left appendage of ours to have changed places with him. But Wanda Jo didn't even notice us. She didn't

see us. We were mere background and bit-players to her. Or just
smoke maybe. For it was Jack alone that she loved.

So of course she helped him. She made neat little precise crib
sheets for him and she learned to compose his term papers in his
own sprawling and childish hand, receiving as reward for this
constant adoration and these daily efforts at school the exclusive
right to ride beside him, to hang on his arm in the middle of the
front seat of his old Ford pickup while he raced and helled up and
down Main Street on Friday and Saturday nights with the gear-
shift stuck up between her creamy white knees.

We envied them all of that then. Such things matter in high
school. They seem primary at the time, essential. At least they
seemed that way to us who were Jack's classmates.

But it was on the football field that he made his real mark during
those years. In public, I mean. For, as I have said already, he was
a hell of a football player: peerless and incredible and brutal. The
whole town thought so. Indeed there are men in Holt today who
will still tell you, even taking into account what he did later, that
Jack Burdette was the best fullback and linebacker that Holt
County ever produced. And no doubt they are right. The coaches
from all the area colleges and universities thought so too; they
began to pay attention to him when he was still only a sophomore.

Consequently it was about then that his father, old John
Senior, began to pay attention to him as well. The old man came
to all of the games and when something happened on the field you
could hear him yelling obscenely from the stands. Afterward he
came down into the locker room and stood around between the
benches, smelling of beer and whiskey and slapping us on the
shoulder while we got out of our pads. He made drunken little
speeches to us. "By god," he'd say. "Goddamn it, you boys, you
sure . . ." And so on. His face would be inflamed with the drama

·

of it all, with his own high emotion and the pregame mix of liquor, and then the spit would begin to fly. Meanwhile we would be waiting for him to finish, or at least to get out of the way, so we could take a shower. But he was proud of all the boys, though he was proudest, of course, of Jack. There was a lot to be proud of. In the fall during those years the old man made money by betting on all of the high-school football games with the men from other towns.

Then in the winter of 1959, about a month after we had played our last game, the old man died. That is, he was killed. By a freight train in the middle of town. Later the railroad company would put up crossing guards and flashing lights, but there were neither of these then.

It was early in December on a Saturday night. The old man had been drinking as usual in the Legion. He had been telling stories at the bar in his loud voice and leaning drunkenly on the barmaids whenever they stood beside him to give their orders to the bartender. Pulling the young girls toward himself into his thick arms, he had kissed their cheeks and had asked them his salacious little joke: don't you want to come out to my car and test my heater? When the girls had said no, he had thrown his head back and laughed.

Thus he had had his usual satisfactory time of it, people say. Then the Legion closed. But outside, when they left the bar, they found that it had begun to snow; it was coming down under the streetlights and beginning to collect along the gutters. So the old man drove home in the snow, just as everyone else did that night, except that driving north up Main Street he would have passed the three blocks of stores, shadowy-looking and quiet now, with the store windows decorated for the holiday with cotton and tinsel and the lamp poles at the corners festooned with Christmas lights. And so, feeling pleased with it all, perhaps even feeling a little satisfied with his own place in the great scheme of things, he must have begun to sing. For he was a great singer when he was drunk. Consequently when he came to the railroad tracks at the center of town he didn't hear the train at all or even see it coming. He drove directly onto the tracks and was hit at once.

The next day, on Sunday morning, most of the men in town, and many of the women and children too, came out to look at the car. In the night the snow had stopped and it was very bright and cold.

I was there too, with my father. At the time he was still teaching me to take photographs for the local newspaper, for the *Holt Mercury,* which he owned and edited. When he woke me that morning he said that I should bring the camera.

He parked the car on Main Street and then we got out and walked along the tracks. There were deep scars in the railroad ties where the iron wheels of the old man's Buick had gouged the ties after the rubber had been torn off. The scars made it look as though some madman had plowed a furrow along the railroad tracks with a single-bottom plow. One of the ruined tires was down in the weeds and there was another one ahead of us where we could see the trail it had made in the snow before it tipped over. I took a picture of it.

Then we went on, walking along the tracks beside the train. Ahead of us we could see that there were people gathered around the smashed Buick. It was shoved free of the train now, into the ditch below the engine. There were men and women peering inside the car and talking to one another.

"You had better take photographs of that," my dad said. "But stand up here so you can get the side of the train in it."

I crowded the boxcars and snapped photographs of what I saw through the camera. Then my dad took several pictures too, to be certain he had something suitable for the front page. Afterward he gave the camera back to me and we went on.

When we arrived at the car it was standing upright in the ditch weeds on its bent rims. The driver's door was crushed in, shoved against the passenger's side. In the door there was the deep

impact, as in a clay mold or a piece of tin, where the train engine
had hit it. All the glass had been popped out and scattered.

Off to the side, George Foley, who was a barber in Holt and
who lived near the tracks, was explaining to two or three other
men what had happened. My dad and I stopped to hear what he
was saying.

He was saying in the night how he had heard a sudden bang
and immediately afterward a continuous screeching; he had
gotten up to see what it was. The train had almost stopped then,
he said, but down the tracks in front of it there was a car that was
caught and the car was still being shoved along ahead of the engine
and there were sparks flying off into the air. So he had gotten
dressed and had run outside down the tracks to the head of the
train. By then it was stopped completely. "But it didn't make no
difference," he said. "It was already too late. He was already
dead."

"How do you know that?" my dad said.

"What?"

"How do you know that he was already dead?"

"Well wouldn't he be?"

"I don't know. I'd like to think he was anyway."

"That's what I mean. If a goddamn freight train hits somebody in the middle of the night and it's going sixty miles a
hour—if that don't kill him outright, I don't know what else
will."

"Probably," my dad said. "What else did you see?"

"Plenty," George Foley said, "I saw enough."

He told us the men were already out of the train engine by
the time he ran up to the car. They were moving about, trying
to pull the car away from the front of the engine by hand, but it
was stuck fast, enmeshed with the engine, and meanwhile the big
headlight still worked back and forth above them, shining down
the tracks into the snow. Then he looked inside the car.

"And my god, he was just meat. That's all he was. He was just hamburger with clothes on. And his clothes, why they was just bloody rags."

Then he told us that the police had arrived. However, there was still some confusion about what to do. It would have been faster to have used cutting torches, but there was gasoline dripping out of the car and they were afraid of starting a fire. Finally somebody thought of hydraulic jacks. Just before morning, then, by working in shifts they were able to pry the car loose and to remove the body. They brought it out in pieces. The police took what they could of it over to John Baker at the Holt Mortuary to prepare for burial.

"And I seen it all," Foley told us. "I seen everything."

Then he was finished. There were others walking along the tracks toward us to look at the car: Ed Taylor and Mrs. Taylor, who had come into town to attend church; they were dressed up. Foley walked over to them and began to tell them his story.

My dad watched him for a moment. "That's the trouble with eyewitnesses," he said. "They just think they've seen it all. And every time they tell it they think they have to improve on what they've already told somebody else."

"Didn't you believe any of it?" I said.

"Maybe. But George Foley likes to hear himself talk. It's how he makes his living."

"I thought he was a barber."

"He is."

"Oh," I said.

"So now I'm going over to the depot," my dad said, "to see if I can find the engineers. I want to hear what they have to say. Then I'll check with the police. In the meantime you can take some more pictures."

He walked away toward the depot. I didn't know what more he had in mind for me to take pictures of. But I moved around to the far side of the car and took several photographs from that angle, with the car in the foreground and the train risen up black and massive behind it. There was still snow on the ground where people had tracked it and the contrast of the snow and the train should have made a good picture, but I forgot about facing into the sun so that later when the photographs were developed it all looked washed out. There was a lot that I didn't know yet.

When I had finished I decided I wanted to look inside the car. I hadn't done that yet and thought I wanted to. Afterward I was sorry I had. There was blood on the crushed dashboard and there were ragged bits of the old man's coat stuck to the driver's door. And hanging from one of the rags was a flap of skin which still had hair growing from it. I felt sick. I walked away from the car back along the tracks toward Main Street.

I intended to wait for my dad in our car, where we had parked it at the curb in front of Kinsey's Hardware. But before I got there I met Jack Burdette.

Jack was alone. He was walking toward me along the tracks in his winter coat; his face looked pasty and he hadn't shaved yet. I stopped when we were close to one another.

"Did you see it?" he said.

"Yes. But I'm sorry about your father."

"Everybody is," he said.

Then I didn't know what to say. I thought of warning him. But I didn't.

He went on and I turned to watch him walk along the tracks. Beside the train he looked cold and dark and solitary. Then he reached the car and I could see that George Foley had discovered him. Foley was already beginning to talk. He put his arm around Jack, while the other people stepped back a little, but I didn't want to watch it. I knew what Foley had to tell him. I went on and got into our car and turned the heater on and waited for my dad to come back from the depot.

· 3 ·

They buried Jack's father on the following Tuesday in the Holt County Cemetery northeast of town. In the nights preceding the funeral there was a wake, then on the day of the funeral there was a Mass of the Dead in the morning at St. John's Church. Afterward, outside, it was very cold standing at the gravesite. Old Father O'Brien said quickly what he had to over the closed casket and spoke in Latin while he scattered ashes. When it was over those of us who attended the gravesite rites filed past Jack and his mother and took off our gloves to shake their hands. Then we went home, or back to school or back to work, and they were left alone.

Things were tight then. Don Nexey, who owned the lumberyard, gave Mrs. Burdette a check equal to two months of her husband's salary—which was generous of him, people said; he wasn't required to do that—but the extra money would not have gone far, probably not much beyond the cost of the funeral and the old man's casket. As a result, in the middle of January Mrs. Burdette, who had never worked outside the home before, took a job at Duckwall's Store on Main Street. They hired her as a clerk. And every day now if you looked through the big display windows you could see her inside the store, wearing a thin green smock

•

over her plain dresses and standing at the cash register or working farther back, dusting and tidying the racks of picture frames and cheap toys. In this way they still had a small regular income each month and I suppose by being very frugal were able to make ends meet. Still I don't think money was the only consideration. At school we began to notice that Jack had changed. He was brooding and surly now. Things had gotten difficult for him.

It had to do with his mother. I think Mrs. Burdette believed that she had been given a new chance. It was as if she thought with the old man's death that she had been given a fresh opportunity. To save Jack, I mean; to prevent his becoming what she had only been able to tolerate in his father—tolerate simply because, given her beliefs and the tenor of the times, the thought of divorce was completely and utterly *in*tolerable. So she tried to assert herself. I suppose she even harbored the notion that Jack might yet turn out to be one of God's children and suffered to come unto Jesus. I don't know. I can't say what went on in her head or how she thought. But I know that Jack was pretty miserable for a time. And I don't think it had a lot to do with grieving over his father's death.

This went on for about two months, until about the end of February. Then he broke with her. He did something which alienated his mother forever and which at least temporarily astonished the rest of us. And looking at it now in retrospect, it seems to have established a pattern for him—or to have confirmed one anyway—a pattern which involved both a sudden move and a rash concomitant act. He left his mother and moved into the Letitia Hotel.

It was an old ramshackle two-story frame building with a deep long porch on its north side. It was built in 1914 by an early resident, an Irishman who had arrived some twenty years earlier as a small boy in the company of his parents. Then the mother died of influenza while he, the immigrant boy, watched, and so years later when he built the hotel he gave it her name out of lingering grief and old affection. It stood (and still stands, though a rooming house now for old men and migrant laborers and drunks) on the corner of Second and Ash streets, a block west of Main. Across the street there is an old hackberry tree which isn't doing very well. The local historical society claims that it was one of the first trees planted in Holt County and they've erected a cement curb around it to protect it.

Jack's room was on the second floor. There wasn't much in it: an old iron bed and wooden dresser and a gauzy-curtained window overlooking Second Street. It didn't have any sink or bathroom; the only bathroom on the second floor was at the end of the hall, a space about the size of a walk-in closet. But it didn't cost much to room at the hotel and he took his meals (when he wasn't eating at Wanda Jo Evans's house or with one of the rest of us) in the little dining room on the first floor.

He paid for these—the rent and the occasional dinners—by working at the Farmers' Co-op Elevator beside the railroad tracks. He had first begun to work at the elevator in the summer when he was sixteen. They had put him to work scooping wheat and unloading grain trucks and running the big augers. Now he began to work there in the afternoons after school and on the weekends as well. The work suited him exactly. It gave him another opportunity to sweat, to display that considerable strength of his, to expand himself amongst the exhaust of trucks and the clouds of grain dust. They were even paying him something for his efforts. Then, too, there was always that rough backslapping of the men who worked there, their sardonic talk and their jokes. For the men liked him, of course: Jack was a local phenomenon. They talked football to him. They remembered each game he had played better than he did himself, and not just the scores but the individual plays and the records he had set as well. They kidded him, they slapped his back; it was a kind of grown-man's adulation, a form of praise he needed and enjoyed.

So now, once he had left his mother's house, he had all of that again, every day. But also, for the first time, he had a room he could call just his and the liberty to come and go from it as he would, with a steady diet of free meals, or at least cheap ones, and enough money left over in his pocket to spend on beer and poker and nickel cigars, and still enough left over to buy gas to put in his pickup and then occasionally even something yet remaining to spend on Wanda Jo Evans. Because he wasn't cheap: if Jack had money he always spent it. So he might take her out to a movie, say, or treat her to a hamburger at the Holt Cafe, with an order of French fries on the table between them to share equally. Then we would see them together: Wanda Jo leaning toward him across the table, her hand with the gripped hamburger arrested before her face, while he talked and ate and chewed and while she went on watching him out of those gray and wondering eyes.

But what I remember most about that time were those evenings in the hotel room. Jack and the rest of us would be playing poker. We would be betting our nickels and dimes at a wooden box upended in the center of the room, under that high old ceiling, under that single dim light bulb suspended from a cord, while off in the corner sitting on the bed Wanda Jo Evans would be bent over the books and the cheap tablets on her lap. She would be attempting to complete Jack's and her own English and math assignments in time to hand them in the next morning, and only now and then would she even stop long enough to look up from under her strawberry hair, to glance quickly at Jack when he laughed or thought to say something that included her.

We played most of these poker games on Sunday nights. There would be beer then too. Jack was nineteen and the rest of us were eighteen now. We were legally of an age not only to be drafted to fight this country's wars but to buy beer too, which if we drank enough of it, and God knows we tried, would give us the necessary recklessness and the urge to shout that we believed were essential for any poker game involving high-school boys.

We had a good time that winter and spring. At school it became a point of honor and a matter of high privilege to say that you had been allowed to sit in, that you had entered Jack's room at the hotel and had lost your dollar or two at cards on Sunday night and had drunk a six-pack of beer. It gave you the right to boast the next morning—on Monday, at Holt County Union High School—to boast and complain of a headache while old Mrs. Lindquist tried once more to explain to us *The Importance of Being Earnest*.

But there was at least one snag in these Sunday night proceedings: the beer was warm. It had to be bought on Saturday night because none of the bars or liquor stores was open in Holt on Sunday. And since Jack's room didn't have an ice chest or a refrigerator (and since none of the rest of us was quite fool enough to store the beer at home in his own refrigerator where his mother would sure as hell find it and ask questions), the beer, by Sunday night, was approximately the temperature of blood.

We attempted several solutions to this problem. We tried, for example, stacking the cartons of beer on the window ledge outside Jack's room. And that kept it cool overnight, but sometimes it kept it too cool: it froze. Then we had Popsicles while we played cards. Which was a funny thing for a while. But the bite was gone out of the beer. It was like kissing your own sister, Bobby Williams said.

"Hell," Jack said. "It's more like kissing my old lady. Which ain't even worth trying once."

In the middle of that next week, then, after midnight, Jack Burdette and Tom Crossland and Bobby Williams and I crowded into the cab of Jack's old pickup. Wanda Jo Evans was there too. Jack was driving and Wanda Jo was sitting on my lap—which was about as close to a high-school boy's notion of heaven as I was ever to come. We drove across town that way. Then Jack eased the

pickup into the alley behind Burcham Scott's old house. When
we entered the alley Jack turned the lights off and coasted to a
stop. Then we got out and whispered to one another and slunk
along in the dark away from the pickup into the old man's
backyard, past his cement-block incinerator and his fallow garden
and finally up onto his back porch, where, pushed off into a
corner, there was an ancient Majestic refrigerator which everyone
in Holt County knew about. It was a part of the legend we'd all
grown up with. We all knew that Burcham Scott was a fisherman,
that he was an old freckled-headed man who had long ago retired
from the pretense of ever doing anything else but fish and we
knew the refrigerator was a part of his equipment. He kept his
night crawlers and red worms in the refrigerator so they would
stay lively and unspoiled until he needed them.

But it was only the middle of March now, too early for
Burcham to begin fishing again, so the refrigerator was empty and
unplugged. We began to slide it away from the wall. Then we tried
to pick it up. But we were fumbling in the dark and the porch
was narrow and we kept bumping into one another. Finally Jack
hissed:

"Get back, you damn morphadites. I'll do it myself."

And he did. He was that big, that strong. He stooped in front
of it, threw his arms around the old Majestic as if it were no more
than some heavy tractable farm girl who had come into town for
a squeeze and a dance, and then stood up with it. He turned,
pivoting, and waltzed off the porch with the refrigerator hugged
up into his arms and carried it out to the alley, while behind him
Bobby Williams and Tom Crossland and I followed like children,
punching one another and giggling.

At the pickup Jack said: "You think one of you runts could
at least open the goddamn tailgate?"

So we drove back across town that night with the old
refrigerator riding up white and square in the back of the pickup,
the four of us sitting around it while Wanda Jo Evans drove, and

at the hotel we didn't even attempt to help him. We merely held the hotel door open while he lifted the refrigerator out of the pickup once more and then carried it against his chest, as if it were still only a farm girl or a crate of peaches, say, on up the stairs to his room. There we opened that door for him too and watched him set it down.

He was panting a little now. There was a thin sheen of sweat on his face. While he caught his breath Wanda Jo plugged it in. Then Jack produced a six-pack of beer. He centered the beer ceremoniously on a shelf in the refrigerator, shut the door, looked around at us, then opened the door again. "There," he said. "Now don't that scratch your ass? Which one of you boys wants a cold beer?"

"Jesus Christ," I said. "It's all the comforts of home, Jack."

"You goddamn right it is."

"And there ain't no place like home," Bobby said.

"No, there ain't," Tom Crossland said. "Oh Dorothy, come and fuck me."

"What in hell's that supposed to mean?"

"Home," he said. "The *Wizard of Oz.*"

"Well watch your goddamn language," Jack said. "There's a woman present."

We all looked at Wanda Jo. Wanda Jo looked lovely. She was smiling at Jack as if what he had said was not only chivalrous but clever.

And that set us off. Snorting and laughing, we pounded Jack on the back and shared the six-pack of beer out among ourselves. And though the beer wasn't cold yet, it didn't matter. It was cold in theory. So we began to tell and retell the story, inventing new twists in the string of events and speculating frequently upon the look on Burcham Scott's old face the next morning when he would walk out onto his back porch. He'd scratch himself and look flat dumbfounded, we said. He'd misplace his worm, Bobby Williams said.

About two o'clock we finished the beer. We left Jack at the hotel with Wanda Jo and went home. The other boys lived out in the country, but I lived in town on Cedar Street.

When I arrived at the house that night and mounted the stairs I found that my father was waiting up for me. That is, he was in bed but he was still awake. "Pat," he said.

"Yes sir?"

"Come here."

I stopped in the doorway. He was lying in bed beside my mother. She was asleep but my dad had been reading. His glasses were pushed up onto his forehead and the reading lamp shone down onto his face. His face looked very white.

"Son," he said. "I've just been wondering."

"About what?"

"Son, you ever figure on making anything of yourself?"

"I hope to."

"Do you?" he said. "That's a comfort. But I'm just curious: when do you plan on starting?"

But Jack Burdette didn't have a father anymore to wait up for him, to question him about his intentions—not that old John Senior would ever have done much of that anyway, even if he were still alive—but now the old man wasn't available even to pretend that he might; and of course Jack had already broken with his mother. So, for him, this episode with Burcham Scott's Majestic refrigerator became just one more piece in the growing legend. It became just one more feature in that local aura that was already following him around high school and about the town. For we had all begun to expect the unusual of him by that time, while he, for his part, had already learned—if acting on bent and sheer heedless volition can be said to be a form of learning—not to disappoint the expectations of anyone. Least of all his own.

Thus he finished his senior year at Holt County Union High School in style. He lived upstairs in the Letitia Hotel. He worked every day at the Co-op Elevator among grown men who admired him. He played poker with his friends in a room he had paid for himself. And on Sunday nights he drank cold beer that had been chilled in somebody else's refrigerator. It was a high-school boy's dream of a dream.

Except that there turned out to be one final hitch in this too: while most of the adults in town and even the high-school principal took a tolerant view of Jack's activities, Arnold Beckham did not. Arnold Beckham was the sheriff. He was one in the long string of Bud Sealy's elected predecessors and he wasn't stupid. He understood that this weekly teenage hell-raising might not only endanger his reelection the next time he ran for sheriff but that it might even reduce the amount of his eventual hard-earned pension. He couldn't tolerate that. Consequently he took measures to protect himself.

One night about midnight, toward the end of April, Sheriff Beckham climbed up the narrow stairs at the hotel and knocked on the door to Jack's room. It was a Sunday night and as usual four or five of us were playing cards. When we heard the knock there was sudden quiet in the room. Jack nodded at Wanda Jo Evans, who rose obediently from the bed in the corner. She had been doing Jack's homework. Now, still carrying a textbook and one of the cheap tablets under her arm, she crossed to the door and opened it slightly.

"Wanda Jo," Arnold said. "You tell that boyfriend of yours to come out here."

Wanda Jo shut the door.

"Now what?" one of us whispered. "Jesus, he's going to tell my folks."

"Stop your crying," Jack said. "I'll handle this."

He stood up from the wooden box in the center of the room

and stepped out into the hallway. We could see Arnold through
the open door.

"Sheriff," Jack said. "What can I do for you?"

Arnold Beckham was a short man with a wiry ring of black
hair above his ears. He looked Jack up and down. Then he began
to speak. It was as if, on his way over, he had prepared a speech.

"Now look," he said. "I know what's going on in there and
I know who's in there with you. And I don't care a damn what
you do or who you do it with. But by god, boy, the first time
somebody calls me up in the middle of the night complaining how
his kid ain't home in bed yet, or somebody else says there's empty
beer bottles scattered all over their petunia patch—well by god,
boy, I'll close you down so fast you won't have time to kiss it
good-bye or even hide your beer. You understand me?"

"On what charge?" Jack said.

"You ain't listening," Arnold Beckham said. Then he did
something none of us expected. He reached up and grabbed Jack's
shirt at the throat and pulled Jack's big face down toward his own.
"I don't need no charge," he said. "On whatever comes to mind."

"Let go. We'll keep it quiet. You don't have to worry."

"No, now," Arnold said. He twisted the shirt tighter in his
fist. "You still ain't listening. Because I'm not going to worry. See?
I'm not the one that's going to worry."

"All right. We'll keep it down. Now let go. You're messing
my shirt up."

"Am I? Well tough titty."

Then Sheriff Beckham stared into Jack's eyes. Their faces
were only inches apart. But finally he released him.

"So is that all you wanted?" Jack said.

"No, that is not all I wanted," Arnold Beckham said. "I'd like
a fishing cabin in the mountains and a young girl waiting on me.
And just now I wisht I was in bed. But that'll do for starters. Now
you mind what I said."

He turned then and we could hear him walking back down

the narrow hallway. But he stopped before he reached the stairs. "And you tell that little girl of yours to go home now. I seen her mom leaving the hospital already." Then he went on.

Jack reentered the room and closed the door. He sat down at the wooden box again. We were all watching him, looking for proof that something had registered. But it hadn't. All Jack said was: "Wanda Jo. You heard what Arnold said. Your old lady's got off her shift at the hospital. So you better leave that homework till tomorrow." Then he smoothed his shirt over his chest once more. And gathering up his cards, he said: "Now who dealt this goddamn mess?"

So the point of all that was wasted on Jack. He had had his first brief taste of law and authority. He had been warned officially. But the warning hadn't meant much to him. It had merely meant that he had to be more careful, a little more circumspect. It never occurred to him that he might have to alter in any real way whatever he wanted to do. I suppose to him it was like a complicated play in football—a double reverse, say, with a fake dive into the middle, by which you could still score, only it would take a little more practice and finesse to do it. It was merely a lesson in subtlety, a brief instruction in the need for secrecy.

And so at the end of May he graduated from high school. We all did: Wanda Jo Evans and Bobby Williams and Tom Crossland and the rest of us.

Jack was almost comical in his cap and gown. The red mortarboard was perched like a pinwheel at the back of his head and the crimson gown he wore was at least three sizes too small for him; it was stretched tight across his shoulders and the hem of it stopped at his knees. He looked a joke, a travesty, like some form of Paul Bunyan who had been gotten up for a kindergartener's promotion or a pigmies' ball. But when his name was called he rose dutifully, even proudly, from his seat in the auditorium.

Then he stomped up across the stage in his cowboy boots and accepted the diploma from the president of the school board as if the diploma were something he actually valued.

In the evening we got drunk with one another for the last time. Afterward we went our separate ways. Bobby Williams and Tom Crossland went to work for their fathers, farming. Wanda Jo Evans stayed in Holt, where she was employed at the phone company as a secretary. And Jack and I went off to college, to study at the university in Boulder. I had in mind to study journalism, in the attempt to begin making something of myself as my father had suggested. And what Jack had in mind was to play football. He had an athletic scholarship, a full ride. The coaches at the university were willing to ignore the Ds on his transcript if he was willing to get his nose dirty. And of course he was.

So we had that in common that summer after graduation: we were both going to college at Boulder. It served as another bond between us. Whenever we met during the summer we talked about college and explained to one another just what kind of splash we intended to make. When we got there, though, it didn't turn out quite the way we intended: one of us sank and the other barely made a ripple. Boulder was a deeper pond than a couple of boys from Holt County had anticipated.

· 4 ·

But it was all right in the beginning. He was a big rawboned kid and when he showed up for football practice in the middle of August he was sufficiently violent to please the coaches. Still it must have been obvious that he wasn't a college-level running back. He was big but he was too slow. So in the second or third week of practice the coaches moved him into the line. That way he could use his strength and aggressiveness and not have to think too much. But he missed the glory. In high school he had carried the ball himself and had had his name featured prominently in the local papers. Now he was a defensive tackle and while he was still pretty good, everyone in college was good; so he wasn't singled out for special attention.

Then school started. I had arrived by that time myself. I had moved into the dorm with another freshman, a scrawny red-haired kid from Chicago named Stewart Fliegelman. I had never met anyone like Fliegelman before. As soon as I'd unpacked my bags he announced that he had come out West as a missionary, to spread the gospel according to Marx. He was full of that kind of youthful enthusiasm. But I enjoyed him a great deal, and the truth is I still miss him. He's a lawyer now in Oak Park, working on a second marriage with two sets of kids to provide for, but about twice a year I call him up and we talk on the phone.

As a roommate Fliegelman was lively, opinionated, verbal, well-read, studious, disorganized, bighearted and politically radical. He used to say that my beliefs were quaint, that whatever charm I had was the direct result of my universal ignorance. Whenever he said such things I told him to go to hell. I told him that coming from Chicago he wouldn't know the difference between bullshit and chocolate pie even if he stepped in it. Then he would jump me and we'd wrestle in the room. By the end of that first semester we were close friends and during the four years that I knew him in Boulder I learned as much from him as I did from anyone else in the world. I'd never tell him that, though. He'd say that I was getting sloppy again. He'd say: "Arbuckle, for once in your life try not to confuse opinion with facts. You're supposed to be a journalist, for Chrissakes."

And so I am. Or at least I try to be. And the IRS, for their part, think so too: they continue to accept my claim to be a newspaperman without ever demanding to see the actual product. Besides, I keep a framed diploma hanging on the wall above my desk to further substantiate my claim. The diploma's been there for more than twenty years. It's dust-coated and spider-webbed now and the paint behind it is darker than the rest. Because, in the end, after four years of college, I came home again. It was my father's idea; he wanted me to help run the paper and eventually to take it over. At the time it sounded like a good thing to do. And so I've been here ever since, for twenty years and more, trying once a week to get out a small-town newspaper for the edification and entertainment of the local populace, if not for the profit and remuneration of its editor and publisher: the *Holt Mercury*.

But that was later. In the fall of 1960 I was in college. And so was Jack Burdette. For a while yet.

After I'd arrived in Boulder and moved into the dorm I'd still see him occasionally. He'd be on campus with some of the others, big muscular kids wearing athletic tee shirts, filling up the sidewalk coming toward you or occupying a table with some of those good-looking long-legged sorority girls, all of them loud and joking, in the University Memorial Center. But I didn't see him very often and we didn't have much to do with one another then.

He was living in Baker, one of the other dormitories. It was like all of the buildings at the university, constructed of flagstone and brick and red tile. For it was a pretty campus, one of the most beautiful in all of this Rocky Mountain region, with the abrupt sides of the Flatirons standing up at the start of the mountains just above town, and on the campus itself the big trees and the old evergreens and all the red-tiled buildings, with still sufficient space between them so that you didn't feel stifled or closed in by the mass of stone or the press of trees. It was a good place for someone like me to be. Boulder—and living with Fliegelman— opened my eyes.

But none of that was true for Jack. He wasn't there long enough. Not that he would have allowed his vision to have been changed appreciably even if he had been. But he didn't get the chance. Within a month after school started he got into trouble. The trouble had to do with a radio.

I first heard about it—or knew about it, that is—when I saw the article in the *Colorado Daily*. They ran it in a little box on the second page. The article said that another freshman named Curtis Harris had brought charges against Jack and that the student judiciary would convene on Friday to hear the case. The article appeared on Tuesday morning. After reading it I went over to Baker to see if I could find Jack in his dorm room. His roommate, another football player, said he didn't know where Jack was; he was probably watching TV.

"But doesn't he have classes?" I said. "It's the middle of the morning."

"What classes?" he said. "Jack doesn't go to classes."

"You mean today?"

"I mean any day. He hasn't been to a class in three weeks. He's going to get in trouble."

"He's already in trouble," I said.

The guy studied me for a moment. "What's that to you? You know him, or something?"

"I know him," I said. "And they should have given Wanda Jo Evans a scholarship too if they expected Jack to go to class."

"Who's she?"

"You wouldn't know her."

"I know some girls."

"But you wouldn't know her. Anyway where's this TV Jack might be watching?"

"Downstairs. Only I don't know if he's even there. I'm not his keeper."

"I'll go see if I can find him," I said.

I went back downstairs.

After looking around for a few minutes I found Jack in one of the rooms next to the dormitory lounge. The door was shut. He was the only person in the room and he was lying on a sofa in his blue jeans and gray tee shirt. He was watching a game show on the black-and-white television and his feet were sticking out over the end of the sofa. When I sat down near him he looked over at me and then turned back to the TV.

"Jack," I said. "How's it going?"

"I can't complain."

"That's good," I said. "But what do you think will happen?"

"About what?"

"About this radio you took."

"How'd you hear about that? You been talking to somebody?"

"It was in the student paper this morning. I came over to see what you're going to do about it."

"What the hell is there to do about it?"

"Well. The paper said somebody named Curtis Harris filed charges against you. That you stole his radio."

"That's a lie. Hell, he wasn't using it so I just borrowed it for a while. And then I didn't give it back to him yet."

"Are you going to?"

"Not now."

"How come?"

"Because. I don't have it no more. The police have it. They took it for evidence."

"All right, then. But what do you think's going to happen?"

"I already told you: I don't know. Besides, what difference does it make?"

"They might kick you out of school. That's one thing."

"I'm sick of school."

"How do you know that? I mean, Jesus, you haven't even been to classes yet."

"I've been to enough. It's just talk."

I continued to look at him. There were dark bruises on his arms from practicing football and there was a scab on his nose between his eyes. Looking at him, he seemed exactly like a kid who'd fallen off a bicycle, like a great big kid who was now consoling himself by watching television from the living room couch.

"But listen," I said. "Think about it for a minute. Isn't there something we can do about this?"

He stopped watching TV, briefly. He looked at me. "Yeah," he said. "You can loan me some money. I missed breakfast. You can do something about that if you want to."

So I did. I gave him a couple of dollars. I was glad to do that much for him and was ready to do more, although I couldn't have said then what it might have been. He folded the bills I gave him and put them away in his jeans pocket. I watched him for a while longer. But when he didn't say anything more I left. He was still lying on the couch watching somebody else win money in a California studio. That seemed to please him.

Then on Friday, when his hearing came up, the student judiciary found against him. It was an open-and-shut case and after they had heard the evidence they recommended that he be expelled from school. There had been a number of thefts on campus already that fall. Consequently the administration accepted the students' recommendation and decided to make an example of him. But it didn't matter to Jack what they did; he didn't contest the charges or even defend himself. In fact he didn't even attend the hearings. Instead that morning he had gone to the Army recruiter on campus and had enlisted; so now he was obligated to two years of military service, and the Army was glad to have him swell their numbers.

He came over to see me before he went back to Holt. He said he didn't have to report to boot camp until the end of October and he thought he'd go home in the meantime and work at the elevator and see Wanda Jo Evans. He wasn't dissatisfied by the turn of events at all.

"Well," I said. "Maybe it's for the best."

"Why not?" he said. "I might even learn something in the Army."

"Take care, then."

"But just a minute. You got any more money?"

"Probably."

"Because I could use something to get home on."

So Jack Burdette went back to Holt County where he was still a hero and where no one knew about Curtis Harris's radio, or would have cared very much if they had known about it; and then at the end of October he went off to Texas, to boot camp at Fort Bliss. I doubt that the irony of that name occurred to him since he wasn't one to pay much attention to such things and I don't suppose the Army is either. Anyway he was there for almost two months. Then I saw him again just after boot camp was finished. Before being reassigned he had come home on leave and I had gone home at semester break. It was Christmastime. Jack looked thinner and harder now, although it might have been just that his head had been shaved; his cropped head made his neck look taller and now his ears stuck out. In any case all the time he was home he insisted on wearing his uniform and his Army cap about the town. He stayed at the Letitia Hotel while he was home, sleeping through most of the day in his room and spending his nights at the tavern with Wanda Jo Evans, the two of them drinking late into the night while Jack told her stories about things he'd already seen and done in basic training in Texas. I don't know how she stayed awake for all of that since she still had to get up early in the morning to work as a secretary at the phone company every day. But she did; she stayed awake; and it was obvious that if anything she was even more in love with him than she had been before. Then he left again, for Fort Ord in California where he underwent two more months of training—as an assistant machine gunner this time—and afterward he was sent overseas to Germany. So none of us saw him again until he was finally discharged late in 1962. He had stories about all of it. He had liked the Army.

In the meantime I was still in college. By the end of my sophomore year I had managed to pass most of the required courses that everyone had to take and so I was beginning to concentrate on journalism. Much of the classwork was mere theoretical posturing, of little practical use once I had returned to Holt two years later to work on the *Mercury* where people were more interested in who had visited whom over the weekend than they were in the ethical paradoxes presented in the First Amendment. But I didn't know that yet. So I attended class regularly and took notes, and when I was a junior I began to cover various campus events for the *Colorado Daily*. It was heady stuff for a while. It was just beginning to be a willful and exciting time on campus and at the paper we had the illusion that we were a part of it all and that we were speaking in the voice of the people even if the people didn't know it yet or want us to. I remember, for example, that it was about this time that Barry Goldwater came to speak on campus and in the paper we said that Goldwater was a fascist, no better than a murderer. After this statement appeared there was a considerable outcry all over the state and finally the chancellor was compelled to remove the student editor who was responsible for it. Then there were demonstrations on campus. The due processes of law had been abrogated and we all felt hot about it. But the editor was never reinstated and it turned out to be a lost cause.

Still I was beginning to get hot about something else just then. I had met Nora Kramer by that time and for a year or more she seemed very much like a lost cause too.

Now I am not very eager to talk about Nora Kramer. And certainly she is less than eager to have me talk about her. For Nora was—and is—a very private person and she will no doubt resent this invasion of her privacy. But I can't help that: like it or not she is a part of this account. We were together for eighteen years, after all, and we had a daughter together. And it was only a good deal later, after Nora left Holt and and moved to Denver, that I turned finally, out of loneliness and admiration and love too, toward Jessie Burdette, who was as different from Nora Kramer as fire is from ice.

But my god, she was a beautiful young woman when I first knew her in Boulder. She had astonishing black hair then. It was as dark and shiny as coal and wonderfully thick and clean. And her skin was so white that it was like porcelain, or like ivory, and it was almost transparent so that you felt that if you were only permitted to look at her long enough you might actually see the slow movement of blood at her temples and wrists. She was a very small person, very bright and intelligent and all neat and tidy, and she seemed as self-sufficient as a bird.

But she was living with her father at the time. Dr. Kramer was a well-known professor on campus. He wore bow ties and dark suits to class every day and taught graduate seminars in the English Department. His concentration was in the Puritans. He was great for John Bunyan and thought *The Pilgrim's Progress* was literature. He had studied at Yale as an undergraduate and I believe he considered the students at Colorado to be beneath his abilities. Nevertheless he had been able to resign himself to teaching at Colorado for more than thirty years. He was not a lot of fun to meet in the living room when I called on Nora for a date.

I never knew her mother. Mrs. Kramer had died a number of years earlier. I have seen pictures of Mrs. Kramer, though. The pictures show her to have been a small woman with dark hair like her daughter's, parted severely to one side, and she appears to have had a thin little mouth, which at least while she was being photographed she held tightly closed. But I know very little about her; Nora did not talk readily about her mother. For Mrs. Kramer had died horribly when Nora was eleven years old. And Nora had seen it happen.

She told me about it once, just once, speaking in a monotone voice as if she were reporting some event which had happened not to her but to someone else, as if what had occurred when she was eleven didn't concern her at all anymore.

It happened that she and her mother had gone to Denver on a Saturday morning to shop at May D & F's, which was a big department store downtown, and it was just before Christmas, a bright clear day, so the sidewalks were crowded with people carrying packages and calling pleasantly to one another, dropping coins into the red Salvation Army buckets. And then while she and her mother were standing at the street corner waiting for the light to change, Mrs. Kramer had been pushed or jostled by the crowds so that she was shoved off the curb out into the path of one of the big city buses that was coming up the street. Mrs. Kramer was able to avoid being hit head-on by the bus, but as it went by, her winter coat was caught by something and suddenly she was being pulled along beside it; then she lost her footing and she was being dragged along on her back beneath the bus. Nora began to run after her. But the bus driver didn't see her, or see her mother either, apparently. Then up the block Nora saw that her mother's coat had torn free, so that she was no longer being pulled along the street on her back. But though her mother had stopped moving, the bus hadn't. And then Nora saw the black wheels of the bus roll over her mother's chest and head. She stopped running then. She began to scream. She screamed and screamed, she told me, until finally someone came and put his coat over the thing in the street, which had been her mother, and she remembers that she continued to scream until the ambulance arrived at last and one of the attendants gave her a shot. Later at the hospital she was asked to provide identification. She was able to do that. But when she was asked whom they should call, she couldn't remember her father's phone number and she began to scream once more.

She told me this story one night in our bedroom, early in our marriage. Afterward I turned in the bed and held her and brushed my hand over her face, expecting tears on her cheeks. But there weren't any tears. And after a while she went to sleep. Then the next morning she would not say anything more about it.

Thus, so far as I know, that long-ago Saturday morning in Denver was the last time that Nora Kramer ever screamed about anything. She would not allow herself to show intense emotion ever again. Not even when Toni, our daughter, was sixteen and there was good reason to show emotion.

But no: I do not wish to cause her further harm. She's had

enough. I am not at all eager to stir up things for her. I am merely glad she seems to be happy again. Still I do feel compelled to make this account of things as accurate as I can. For my own reasons.

But perhaps it's enough to say that after two years of dating Nora Kramer in Boulder, after two years of turning myself inside out for her, so that I hardly knew myself who I was anymore, and after meeting her father repeatedly in the living room where he would be sitting in a chair beside a lamp, reading Bunyan and maybe a little of Milton too, a little of *Paradise Lost* for variety's sake, to clear his palate—those nights when I tried to make conversation with him while he read and while I waited for his black-haired daughter to come down the stairs so we could leave the house and go outside where I thought I might remember how to breathe once more—after all of that Nora and I were married in the summer of 1964 and we moved to Holt where I began to work for my father on the local paper. But Nora didn't like Holt very much, even from the beginning. It wasn't a thing like Boulder and Denver were. And I recall now what Stewart Fliegelman said about our prospects.

"What's wrong with you?" he said. "You still think she's some kind of violin and you just haven't learned the fingering yet?"

"What'd you say?"

"I said, 'She isn't a violin,' for Chrissakes. Aren't you listening to me?"

"I'm trying to," I said. "But it's so goddamn loud in here I can't hear anything. And you never make any sense anyway."

Then Fliegelman leaned across the picnic table and started to shout into my face.

We were sitting in the Sink, one of the student bars on the hill near campus. You sat on wood benches at picnic tables; the tables were all carved and scarred on top and around you all of the walls and the low ceiling were painted black. There were beatnik sayings and slogans on the walls, spray-painted over the black in dripping colors, and toward the back there was a room which had a dirt floor. It was always crowded in the Sink, but it was especially crowded on Friday nights when everyone was trying to make a date for the weekend: an intense place then, packed and smoky and loud and really filthy and still wonderful, with students drunk on the seventy-five-cent pitchers of beer and shouting to people three feet in front of them above the scream of the jukebox. It was the place to go on a Friday night if you were a student in Boulder. It and Tulagi's. Tulagi's had a big dance area and live music while the Sink had atmosphere and also Sink Burgers with special sauce that ran down your chin.

That evening I had just come in and I had sat down on the picnic bench, after a date with Nora Kramer, looking characteristically confused and hang-faced, no doubt, wanting consolation and understanding, or at least a Sink Burger, and now Fliegelman was shouting into my face about violins.

"Because there isn't any music there," he shouted. "You hear me?"

"I hear you. But what the hell are you talking about?"

"It's an extended metaphor, for Chrissakes. Don't you know what that is?"

"What?"

"It's what you and Nora Kramer aren't. That's what it is."

"Jesus Christ," I shouted back at him. "You're drunk, Fliegelman. You're from Chicago and you're drunk and you're full of shit."

"Like hell," he said. He sat up straight from the picnic table as if I'd said something which offended him. "It's beer. And I've done all I can for you, Arbuckle. I'm going to go liberate my bladder. It's my right as a citizen." Then he stood up from the table and made his way drunkenly back across the dirt floor toward the rest room, moving through the dense pack of student bodies as if he were some redheaded gnome at a bacchanal.

Well, our generation was full of talk of rights and liberation then and of music too (though more about electric guitars than of violins), and as it turned out, although I paid no serious attention to him at the time, Stewart Fliegelman was right about Nora Kramer and me. There wasn't any music there. Nor much that resembled liberation. And as for Fliegelman himself, his first attempt at marriage wasn't exactly Beethoven's *Ode to Joy* either.

· 5 ·

Jack had been home from the Army for almost two years by the time Nora and I moved to Holt. After graduation in June we were married in Boulder in the Episcopal church. Stewart Fliegelman stood up with me and Nora had a friend of hers as attendant. Then when it was time for Dr. Kramer to escort his daughter down the aisle toward the altar he did so without once looking at her—it was as though he just happened to be passing through the church on his way to work, or as if he were still deep in thought about Milton and Bunyan—and Nora looked lovely too, in her white veil and white dress and with her dark hair pulled away from her face like a young girl's. Afterward, though, perhaps as an offering of consolation to her (for the old man certainly felt she deserved consolation, marrying me), he insisted that we take a week's honeymoon in New York at his expense.

So we flew to New York, attended a play on Broadway, saw the sights, ate in restaurants with male waiters in white jackets standing over us, and we held hands under the table—all as you're supposed to do—and it was in New York that we began those icy exchanges in bed which not only characterized that first week of our marriage but the next eighteen years as well. Then in the middle of that week Nora got sick with something, a summer cold or the flu, so we cut short the time in New York and flew home again. The change in air pressure in the plane caused her ears to pain seriously, I remember, and her face was chalk-white when we walked down the ramp. We stayed that night in Boulder with her father and the next day when Nora felt better we drove the three hours east to Holt. The day after that I went to work at the paper and Nora began to plant rosebushes behind our house in the dirt along the garage. It was not a pleasant beginning for either one of us.

But Jack Burdette seemed to be doing very well. He was home from the Army and it was obvious that he still thought of himself as having had a very good time for those two years while he had been in the service. That is, being a soldier, he had perfected his beer drinking and his poker playing and he had seen something of the nightlife in the towns near the bases he was sent to. Also, he had discovered that money, if he had enough of it, would buy many things that he hadn't known before that it would buy, not excluding the temporary services of other human beings. He told us that he had developed a respectful view of the healing powers of penicillin. We heard all about it once he was home again. There was one story in particular that he told. It involved three German girls and two bottles of champagne and one hotel bed, the kind of arithmetic Jack said he understood. "Them German fräuleins won't refuse you nothing," he said. "You ought to try one yourself."

Thus the Army had served as a kind of finishing school for Jack, a form of postgraduate work in the essential life skills. They had even given him a diploma in the guise of an honorable discharge to prove that he had passed, to show that he had learned their fundamental lessons.

Late in 1962 then, after spending his last paycheck in a final protracted binge, he had returned to Holt. He was heavier and stronger now, beginning to spread out and to take on mass, to develop a heavy gut which daily beer drinking had something to do with, and certainly he was more experienced than he was when he left, but he was probably not any wiser. That didn't matter, though; Wanda Jo Evans was still here and so was his job at the Co-op Elevator. In short time he had taken up both.

In the meantime Wanda Jo Evans had undergone some changes herself. She had reached full bloom now. She had attained a kind of pinnacle of home-grown loveliness. I do not mean that she had become sophisticated in any way; it was not that at all; it was simply that she was even more beautiful than she had been before and that she was still warmhearted and utterly devoted to Jack. At twenty-one she had reached that brief moment of physical perfection. The baby fat was gone, her strawberry blonde hair grew long and full to her shoulders, and now each morning when she walked to work at the phone company she wore nylon hose and heels and a nice skirt and blouse. Consequently it was at about this time that some of the men in town began to make it a point to be drinking coffee at the front tables at the Holt Cafe so they could stare out the windows and watch her walk across Main Street. The men hoped that a sudden gust of wind would rise and lift her skirt to reveal more of her legs, or that a sudden breeze would come up and blow her skirt tighter against her thighs. Failing these, they were there every morning anyway, to watch her mount the curb when she reached the other side of the street. For she was something to see. But she was still a very nice girl, still entirely innocent and guileless, and she herself cared only about seeing Jack Burdette.

When she had begun to earn money as a secretary after she had graduated from high school, she had moved out of her mother's home and had rented a tiny one-bedroom house of her own. It was over there on Chicago Street on the east side of town where there are mainly small one-story frame houses painted white and yellow and sometimes pink, with little gray slap-sided toolsheds in back along the alleys and vacant lots between the houses, with here and there an old wheelbarrow or an old car, a DeSoto or a Nash Rambler, say, rusting on blocks among the pigweed and redroot under the stunted elms. She worked steadily, efficiently, at the telephone office every day, and she kept her little house clean, mowed the lawn on summer evenings, shoveled the snow off the walks in winter, and for two years while Jack was gone she composed letters to him, following him from El Paso to San Francisco and then to Germany, all by mail, by letters—letters which Jack himself only rarely answered and then only to allow, as he would, I suppose, that he was in California now or that he had arrived in Germany, or perhaps (and this is more likely, knowing Jack) simply to complain that he had lost his weekend pass for some minor infraction of military rules and so had nothing better to do with his time than to scribble her a brief note on Army paper while he waited for the other men to come back so he could begin to play cards again.

But finally in the winter he had returned to Holt once more and it was all right again. Or perhaps for Wanda Jo it was better than all right, since for the next eight years she continued to go out with him, believing all that time that he would marry her yet.

Well, it was an abject kind of love. And it took many forms. But clean socks was at least one of them.

I think it must have been a matter of barter to Wanda Jo, a kind of romantic transaction. It was as if she believed that washing his socks and laundering his shirts was not only the obvious and logical progression from making crib sheets for him when they were in high school, but that now doing his laundry each week was also the fair means of exchange for the privilege of going out with him on Saturday nights. Because for eight years, Jack would park his car in front of her house on Chicago Street, on those Saturday nights, and then he would get out and saunter up to her house and under his arm he would carry to her front door a brown paper bag—a bag which would never contain roses or carnations or even a handful of daisies but which instead would always be

·

stuffed to overflowing with another week's accumulation of his dirty clothes, his dirty socks and his greasy shirts. Then Wanda Jo would open the door to him and take that paper bag from his hands. It was as if she thought he'd brought her a gift, a present, a romantic offering, as though she believed he'd given her something which was actually valuable and considerate. And of course in return she'd have something to give him too; she'd hand him that other paper bag, the one with his clean clothes in it—his sour socks and his old work shirts and his soiled jeans transformed now, sweet-smelling, washed and tumble-dried and still fragrant of soap, as though in the intervening week she'd managed to perform some miracle or magic. And in truth she had: she had accomplished a kind of domestic and loving alchemy.

Then Jack would say: "Thanks, Wanda Jo." Or he might even become extravagant; he might say: "Thanks a lot, kid."

So they'd leave her little house on Chicago Street then. They'd walk out to his car together, with Jack's big arm draped over her smooth silky shoulder under her strawberry hair, and at the car Jack would throw the sack of clean clothes into the backseat. Then they'd go out for the night, to drink at the tavern on Main Street or to drink and dance at the Legion on Highway 34. It was all a weekly occurrence; it happened every Saturday night. And afterward, after the bars had closed and after Jack had told his last joke to the last man still there in the bar who was still sober enough to laugh in the right places, they would usually go back to Wanda Jo's house again. Then for an hour or two there would be another kind of exchange in the back bedroom where, we understood, Jack would teach her the tricks he himself had paid to learn while he was in the Army. And none of us doubted that Wanda Jo was obliging about that too. Because she loved him. Because she still thought of him as a big black-haired man with a good sense of humor. She was willing to wait for him for all those years—for him to make up his mind about marrying her— because she still believed he would eventually. She hadn't any-

·

thing else in mind for herself. Jack Burdette was the sum total of what she hoped for in life. She told me that once.

It was on one of those Saturday nights. It was in March or April, toward the end of winter, after Jack had been back in Holt for six or seven years.

I had been working late at the *Mercury* rather than going home to Nora and a silent house. Nora would be reading as usual, wrapped up in an afghan in the front room, and Toni, our little girl, who was two or three then, would already be asleep in her bed upstairs under a white comforter. So I had gone back to the office after supper to try to work on an editorial I was writing for the next week's issue of the paper, and afterward I had walked up the block to the Holt Tavern on Third and Main streets. I wanted noise and laughter; I wanted to drink a beer among friends before going home again. At the tavern I stood at the bar talking to Bob Sullivan for a while.

Bob Sullivan was a semiretired farmer who had moved to town recently, and at the moment he was seriously disappointed in his granddaughter Amy. She had married a local boy named Jerry Weaver six months earlier. "And the kid wasn't any good for her," Sullivan said. "I told her so. Here she's just a year out of high school and then this Weaver kid talks her into a church wedding before she even has time to turn around good and see what else there might be in the world waiting for her."

"How old is she?" I said.

"Nineteen."

"It's pretty young to get married."

"That's what I mean." Sullivan said. "But do you think you can tell these kids that?"

"No I don't."

"Well you can't."

Sullivan ordered another Jack Daniel's on the rocks. After it was on the bar in front of him he drank half of it at once.

"So," he said, "after I see she's going to go through with it,

•

I decided: hell, all right, then, I'll make it easier on her. I'll buy her a nice double-wide trailer as a wedding present. And I did. It was brand-new too when I give it to her."

"That was good of you."

"Because you don't think that kid has any money, do you?"

"His family has two or three sections of wheatland. They ought to have some money at least."

"But do they spend it?"

"I wouldn't know."

"They don't. And now I wish I didn't either. I'm going to tell you why."

"I'm still listening."

"Because," Bob Sullivan said, "the last time I go out to Amy's house it was a month ago Sunday afternoon. I sit down at the kitchen table like I usually do and Amy brings me a cup of coffee. And after I've litten a cigarette to smoke with the coffee, she looks across the table at me and says: 'Grandpa,' she says, 'I wish you wouldn't smoke in my house anymore.' 'What?' I say. 'Grandpa,' she says, 'I just would appreciate it if you wouldn't smoke in my house anymore.' 'You would, would you? Well I'll be damned.' 'Because it's a house rule,' she says. 'Is that right?' I say. 'Yes,' she says, 'it is. Jerry and me made up that rule last week after you was here the last time. I'm sorry, Grandpa.' 'So am I,' I say. 'And I'm getting sorrier.' Then do you know what I did?"

"No. But I can guess."

"I stood up and went outside. That's what I did. I drove home again mad as hell about it. And I haven't been back there since. What do you think of that?"

"It sounds pretty sudden to me."

"That's what I think. Because I'd already taken out my lighter and litten my cigarette. It wouldn't be so bad if she had just told me before I'd already litten. But she never."

"She'll probably get over it," I said.

"I don't know. It's been more than a month."

"Give it awhile longer."

"Sure. But do you know what, Pat?"

"No."

"Do you know what the damn hell of it is?"

"No I don't."

"I miss her. That's what the damn hell of it is. I miss Amy. I miss going out there, talking to her and drinking coffee with her. And tomorrow it's going to be Sunday afternoon all over again too."

Then he looked at me and I shook my head. He drank the rest of his Jack Daniel's and afterward he sat there at the bar stirring the ice in the glass with his finger. Finally he stood up very slowly and went back to the rest room.

While he was gone I moved farther down the bar. I ordered another beer. Toward the back, sitting at a table by herself, I saw Wanda Jo Evans. She waved at me and I walked back to her table and sat down in the chair next to her. Jack Burdette was standing over by the pool table talking to a circle of men, heavy, solid, massive, an imposing presence, standing there talking, gesturing with a full glass of liquor in one hand and a cigarette in the other, his face far above those other faces, florid now and animated, his eyes a little bit shiny. The men were all watching him while he talked.

"You're looking lovely tonight, Wanda Jo," I said. "Is that a new dress?"

"Do you like it?"

"Yes. You look terrific." And she did of course. The dress she was wearing was a pale green color, which set off her hair, and it was made of a soft material which fell smoothly from the shoulder down over her breasts and hips. There were little buttons down the front of it.

She smiled. "You don't look so bad yourself."

"I'm losing my hair," I said. "Look at this." I slapped myself on the forehead where my hairline had been. "If I don't quit this pretty soon I'm going to be a walking cue ball."

"Jack's losing his hair too."

"But he's got more to lose. He could transplant some off his chest and nobody'd even notice."

"I'd notice," she said. Then she laughed. She'd drunk enough to be amused by the thought of that. "He *is* awfully hairy, isn't he?"

"He's the missing link," I said.

We looked over at Jack where he stood beside the pool table. He was telling another joke or retelling one of his stories, and the men standing around him were waiting for the punch line. Jack had their complete attention. A barroom and a male audience were Jack's element.

Wanda Jo turned back and began to twist a straw between her fingers. "I saw your wife and little girl on Main Street yesterday," she said.

"Did you?"

"Yes. What's your little girl's name again?"

"Toni."

"Toni. Well she's cute. And she had the prettiest little dress on. I wanted to hug her."

"She's got some of her mother's good looks at least. But she's stubborn as hell. Maybe you could come over and help us out at nap time."

"I would," she said. "Just let me know." She was serious. "Anyway I think you're lucky."

"Oh? I don't know," I said. Because I didn't think of myself as being lucky. Not in marriage anyway. But of course Wanda Jo meant that I was lucky being a father. I would have agreed with her about that. At least at the time I would have. Toni was what kept Nora and me together.

"But I hope to have children myself," Wanda Jo said.

"Do you?" I said.

"Don't you think I'd make a good mother?"

"Of course."

"I think I would. Only it's getting so late. Sometimes I wish Jack would just hurry up and make up his mind. He says he will but then he keeps putting it off."

"That sounds like him."

"Did you know we were going to be married last summer?"

"No."

"We were. I bought a dress and wedding invitations. But Jack decided he wasn't ready yet."

"I don't suppose he was."

Wanda Jo stopped twisting the straw and looked at me. "Of course he will eventually. I have to think that. Otherwise, what else is all this for?"

"He'll come around. He's just not done playing yet," I said. Then I took her hand; I squeezed it and she smiled. But the smile didn't last long; it didn't change anything in her eyes. Afterward she looked unhappy again.

"Let's have another drink," I said.

So we talked about other things for a time and drank another round or two. And in the end Wanda Jo Evans became drunk while Jack Burdette went on talking to his circle of male friends.

Finally I decided to go home. It was after midnight and they were closing the bar. When the lights were turned on Jack came over and put his arm around Wanda Jo and they walked out to his car together. Outside on the sidewalk he said something which made her laugh, but her laughter was too loud and you could hear it along the storefronts, hanging in the air like fog. I stood on the sidewalk and watched them get into the pickup. Then they drove over to Chicago Street.

So it might have gone on indefinitely. It had already gone on that way for most of a decade. Then in 1970 Doyle Francis turned sixty-five and decided he wanted to retire. And Doyle's retirement turned out to be the first in a series of events which ended it for Wanda Jo Evans, although neither she nor anyone else knew it at the time.

Doyle Francis was the manager of the Farmers' Co-op Elevator in Holt. He had been the manager for more than thirty years—for as long as anyone could remember—and he had worked hard and he had performed valuable service. But now he was tired. He wanted out. He wanted to play golf and to see if he could raise asparagus in the garden behind his house. Consequently early that summer he had notified Arch Withers and the other members of the board of directors of the Co-op Elevator that he would retire in the fall, after corn harvest.

In November, then, about two weeks before Thanksgiving, the board invited all of the local farmers who were shareholders in the elevator, and all of the Co-op employees and the mayor and the town councilmen and all of their wives, to a banquet to be held in Doyle's honor at the clubhouse at the golf course east of town. And Nora and I went too, so I could cover the occasion for the *Mercury*. I don't suppose such an event would have received much play in the *Denver Post* or the *Rocky Mountain News* or, for that matter, in any other newspaper along the Front Range, but in Holt, on the High Plains, it was front-page news. It was a matter of local concern to see how Doyle's retirement would affect things at the elevator.

At the banquet there were the usual long rows of tables set up with chairs along either side and there was a head table established up front. For dinner we had the customary roast beef and mashed potatoes and green peas and coffee and a form of fruit cobbler. Afterward we listened to several brief speeches and testimonials. Then a few of the farmers who were present stood up voluntarily—but a little awkwardly too, with their white foreheads shining fresh and clean for the occasion, under the clubhouse lights, with their big calloused hands showing red beyond the cuffs of their suit coats—and once they had stood up they began to tell stories and jokes at

Doyle's expense, stories about Doyle which everyone in attendance had heard three or four times before and in more profane and expansive versions. But it was a success nevertheless. And of course Doyle took all of this good-naturedly. Then Arch Withers, the president of the elevator board, called Doyle up to the lectern so he could present Doyle with a gift. It was a sizable box wrapped in silver paper and a red bow. Everyone was watching him open it, although Withers and the other members of the board who were sitting with their wives at the head table were more than just watching him: they appeared to be beside themselves. There wasn't a straight face among them. But finally Doyle got the silver wrapping off the box and opened it. Peering inside, he looked bewildered at first, dumbfounded; then he grinned and reached inside and held up the contents of the box for all to see. And what he showed us was not the usual pocket watch or a brass pen and pencil set that would gather dust on some desk. No, it turned out that the board had presented him with a good sturdy outdoor hammock to lie in—and a five-year subscription to *Playboy* magazine to read while he was lying in the hammock. Doyle grinned largely. Then he spoke:

"Boys," he said, "I'm afraid you flatter me. The sad truth is, I'm too fat for one and too old for the other."

Everyone laughed. Then one of the board members called out: "Yeah but, Doyle. What we want to know is, which one is it you're too fat for?"

Then people did laugh. They turned to look at Doyle's wife who was sitting at the head table beside Doyle's vacated chair. She was a small plump kindly woman with white hair, and now her face was suddenly red and her hands were playing in embarrassment with a clubhouse napkin. Doyle spoke again:

"Course," he said, "I suppose I could always lose some weight. I mean I might even manage to get skinny again. Don't you think?"

．

People laughed once more, and when he carried the box over to his chair and set it down and then bent and kissed his white-haired wife loudly on one of her red cheeks, kissing her with obvious good humor and genuine affection even after more than forty years of marriage, people applauded.

So that much of Doyle Francis's retirement banquet was a success. People in Holt felt good about it. And I believe they felt good about the final proceedings that night too.

Because what happened next was the public announcement that Jack Burdette had been chosen to succeed Doyle Francis as manager of the Co-op Elevator. Arch Withers made the announcement. Leaning heavily on the lectern, speaking solemnly to the audience, he said that he and the board recognized that it would be hard to fill Doyle's shoes, but that they had decided to look no farther than right here at home. After thinking about it thoroughly they had come to a unanimous decision; they had all agreed to promote Jack to manager.

People applauded once more. Everyone approved. And while Jack walked up the lectern to shake hands with Arch Withers, one of the farmers in the audience said: "Well at least his feet are big enough. Burdette ought to be able to fill Doyle's shoes, or anybody else's, with them big boats."

Sitting in the middle of the' room at one of the long tables, Wanda Jo Evans might have said something about Jack's having clean socks too. But she didn't—although when I looked at her there were tears shining in her eyes, tears of love and approval, I suppose, but also of private expectation. For I think Wanda Jo Evans must have thought that now, with his promotion, Jack might want to settle down, that he might be ready to make their relationship—that almost-eight-year-old Saturday night transaction of theirs—not only a weekly exchange but a daily and permanent condition.

*   *   *

Then it was 1971. It was spring. Jack had been the manager of the Co-op Elevator for about six months. At the beginning of April that year the board decided to send him down to Oklahoma, to Tulsa, so he could attend a weekend convention for the managers of grain elevators. It was the board's belief that it would be worthwhile for him, and the elevator too, if he would attend the convention, sit in on the seminars and workshops, and then return with the latest predictions about the futures market as well as any new information he might collect about the prevention of grain dust explosions. An under secretary of agriculture, several economists and university scientists were to be there, to lead the workshops and seminars.

So Jack drove down to Tulsa. He went alone, driving one of the company pickups with two or three different company charge cards in his pocket. He left on Thursday. The convention was to begin at noon on Friday at the Holiday Inn, and it was understood that he would stay through the weekend, return on Monday sometime late in the afternoon or early evening, and then make his report to the board at a special meeting on Tuesday. And apparently Jack arrived in Tulsa on Thursday evening just as planned. He found the Holiday Inn, checked himself into the motel, located the dining room and the bar, hobnobbed with some of the other elevator managers, listened to their stories and told some of his own, went to bed at a reasonable hour, and afterward there is reason to believe that he even attended some of the meetings on Friday afternoon and again on Saturday. But by Saturday night, apparently, he had had enough.

I don't know; perhaps he was just bored. Perhaps he was tired of it all already. Attending convention workshops and seminars would no doubt have been too much to him like taking high-school classes and college instruction. There would have been all that talk in those close windowless rooms, with the pitchers of ice water and the urns of coffee set out on a table in

the back, but nothing stronger, nothing for a man to drink really:
those experts up at the front of the room talking on and on,
speaking learnedly, humorlessly, professionally about corn futures
and grain dust explosions, with the accompanying racks of charts
and diagrams beside them and the sheaves of documented sci-
entific research, all of which he was not only supposed to believe
and make sense of but to take careful notes about too with that
ballpoint pen and that new tablet they would have given him,
sitting there at some table with his big muscled arms resting out
over the table in front of him like two oversized ham steaks while
he calculated the hours and minutes until dinnertime and the first
drink of the evening, though not necessarily in that order. And
meanwhile the experts would still have been talking and he would
still have been trying to stay awake. Consequently I believe he
must have been good and bored by Saturday night, tired of it all.
But also, I know, by that time, he had met Jessie Miller. And Jessie
Miller, as she was known then, would have been enough to make
him want to disappear even if he weren't bored.

　　She had been hired by one of the sponsors of the convention
to stand behind a table set up in the lobby. She had been instructed
to wear a white blouse and a black miniskirt, to smile congenially,
to pass out glossy colored brochures, and to show continuously
a film extolling the virtues of a particular species of hybrid seed
corn. And she had been doing all of this faithfully all of Friday
afternoon and all of Saturday. So Jack must have met her, or at
least have talked to her, several times already.

　　Then on Saturday evening, after he had been released at last
from the last workshop late that afternoon, he began seriously to
charm her. For he was capable of charm. I may not have made
that clear, the fact that Jack Burdette could be attractive to
women, that he was capable of exercising considerable charm and
persuasiveness where women were concerned. Still it's true; on
those occasions when it mattered to him what women thought
of him and whenever it made any difference to him how they

responded to his talk—that is, when he wanted something from a woman—he was in fact capable of great leverage and conviction. But he had that effect on men too. He dominated any room he entered. But it wasn't all conscious and deliberate on his part. Most of it was a matter of impulse and instinct, the result of native vitality and energy. He was full of himself. Domination came naturally to him. And in any case, he was huge, and he still wasn't bad-looking at that time. He hadn't gotten sloppy yet.

So he began to charm her. She was just twenty years old in 1971 and he was already thirty. He wined her and dined her, bought her steak in the dining room and danced with her in the lounge until late that night, swirling her around the floor to the live music played by the country band hired by the sponsors of the convention, and he mixed it all with a variety of expensive wines which he charged on the Farmers' Co-op Elevator's charge cards. Then he disappeared with her. They went upstairs to his motel room and didn't come out until Monday morning—not until everyone else at the convention had already checked out and had gone home—leaving the motel room only then to have their blood tested and afterward to locate the nearest justice of the peace before returning once more to the privacy of Jack's room at the Holiday Inn.

Thus he didn't return to Holt again until late Wednesday night. And when he did return he was already married. He moved Jessie into his old room at the Letitia Hotel, just a block off Main Street.

This surprised and astonished everyone in Holt. But it was more than mere surprise and astonishment to Wanda Jo Evans. To her it was nearly a lethal shock. And it wasn't even Burdette who informed her of the fact that he was married now. On the contrary, she discovered this in the same way that everyone else in Holt did: by hearsay on Thursday morning, after he had returned from Oklahoma and had already spent that first night with Jessie in the Letitia Hotel.

Still Wanda Jo knew that he was going down to Tulsa. She was aware that the board had sent him to the convention. But I don't believe she thought much about it. No one did. It was simply part of his new responsibilities as manager of the elevator. To Wanda Jo, then, it must have been merely that he would be gone for the weekend and that she would miss their weekly dancing and drinking and later their lovemaking in the back bedroom. So perhaps while he was gone she decided to make good use of her time. Perhaps she gave her little house a thorough cleaning; maybe she had a permanent curl put into her hair and did things like balance her checkbook and sew buttons on one of Jack's shirts. Then it would have been Monday and Jack would have been due to come back.

Except that he didn't come back on Monday. He was still in Tulsa on Monday. He was busy. He was occupied. He was having his blood tested. He was pulling strangers in out of the courthouse hallways to act as witnesses, and he was standing up in front of an unknown justice of the peace, promising the twenty-year-old girl beside him whom he had known now for maybe forty-eight hours that he would continue to love her and take care of her, whether they ever got rich or not, whether they managed to stay well or happened to turn sick, till death did them part. So it was late on Wednesday night before he returned to Holt. It was long after midnight and consequently for another night Wanda Jo Evans must have given up waiting for a phone call that didn't come and she must have gone to bed at last, in confusion and wonderment, beginning now to worry. But finally she must have gone to sleep. Then the next day she discovered that he was married.

It was Joyce Penner, one of the women at the telephone office where Wanda Jo worked, who told her. Joyce heard about it in the bakery. About nine-thirty that morning Joyce walked around

the corner to Bradbury's Bakery on Main Street, to buy sweet rolls
for the women in the telephone office, and by that time people
in town were already talking about it. So, as we all heard later,
Joyce went back immediately, without even buying the rolls for
the women. Reentering the telephone office she leaned over
Wanda Jo's desk and said: "Honey, come back to the ladies' with
me."

"What's wrong?" Wanda Jo said. "Is something wrong?"

"Just come back to the ladies' with me."

"Well. Something must be wrong," Wanda Jo said.

But Joyce was already walking away from her, past the other
women at their desks. Wanda Jo stood up and followed Joyce
back to the rest room, to that little square pragmatic space where
there is no window, where there is barely room enough for one
person and the fan comes on according to code when the light
switch is turned on and it makes a tinny noise, and then Joyce
locked the door behind them and told Wanda Jo to sit down.
"Why?" Wanda Jo said.

"Just do," Joyce said. And then she told her.

So I suppose bad news can be lethal for some people.
Especially if it is sudden and unexpected. That is, if you are not
used to it, if you have gone along passively, hoping for the best
despite all the evidence to the contrary, if you are twenty-nine
years old and still believe that a man will marry you simply because
you have washed his dirty socks for eight years and have slept with
him on Saturday nights during all that time, then I suppose bad
news can kill you. In any case it was something like that for Wanda
Jo Evans. Because, in a way, Wanda Jo Evans did die that Thursday
morning in April. I do not mean that she slit her wrists with a
lady's razor that she happened to be carrying in her purse, nor that
she did anything so suicidal as to stab herself with a fingernail file.
I simply mean that she stopped caring what happened to herself
anymore.

It began immediately. For the rest of that morning she sat in the telephone office rest room, staring at the tiled floor, wiping her nose on cheap toilet paper, crying quietly, her recently curled strawberry blonde hair fallen forward about her abashed and stricken face and her slim white neck bowed and exposed as if she were waiting for some final blow of some Holt County inquisitor's ax. All of that—that dreadful individual remorse and despair and submission—while the fan overhead went on making its maddening little noise and while the other women out in the front office continued to talk about her and to send a representative from among themselves every fifteen minutes or so to check on her. She stayed in the rest room all that morning. Then at noon one of the women drove her home.

For the rest of that spring she drank. In the evenings she went home after work and sat in front of the television, drinking cheap wine or vodka until she fell asleep. And on the weekends that spring she went out to the bars in town, going out alone now to the same places where previously she and Jack had gone together. Invariably she drank until the bars were closed. Then, in time, she began to take someone home with her too. She brought them back to that little bedroom in the house on Chicago Street, and the bed wasn't even made anymore and the sheets smelled of sweat and the stale smoke of old cigarettes. But none of that was important to her now. It was only important to her that he—whoever he was, and there were a lot of them during those months of late spring and early summer, and even occasionally more than one at the same time—it was only important that he do his own laundry. She insisted on that.

By June she was a mess. She was completely lost and pitiable. And people in Holt did pity her too—the women, in particular, but some of the men as well, when they thought about it. They all felt sorry for her. But no one knew what to do for her either. Finally, however, some unexpected help came from the outside. It came in the guise of a little mousy middle-aged man who wore horn-rimmed glasses and a white shirt and tie: a Mr. T. Bleven

McGill. He was a telephone company supervisor and it turned out that he had a heart. T. Bleven McGill persuaded Wanda Jo to apply for a transfer to another office. Thus, at the end of June in 1971, she moved to Pueblo. And so far as I know she is there still.

But before she left she did one thing—something which has become a part of Holt County legend too—she delivered that last brown paper bag of clothes to Jack. They were all clean and dutifully laundered of course. In fact they still smelled faintly of soap. She had washed them during that week just prior to the time that Jack had gone down to Tulsa to the manager's convention, and naturally when he returned he hadn't thought to pick them up. Now Wanda Jo presented them to him one afternoon while he was at the elevator office. Bob Thomas and several other men were there too. She didn't say anything to Jack, nor to any of the others. She merely set the bag on the counter, looked at Jack, stared at him, met his eyes, and then swept her glance over the other men. Finally she turned and walked out.

After she had gone Burdette looked inside the paper bag. He recognized the contents; they were his clothes all right, but they had been changed. They had been cut by a razor or by a pair of scissors, sliced methodically, bitterly, into tiny pieces, the biggest of which was no larger than a single square in a checkerboard or a little girl's hair ribbon: all his socks and shirts and pants and underwear. Burdette dumped the things out onto the counter.

"Huh," he said to other men in the office. "You reckon this means we're through? You suppose this means she won't be doing my laundry no more?"

Bob Thomas and a couple of the men laughed.

"But hell," Jack said. "She was a nice girl. Only she always was a little short on a sense of humor."

PART TWO

PART TWO

· 6 ·

She was the exact opposite of what people in Holt thought she would be. That is, she was the exact opposite of what people in Holt thought she would *have* to be. If Burdette was going to marry her, if he was going to leave someone as beautiful and selfless and long-suffering as Wanda Jo Evans was and then marry someone else, she would have to be something. At the very least she would have to be some husky-voiced Oklahoma version of Jayne Mansfield or Marilyn Monroe.

She wasn't, though. She wasn't like that at all.

Still from the very beginning Burdette himself misled people about her. That Thursday morning in April, after he had come back from Tulsa the night before and had then returned to work at the elevator the next day, he told Arch Withers about her. And what he told Withers at least implied that she was the kind of woman people still expected her to be. Also, since it was from him, from Arch Withers, that people first heard about her and since no one had met her yet or had seen her on Main Street, and wouldn't see her or meet for another three or four hours—not until noon when she would leave the Letitia Hotel and meet Burdette at the Holt Cafe for lunch—for the length of that one morning (which was still the same morning that Wanda Jo Evans was crying privately, miserably, in the telephone office rest room) people in Holt assumed that she would have to be blonde at least, even if she wasn't also brassy and vacuous and loud, a kind of empty-headed lipsticky Sooner starlet.

That Thursday morning back in April, Arch Withers had been waiting for Burdette near the rough plank steps leading up to the elevator office. He was standing on the gravel in the morning sun, leaning up against the fender of his old black pickup, chewing on a flat toothpick and cleaning his fingernails. By the time Burdette arrived at eight o'clock that morning Withers had been waiting for him for nearly an hour. Then Burdette drove up in the company vehicle he had taken down to Tulsa. He got out and walked over to Withers.

"Well," Withers said. "What happened? Did you get tired of motel food and decide it was time to come home again?"

"No. I liked their food all right," Burdette said. "Their beds was satisfactory too."

"So it wasn't that. Well that's something at least. I wouldn't want to think you missed any meals or lost any sleep on our account—just because you finally come back two days after you was supposed to and never called nobody the whole time and never even answered the phone when somebody else tried to call you."

"Arch," Burdette said, "you sound a little upset."

"That so?"

"Yeah you do. And it doesn't become you."

"Then you'll have to excuse me," Withers said. "Maybe I ought to apologize. Because I'm not upset, goddamn it. I'm mad. Just where in the goddamn hell have you been all this time anyhow?"

Burdette told him about Jessie Miller then, about meeting her

in the Holiday Inn lobby where she was showing that continuous
monotonous film about hybrid seed corn. He told Withers about
dancing with her. "She was pretty good-looking too," he said.

"Was she?" Withers said. "Then I guess I'm glad for you. But
what the hell's that got to do with anything?"

"Quite a lot," Burdette said.

"How do you mean?"

"Well. I married her."

"What?"

"I married her."

"The hell you did."

"That's right. I'm a old married man now. Like everybody
else."

"I'll be a son of a bitch," Withers said. "I thought you had
better sense."

Then, as Arch Withers told it later himself, he chewed his
toothpick for a while and studied Burdette, looking him up and
down as if Burdette were some sudden bump in the evolution of
humankind, and not an attractive one necessarily but as if he were
a talking mannequin, say, or an enormous and potentially dangerous aberration.

But finally Withers accepted this new fact and went on. He
said: "All right, then, so you're married. You married some
good-looking girl in Oklahoma. But Jesus Christ, man, didn't you
even go to a single meeting we sent you down there to go to?"

"Sure," Burdette told him. "I went to some of them. I went
to a goodly number. I didn't meet her till Saturday."

"Then how come you never come back until Wednesday?
You was supposed to report to us here on Tuesday."

"I remember," Burdette said. "But you don't expect them to
open that office of theirs on the weekends, do you?"

"What office?"

"The one so we could get our blood tested."

"You mean you got married on Monday?"

•

"That's right."

"But that still leaves Tuesday."

"No it don't."

Withers stared at him.

"Tuesday was our honeymoon," Burdette said. "We was still in bed on Tuesday."

Withers took the toothpick out of his mouth then and threw it away. He said he didn't have any more use for it now. It didn't taste good to him.

Nevertheless he went on once more. "All right," he said, "I guess some kind of congratulations are in order. And I do congratulate you—I wish you both well. Still I'm only going to hope for one thing."

"What's that?"

"I'm just going to hope that this doesn't spoil your good judgment."

"It never has before."

"Goddamn it—you haven't never been married before either."

"That's a fact," Burdette said. "I haven't even been to Tulsa before. It might get to be a habit."

Burdette slapped Withers on the back then. But Arch Withers still wasn't amused. He climbed into his pickup and started it. Through the open window he said: "How *was* your blood anyway? That report you had. It might be of interest to the board."

"Arch," Burdette said, "it was hot. You just wouldn't believe how hot it was." He began to laugh. "And hers was too," he said.

Then Withers drove away, across the gravel out onto the road and over to Main Street to Bradbury's Bakery. For an hour before going home again, before returning to the tractor waiting for him in the half-plowed field which he admitted he had left for too long already over this damned business, he sat drinking black coffee and eating cream-filled doughnuts while he told some of us what he had just heard. He said he believed that Burdette had stopped laughing as he drove away but that he was pretty sure Burdette was still grinning.

"So," one of us said. "He's married now, is he? Well hell's bells."

"Except you mean wedding bells, don't you?" one of the others said.

"No, I don't. I mean, that son of a bitch. I wonder what she looks like."

As a result of all this there was a considerable crowd at the Holt Cafe on Main Street that Thursday noon. People in Holt knew Burdette ate lunch there and they hoped that his new wife would join him. They wanted to see this new woman for themselves. They wanted to examine her and confirm their expectations. By twelve o'clock all of the tables and booths at the cafe were occupied and there was an increasing number of people standing up at the front door waiting for the possibility of a vacated table. Meanwhile the special of the day—Swiss steak and potatoes and green beans and hot apple pie—had already been used up.

Then a little after twelve Burdette walked in. He stood just inside the doorway a moment, scanning the tables and booths, looking across the steamy overfilled room for a place to sit. A couple of the local men waved at him, motioning for him to come join them at a center table opposite the salad bar. He acknowledged the men, but then he walked past their table and over to a booth in the corner. There was a young woman sitting in the booth, alone.

She had come in earlier. I believe she had been there for about thirty minutes; maybe more than that. When she had entered the cafe late that morning people had noticed her—anyone new in town would be noticed—but I don't think they had thought much about it. I suppose they—we—had all assumed that she

was just some single woman from out of town who was passing
through Holt on Highway 34 and that she had only stopped for
lunch and maybe for an hour of rest at the cafe. Still there were
people who were annoyed with her too; those men and women
who were standing up at the doorway kept glancing at her,
indicating by their quick harsh glances that she ought to have the
decency to get up and leave. She was occupying an entire booth
by herself, a booth which they themselves had more immediate
and urgent need of.

Then Burdette did something which surprised everyone in
the cafe. He sat down with her—not across from her but beside
her—and he put his arm around her. He pulled this new unknown young woman to himself and kissed her.

And suddenly it was as if you could actually hear the insuck
of breath from the men and women sitting in the cafe that noon
when they realized who she was, when they understood who she
had to be. It was like that moment that comes in a movie when
everything—music, motion and sense—is stopped for a few
seconds and the figures on the screen are held temporarily in silent
stasis and arrest. People in Holt felt shocked. She wasn't anything
like what they expected her to be. There were some in the cafe
who even wondered if she weren't part Indian.

For Jessie Burdette, it turned out, was a very quiet and solitary
woman. She had brown eyes and dark brown hair and beautifully
clear skin, and she was of less than medium height and she was
quite slim, but she wasn't petite. She didn't make you think of
girlish debutantes or of retiring primroses. She wasn't even pretty
really. That is, she was attractive, she was very attractive; and
later, thirteen years later, when I came to know her well I thought
she was the most attractive woman I'd ever known and absolutely
the finest person. And in the end I was ready to do anything at
all for her. Still she was not pretty in any conventional sense. She

wasn't at all the positive and cute, sunny little pert-nosed girl next door; nor was she any form of that brash California idea of female pulchritude either. Instead she was rather small and dark and quiet and obviously strong-willed. She seemed capable of a great deal. She seemed independent. Even on that first day, when I saw her for the first time in the Holt Cafe, there seemed to be a quality of aloofness about her, as if she preferred really to be left alone, or as if she knew very well what she wanted and if that happened to preclude being close to others—so that she must always seem a little set off and separate from other people in Holt, or, for that matter, from people anywhere else in the world—she was willing to accept that too.

So I don't know why she married Jack Burdette. Not absolutely, at any rate. On the other hand, as I've suggested before, I think I do know why Burdette married her: out of boredom. He decided that charming Jessie was at least preferable to attending any more convention workshops. Then, too, he had those company charge cards in his pocket. He wouldn't have wanted to waste an opportunity to spend money which did not belong to him, especially if it was simply a matter of having to scribble his name on a piece of paper. But I can't say absolutely why Jessie married him.

I suppose part of it had to do with the fact that she was only twenty years old in 1971. She was still very young, although she was not entirely ignorant of the ways of the world and men. She had had some experience of both, some limited experience. But the point is, she was very young even so. She was not much more than a girl yet. Besides, she had lived her entire life in Tulsa. And I don't think, at twenty, that Jessie Burdette believed that Tulsa was all there was in the world worth seeing.

So in April that year Jack Burdette arrived at the Holiday Inn. He was a big man and jovial, and he was ten years her senior and he was from Colorado. And so he charmed her. And then, rather than return to any more convention workshops, he proposed marriage to her. And, for her own reasons, she accepted. But there was one other little bit of play in this weekend romance too: sometime during those days and nights in the motel room Burdette managed to convey the impression to her that Holt was better than it is. He told her, for example, that you could see the mountains from Holt.

You can't of course. You have to drive at least forty miles west of here to see the mountains. And then it has to be a very clear day, coming after it has rained or after the wind has blown hard for five or six hours so that the brown cloud hanging over Denver has been driven away or been blown off, and then what you see of mountains is merely a faint blue jagged line on the horizon some hundred miles farther to the west. But to Jessie Burdette, as later she would describe the manner in which Jack had told her about it, Holt County would at least have seemed different from Tulsa, Oklahoma. And she thought she had good reason to want out of Tulsa, Oklahoma.

She was the oldest of three children. The two others were boys, younger than she by five and six years. Her mother was an invalid, confined to a wheelchair, and her father was an implement salesman who was gone from home most of the time. As a teenager then, after her mother was crippled, she had spent many hours taking care of her mother and her two little brothers. She knew a great deal about cooking and cleaning and washing clothes and changing bedpans and emptying urine bags, and she had worked part-time in the evenings at fast-food restaurants, and she had even saved a little money to buy material to make clothes for herself. But she didn't know much about fun. It was all a kind of gray reiteration of things to her, an endless unhappy routine. Then she graduated from high school. And after graduation she had worked as a temporary secretary on several occasions. But none of that was taking her anywhere. Then it was about this time that her father, because of business associations, heard about the weekend job at the elevator convention at the Holiday Inn. So she

WHERE YOU ONCE BELONGED   89

applied for the job and she was hired to show the film about hybrid
seed corn in the motel lobby. She wore the miniskirt they required
her to wear and the short-sleeved white blouse with the low
neckline, and all the time she managed to smile congenially at the
men at the convention. Then Jack Burdette showed up and began
to talk to her. And soon it was more than just talk, and then on
Monday he married her.

So for the next five years, after seeing her for the first time in
the Holt Cafe that Thursday noon, like everyone else in town I
still only saw her infrequently. And then it was only causally,
remotely, as from a safe and necessary distance. On those occasions when she happened to be shopping on Main Street, or on
those rare weekend nights when she would agree to go out to the
bars with Burdette, I would see her, just as everyone else did, and
pay attention to her.
     She was still doing some of that then—going out to the bars,
I mean. During those first seven or eight months after Wanda Jo
Evans had left town and while she herself was still new among us,
we would see her every once in a while at the Legion or at the
Holt Tavern on Saturday nights. And we would all watch her then.
Typically, she would be sitting quietly in a corner booth by herself,
sipping some sugary drink very slowly while the ice in her glass
melted away, thinning the pink liquor to mere colored water,
while Burdette himself (since marriage hadn't changed him; since
marriage was merely a change in his weekend companion, not a
real break in his Saturday night routine, that masculine habit and
custom of his) would be standing off at the end of the bar away
from her, drinking whiskey or scotch, the center of that constant
and admiring group of backslapping men, while he told his jokes
and stories and they all laughed.
     That wasn't often, though; we didn't see much of that. Jessie
Burdette did not go out to the bars very regularly. And when she

did go out she was always pleasant and would talk to you if you said something to her, but she would never volunteer anything herself. Instead she seemed to prefer to sit quietly sipping her watery drink, watching others have what she maybe didn't even consider then as being a very good time.

But in the meantime the local women had begun to work on her, to pay special attention to her. I suppose the women in town wanted to be friendly. They began to ask her to join their social clubs and their church organizations. Wouldn't she like to come to tea, to join Rebecca Circle, to play bridge, to be a member of the Legion Auxiliary, to golf with them on Saturday mornings, or maybe—wouldn't she like to participate in Bible study?

But she wouldn't, she told the women. She refused them outright, although when they called on her she was pleasant about it all. Nonetheless she was certain about it too.

So the women felt a little hurt by this, a little bit rebuffed and rejected. It put them off. But a month or two later they decided to ask her again. She only needed more time, they told one another; she was merely being polite. She probably wanted to settle in more thoroughly and to look about her, as anyone would, moving to a new town. With the passage of time, she would feel differently, they said. In the middle of fall that first year they began to ask her again.

But again she refused their invitations, rejecting that female attempt at communal neighborliness and sociability a second time. She hadn't changed her mind at all, it turned out. While we understood that she was still quite cordial to them, in that typical, quiet and pleasant manner of hers, she was also absolutely certain about it. She was not in the least bit interested.

And now the women felt more than a little put off. They were offended. They felt wounded by her rejection. As a result, they stopped asking Jessie Burdette to join anything at all.

*   *   *

Then in March of 1973, almost two years after she had arrived in town, she had a baby. She delivered a little boy whom she named Thomas John. Later, when that became too much of a mouthful, she shortened it to TJ. He was a handsome little boy. He had his mother's dark hair and her sober brown watchful eyes. And it was obvious to us, seeing them on Main Street, what she thought of him. She was delighted with him. We would see them together: the young woman, small and quiet and trim again after her pregnancy, pushing the handsome little boy along the street in a baby carriage, the two of them going in and out of the stores, looking as content with themselves as if nothing else mattered. She would be smiling at him too, talking to him quietly as though he could already understand what she was saying. Then later when he was a little older and when it was summertime we began to see them in front of the house on Gum Street (for Burdette had made a small down payment on a two-bedroom house by that time; it was in the middle of town, near the railroad tracks)—this new mother and her little boy would be playing together on a blanket spread out on the grass in the shade under the elm and hackberry trees. He was a little more than a year old when she delivered a second child.

This one was a boy too, named Robert and called Bobby, who was almost the exact twin of his older brother: a handsome little boy with the same brown hair and the same brown watchful eyes. She was pleased with him as well. She was delighted with both of her sons.

Consequently there were three of them now for us to watch in town. Three of them to notice on Main Street or to observe in the yard in front of the house, playing games on the front lawn or making little farmsteads in the dirt with miniature cows and horses and bits of sticks—this young woman whom nobody knew at all yet, whom we had expected in the beginning to be some playgirl, some Oklahoma Monroe or Mansfield with a heaving bust and a cinched-in waist above wide hips and long legs, but who, it happened, wasn't like that at all.

Thus there developed a kind of mystery about Jessie Burdette in Holt. None of us knew what to think of her. Who was she, really? We didn't know. It was as if she were some fine and exotic bird that had flown in here one spring and had then decided to stay—but one which didn't seem to expect any sustenance or even association from anything or anyone around her.

So for five years she was left almost entirely alone. She was merely here, living in a town of three thousand where everyone knew everyone else. And no one knew her.

Then everything changed, for her and for those of us who were still watching her. It had to do with her husband. Sometime in the middle of the afternoon on the last day of December in 1976 Jack Burdette disappeared. And in the end he did not return to Holt for a very long time, not until a great deal of damage had already been done.

· 7 ·

At first people in Holt were not alarmed by his disappearance. On the contrary, they were rather amused by it. They thought of it as a kind of joke, as another of his sudden and outlandish acts which in time would be explained, or at least accepted, as just another installment in that ongoing legend that followed him about the town.

Then he'd been gone for about a week. And it began to get about—in the bakery and the pool halls and the tavern, wherever people were talking—that he had charged some things on Main Street before he left.

We learned that on that Friday afternoon on the last day of December he had gone into Foster's Jewelry Store and after looking at several men's rings and old-fashioned pocket watches he had chosen the most expensive 14-carat gold Bulova wristwatch that Lloyd Foster had to offer. And he hadn't paid for it; he had merely signed his name to a charge slip. Then he walked out of the store with the new gold watch on his wrist and went next door to do the same with Ralph Bird.

And there, at the Men's Store, he charged a new maroon sport coat and a pair of good gray wool slacks, a leather belt and three

long-sleeved oxford-cloth shirts—all of which satisfied Ralph
Bird so well (since Bird hadn't expected to conduct any business
at all in that dead time following the Christmas rush) that he
decided, uncharacteristically, to throw in a good new striped tie
to boot.

And Burdette thanked him. He slapped Ralph on the back and
signed his name to another charge slip. Then he walked out of the
Men's Store wearing the coat and the slacks and the belt and one
of the shirts—with the other things (the two extra shirts and the
bonus tie and his old clothes) all stuffed into a plastic store bag.
Once he was outside, he walked up to the corner to Schulte's
Department Store.

But we discovered that he wasn't quite so successful there.
It happened that old Mrs. Thompson was the only clerk available
at the moment and it was she who waited on him. In no uncertain
terms Mrs. Thompson informed Burdette that the store had
specific limits on how much they would allow anyone to charge.
Burdette took this amiss. "But look here," he said. "You know
me. You know who I am."

"I certainly do," Mrs. Thompson told him. "I've heard more
about you than I ever want to, ever since you were an ornery little
boy. Your mother is a friend of mine."

Consequently, at Schulte's, Burdette was somewhat ob-
structed in his Friday afternoon shopping; that is, he was allowed
to charge only a pair of dark socks and a set of blue underwear.
And before he left the store he must have thought better of
changing into the socks and the underwear and wearing them out
onto the street. Mrs. Thompson was still watching him.

Despite these new stories about Burdette which everyone in
town heard and afterward repeated, people in Holt were still not
alarmed. They were still amused by his disappearance and by his
post-Christmas shopping spree. If nothing else, there was a good
deal of joking and fun to be had at Lloyd Foster's and Ralph Bird's
expense. People said that either man could profit by hiring Mrs.

Thompson to clerk in his store. They said Mrs. Thompson would at least have cut their losses.

But then that first week of Burdette's disappearance turned into a second week. And then gradually the jokes in the bakery and the pool halls and the tavern began to grow stale and there began to be other people in Holt, besides Ralph Bird and Lloyd Foster, who were growing doubtful that Burdette was ever going to return. No one had any idea where he was and there wasn't anyone in the county who could imagine what was keeping him away.

It was the middle of January then. It was late on a Friday afternoon and it was at this time that Jessie Burdette came into the office of the *Holt Mercury*. During the afternoon it had been snowing and now it was very cold outside. There was little traffic on Main Street and the wind was blowing the dry wisps of snow along the sidewalk. Above the storefronts it was beginning to turn dark.

Jessie Burdette came into the *Mercury* just before five o'clock. She had the two little boys with her. TJ was almost four years old then and Bobby was almost three. They came in bundled up in their winter clothes, the boys in matching snowsuits and Jessie in a navy blue wool coat which was still loose enough that she could button it over her stomach; for, although we didn't know it yet, she was pregnant again; she was already in her fourth month. Inside the office she sat TJ and Bobby down together on a wooden chair against the wall. The little boys looked handsome as ever and red-cheeked. She unzipped their snowsuits and smoothed the hair back from their foreheads. "Now sit still, please," she told them. Then she stepped up to the counter and waited for Mrs. Walsh.

Mrs. Walsh was the office receptionist. My father had hired her to work in the office twenty years earlier as copy editor, and she had stayed on all those years although my father himself had

retired in 1970 and had left the daily management of the paper
to me. Now she stood up from her desk and approached the
counter. From across the room I watched her talking to Jessie
Burdette.

"Yes?" Mrs. Walsh said. "Can I help you?"

"I want to print something in the paper."

"Is it an ad?"

"No. It's not an ad."

"Ads are fifty cents per line."

"It's not an ad, though."

"What is it, then? Do you have it with you?"

I watched Jessie reach into her coat pocket and draw out a
sheet of yellow tablet paper. She began to unfold it on the counter.
When it was completely unfolded she pushed it across the counter
toward Mrs. Walsh.

Mrs. Walsh picked it up and held it close to her face under
the light. Immediately she put the paper down again. She stood
up very straight. "Why," she said, "we can't print this. This is . . .
We can't print this."

"I intend to pay for it," Jessie said. "Is that the problem?"

"No that is not the problem."

"What is the problem, then? Why can't you print it?"

"It's simply unprintable."

Jessie looked past Mrs. Walsh, looking across the room at
Betty Lucas who was typing at her desk, and then at me. "Is there
someone else I can talk to?" she said.

"What?"

"I'd like to talk to someone else, please."

"But they'll just tell you the same thing I have."

"What about Mr. Arbuckle? He's the editor, isn't he?"

"Mr. Arbuckle is busy."

"I'd like to talk to him."

"But I've just told you. He's busy."

"Yes, but would you ask him to come over here?"

I stood up from my desk and walked across the room to the counter. Mrs. Walsh had begun to shake. The dark veins at the side of her head stood out beneath her white hair. "Is there something wrong, Mrs. Walsh?"

"This young woman thinks we will publish this in the paper."

"What is it?"

"Here," she said. "You read it. I refuse to." She handed the tablet paper to me.

"Thank you, Mrs. Walsh," I said. "Maybe you can begin closing up now."

She turned and sat down at her desk. I could hear her behind me. She was upset. She had begun to whisper in the direction of Betty Lucas.

I read what was on the paper. It was a brief notice. It had been written in pencil and the paper it had been written on had been folded many times, into small squares, and at the edges it was frayed and ragged as though she had been carrying it around in her pocket for a week waiting for the right moment to bring it in. Then I looked at Jessie. Her eyes were very brown and her cheeks were still red from having been outside in the cold. I thought she looked very beautiful. There were bits of dry snow on the shoulders of her blue coat.

"Yes," I said. "I've heard your husband was gone. I suppose we've all heard that much. But I take it you haven't heard from him yet either. Is that what this is about?"

"No. I haven't heard from him."

"Where do you think he is?"

"I don't know. I haven't any idea where Jack Burdette is."

"You've notified the police, though?"

"Yes. But yesterday there was a bill in the mail."

"A bill?"

"For some clothes he charged," Jessie said. "So I called them back and told them they could stop looking for him. He isn't lost."

"I see," I said. "I think I do, anyway." Because it seemed

obvious to me now, having read what she'd written on the piece of tablet paper, that she had come to a thorough understanding about the charges Burdette had made on Main Street and also about what those charges indicated about his disappearance. She hadn't had to be present for the jokes and the talk in the bakery, or later to be there to hear the growing alarm people felt. She seemed to understand all too well what those things would mean to her as his wife in Holt.

I looked outside for a moment. On Main Street it was fully dark now. The streetlights had come on and it was snowing again. Behind me Mrs. Walsh and Betty Lucas had begun to put their coats on, preparing to go home for the evening. I waited until they had gone out through the back room into the alley. Then I turned back to Jessie.

"I wonder, Mrs. Burdette," I said, "I wonder if you don't think this is a little bit drastic? After all he might come back. Don't you think? Maybe he's just taking a vacation."

"No," she said. "I don't think that. I've stopped thinking that. It's been two weeks."

"Yes. But two weeks aren't a lifetime."

"They're long enough."

"And so you still want me to print this in the paper? You do want that?"

She began to open her purse. "How much is it?"

"But wait a minute," I said. "I haven't said I will yet."

She looked at me. Her eyes were very large and dark. I picked up the penciled notice once more, reading it again while she turned to see that the two little boys were still seated quietly on the chair behind her. They were watching her like little birds.

Finally I said: "Very well, then. I'll agree to print this. Although I don't think it will do you any good. In fact I'm afraid it will do you a great deal of harm in town."

She still wanted it printed. So I took out a form from a shelf

•

under the counter. I copied her note onto the form as she had written it and afterward she paid for it.

She began to prepare TJ and Bobby to go outside again. They sat solemnly in front of her while she knelt to zip up their snowsuits; she helped them pull their mittens on.

I was standing behind the counter, watching her. Her blue coat was smooth and neat across the hips and her hair looked dark and lovely. "Listen," I said, "will you let me drive you and your boys home? I'm leaving now anyway."

She looked out the front window. Outside it was worse: it was snowing harder and the wind was blowing the snow horizontally along the street. "If it's not any trouble," she said. "I don't want them to get cold again."

"I'll get my coat."

Thus she allowed me to drive them across town to Gum Street that first time because it was snowing and because it was cold outside. I don't recall that we said anything of significance. TJ sat on the seat between us and she had Bobby on her lap and I suppose during the six- or seven-block ride one of us managed to say something about the accumulation of snow. It was a quiet and awkward ride. But at the curb when I stopped to let them out I remember watching her take the boys up the sidewalk into their small house in the snow and I recall how she looked in her blue coat when she opened the door and then how the house itself looked after she had turned the lights on. Afterward I drove home again to the house where Nora and Toni were waiting for me to eat supper with them. But I wasn't very much interested in supper just then, nor in going home again, nor even in my wife and daughter. I suppose by that time I was already a little in love with Jessie Burdette.

So in the following week I ran her notice as a kind of display ad on the back page of the *Holt Mercury* just as she had wanted it. I offset it with the announcements for Sunday church services and the obituaries for two longtime Holt County residents. Her notice said: *I'm not responsible for whatever Jack Burdette did or will do. He's no good. It doesn't matter what people say. He's a son of a bitch and I don't care anymore.*

I had my own reasons for printing it.

This public declaration of hers caused a stir in town when people read it. My father, for one, called me on the phone and said I was crazy to print such a thing. What did I think I was doing? It was unprofessional, he said; it was bad business practice. This was Holt County, Colorado, not San Francisco, California. Did I think he'd turned the paper over to have it ruined?

Of course other people in town felt similarly, as I knew they would, although their annoyance and their objections had more to do with moral considerations than with any concern over practical issues. Some of the older women were particularly incensed: they wrote letters to the editor about the appearance of profanity in the *Holt Mercury*. They didn't like it, not the profanity nor the public display of raw emotion, and a number of the women canceled their subscriptions as a result.

Nonetheless, the commotion Jessie's notice caused in Holt County that week was soon forgotten. It was a minor episode compared to what happened in the weeks and months that followed. And all of that got into the paper too.

Then there was one other small event which reflected on what was printed in the *Mercury* at about that time. It was in a minor key. It had to do with Jack Burdette's mother.

She was an ancient woman now, gray-haired and very thin and even more severe than she had been before, but still living alone in the house on North Birch Street and still attending the Catholic church on Sunday mornings when she was able. After her son had been gone for about a month, in a kind of desperate form of masculine absurdity—since no woman would have even considered such a thing—several of the men in town decided that they would call on old Mrs. Burdette to ask her some questions. They thought it would be worthwhile to inquire if she had heard from her son. They hoped, if nothing else, that she might be able to suggest where he had gone.

So one afternoon they walked up onto the front porch and rang the doorbell. But after Mrs. Burdette had opened the door to them she didn't ask them in. She merely waited inside, in the dark front hallway of the house, listening to their questions and foolish talk from beyond the scarcely-opened door. They continued to explain to her what they had come for. Then they stopped talking; she hadn't said anything yet. She had simply stared at them out of those clean little wire-rimmed glasses while she studied one face and then another. She didn't seem to know or even to care what they were talking about. In exasperation, one of the men said to her: "But, Mrs. Burdette, look here: you do know Jack's gone, don't you? You do read the local newspaper? Why, it's been in the *Mercury*. Haven't you seen it?"

When she spoke finally, her voice sounded harsh and rusty, as if she hadn't used it in days. "I don't know anything about your newspapers," she said. "And I don't want to. I read the Bible."

Then she shut the door in their faces. They could hear her locking it. Afterward they could hear the faint sound of her steps retreating into the interior of the silent house. So the men were left standing on the front porch. They felt foolish. They looked at one another and moved quickly down off the porch like little boys who had done something silly.

In any case, by the end of January the alarm in Holt had turned at last to shock and fear. People had finally grown afraid that something serious had happened to Jack Burdette and they were disturbed to think so. They still liked Burdette and thinking something bad had happened to him made them feel less secure for themselves in their corner of Colorado. The police had begun to send out all-points bulletins across the state, hoping that might turn him up. But nothing did. Burdette had disappeared without a trace.

Meanwhile at the Farmers' Co-op Elevator things were a mess. Without Burdette there to manage the elevator every day, nothing was getting done properly and Arch Withers and the other members of the board of directors didn't know what to do. Finally they decided to ask Doyle Francis to come back. They wanted Doyle to run things again, on a temporary basis, so that the routine shipment of corn and wheat might continue once more, until Burdette turned up, or until . . . well, until they had to hire his replacement. Still they refused to think it would come to that.

Then, about the middle of February, that private feeling of shock and fearfulness in Holt turned suddenly to hostility and public outrage. For, by that time, Doyle Francis had had sufficient opportunity to examine the books at the elevator. And in going over the books he had discovered that something was wrong. He called a special meeting of the board to tell them about it. It was on a Tuesday afternoon.

"Jesus Christ," he told the men when they were assembled before him in his office. "What in the goddamn hell were you boys thinking of anyhow?"

"What do you mean?" Arch Withers said.

"Didn't you even check on him? Didn't you even think to look at these books yourselves?"

"Of course we did. We looked at them. Charlie Soames went over these books every year with us. So did Jack Burdette. What's wrong with them?"

"Plenty," Doyle said.

"Like what, for instance?"

"Like this, goddamn it." Doyle pointed to the books spread

•

out before him on the desk. "As near as I can tell, you're missing about a hundred and fifty thousand dollars. That's what's wrong with them."

"What? Hold on now. You mean to say—"

"I mean that's just an old man's estimate. It's been going on for three or four years."

"What's been going on? What are you talking about?"

Doyle explained it to them. In careful, rational detail, he showed the men sitting across from him what had happened, how the books had been manipulated, how they had been juggled by someone who knew what he was doing. But just a little at first, Doyle said, pointing to the pages of neat figures, then in larger and larger amounts as the months passed. And all very cleverly, in a kind of sleight of hand, as a CPA might do it if he had in mind to do something neat and criminal. Doyle said it had taken him days to understand how it had been done. Finally he had, though. "Oh, it was careful," he said. "I'll give them that much."

The men sat silently, looking at the opened books on the desk. They picked at their hands and refused to look at one another. For his part, Doyle Francis sat back in his chair watching them.

At last Arch Withers said: "All right. If what you say is true, who did it? Who's them?"

"What?"

"You said them. Who do you mean by that?"

"Who do you think I mean?"

"How the hell do I know? Do you mean Charlie Soames?"

"Why not? Charlie did the books, didn't he? He did the books when I was here before and I assume you boys kept him on after I left."

"That son of a bitch," Bob Wilcox said. Wilcox was the young man on the board. "Goddamn that old—"

"And Burdette?" Withers said, interrupting him. "What about him? Was he in on this too?"

"Of course he was. Don't you think he had to be? Why else was he going to charge those new clothes on Main Street and then disappear and not come back home again?"

"By god," Wilcox said. "He's another son of a bitch. We ought to—"

"Shut up," Withers said. "It's too late for any of your hysterics."

"That's right," Doyle said. "It's too late for a lot of things. Except I believe that Charlie's still in town, isn't he?"

"He's still in town."

"Then I'll go get him, if none of you will. I'll bring that—"

"Damn it," Withers said. "I already told you to shut up. Now do it." Young Bob Wilcox started to say something more, but Withers turned and stared at him. Then Wilcox closed his mouth tight and Withers turned back to Doyle Francis. "So what do you suggest we do about this? You seem to of thought about it."

"Oh yes. I've thought about it," Doyle said. "It's about all I have thought about for the last two weeks."

"So? Are you going to tell us what to do or not?"

"There's only one thing to do. We let the sheriff's office handle it now. We call Bud Sealy and tell him to go over to Charlie Soames's house and arrest him and lock him up and then we wait for the trial. What else is there?"

"But there's still the money, isn't there? What about the money?"

"What about it?"

"Well goddamn it. It was our money. It was all us share-holders' money."

"Sure it was," Doyle said. "And you can tell that to the judge too, when you get the chance. But I don't suppose that will get it back for you. Jack Burdette's been gone for a month a half and god only knows where he's gone to. But wherever he is, he's already begun to spend it. You can count on that."

There was silence again while this new thought sank in. The

men stared hatefully at the accountant's books on Doyle's desk. After a time, Arch Withers roused himself once more.

"Go on, then." he said. "What are you waiting on? Make your goddamn call. Call Bud Sealy."

"No," Doyle Francis said. "I don't think I will. I think one of you boys ought to be able to call him. It's your funeral. I've been thinking about this mess for too long already."

So Arch Withers, as president of the Farmers' Co-op Elevator's board of directors, called Bud Sealy from the manager's office that Tuesday afternoon, with the books still spread out on the desk before him and while Doyle Francis and the other men watched him.

And subsequently that same afternoon Bud Sealy arrested Charlie Soames at his home in the six hundred block on Cedar Street, where Soames had a small office at the back of the house. Sealy drove over to the house, parked and knocked on the door. He was let in by Mrs. Soames. She was an excitable old woman with heavy breasts and meaty arms. She led the sheriff back to Charlie's little office and stood in the doorway.

When Sealy entered the room—it was all neat and tidy as ever—Charlie Soames seemed to be waiting for him. He was sitting at his desk with his hands folded and he seemed to have everything in order. It was as though he had prepared himself for Sealy's arrival, as if he were glad that it was over now. "So you know," Soames said.

"Yeah. I just got a call from Arch Withers."

"It took them long enough. I expected you a month ago."

"I'm here now. Are you ready?"

"Yes."

"Ready?" Mrs. Soames said. "Ready for what?" She was still standing in the doorway, displacing air. Her hair stood out from her pink head. "Where are you taking him?"

"Your husband's got himself into trouble."

"My husband? What do you mean? What could he do?"

"Enough," the sheriff said. "Now maybe you'd better go into the other room for a minute."

"I'm not going into the other room. So he has done something. The old fool! He's done something and now what am I supposed to do?"

"For one thing," Sealy said, "you're going to be quiet."

"I didn't do anything. You can't tell me in my own house to—"

"Yes. You're going to be quiet. Or I'm going to gag you."

Mrs. Soames glared at the sheriff. "You wouldn't touch me. You wouldn't dare touch a lady."

"Try me," he said. He took a step toward her and she backed up.

"Oh!"

Then she began to shriek. Sealy shut the door on her. They could hear her excited noises. But after a moment the noises stopped.

"That's better," he said. He turned back to her husband.

Charlie Soames was still seated silently at his clean desk. It was as if he had been waiting for this too. Now he stood up and Sealy told him he had the right to remain silent. Then he put handcuffs around Soames's thin wrists. Afterward they walked out of the tidy little office and on through the house. Mrs. Soames was waiting for them in the dining room; she followed the two men toward the front hallway. When they stopped at the door so the sheriff could open it, Mrs. Soames began to shriek again. She rushed her husband and began to slap at him, at his face and neck. Soames fell down under her hands. She slapped at his head. Finally Bud Sealy shoved in between them, pushing Mrs. Soames away.

"Quit that," he said. "What do you think you're doing? Goddamn it, stop that now."

He lifted the old man by the arm and they went outside. Mrs. Soames followed them out onto the front porch. She stood watching angrily as the car drove away.

When they arrived at the courthouse Sealy walked Charlie Soames down to the basement to the sheriff's office and booked him for the suspected embezzlement of Co-op funds. Afterward he fingerprinted him and then he led Soames back to a cell. He stood over him while the old man sat down on the cot. Soames looked very small and tired. But he wasn't quite defeated yet.

"Well," the sheriff said. "You want to tell me about this?"

"What's there to tell?

"Oh there ought to be something."

"Do you mean you want a formal confession?"

"Something like that."

"What do you want to know?"

"Well. For starters—I'm just curious—why in hell didn't you take off too? You had your chances, didn't you?"

"You mean why didn't I leave?"

"Sure. Like Jack Burdette did. You and Burdette were in this together, weren't you? Why didn't you jump up and leave when he did? You could of left with him."

"Him," Charlie Soames said. The mention of Burdette seemed to awaken something in him. He sat up straight, agitated now. "Why that man . . . that—"

"What about him?"

"He didn't even tell me he was leaving. We agreed on it. He promised me. He wasn't supposed to leave yet. Then he—"

"Sure," Sealy said. "Then he."

"But you don't understand."

"Don't I?"

"No. Because we were waiting for it to amount to two hundred thousand. That's why. And I kept telling him we ought

to leave now. I told him we have to take it and get out now. Before
the auditors find out, I said. They were getting suspicious. I could
tell that. I knew they were. I tried to tell him. But my god, that
man kept saying: 'Just another fifty. Just another fifty.' Like it was
play money or something. Oh, he didn't understand the risks. He
didn't understand anything. And it was his idea from the beginning. I let him talk me into it. But I was the one that had to do
the books, wasn't I? Not him. And he kept promising me: 'Wait
until it's two hundred thousand, then we'll leave together.' That's
what he said. We agreed on that. He promised me. But then
he—"

"Yeah," Sealy said. "Well. You poor dumb old son of bitch.
So he didn't tell you he was leaving either."

"I thought I could trust him."

"Of course. Except you weren't the only one in town that
thought that, now were you?"

"I trusted him, though. And what was I going to do now?
Where was I going to go? He had the money. He took everything.
He withdrew it all out of the bank over in Sterling. And—"

"Sterling? You mean you kept the money over in Sterling?"

"That's where we had our account. I thought it would be
safer. But I still thought I could trust him. I still believed he was
trustworthy."

"That's right," Sealy said. "Because he promised you. Because
you agreed on it."

Soames stopped talking for a moment. He looked at the
sheriff.

"But wouldn't you have said he could be trusted? Didn't you
think Jack Burdette was a trustworthy man?"

"I don't know," Sealy said, "Probably. But I might of said the
same thing about you too, Charlie. And now look at you. Jesus
Christ, look how you turned out."

*   *   *

By evening everyone in Holt County knew about the arrest of
Charlie Soames. They had heard about the embezzlement of
Co-op funds and about his three-year involvement in it. So the
panic and outrage had already begun. The Co-op Elevator was
owned in shares by half the people in the area and they all wanted
blood.

They would have preferred Jack Burdette's and Charlie
Soames's blood, both, but Burdette had disappeared. Burdette
was already in California, lost somewhere in the streets of Los
Angeles. The police had finally managed to trace him that far, but
then they had lost track of him. Consequently people in Holt
began to understand that they were going to have to content
themselves with the arrest of his accomplice, with the indictment
and conviction of old Charlie Soames, and then with his rightful
punishment. They expected to get something satisfying out of him
at least.

And that was awful, really. Charlie Soames was already
seventy years old by that time. Like Jack Burdette, he had grown
up here. And everyone knew him just as they thought they had
known Jack Burdette, except that Soames hadn't any of Burdette's flair for sudden and outlandish acts. He was merely an old
man who had always lived here. He had spent his entire life being
steady and normal and unremarkable. For almost half a century
he had been a bookkeeper and accountant for various businessmen in town, and at forty he had married a woman who was only
a year or two younger than he was, a woman who dominated him
completely, and together they hadn't been able to have any
children. Or perhaps they hadn't even tried to have children. No
one knew about that. His wife liked to talk, but that didn't happen
to be one of the topics she liked to talk about. No, the truth was,
Charlie Soames's entire life had been about as gray as a man's life
can be. Now suddenly he had done this.

So he was arrested. And in very short time he was indicted.
Then he posted bail and he was released to await the trial. He

made the bail payment out of his own meager life's savings, out of money which he had accumulated over years of frugality; it had nothing to do with the embezzlement; he had earned this particular money by doing bookwork for others—the police had checked. So he was released and then he went home again to his wife. But that must have been worse than sitting in a cell in the basement of the Holt County Courthouse on Albany Street. He would have been left alone for a few hours in jail. There would have been silence there. But now, once he was home again, Mrs. Soames must have made it hot for him. She was capable of that. She must have ground him like hamburger.

Perhaps that was why, about a week after he was released, he showed up on Main Street once more. It was in the middle of a weekday morning. He walked into Bradbury's Bakery to have coffee. I don't know, perhaps he had in mind to test the water, to take a kind of reading of Holt County feelings about things. The bakery was crowded as usual at that time of day. Businessmen and housewives and store clerks and one or two farmers were drinking coffee and eating doughnuts, sitting about the room at the various tables. They were all talking.

Then Soames walked into the bakery and everyone got quiet. They watched this small tidy familiar old man fill his coffee cup at the urn at the front counter, watched him pay for it and then turn to find a seat. Across the room there was a vacant chair at a table near the wall. Ralph Bird and a couple of other men happened to be sitting at the table. Soames approached them.

"Wait just a goddamn minute," Ralph Bird said. "Where do you think you're going with that?"

Soames stood beside the table staring at him.

"Get the hell out of here. You ain't sitting here with us."

Soames looked at the other men. He had done books for each of them. They stared back at him.

And he was just an old defeated man now and he knew everyone in the room. His hand began to shake. The coffee in the

·

cup spilled out over his hand and shirt cuff and dripped onto the floor. He was making a mess. He continued to stand there, his hand shaking and the hot coffee burning his hand, while his eyes clouded over. His eyes seemed to lose their focus.

At last one of the girls came out from behind the counter and removed the cup from his hand. "Here," she said, "give me that." It was as if he were a child. She wiped his hand with a dishrag and knelt to wipe the floor.

Then Soames looked once more at the people in the bakery. They were still watching him. He turned and walked out of the store onto the sidewalk. They could see him through the plate-glass windows. He stood for a moment, looking up and down the street. Finally he went home again.

At his home on Cedar Street he entered by the front door and climbed the stairs to the attic. His wife was at the back of the house, peeling carrots at the kitchen sink. Later she would tell people that she didn't even know he was home yet. He was always so quiet.

She did hear the explosion in the attic, however. Several other people did too. The neighbors heard it.

Because, after he had mounted the stairs, he had entered the dusty box-filled room and had sat down on an old trunk near the chimney, under a single dim light bulb suspended from one of the rafters. Sitting on the trunk, he had put a shell in the chamber of an old .22 single-shot rifle. Then he had placed the butt of the rifle on the floor between his feet and had closed his tired little mouth around the gun barrel. And whether he paused once to look about him, as people do in movies, to take one last look out the attic window toward the tops of the trees standing up in the backyard, no one knows. We simply know that he fired a single sphere of lead up through his palate into his brain and that this little sphere of lead destroyed him.

It destroyed him, but it didn't kill him. The bullet had lodged in his brain in such a way that he was still alive.

He was slumped against the chimney when his wife ran upstairs to find out what had caused the noise. The gun was still between his knees. There was considerable blood running down onto his shirtfront and his head was thrown back horribly. He was still breathing, though. There were red bubbles coming up out of his mouth. Looking at him, Mrs. Soames became hysterical. She began to scream. Then the neighbors arrived and it was one of them who called the police.

They flew him immediately to a hospital in Denver. And in Denver the surgeons did what they could; they closed the hole in the roof of his mouth and made other repairs. But in the end they decided to leave the bullet where it was. They said it might kill him to try to remove it. Afterward when he was well enough to be released from the hospital he was brought back home again to Holt.

And so he looked all right, more or less, when we saw him again. He still resembled himself; he was still a neat tidy little old man. It was only his eyes that looked different. His eyes appeared to be blank now, expressionless, as if there was nothing behind them. He could eat and he could drink liquids. He could still function. He could even talk a little, in a harsh lisping monotone. But it didn't matter if he could talk. What he had to say now was all nonsense, mere jabber and repeated dribble about nothing.

So old Mrs. Soames didn't know what to do with him then. She dressed him and fed him every day, and sat him on the swing on the front porch. And occasionally she stood him out in the front yard where he could hold a garden hose in his hands. But, if she let him, he would stand there all afternoon, slapping water on the grass. He seemed to like playing with water. Then people would walk by the house and see him. And sometimes they would say something to him, something cruel and nasty, something vindictive like: "You old son of a bitch. Why don't you try it again? Why don't you use a deer rifle this time? Just try it once. Oh, goddamn you, anyway." And Charlie would simply go on spraying the grass with water while some of it ran off his elbow onto his shoes; he would nod and jabber at the people passing by and he would seem to listen to their talk, cocking his head like some ancient, confused little bird. And when they moved away down the street he would even seem to follow them with his blank eyes. But none of that meant anything to him. It was all a mere show to him, a display of shadows that happened to move and talk. None of it held any significance.

If he had only known it then, I suppose he might even have been happy. He couldn't understand anything his wife or anyone else in Holt had told him, and he couldn't recall the first thing about debits and credits and about double entry bookkeeping. Consequently he knew nothing at all, nothing whatsoever, about his involvement in the embezzlement of Co-op funds.

So he was in a perfect state now: he was mad. He couldn't be bothered anymore and he was completely beyond the reach of the law. There wasn't any way to punish him for what he had done. He was beyond all of that. Any thought of putting him on trial was out of the question.

· 8 ·

Now people in Holt felt they had to turn elsewhere for some form of restitution. They felt doubly cheated. Burdette had disappeared at the end of December and every day he was gone it became more obvious that the police were never going to locate him and bring him back. Now his accomplice wasn't even going to be put on trial.

So in time people began to turn on his wife, on Jessie. They wanted satisfaction from someone and she was still here, she was still in Holt, and it made it easier that they thought of her as an outsider. She had been in Holt for almost six years, but she had always been too aloof for her own good, people said. From the day she had arrived she had held herself apart. It was as if she felt she were too good for them—that's what people thought. So they were naturally a little in awe of her, and a little antagonistic. They didn't understand her; they thought of her as that woman Jack Burdette had discovered in some Holiday Inn in Oklahoma, that small quiet overly independent woman he had met and married in Tulsa when he should have married Wanda Jo Evans, a local girl whom everybody liked and admired. No, she had not grown up here,

•

and there wasn't anyone in town who knew very much about her.

So perhaps it was inevitable, given the pitch of emotion and the nature of people, that since there was no one else in Holt who was still available to them, they turned on Jessie Burdette. They were outraged by what had happened and nearly everyone had been affected by it in some way. They began to associate the problems at the elevator with Jessie's arrival. The notice she had printed in the *Mercury* ended up not making any difference to anyone. Too much had happened since then, and now no one quite believed her.

Thus for three or four months that spring Jessie Burdette became public property. There was a kind of general insanity in Holt, a feeling that almost anything was possible. It was as if people had declared open season on her and thought of it as a matter of community honor.

At first there didn't seem to be anything you could put your finger on. There seemed to be merely an increased watchfulness whenever she was present, an intensified correctness and communal coolness toward her whenever she appeared on Main Street. People talked to her now only when they had to, at the checkout stand in the grocery store, or at the gas station when she paid for gas. No one voluntarily greeted her.

Then one evening someone in a car ran over TJ and Bobby's orange cat in the street out in front of the house. The little boys found it the next morning on the front step. Its death might have been an accident but whoever had killed it had brought the cat to the house without stopping to apologize or to offer any explanation. The cat was badly mangled; its fur had been torn open, exposing its insides, and it had been placed where Jessie and the boys were sure to see it. The boys were badly upset by this. Jessie helped them bury it beside the fence in the backyard.

Still, despite this increasing hostility, she continued to stay in Holt. I am not certain why that is, even now. Most of us, I think,

would not have stayed here even for a week, not if we felt we had
any alternative. But perhaps that had a good deal to do with it,
the fact that she felt she had nowhere else to go. There was
nothing for her in Oklahoma anymore; her parents had divorced
and now her mother was in a home for invalids and she hadn't
heard anything from her father in years. She wasn't even certain
where he was. As for her brothers, they had both enlisted in the
military as soon as they had graduated from high school, so she
couldn't have gone to them even if she had wanted to. And in any
case, she didn't want to. She seemed to want to stay in Holt, to
see this out for her own reasons. It was as if she were determined
to react even to these events in her own quiet and independent
way, as if her opinion of herself depended upon this alone. It was
as if she were trying to prove something.

So it was tragic finally. In the end it became more than just
a matter of money. When it was over it was so painful to think
about that there were very few people in Holt who ever wanted
to remember it.

It began in April. At the beginning of April that year she appeared
one afternoon at the elevator beside the railroad tracks. She
walked up the plank steps into the outer office and scale room
and told Bob Thomas she wanted to see Doyle Francis. This
surprised Bob Thomas. It was just after lunch and Bob had eaten
too much as usual and was half asleep. He was slouched at the desk
behind the counter, shuffling through some shipping receipts.
When he looked up there she was. "What?" he said. "What'd you
say?"

"I'd like to see Doyle Francis, please. I believe he's still
working here."

"I'll go get him. No, I'll go tell him. Hell. You wait here."

She had her information right; Doyle Francis was in fact still
working at the elevator. In the three months since her husband

had left town, the board of directors had begun to advertise for
a new manager, as they had promised Doyle Francis they would,
but they hadn't hired a permanent replacement yet because in the
intervening days and weeks they had become suspicious of their
fellow man. Deeply, excessively suspicious. They had begun to
insist on researching each applicant's past—and not just his work
experience, as is customary when hiring somebody new, but his
ethical and moral and religious history as well. It was as if they
had begun to suspect everybody, to believe every man in the world
who applied for the manager's job at the elevator wanted only to
take their money, to skip town with it. In the end, however, what
they really only wanted to ask these men was: "Goddamn it, if we
hire you now, how long are you going to be here working for us
before you think you have to add to what we pay you, before you
turn out to be another son of a bitch like Jack Burdette did? You
ought to at least be able to tell us that much."

No one blamed them for this attitude, for this new profound
mistrust of others; most of the people in Holt felt similarly. But,
because of the board's suspicions, Doyle Francis was still there in
April, still waiting for the board to hire someone else so he could
relax into retirement again. That afternoon he was still in his old
office when Bob Thomas burst in.

"She's here," Bob said. "She wants to see you."

"Who does?"

"Her. That son of a bitch's wife. She's out there in the scale
room."

"What does she want?"

"How the hell do I know? She just said she wanted to see you.
That's all she said."

"Well," Doyle said. "Show her in, Bob. Or are you scared,
if we get too close to her, she might steal your pocketbook or
something?"

"By god," Bob said. "I don't trust none of them no more.
That's a fact."

"Never mind," Doyle said. "Ask her to come back here. Go on now, try to act like a gentleman for once in your life."

"I don't need to act like no gentleman. Not with her, I don't."

He turned and went back out to get Jessie. She was still standing at the counter.

"He said he'd see you. Come on, I'll show you where he's at."

"Thank you," Jessie said, "but I know where the manager's office is."

"Well don't take too long. Some of us got to work for a living."

Jessie walked around the counter and down the narrow hallway past the toilet and the storage room. She was wearing slacks and a loose green blouse. When she entered, Doyle Francis stood up. He was one of the few men in town then, at least of those connected to the elevator, who still treated her with respect and minimal courtesy. He offered her a wooden chair with armrests.

She sat down heavily, a little carefully—she was still pregnant then, still carrying that little girl of hers that Burdette had left her with; she was in her seventh month. She set her purse on her shortened lap, in front of her stomach.

"Now, then," Doyle said. "What can I do for you, Jessie?"

"I don't want anything. If that's what you think."

"No," he said. "I don't think that. They don't pay me enough to worry about what other people think."

"Well I don't," Jessie said. "I didn't come here to ask for anything. I came here to give you something."

"Oh?" he said. "What is it you want to give me?"

"Not you. The board of directors. The elevator. All these people."

"What is it?"

"Here." She opened her purse and withdrew a legal document. She pushed it across the desk toward him. Doyle picked it up, looked at it.

"Wait a minute," he said. "Hold on now. This is some kind of a deed, isn't it?"

"They said it was legal."

"Who said it was legal? What are you talking about?"

"The people down at the bank. They said I could sign it over to whoever I wanted to, even if Jack wasn't here to cosign it. They said considering the circumstances it would be all right."

"Did they now?" Doyle said. "I'll bet they did too."

He looked at the document again, read it this time. It was a quitclaim deed transferring the title of a house and property over to the board of directors of the Holt County Farmers' Co-op Elevator. Her signature was at the bottom in fresh ink.

"All right, then," he said, "I suppose it is legal. I wouldn't know; I'm not a lawyer. But then I don't suppose anybody around here would protest it very much, would they? Even if it wasn't legal?"

"No. They wouldn't protest it."

Doyle laid the deed down on the desk. He folded his hands over it. He said: "How old are you, Jessie?"

"I'm twenty-seven."

"And you have two boys?"

"Yes."

"How old are they?"

"They've just turned four and three. But why are you asking me these—"

"And you're going to have another one pretty soon, aren't you?"

"In June," she said. "But—"

"Do you believe in hell?" he said. "Is that it?"

She stared back at him.

"Is that why you're doing this? Because, let me tell you, I don't think there is any hell. No, I don't. And I don't think there's any heaven either. We just die, that's all. We just stop breathing after a while and then everybody starts to forget about us and pretty soon they can't even remember what it is we think we did to them."

"I don't know what I believe," she said.

"Then why are you doing this? Will you tell me that?"

"Because," she said.

"Because? That's all. Just because."

She continued to stare back at him, to watch him, her eyes steady and deep brown.

Finally Doyle said: "All right, you're not going to tell me. You don't have to tell me; I think I know anyway. But listen now. Listen: let an old man ask you this. Don't you think you're going to need that house anymore? I mean, if you give it up like you're proposing to do, just where in hell are you and these kids going to live afterwards?"

"That's my concern," she said. "Isn't it?"

"Yes, of course it is, but—"

"And you agree it's legal, don't you?"

"Yes. As far as I can tell."

"So will you please give that piece of paper to the board? You can tell them we'll be out of the house by the first of May."

"But listen," he said. "Damn it, wait a minute now—"

Because Jessie had already stood up. She was already leaving. And Doyle Francis was still leaning toward the chair she had been sitting in. Those good intentions of his were still swimming undelivered in his head and his arms were still resting on that quitclaim deed on his desk. She walked out through the hallway and on outside.

In the scale room Bob Thomas watched her leave. When she had driven away he went in to see Doyle. "Well," he said, "she was here long enough. What'd she want?"

"What?"

"I said, 'What'd she want?' Burdette's wife."

"Nothing. She didn't want anything."

"I don't believe that."

"I don't care what you believe. That woman doesn't want a goddamn thing from any one of us."

"What do you mean she doesn't want anything? She's a Burdette, isn't she?"

"I mean," Doyle Francis said, "get the hell out of here and leave me alone. Goddamn it, Bob, go find something else to do with yourself."

For some of the people in Holt that was enough. I suppose they felt about it a little like Doyle Francis did, that she deserved the magnanimity of their good intentions. Privately, they understood that she was innocent, or at least they knew that she was ignorant. It wasn't her fault, they told themselves; she wasn't involved. They could afford to be nice to her. Anyway, they could refrain from actually wishing her harm.

For others, though, who were more vocal and more active, it still wasn't sufficient. These people argued that the house didn't amount to enough. It didn't matter that it was all that she had, that it was the sum total of her collateral and disposable property. It was merely an old two-bedroom house in the middle of town. It needed tin siding and new shingles; it needed painting. Besides, there was still a fifteen-year lien against it when she signed it over, so that when the board of directors became the fee owners of the house and then sold it at public auction, it didn't even begin to make a dent in that $150,000 that her husband had disappeared with. No, they weren't satisfied. A house wasn't alive and capable of bleeding, like a human was. It wasn't pregnant, like Jessie was.

In any case, by the first of May she and the two boys had moved out of the house as Jessie said they would—they had rented the downstairs apartment in the old Fenner place on Hawthorne Street at the west edge of town—and it was Doyle Francis who helped them move. They used his pickup. Jessie accepted that much assistance from him at least, although afterward she sent him a freshly baked chocolate cake on a platter, to square things, to keep that balance sheet of hers in the black.

Well, it was a nice enough apartment: they had five rooms—a kitchen, a living room, two small bedrooms, and there was a bathroom with a shower off the kitchen. They also had use of the front porch, a wide old-style porch with a wooden rail around it and with a swing suspended from hooks in the ceiling. From the porch, they could look west diagonally across the street toward open country since that was where Holt ended then, at Hawthorne Street: there was just Harry Smith's pasture west of them, a half-section of native grass in which Harry kept some horses. So it was a good place for her boys to grow up; they would have all that open space available to them across the street.

When they had settled in and after new curtains had been hung over the windows—heavier ones to block any view from the street—Jessie began to take care of the money end of it as well. She began to earn a living. She took a job at the Holt Cafe on Main Street. Six days a week she worked as a waitress, rising each morning to feed TJ and Bobby and to play with them until just before noon when the sitter, an old neighbor lady—Mrs. Nyla Waters, a kindly woman, a widow—came to watch the boys while Jessie worked through the noon rush and the afternoon and the dinner hour, and then returned again each evening about seven o'clock to bathe and put the boys to bed and to read them stories. She often sang to them a little too, before they slept.

And working in this way—being pregnant and having to spend that many hours away from her children—was not the optimum solution to all her problems either, of course, but she didn't have many alternatives. She refused to consider welfare. Accepting Aid to Dependent Children, or even food stamps, was not a part of her schedule of payments—that local balance sheet of hers, I mean—since any public assistance of this kind came from taxes. A portion of that public tax money would have originated, at least theoretically, in Holt County. She knew that.

And she didn't want anything from people in Holt. Not if she hadn't paid for it, she didn't. Doyle Francis was right about that.

But then, toward the end of spring that year, she discovered a way to make the final payment. She began to go out dancing at the Holt Legion on Saturday nights.

But no one would dance with her at first. She came down the stairs that first Saturday night early in May and walked over to the bar, lifted herself onto a barstool, ordered a vodka Collins, and waited. And nothing happened. Maybe it got a little quieter for a moment, but not very much, so she couldn't be certain that she'd even been noticed. She looked lovely too: she had made herself up and had put on a deep blue dress which was loose enough that her stomach showed only a little, as if she was merely in the first months of pregnancy; she was wearing nylons and heels; her brown hair was pulled away from her face in such a way that her eyes appeared to be even larger and darker than they were ordinarily. Sitting there, she waited; no one talked to her; nothing happened; finally she ordered another drink. On either side of her, men on barstools were talking to one another, so she swung around to look at the couples in the nearby booths. They were laughing loudly and rising regularly from the booths to dance. Maybe they looked at her; maybe they didn't—she didn't know. So that first night she sat there at the bar, waiting, for almost two hours. Then she went home.

The second time, that second Saturday—this would have been about the middle of May now—she drank a small glass of straight vodka at home in the kitchen before she went out. Also, she was dressed differently this time. There was more blue makeup over her eyes and she was wearing a dark red dress with a low neckline which showed a good deal of her full breasts, a dress which made no pretense of disguising her pregnancy; it was stretched tight across her stomach and hips. Preparing to go out, she combed her hair close against her cheeks, partially obscuring her face, and then she entered the Legion again, walked down the steps into that noise and intense Saturday night revelry a second time. And as before, she mounted a barstool, ordered a drink, and then she turned around, with that short red dress hiked two inches above the knees of her crossed legs, with a look of expectation, of invitation almost, held permanently on her beautiful face.

Well, it was pathetic in its lack of subtlely. But subtlety and pathos are not qualities which are much appreciated at the Legion on Saturday nights, so she only had to sit there for an hour this second time before Vince Higgims, Jr., asked to her to dance. Vince was one of Holt County's permanent bachelors, a lank, black-haired man, a man considered by many of us to be well-educated in the ways of strong drink and ladies in tight dresses. "Come on, girl," Vince said."They're playing my song."

They were playing Lefty Frizzell's "I Love You in a Thousand Ways," with its promise of change, the end of blue days—a song with a slow enough tempo to allow Vince, Jr., to work his customary magic. He led Jessie out onto the crowded floor and pulled her close against his belt buckle; then he began to pump her arm, to walk her backward in that rocking two-step while she held that permanent look of invitation on her face and he went on smiling past her hair in obvious satisfaction. They danced several dances that way, including a fast one or two so that Vince could demonstrate his skill at the jitterbug—he twirled her around and performed intricate movements with his hands— then they cooled off again with a slow song.

And that's how it began: innocently enough, I suppose, because unlike some of the others in town, at least Vince Higgims meant Jessie Burdette no harm. I doubt that Vince even had hopes of any postdance payoff. It was merely that he was drunk and that he liked to dance. The same cannot be said about the others, however. These other men were still remembering the grain elevator.

They all began to dance with her. It was as if Vince had broken some taboo, some barrier of accepted behavior, so that now it was not only acceptable to dance with Jack Burdette's pregnant wife, it was required; it was a matter of community honor and restitution. And so, ten or fifteen men took their turns with her that night. They danced her hard around the floor. They swung her violently around; they held her clenched against themselves, forcing their own slack stomachs against her swollen hard one. From that point on they danced every song with her. And all that time Jessie seemed to welcome it, to smile and speak pleasantly to all the men who held her. When it was over, though, when the band finally stopped playing and the lights were turned on once again, she was very pale; she was sweating and her dress looked wrinkled, worn out, stained, as if it had been cheapened. She went home exhausted.

But the local routine was established now—that three-week-long Holt County system of payment was initiated and accepted. And so the third time, that third Saturday night in May, it was just the same—only it was worse. This time the men not only danced with her in the same fierce vindictive manner but they also insisted on buying her drinks. She was wearing that same red dress too, washed and pressed again but showing the additional week of pregnancy. It looked tighter on her now, riper, as if the seams would burst at any moment, while above the deep neckline the blue veins in her full breasts showed clearly. Nevertheless, she danced with every man who asked her. They danced and danced—waltzes, jitterbugs, country two-steps, a kind of local hard-clenched fox-trot—anything and everything the men thought they knew how to do, regardless of the violence and energy it required. And this dancing, if you can call it that, this intense communal jig, stopped only when the band stopped. Then, during those ten minutes of brief rest between sets, they drank. They sat her on a barstool and three or four of them stood around her, telling jokes and buying drinks—taking turns with this too, ordering her double shots of scotch or whiskey or vodka—it didn't matter what the combination or how unlikely the mix—they ordered liquor for her to drink and insisted that she drink it. And she did that too. She accepted it all, seemed to welcome it all, as if she were privately obliged to honor any demand.

Of course by the evening's end she was even more exhausted this time than she had been the previous Saturday night. Also, she was very close to being drunk. When the lights came on at last, when the last man stopped dancing with her, she could barely walk off the dance floor. She was weak on her feet; there was a drunken waver in her step. She didn't say anything, though. Nothing in the way of complaint, I mean. And when that last man thought to ask her if she were coming back again the next week, she said: "You want me to, don't you?"

"Why course," he said. "Don't you know I'll be here? We'll all be here."

"Then I will too," she said.

And she was. Only, by this time, many of the women and at least some of the men in town were growing a little uneasy, a little uncomfortable with this particular form of weekly gambol and amusement. So not everyone showed up the following week, that last Saturday in May. Jessie did, though. It was the last time that she went to the Legion for a long time.

But again it was the same. She was wearing that same red dress, as if it were a uniform now, an essential part of the routine, and there was the same excessive amount of makeup on her face. She was drinking too—it was obvious in fact that she'd been drinking heavily even before she arrived at the Legion. She entered the bar-and-dance room about nine o'clock and didn't even bother this time to lift herself onto a barstool. She merely waited inside the door, with the music and smoke and laughter already at full strength around her. She didn't have to wait long: two or three men discovered her at the same moment and ushered her in.

"What are you drinking?" one of them said.

"Don't you want to dance first?"

"No, let's have a drink. I'm buying."

"All right," she said. "A whiskey sour, then."

"Make it a double," he said.

She drank it fast, as if it were no more than water or lemonade, as though she was no more conscious of what she drank than she was of the banter around her. When she had finished it, she set the glass down and said: "Now who's going to ask me to dance? I thought you boys knew how to dance."

"I'll show you how to dance," one of them said. "Come on."

This was Alden Haines, a man of forty-three who was only recently divorced and who farmed a couple of irrigated circles of corn east of town. He was not a bad man really, but he was still angry at the time about the divorce: his wife had been the one to initiate the legal proceedings. More to the point, he was a shareholder in the Farmers' Co-op Elevator. "See if you can keep up with this," he said.

He took her out onto the dance floor. Pushing roughly through the other couples, he began immediately to swing her about the floor in circles and abrupt spins. Jessie kept up with him, moving him back and forth or circling at the end of his outstretched arm. Watching her, she seemed almost feverish with intensity, as if she were resolved to test some private limits. When the dance ended, she and Haines were both sweating. The band played a slower song next and Haines pulled her close to himself, clenching his hands behind her back while she held tightly to his neck. He rocked her backward across the floor in time to the slow music. Neither of them talked. When the song ended, someone else cut in, and so it began again, with the same intensity, with

the same feverish resolve. It went on in that way until the end of
the set.

Then the band broke for ten minutes and the local men
bought her drinks again at the bar. While they stood around her,
not speaking to her very much but merely talking and joking
among themselves while still paying close attention to the level
of liquor in her glass, the rest of the people in the Legion that night
were also ordering fresh drinks. The two or three barmaids were
kept busy carrying trays of glasses and bottles out to them in the
booths. Across the room somebody started throwing ice cubes at
one of the barmaids to get her attention. "Stop that," she called.
"I see you—I'll be there in a minute."

Then the ten-minute break was over. The band resumed
their places at the far end of the room and began to play. And
Alden Haines led Jessie out onto the floor again. It was a fast
song, the band's rendition of "That'll Be the Day." He swung
her violently out at the end of his arm—and that was the end
of it. Almost before it had begun, it was finished, completed. I
suppose it was the ice cubes on the floor. Or perhaps during
the break someone had spilled beer or liquor in the dance area.
No one was certain what it was. But in any case, her foot
slipped on something wet and she went down. She tried to
catch herself when she fell but she couldn't; she fell forward,
hard, and didn't get up immediately. Afterward she lay there in
her red dress while the people around her stopped dancing.
She turned onto her side, pulling her legs upward against
herself. Haines leaned over her.

"You all right?" he said. "Can you get up?"

He lifted under her arm, helping her to stand. She was very
pale. She was sweating again now, her face shining like wet chalk
in the dim light. In the center of the dance floor she stood
unsteadily on her feet while Alden Haines held her arm and people
watched. "I think I need to go to the rest room," she said.

"You want me to walk you upstairs?"

"No. I want to be alone."

Later it was obvious that the pains had already begun while she was so still on the dance floor—those who were there remember seeing her eyes focus peculiarly, a kind of brief intermittent stare—but she refused any assistance. She walked off the dance floor by herself, past the bar and up the stairs to the rest room near the front entrance. She went inside, into one of the toilet stalls, and sat down. They waited for her to come back. When she was still there ten minutes later, a couple of women went in to check on her. She was still seated on the toilet, still conscious but quiet and very white. She was bent forward over her knees. There were clots of blood in the toilet. One of the women came outside into the hallway and said they should call the ambulance.

The ambulance got there in five or six minutes. The attendants went in and brought her back out in a wheelchair, tipping it backward to get down the front steps, and then they pushed the chair up a ramp into the ambulance and drove to the hospital. None of that took very long—the hospital is only three or four blocks east of the Legion—but it wouldn't have mattered if it had taken an hour.

When they arrived at the hospital, they wheeled her into the emergency room and Dr. Martin laid her down on a bed and examined her. He lifted her dress and noticed the blood. Then he listened for fetal heart tones. He couldn't hear anything, though: the little girl inside her was already dead. Afterward he said the placenta and uterine walls had separated. When she fell, she had gone immediately into labor, and because its source of oxygen had been cut off, the baby had died within minutes—probably during the time Jessie was still in the rest room. He didn't tell her that, though. He didn't want to upset her: she still had to deliver the baby.

They gave her Pitocin to help stimulate the contractions. But she was in labor for nearly ten hours and there was additional loss of blood and she might have died. But finally she delivered the baby late on Sunday evening.

Afterward they held it up so she could look at it for a moment. The little girl was ashen but otherwise it looked quite normal. Jessie reached up and touched one of its feet. Then they took it away and one of the nurses said: "I'm so sorry, Mrs. Burdette."

So people in Holt thought she would cry then. They thought she would break down at last. I suppose they wanted her to do that. But she didn't. Perhaps she had gone past the point where human tears make any difference in such cases, because instead, she turned her face away and shut her eyes and after a while she went to sleep.

She stayed in the hospital for most of that next week. Mrs. Waters, her neighbor, took it upon herself to care for TJ and Bobby during that period. The old woman brought them in to see their mother as soon as she was able to have company and Jessie talked to them every day and held their hands and brushed the hair off their foreheads. She refused, however, to talk to any of the hospital staff about the little girl she had delivered and she refused absolutely to talk to a local minister when he came to her room to visit her. She preferred to lie quietly, looking out the window. When the week was over, they released her and she went home again, to the old Fenner house on Hawthorne Street. And then in another week she returned to work at the Holt Cafe. In the following months she continued to refill the townspeople's cups with coffee and to bring them steak and potatoes from the kitchen.

And so I don't know what monetary value people place on baby girls in other areas, but here we learned in May that year that $150,000—less the resale value of a two-bedroom house in the middle of town—was a figure that seemed appropriate.

· 9 ·

That was in the spring of 1977. Afterward things in Holt returned to a quiet normalcy. Jessie continued to live at the west edge of town with her sons. The two boys were growing up and she went on working every day at the Holt Cafe and gradually people in town stopped talking about her husband. Of course Charlie Soames was still here. He was still nodding his head and lisping nonsense while he watered the grass or sat on the front porch swing. But in time people grew used to his altered presence, so that it was no longer maddening to see him. They began to forget about his part in the events of that spring. They thought of him now, if they happened to think of him at all, as just an old empty-headed man who lived in town on Cedar Street. Matters in Holt grew quiet and routine once more.

Then in the summer of 1982 another series of events began which ultimately had relevance for this story. These events began with the death of another girl in Holt.

She was a beautiful child. She resembled her mother. She had Nora's rich black hair and white skin, and she was small-boned and bright and neat looking, and she had her mother's blue eyes. But she was like me too, in some ways. She didn't like to stay home. She wanted to be out where there was something happening; she wanted to know things.

So she was a favorite among her friends, and when she was a teenager she was out of the house most of the time, going places, even if it was only to ride up and down Main Street in someone's car. She and her mother were very close, however. And I believe Nora was silently pleased that Toni was unlike herself in that one regard at least, that she was lively and gregarious and had friends, because Nora had very few friends and was often very lonely in Holt. Nora had never liked living here; it was too raw for her; there wasn't the slightest hint of any culture that she could recognize. Consequently she spent much of her time alone, gardening in the backyard, growing roses, and she read a great deal. Then too, she would often drive to Boulder for a weekend, to visit her aging father, Dr. Kramer, the old professor. Afterward she would come back to Holt and appear to be cheerful for a day or two. But it would never last. After eighteen years of marriage we had achieved an unhappy and silent compromise: for Toni's sake we stayed together. We didn't talk about the future and while we were generally kind in our daughter's presence and made a pretense at being contented, we were essentially indifferent to one another. But in the summer of 1982 even that seemed too much to pretend about any longer.

It was the custom in Holt County for graduating high-school seniors to have a keg party out in the country on the night of graduation. Usually some of the parents sponsored the party, thinking it would be better to have adults in attendance to ensure that the kids didn't do anything too crazy, to see to it that when they left in the early hours of the morning someone in the car was sober enough to drive home. Besides the beer, the parents provided a midnight breakfast, enough for everyone, and such an arrangement had always worked satisfactorily. Afterward there would be something eventful for the kids to remember, to mark their passage into adulthood, and no one got hurt.

Toni, our sixteen-year-old daughter, had gone to the party that year. Not that she was graduating yet—she had just finished her sophomore year at the Holt County Union High School—but she was dating a boy who was a senior and so she had gone with him. He was a nice kid. Nora and I both liked him. He was generally a responsible boy and he had treated Toni with affectionate kindness. They had been dating for almost a year. His name was Danny Pohlmeier.

The night of the party Nora and I had gone to sleep as usual, after watching the ten o'clock news. Then about four o'clock the police woke us. It was Dale Willard, the deputy sheriff, who came and knocked on the door. I put my pants on to go downstairs. Willard was standing on the front porch in the dark. I turned the light on. Under the porch light Willard's face looked pasty and tired. "There's been an accident," he said. "You'd better come down to the hospital."

"What's wrong? Is it Toni?"

"It doesn't look very good."

"You mean she's badly hurt?"

Willard didn't say anything.

"Tell me," I said. "Is she badly hurt?"

"You better come down to the hospital. I don't know how to tell you this."

"You mean it's worse than that."

Willard looked at me quickly. "I'm sorry," he said. Then there wasn't anything more to say. He turned and walked off the porch. But he stopped again and turned back. "I'll wait for you in the car. If you want me to."

I stood watching him a moment. He walked on out to the county's blue police car where it was parked at the curb and got in and closed the door quietly and then sat waiting with his hands on the steering wheel, looking straight ahead out through the windshield. I couldn't move yet. It was cool outside on the porch. There was a slight breeze blowing. The stars were very high and clear overhead. *Oh, god.* Finally I went back upstairs to tell Nora.

She was awake, sitting up in the bed in her nightgown. Her hair appeared very black against her nightgown and her pale shoulders. "Who was it?" she said.

"Dale Willard."

"What did he want? Doesn't he have something to do with the police?"

"He's the deputy sheriff."

"What did he want?"

"It's about Toni," I said. "She's at the hospital. He said Toni's been hurt."

"No," Nora said. "Oh no. No."

She didn't say anything more. Her eyes widened and then narrowed, and her lips moved, but there was no other sound now. She seemed to be holding herself from any further display of emotion. She got dressed and we went downstairs.

Outside Dale Willard was still sitting in the county police car in front of our house.

"Do you want to ride with him?" I said. "He's waiting for us." Nora shook her head.

So I walked over to the car and told him we would drive ourselves. We got into our own car and drove to the hospital. The streets were empty and quiet and the houses were all dark, but Dale Willard followed us anyway. I believe he felt responsible for seeing that we got there safely.

At the hospital one of the nurses met us at the back entrance and showed us into a waiting room. Then she left. In a moment Dr. Martin came in and we stood up while he told us about it. One of the other kids in a car driving home from the party half an hour later had discovered them. Toni and the Pohlmeier boy had left the party together, at about two-thirty, and apparently he was driving too fast and he had gotten over too far onto the loose sand at the side of the country road. Then he must have tried too quickly to correct it—the car had rolled over four or five times. They couldn't be sure how many times it had rolled over, but when it had stopped it was in the barrow ditch, upside down. There was glass everywhere and the roof was smashed down level with the hood and trunk.

"Where is Toni now?" I said.

Dr. Martin ignored that for the moment. He went on. He said he thought that Danny Pohlmeier was going to live. There was a good chance of it, he said. He was a healthy young boy. It was too soon to tell, though. They were making arrangements to fly him to Denver.

"Where is Toni?" I said.

Dr. Martin looked at Nora. "We have your daughter in a room just down the hall here. But I don't think she suffered. It was too sudden. I feel certain she didn't suffer."

"Where is she? We want to see her."

"I don't think you do."

"Yes," I said. "We want to see her."

He looked at Nora again. She was standing very rigidly, watching him. "Very well," he said.

I took Nora's arm and we followed Dr. Martin down the hallway to one of the rooms in the emergency area. Inside on an examining table there was a small figure with a white sheet pulled over it.

"We want to be alone now," I said.

Dr. Martin took my hand and pressed it and put his arm around Nora's shoulders. He was going to say something more but evidently thought better of it. He went out and shut the door.

After he was gone Nora lifted the sheet. We could see Toni's poor face then. Her black hair was matted at the side of her head and her face was swollen and discolored. Her eyes were only half-shut. Her face had been badly cut up and she had bled from the nose and mouth. There was dried blood in her nostrils and there was more blood at the corners of her mouth.

"Oh god," I said. "That's enough, Nora. Put it back now. Jesus god."

But Nora lifted the sheet so that she could see all of Toni's body. They had cut her clothes off. Our daughter looked very small and broken. Nora moved her fingers gently over the bruised arms and then she walked over to the counter and pulled a Kleenex from a box and moistened it with her tongue so she could removed the dried blood from Toni's mouth. She bent and kissed the forehead and put the sheet back.

After that we went home again. It was beginning to be daylight now. And later in the morning John Baker, who owned the mortuary, came to the house and we made the arrangements for the funeral. A couple of days later Toni was buried in the Holt County Cemetery northeast of town.

It was a large funeral; all of her friends from school were there and many of their parents and various townspeople. There were a great many flowers at the altar of the church. The minister spoke and there was some music, I remember, and afterward, at the cemetery, after the brief prayers and rites, people filed past us to shake our hands while we stood in the shade under the green awning at the gravesite. For the funeral John Baker had done what he could with Toni's face, but it was not recognizable. It was merely the mask of a dead child, caked with powder and waxen-looking. So we had not permitted the casket to be opened and we had not allowed anyone to view her at the mortuary in the evenings before the funeral. When it was all finished and everyone had driven away, Nora and I went home again to a house that seemed utterly quiet. None of the public ceremonies had helped.

*   *   *

But as it turned out Danny Pohlmeier did live, as Dr. Martin said he might. He was in the hospital in Denver for two or three months and then he was in a cast for another half year or so. When he was home again he came to the house one night to talk to us. He sat on the couch and cried into his hands while he told us about it. After he had stopped talking there was nothing more to say. We walked him to the front door and he left. Nora and I did not blame him for what had happened. We did not feel that way about it. He was a nice boy and it was obvious that he felt very badly. Still we never mentioned his name to one another again.

In fact we were hardly speaking at all. It was an awful summer. Nora was quieter and even more withdrawn than she had ever been. She couldn't sleep at night and she had begun to take things to make her sleep. Then she would get up late in the morning with a headache and move silently about the house. In the evenings she would still garden a little, among her roses, pulling weeds and dusting the flowers with insecticide, but she wasn't much interested in her roses anymore and she had begun to wear white gloves whenever she worked outside. They were the same gloves she had worn previously to church and for women's society meetings; now she was using them to protect her hands from the soil in the backyard. It was as though she were afraid of being contaminated by even that much of Holt County. Finally at the end of summer we agreed that it would be better if she left town for a while.

We gave people another reason for her leaving, however. Earlier that spring her father had been forced to retire from teaching at the university and he had decided that he wanted to move to Denver, to be in a larger city. He needed help to make the move. So at the beginning of September, Nora went to Boulder to assist in making the arrangements. We were both relieved that she was going to be gone for a time.

Then she refused to come back. It was at this time that Nora

·

rented for her father the large apartment on Bannock Street, on the ground floor of an old Victorian house. It was a roomy place. It had leaded windows and outside there was ivy growing on the brick walls, with a black wrought-iron fence separating the house from the sidewalk and street, and evidently the whole thing suited the old man so well that he was quite pleased with his daughter and even told her so. Consequently Nora stayed awhile longer to help him establish his desk and his books. Then she decided to stay with him permanently. She took a job at the city library downtown and returned every evening to cook supper for him. It was an arrangement they both seemed to like. She wrote me a letter about it. That was how I learned that she was not coming back.

I wasn't certain how I felt about this. The truth is, I did not miss her particularly. It was easier in the house without her there, without having to watch her every day. But a week or two later, on a Sunday, I drove to Denver to see them. I took Nora and the old gentleman out to eat at a restaurant. It was a place they suggested. There were white linen cloths and linen napkins folded in cones on the tables and heavy silverware beside the white plates. There were several wineglasses too. Dr. Kramer ordered the wine and when the waiter brought the bottle to the table the old man made a bit of dignified show, sniffing the cork and feeling it with his papery fingers. He decided the cork was sufficiently moist and told us it proved that the bottle had been placed on its side, that the cork hadn't been allowed to dry out. Then the waiter poured wine into his glass and he tasted that and it seemed that the wine was satisfactory too. We all had a glass of wine.

So it was a long complicated meal of four or five courses. But Nora and the old man appeared to enjoy it. I had to admit that Nora's face looked lovely again; the rigid control she had held on herself during the summer seemed to have been relaxed and she looked almost girlish once more. She sat beside her father and was very attentive to him. They discussed each course as it was brought by the waiter, sampling the food the other had ordered and making comparisons. Later we had dessert and coffee. Then we were finished with dinner and so we drove around in the city for an hour, across town through the city park and past the zoo and the museum, and back through the Cherry Creek retail area toward Broadway and Bannock Street. At the apartment again, Dr. Kramer decided he would take a short nap.

"Of course," Nora said. "Why don't you rest for a while, dear."

"But don't let me sleep too long. You know I mustn't sleep too long."

"No. Just for an hour."

"No more than that."

"I'll wake you in an hour. Then we'll have some tea."

She followed him into the bedroom. Through the opened door I could see her bending over him, removing his shoes and covering him with a blanket. They were quite affectionate with one another; they called one another "dear."

When she came back to the living room I said: "Why don't we take a walk now? I need some air and I want to work off this dinner. Maybe we can even talk a little."

It was early evening then. It was in the fall of the year and the trees standing up in front of the old houses in the neighborhood were just beginning to turn. The apartment they had rented was in an old established area of Denver. Formerly it must have been an attractive part of town; there were many large brick houses, built before the turn of the century, but the houses were nearly all divided into apartments and the streets were lined with cars. We walked five or six blocks south along Bannock Street and then turned west where we could see the mountains, high and blue-looking out beyond the city, and then north, and then east again to make a circle. It felt good to be walking. It was pleasantly cool outside and we saw a number of Hispanic families sitting out on the big porches of the neighborhood houses, playing music and drinking beer and talking, while handsome little black-haired kids played games in the yards or rode bicycles on the sidewalks, and I thought there was a sense of real life in the neighborhood, of things happening which would be interesting to know about. But soon Nora was ready to return to the apartment and her father. "I should wake him," she said. "If he sleeps too long, he won't be able to sleep again tonight."

"Let's go back, then. If that's what you want."

"Yes, I do."

We walked a little farther.

"And this *is* what you want, isn't it? You want to stay here and live with your father? And work at the library?"

"Yes. You wouldn't like it. I know you wouldn't, but I do. It suits me."

"Well. I hope you'll be happy."

"Oh please. Don't be that way."

"I'm not. I do hope you'll be happy. I mean that."

"Because I tried," she said. "I did try, don't you think I did?"

"Yes. I think you did. I think we both did."

"Thank you for saying so." She touched my arm and then took her hand away.

"Yes. Well. I miss Toni. I can't help but miss her."

"I know," Nora said. "I miss her too."

Then we arrived at the apartment. We stood on the sidewalk in front of the iron fence.

"Do you want to come in?" she said.

"No. I don't think so. You go ahead."

"Thank you for dinner."

"Good-bye," I said.

She went on up the steps into the apartment. I stood for a moment longer watching as the lights were turned on inside. Then she pulled the curtains shut and I got into the car and drove home, out of Denver onto the High Plains toward Holt.

*   *   *

After that I was lonely for a while. I do not mean that I missed Nora herself very much, but it was the absence of there being anyone else at all in the house. I suppose after eighteen years, even if it is an unsuccessful marriage, you still miss the sound and presence of someone's being there when you go home. I missed Toni horribly.

Finally I began to eat supper at one of the local restaurants to delay going home, and often I ate at the Holt Cafe. Jessie Burdette was still working there. She looked very attractive in her yellow blouse and dark slacks, with her brown hair pulled back away from her face in combs. She was thirty-one years old then. She was very competent as a waitress, and it was pleasant to see her and to talk to her briefly in the evenings.

So the fall passed in that way. I worked steadily at the newspaper office every day, editing and publishing the *Holt Mercury,* printing whatever was profitable and of interest locally without attempting to do anything that would take much effort, just the routine small-town-weekly-newspaper kind of thing. Then one evening at the Holt Cafe, after I had eaten supper, when Jessie brought the bill to the table I asked her if I could drive her home when she got off work. The evening had turned cool and I knew that she usually walked home.

"I'm sorry," she said. "But I drove this time. I was late leaving the house so I decided to drive."

"Oh. Well maybe another time."

"Yes," she said. "Why don't you ask another time? But do you want anything else? Any dessert?"

"I guess not."

She put the bill on the table and carried the dishes back to the kitchen. I finished my coffee. *Well that was foolish,* I thought. *She doesn't need you bothering her.* I got up and walked over to the register to pay. Jessie was clearing another table. I waited for her, then she came back and rang up the bill and made change and I started to leave.

"But, Pat," she said. "Wait. Would you like to come to the house? I could make some fresh coffee."

"I would, if it's all right."

"I'll be here another hour or so."

"Okay."

"Say about seven-thirty?"

"Okay."

She laughed. "Sure that's okay?"

I grinned back at her. "I'm real quick. I guess I'm out of practice."

"I know you are," she said.

I walked on outside. I thought of taking something to her, some cake or cookies to go with the coffee, but the bakery was closed and only the bars and liquor stores and the 7-11 were open now at this time in the evening. So I went back to the office and worked for an hour and then waited half an hour longer; then I locked up again and drove over to her apartment on Hawthorne Street.

TJ and Bobby were watching television in the front room when I walked up onto the front porch. I could see them through the window. I rang the doorbell and Jessie came to let me in. "This is Mr. Arbuckle," she said. "He owns the newspaper." Her sons looked at me. "Can't you say hello?"

"Hello," they said. Then they turned back to the television.

Jessie led me out to the kitchen. It was clean and bright, with space enough for a large table and four chairs. "Do you want to sit down?" she said. "I'll get the coffee started."

"You have a nice place here," I said.

"It's all right. Anyway, it's not too expensive."

I watched her making the coffee. She had changed clothes since coming home from the cafe; she was wearing a long-sleeved blue pullover now and faded Levi's and her hair looked freshly combed. When the coffee began to perk she sat down across from me at the kitchen table.

I don't know what we talked about that first evening—well yes, I do know. We talked about ourselves, about her childhood in Tulsa, her crippled mother and about her brothers and her father, and I told her a little of growing up in Holt. It was awkward at first. We drank several cups of coffee and at nine-thirty Jessie said, "Excuse me a minute," and went into the front room. She told the boys they had to go to bed now. They turned the television off and came through the kitchen to enter the bathroom. I was still sitting at the table and as they passed through the room they looked suspiciously at me. When the bathroom door was shut I could hear them brushing their teeth and whispering to one another. Then they came out and stood beside the table while Jessie kissed them. "Go to bed now. And no funny stuff. Okay?"

They looked at me once more. "Good night," I said.

"Good night," TJ said. He poked at Bobby.

"What?"

"You're supposed to tell him good night."

"I don't even know who he is."

"Tell him good night anyway."

"Good night," Bobby said. Then he walked out of the kitchen and TJ followed him.

"Oh my," Jessie said. She laughed and made a face. "Such manners."

"It's all right. You've done a terrific job raising them. They're good kids."

"Do you think so?"

"Yes. You have a right to be proud of them."

She reached across the table and touched my hand. "Thank you. You're a nice man. Did you know that?"

"I'm not so nice."

.

"You seem to be."

Later I stood up and Jessie walked with me to the front door and out onto the porch. We stood looking out across Hawthorne Street toward Harry Smith's horse pasture. There was a half-moon and you could just make out the shapes of soapweed and sage against the dark native grass.

"Thanks for the coffee," I said. I started down the steps.

"Pat."

"Yes?"

"Do you think you'll be eating at the cafe tomorrow?"

"I don't know. Probably."

"Then I probably won't drive my car to work."

"Then I probably will drive mine," I said.

"There," she said. "You see? You're not as much out of practice as you thought."

I laughed. It was the first time I'd laughed in months. "Maybe it'll all come back to me."

"I think it will."

After that it was a wonderful fall and winter. I wasn't lonely anymore, and I think perhaps they were good weeks and months for Jessie too. After that first evening we saw each other nearly every day. When she had finished work at the Holt Cafe I would drive her home to the apartment, and then while the boys watched TV or did schoolwork we would sit in her kitchen and talk. We talked for hours. I had never talked with anyone as much as I did with her, telling her things I had not told anyone before, things which I hadn't known I'd thought until I heard myself saying them to her. It was a new experience for both of us to be unguarded with someone, and as the months passed I began to stay at her apartment later into the night, talking and drinking coffee, and then after the boys were in bed and asleep often we would move back to her bedroom. She was a beautiful woman and very warmhearted and generous in bed, and I looked forward to seeing her every day, to talking to her and being with her. I thought about her constantly.

She had Sundays off and during the week we made plans to do something together with the boys. We took drives out into the country, or drove to another town or went to a movie, and if there had been a rain or if the wind had blown hard we hunted arrowheads in the bare fields of the farmers I knew. In the spring TJ and Bobby each found a number of pieces of flint and a few complete points. We ordered books about Plains Indians and about arrowheads and read them together, and one Sunday we spent an afternoon constructing a glass display case to put the points in. The boys lined it with dark velvet. They were pleased with what they had made and I believe they came to think that I was all right too. I certainly thought they were. They were wonderful little boys and I was crazy about their mother.

There was one day in the summer that we drove to Denver. It was a Sunday in August. We left Holt about noon, driving west across the High Plains past fields of wheat stubble and green corn and the dry pastures, and after a while we began to see the mountains rising up toward us, and then in a couple of hours we were in Denver. We wanted to make an afternoon of it, to take the boys to Wet World where there was a water slide, and afterward we planned to eat at Casa Quintana.

It was about two-thirty when we arrived at Wet World on South Colorado Boulevard. We took our swimming suits and went inside. I bought the tickets at the counter and took the boys back to the men's dressing room while Jessie went to change in the women's. The boys were bashful getting undressed in front of me; they turned their backs and pulled their suits up and draped towels around their necks. When we were ready we went outside and waited for their mother. Then she came out, and my god she looked lovely. Every time I saw her I felt the same way. She was wearing a two-piece suit, with the towel wrapped around her hips. She was naturally brown-skinned and now late in the summer she was a wonderful dark color.

"Good lord," I said.

"What's wrong?"

"Nothing at all."

"What's wrong, though?"

"It's just you. You look beautiful."

We went back to the water-slide area and climbed the flights of stairs to the top. There was a long line of people waiting to go down. You went down through a tube, through fast twists and swoops, sitting on a piece of plastic with a stream of cold water pushing you and at the bottom you shot out into the swimming pool. As people disappeared, going down, you could hear them screaming and hollering. The line kept moving forward, then it was our turn. "Who wants to go first?" I said.

TJ's and Bobby's eyes looked huge. They stood on the platform staring down into the water slide where it made its first turn.

"It's all right," I said. "You'll see."

"Does it hurt?"

"No. You won't get hurt. It's fun."

"Okay," TJ said. "I think I can try it."

I gave the attendant the tickets and he handed us the plastic pieces to sit on. TJ sat down on the plastic and inched himself toward the lip of the platform, then he was over the lip and the stream of water caught him and he went down fast, screaming.

"Next," the attendant said. "Who's next? There's people waiting."

"What do you think, Bobby?" I said.

"Can I try it with you?"

"Yes. Come down with me once, then you'll be all right."

I sat down on the plastic rug and took Bobby on my lap. I winked at Jessie.

"See you boys at the bottom," she said.

I pushed us off the platform, leaning back, holding Bobby with one hand and pushing off with the other; then the water caught us and we went down in a wet rush around the first turn, banking up onto the side and shooting ahead, then more twists and sudden dips and a long fast straight run and a sudden turn up onto the side, the water carrying us and Bobby and I both yelling, and another swoop and then a short run and finally out, flying, still seated on the plastic rug but suspended in air now, and then down into the pool. We went under, I held Bobby around the chest and swam to the surface. When we came up Bobby's eyes were as bright as glass. "How'd you like it?" I said.

"I'm going by myself next time."

We turned to watch for Jessie. But one of the lifeguards standing at the side of the pool motioned us out of the way, so we wouldn't get hit. We swam over to the edge where TJ was. We climbed out and waited. But she didn't come.

"Where's Mom?" TJ said.

"I don't know. She was right behind us."

"What's taking her so long? "

"I don't know. Keep watching."

Then suddenly she came flying out of the tube with a big fat man in yellow trunks just behind her, the two of them sitting briefly on air, his legs around her, and then they sat down into the water in a tremendous splash. They rose to the surface and Jessie swam over to us. "Sorry," the fat man called. "Did I hurt you? I'm sorry." Jessie shook her head and waved at him. She was laughing.

"What happened?" I said.

"Oh," she said. She looked toward the man in yellow trunks; he was climbing up the ladder out of the pool, pulling his trunks up over his fat bottom. "I got stuck about halfway down and I couldn't move."

"Wasn't there any water?"

"Yes, but I lost the piece of plastic. Then that man came down and smacked into me, with his legs around me, and we came down the rest of the way like that."

"Did he hurt you?"

"No it was just funny. And he kept yelling: 'I'm sorry, lady. I'm sorry.' But it wasn't his fault. He *was* awfully big, though."

"Well," I said. "It's a little unorthodox, but you did make a splash."

"I think we did," Jessie said.

"But, Mom," TJ said. "Don't do that again. It's embarrassing."

"I didn't mean to."

"I know. But it's embarrassing."

"Very well. Next time I'll let Pat follow me. Will that be all right?"

"It's certainly all right with me," I said.

"But you should have heard him," Jessie said. " 'I'm sorry, lady. I'm sorry, lady.' God, it was funny."

Jessie began to laugh again. Her sons stood beside her, looking up into her face. I don't think they had ever seen their mother look so amused and animated. She was having a good time. We all were.

We stayed at Wet World for most of the afternoon. Jessie and I went down the slide several more times with the boys, then we got out and dried off and sat at a table watching them. The boys swam and played in the water, diving after a piece of tile, and finally they rode the water slide a few more times. Then we got dressed and walked out to the car. We were very hungry.

It was about five-thirty now. We drove across town to West Colfax, to the shopping center where Casa Quintana was. It was a large Mexican restaurant where the food was satisfactory, but the primary attraction—for little boys—was the entertainment and the decor. The rooms had been plastered to give them the appearance of adobe, as in a Mexican village, and sitting in the rooms you were meant to have the feeling of being in a peasant's house. Most of the rooms looked out at a central square where there was a sunken pool with a clifflike platform above it. Also in one area there was a cave which kids could explore. We walked inside the lobby and stood waiting for half an hour for a table. I gave the hostess our name and told her we wanted a place near the pool, so it took a while for a table to be available. Then there was one and we followed the hostess back through a couple of the rooms to a booth. "Your waitress will be with you in a minute," she said. From where we were sitting we had a clear view of the pool and adobe cliff.

After the waitress had come and we had ordered, some mariachi singers came through the rooms, singing sad songs in Spanish. They were dressed in Mexican costumes with braid and silver and wore big decorated hats. They stopped at our table and sang to Jessie in high voices.

"Ask them to sing something happier," she said.

"I don't know any Spanish songs. Just 'La Cucaracha.' "

"You would," she said. She smiled at the singers. When they were finished we applauded and they went on.

In a little while the waitress brought us our food. There was a small Mexican flag on a stick on the table and if we wanted anything more we could run the flag up and she would see it and come back. When we had finished eating I said: "Don't you boys want some sopapillas now?"

"What are they?"

"They're like pockets. They're made of dough and deep-fried. You can put honey inside them."

"Okay."

.

"Run the flag up, then."

They ran the flag up the stick and the waitress came over to the table.

"These boys want a sopapilla," I said. "So do I."

"Three of them?"

"Do you want one, Jessie?"

"Of course."

"Four of them. With honey."

The waitress cleared our plates and went back to the kitchen to put in the order. While she was gone there was a sudden racket on the cliff above the pool. Two men were arguing with one another, shouting nonsense and pretending to fight; then they each pulled guns and shot tremendously several times, but threw the guns down when they were empty and began to fistfight. They struggled on the lip of the cliff again until one, the bad one, was slugged hard and he fell forward in an arc off the cliff and dove into the pool. Then he climbed out, streaming water, and he and the man above him yelled again at one another while people applauded and whistled. I looked at TJ and Bobby. They were stunned.

"They were just fooling, weren't they?" Bobby said.

"I don't know," I said. "What do you think?"

"There wasn't any blood."

"Wasn't there?"

"I didn't see any blood," Bobby said.

"Well. It looked pretty real to me."

"They were just fooling," TJ said. "You could tell because of the way he dived."

They looked at me solemnly, studying my face. Finally I winked. Then they grinned.

Afterward we ate the sopapillas, leaning over the table, dripping honey onto the plates. Jessie and I ordered coffee while the boys explored the cave in the back room where there was a cache of jewels and other gems studded in the plastered roof.

Later they came back talking excitedly and I paid the bill and we left. It was getting dark outside now and the air was cooler again, as it always is in the evening in Colorado even in the summer.

When we were in the car, TJ leaned forward from the backseat and said without being prompted: "Thank you for taking us to these places today."

"Oh. Well, you're welcome. It was your mother's idea too."

"Thank you, Mom," Bobby said.

"We had a good time, didn't we, honey?"

We went home then. It was almost eleven-thirty by the time we arrived in Holt. On the way TJ and Bobby went to sleep in the backseat while Jessie and I talked quietly and looked out at the flat dark open country and held hands. She slept a little too, leaning against my shoulder. Then she woke again as I slowed down, driving into town. I stopped at their apartment on Haw-thorne Street and we walked the boys inside to their bedroom. They were asleep on their feet and I don't think they really woke up. Jessie opened their window and left the door open so there would be a cross draft of air.

When we were back in the living room I said: "I'd better go home now. It's late."

"Are you very tired?"

"I'm tired, but it's been a wonderful day. I think the boys had a good time."

"They did," she said. "But why don't you stay the night? You never have."

"I haven't wanted to cause you any trouble."

"It isn't any trouble. But I suppose you mean the people in town."

"I didn't want them to see me leave in the morning. It seems different if I leave in the night."

"Don't you think they talk about us anyway?"

"Probably."

"What difference can it make, then?"

"I don't know. I'm being stupid, I guess."

"You're not being stupid. You're just trying to be nice. Now are you going to take me to bed or not?"

"Well hell," I said. "If you insist."

"I do," she said. "Come to bed, please."

We went back to her bedroom. We felt very close when we were in bed together, and then afterward, before we slept, we looked out the opened window toward the streetlamp while the light played on her face and her shoulders and breasts, and we talked a little, and at last went to sleep with her head on my arm and her dark brown hair, like silk, smooth against my face.

That was in the summer on a Sunday in the middle of August. Then in the fall on a Saturday afternoon in November, Jack Burdette suddenly appeared in Holt once more.

· 10 ·

No one believed it at first. Then suddenly it was true: he was back in town again after eight years. He was driving a red Cadillac and after he had been sitting in the car for an hour on Main Street while people went by in front of him, shopping, paying too little heed to what they saw to understand who it was, Ralph Bird had finally recognized him. And so in the early evening Bud Sealy arrested him and hit him once in the back of the head with a gun and then forced him into the backseat of the police car and drove him around the corner and up the block to the courthouse on Albany Street and put him in jail.

So the local phenomenon was home again. The native son had returned. Only he was behind bars now, locked up in a cell where he couldn't get out, and people were glad that he was. They began to talk about him immediately. They told one another they would get something satisfactory out of Jack Burdette yet.

As for Jessie and me, we heard about it that same evening, on the Saturday of his return. We were in her apartment in the old Fenner house at the edge of town, watching a movie on television

with TJ and Bobby. It was eight o'clock by that time. Jessie had
come home tired from work so we had decided not to go out.
Then the phone rang.

Jessie went out to the kitchen to answer it. When she came
back she said it was for me.

"Who is it?"

"I think it's Bud Sealy."

"What does he want? They were just getting to the good part
in this movie."

"Should I tell him you'll call him back?"

"No. I'll talk to him."

I walked out to the kitchen and picked up the phone. "Bud,
is that you?"

Bud Sealy sounded grim and official. "Listen, Arbuckle," he
said, "I'm going to tell you something first. Then you can tell her
yourself if you want to."

"Tell her what?"

"You're not going to like it. I don't like it much myself."

"What is it?"

"Her husband's back in town."

"What? You mean Burdette's here in Holt?"

"That's right. The son of a bitch come back. You ought to see
him. I got him locked up in jail."

"Jesus Christ. What's he doing back here?"

"Hell if I know. He isn't saying."

There was silence for a moment.

"You still there?" Bud said.

"I'm still here."

"Yeah. Well, I thought you ought to know. There's going to
be a hell of a mess about this."

We hung up then. I stood looking out the kitchen window
into the backyard. It was dark outside and the trees looked black
and still. Then while I stood at the window it all began to race
in my mind. Everything was changed now.

I was still standing at the kitchen window when Jessie came out to see what was taking me so long. She put her arm around my waist. "Is something wrong?" she said.

"Yes. I'm afraid so."

"What is it?"

"Oh Christ," I said, "Jessie."

"What's wrong?"

"Sit down, please. Will you?"

I pulled out a chair for her at the table and sat down beside her. Jessie watched me steadily while I talked. She did not seem to be greatly upset, nor even much at a loss by what I said. And in the months that have passed since that night I have had time to think about it and I believe that it was not so much that she expected him to come back any more than the rest of us did. It was more, I think, that she had managed to achieve a kind of distance and poise of her own, a perspective from which she no longer allowed herself to worry about things she couldn't control. She had been made to suffer so much that spring after he had left, she had had to endure so much that in the end when she had survived it all she was stronger than she had been before and now she saw things differently than the rest of us do. She would no longer permit herself to worry about someone who was supposed to be a thousand miles away—even if he was suddenly back in Holt, a short five-minute drive across town.

Nevertheless when I had finished talking she said she didn't want to see him again. She did not want to have anything more to do with him.

"No. You won't have to see him again," I said.

"And I don't want TJ and Bobby to see him."

"No. But I'll have to. There needs to be something written for the paper about this."

"Will they put him on trial?"

"I don't know. They will want to. It depends on what evidence they still have."

She stared at the white enamel on the kitchen table. After a while she said: "I need to tell TJ and Bobby."

"Yes."

"I better tell them now."

She went back into the front room. She turned the television off and I could hear her talking to them; I could hear the questions they asked and then her quiet voice talking again, reassuring them. I sat at the table thinking about it all.

That was on Saturday night. On Monday I went over to the courthouse to see Jack Burdette. Jessie had called in at work and she had kept the boys home from school. We thought it would be better to let some time pass. The boys were frightened and upset. Nevertheless they went back to school and Jessie went back to work the next day. They were not trying to avoid things indefinitely.

On that Monday afternoon when I got to the courthouse there was a group of men, hangers-on and old local men retired from work, standing around in the parking lot in their adjustable caps and their long-sleeved shirts looking at Burdette's car. The police had moved it from Main Street on Sunday morning and it stood now, long and shiny and red, gleaming in the lot behind the courthouse. Parked beside the cars from town, it looked an affront. The men were talking and gesturing to one another.

"We ought to take a torch and cut this goddamn thing into pieces," one of them said.

"And parcel it out," another said. "The son of a bitch. It was our money."

I went on into the courthouse and down to the sheriff's office. Bud Sealy was sitting behind his desk, slouched back in his chair reading a magazine. He looked tired. I told him I wanted to talk to Burdette.

"Go ahead," Sealy said. "You can try it."

"Isn't he talking?"

"Not much. Not since the other night when I brought him in. We had a little talk then."

"But hasn't he said anything?"

"Sure. But nothing you'd want to print."

"I need to try him anyway."

"Of course. You two was friends once, wasn't you? He might talk to you."

I walked back into the jail. I had been there a number of times before, for newspaper stories, and as always the jail smelled sourly rank and oppressive. There were three empty cells, then the last one where Burdette was. I could see him through the bars.

He was lying on a cot which was too short for him so that his feet hung over the end uncomfortably. His feet were bare and calloused and he was still wearing the same wrinkled plaid shirt and dark pants he had worn when he had arrived on Saturday. Over in the corner of the cell there was a small sink and next to it a lidless toilet. He looked very bad, though, so that I don't know that I would have recognized him if I hadn't known in advance who it was. He looked wasted now, massively fat and excessive, sick-looking. I thought in fact that he must be sick; his skin was the yellow color you associate with serious illness and there were deep circles under his eyes. Most of his hair had fallen out in the years he had been gone so that the top of his head shone under the light now, and on his face there was a look of disgust, a kind of unaccustomed cynicism, as if nothing in the world interested him at all anymore.

Then he spoke. And I knew that I would have recognized his voice. "That you, Arbuckle?" he said. "I been laying here wondering if you'd come to see me."

"Yes. I've come to see you. You're news, Jack."

He grinned at me. "You mean this isn't a social call?"

"I need something for the paper."

"Well," he said. "You look about like you always did. Life must agree with you, Arbuckle."

"It does," I said. "But you don't look so well. What's wrong with you? Are you sick?"

"No. Hell. I'm all right. I'll be a whole lot better once I get out of this goddamn place."

"If you do get out."

"Oh, yeah, I'll get out all right. They can't hold me."

"They think they can."

"They can't, though. That's a fact."

"Maybe," I said. "We'll see."

He began to light a cigarette. His movements were slow and ponderous. When he had it lit he tossed the match onto the floor, over into the corner where there was already a pile of cigarette butts and matches. "What'd you want to know anyway? Since you're here."

"It doesn't matter really. Whatever you want to tell me. Except that I don't understand what made you come back. Didn't you like California?"

Now for the first time he sat up. Perhaps the memory of his years on the West Coast still interested him. It was hard to tell; he was so bloated and wasted-looking.

"Arbuckle," he said, "you ever been out there? To California?"

"No."

"You ought to sometime. It's a hell of a place."

"So they say."

"Yeah, it's a hell of a place. Only it's expensive. You can spend a lot of money out there. They got things in California you never even heard of."

"Probably."

"Lots of things."

"Well, you had lots of money," I said. "What happened to it? Did you run out?"

"Sort of," he said. Then, unexpectedly, he began to laugh. "But don't you think they'd let me have some more?"

Apparently the thought of that amused him. His eyes squinted shut and his gut shook; his heaving weight made the cot bounce. "Why not?" he said, going on. "This is my hometown, isn't it? Don't you think they'd let me take some more?"

"No," I said. "I don't think they would." I knew of course that he was joking, that he wasn't stupid, but I didn't care. I had other things on my mind. I told him there were people in Holt who hated him now. "They haven't forgotten anything," I said. "I doubt if they'd give you five cents to leave on. Assuming you were allowed to leave."

"No? I would of thought they'd of forgot by now. But hell, never mind about that. What about you?"

"I don't know what you mean."

"I suppose you hate my guts too."

"Maybe."

"Do you?"

"Look," I said. "You never cared what anyone thought of you before. What difference could that make to you now?"

"You're right," he said. "It don't make no difference." Then his face changed again. There was the show of effort in his eyes, as if he were concentrating. "It's just that I hear you been seeing my wife."

"What?"

"Yeah. That's what I hear. I hear you been seeing my wife. I hear you been seeing Jessie."

"She isn't your wife. Not anymore."

"Oh, yeah. Jessie and me—we're still married."

"You ruined all of that a long time ago. She doesn't want to see you again."

"Sure. We're still married."

"Listen, goddamn it. You leave her alone."

"And I still got my kids here."

"You haven't got anything here. You don't have a goddamn thing in Holt anymore."

"Yes," he said. "I still got my family here. I can count on that much. And this is still my hometown."

"Listen. You must be crazy. You listen to me, goddamn you."

But he didn't listen; instead he began to laugh again. He lay back on the cot with his feet hanging over the end. He was pleased with himself. His heavy sick-looking face smiled out at me from behind the bars. "Anything else you want to know, Arbuckle? Did you get what you needed for your paper?"

"Go to hell," I said.

And that amused him too. It was all amusing. It seemed pointless talking to him anymore. Finally I left.

Then on Tuesday, Arch Withers paid him a call. Over the years Arch Withers had become an embittered man.

After Burdette had disappeared at the end of December in 1976, Withers had gone on serving as president of the Farmer's Co-op Elevator's board of directors and he had finished his term of office, but when he had run for reelection two years later people who owned shares in the elevator had not reelected him. In fact he had been defeated by a large margin, and the loss had affected him deeply. He still farmed north of Holt, but now he didn't come into town very often; instead he sent his wife when he needed something and he never sat drinking coffee at Bradbury's Bakery. He was lonely and isolated, living in a place where he had always felt accepted and admired.

That afternoon when he arrived at the courthouse some of the old men who had been there the day before were there again, standing in the shade, looking out at Burdette's red Cadillac, still talking and gesturing. They watched Withers park his black pickup in the parking lot, then he approached and passed without saying anything to any one of them. When he entered the sheriff's office he demanded that he be allowed to see Jack Burdette. "Let me talk to him," he said.

"Now, Arch," Sealy said. "He don't have any of it left. You know that. Hell, would he of come back if he did?"

"Just let me see him."

"But I can't let you into his cell."

"I don't plan on going into his cell."

"Sure, but if I let you see him, you better not try anything. You hear me? I'll be watching."

"All right. Now where is he?"

So Sealy agreed to let Withers see Jack Burdette. He led Withers back into the jail and then stood guard in the doorway while he began to talk. And it was merely quiet and semirational talk at first, a kind of review of things. But Burdette must have seemed even less interested in what Withers had to say than he had the day before when I had talked to him, and evidently he was considerably less amused. Again he lay stretched out on the sunken too-small cot, lying there heavy and dull, yellow-faced, smoking cigarettes, barely listening while Withers talked on and on. By this time he must have been tired of it all. It was as if he were merely waiting for something. Withers' talk must have seemed to him to involve only some minor misunderstanding between them, an old dispute of no particular significance. Except that it was more than that to Withers, of course. He kept talking, trying to push Burdette into some kind of response. There wasn't any response, though. Burdette simply lay waiting for Withers to cease talking.

So in time Withers grew hot. He began to shout, to curse: "Goddamn you, Burdette. Goddamn you."

And Jack Burdette still seemed utterly uninterested, as if he couldn't be bothered by any of this. Finally he did manage to rouse himself a little, however. He raised his head. "Withers," he said. "I wish you'd shut your goddamn mouth."

"By god——" Withers said.

"I never came back here to hear about your goddamn elevator. Leave me alone. You're starting to get on my nerves."

Arch Withers went a little crazy then. He began to shake the bars, shouting for Sealy to come forward and unlock the cell so he could go inside. "I'll kill the son of a bitch," he shouted. "I'll kill him."

"Sealy," Burdette called. "Get him out of here. I heard enough of this."

"I'll kill him."

"I don't have to listen to this, Sealy."

"Unlock this thing."

"Sealy, you hear me?"

It went on in that way, a violent refrain, until at last Bud Sealy moved down the alleyway toward Withers and tried to lead him away. "Come on, Arch," he said. "Let's go."

"I'll kill him."

"No. You had your say."

"By god—"

"Let's go. Come on now."

Suddenly Withers began to struggle. He fought Bud Sealy in the alleyway of the jail, shouting still, swinging his arms. Sealy shoved him against the bars of the cell, pinning him there, his heavy forearm under Withers' chin, and then he pushed him out of the jail back into the office. Withers stood before him, panting.

"Goddamn it, Arch. What in hell you think you're doing? You want me to arrest you too? I had enough of this."

"He's not even sorry," Withers said.

"What did you expect? Did you think he would be?"

"He don't even care about any of us."

"Listen, go home now, Arch. You're through here. Understand? Go on home."

But Withers seemed too exhausted to move. He appeared to be spent and defeated. It was as if he had been waiting for years for just this moment and now it had meant nothing at all: Burdette wasn't even sorry. Finally Sealy had to take Withers by the sleeve and walk him out of the office and up the stairs toward the exit.

Outside, next to the courthouse, the local men were still standing in the shade in the November afternoon. When Withers appeared in the doorway they wanted to know what had happened. But he wouldn't talk to them. He walked slowly past them, down the sidewalk. Their heads turned to follow his progress across the parking lot, past Burdette's Cadillac and on toward his black pickup. They watched as he climbed into the vehicle and shut the door.

When he was gone one of them asked: "What happened down there, Bud?"

"Nothing happened."

"But didn't Withers talk to him?"

"Maybe. But Burdette wasn't listening to him."

"What'd he talk about?"

"What do you think he would talk about?"

"Of course. Well, he's had enough time to think about it anyway. I bet he made a little speech to him, didn't he?"

Sealy studied him for a moment, studied them all. "Look," he said. "You boys better go on home too. There ain't nothing going to happen here. Go on home and see if the wife's got dinner yet. I seen enough of you for one day."

After that nothing did happen for a while. For the rest of the week Burdette stayed in jail, lying on the cot in his cell, waiting, sleeping much of the time, his plaid shirt and his dark pants growing daily more rank and wrinkled, while in town along Main Street people talked endlessly about him, at the tables in the bakery and across the street in the tavern, and everyone seemed to know something about it.

But by the end of the week it became clear that something had been occurring elsewhere. Over in Sterling in the district

attorney's office something significant had been going on: the
wheels of Colorado state law had been turning and what they had
turned up was proof that Burdette was right. He couldn't be held;
the statute of limitations had run out. If he had been out of the
state for five years, and if an additional three years had passed, he
couldn't be prosecuted. He was free to go.

Bob Witkowski, the district attorney, called Bud Sealy on
Friday afternoon to inform him of that fact.

"What?" Sealy said. "What's this? You mean, here that son
of a bitch stole a hundred and fifty thousand dollars from people
and now you're telling me I can't hold him?"

"That's right. That's what it amounts to."

"I don't believe it."

"You'd better believe it. That's the law. And you'll be
breaking it if you keep him. You've already been acting illegally
by locking him up for a week."

"So you're telling me now I have to let him go? That's how
the law reads?"

"That's right. Release him, Bud."

"Well, Jesus Christ Almighty. That son of a bitch. He knew
all along."

Sealy slammed the phone down and stared at the wall.

By nightfall, though, Bud Sealy had gathered his senses and had
decided to act intelligently. To avoid any possibility of interfer-
ence from people in town—there were a number of hotheads in
Holt who might drink enough to think they ought to try something, and it was just the beginning of pheasant season so there
were plenty of shotguns available in the racks behind the seats in
the pickups—he and Dale Willard secretly moved Jack Burdette
out of his cell and drove him out to the county line. It was long
after dark. Sealy had handcuffed Burdette again and had shoved
him into the backseat of the police car behind the protective grille.

Burdette had objected, had cursed and shouted, thinking that Sealy was going to ride him out into the sandhills and kill him. But Sealy had told him to shut up and finally he had. Behind the police car Dale Willard followed in Burdette's red Cadillac.

When they were across the county line they turned off onto a gravel road. Sealy got out and unlocked the back door. "Get out," he said.

"Bud. Now listen."

"Get out, you son of a bitch."

"Bud. Listen to me. You better listen."

"Goddamn you." Sealy withdrew his gun and shoved it under Burdette's chin. "Move."

Burdette slid slowly out of the car and stood up onto the road. He began to rave. "Willard," he said. "Willard, you're here. You know that. You're going to be involved if you let this happen. You know that, Willard."

"Shut up," Sealy said. "We're all involved. Now turn around."

"Willard. Don't let this happen, Willard."

"Unlock him," Sealy said.

Willard removed the handcuffs. He handed them to the sheriff.

"Now," Sealy said, "get the hell out of here, you son of a bitch. And don't you ever come back."

"What?"

"I'm letting you go. You don't know how lucky you are."

"What? So you found out. You can't hold me."

"Something like that."

"I knew you couldn't. I told you—"

"Shut up."

Burdette stared at him.

"And don't you ever come back here again," Sealy said. "You hear me? I'm warning you. Don't you ever come back here. By god, you won't be so lucky the next time."

Jack Burdette looked once more at the sheriff, then again at Willard. He walked over to his car. The engine was still running. He got in and backed the Cadillac onto the highway. Then he honked once, in apparent farewell, a kind of final affront, and roared away. It was not quite midnight then.

The next morning there was a new, even more intense feeling of public outrage in Holt when people discovered that the red Cadillac was gone and that Burdette had been allowed to leave. For a long while that morning groups of men and boys stood in the parking lot at the courthouse where the shiny red car had stood all week. They swore to one another that they would do something yet; they would take some action. But no one could think what it should be.

Meanwhile Bud Sealy sat in his basement office looking out at them from behind his barred window. For several hours they stood there talking impotently and disgusted; finally about noon they began to disperse, to wander home for lunch. After everyone had gone, Sealy called his wife and told her to bring him some coffee and a sandwich. He didn't want to leave, he said; he expected them to come back. And after the noon meal many of them did. They began to talk again, to gesture and swear. In the end, however, nothing happened. It was too late for the local men to do anything about it.

Throughout that morning, though, there had been the fear that something might occur, that someone might be crazy enough to attempt something violent. So about midmorning I suggested to Jessie that we leave town for a couple of days. I had been staying at her apartment all week, out of a sense of protectiveness, and now we decided to take the boys and drive to Denver, to stay in a motel, and drive up into the mountains somewhere. The aspen would have already turned but it would be pleasant in the mountains, I told her, and quiet. She thought that would be a good idea. She called the cafe and told them she wouldn't be coming in. Then we packed and left.

In Denver we took a couple of rooms at a motel on Interstate 70 near Stapleton Airport. There was an indoor swimming pool connected to the motel and the boys swam for awhile, practicing their dives, while Jessie and I watched them and had a drink. There was also a couple from Texas swimming in the pool who said they were on their honeymoon from Nacogdoches. They seemed very young and happy. The girl was plump, with a pretty round-cheeked face, and her husband kept pulling her into the water and squeezing her and whispering into her ear; then she would splash him and laugh and swim away. Later they climbed out and walked back to their motel room, with his arm around her waist, and we didn't see them again.

When TJ and Bobby were finished swimming they took a shower and we ate an early supper in the motel restaurant. Afterward we went out to a movie. We drove across town to a theater in a shopping mall and had popcorn and Cokes and sat in the dark theater watching the screen. But I couldn't keep my mind on the story. They had done what they could to make it seem plausible that an Amish girl would fall in love with a city detective and there were many dramatic scenes and wonderful photography, with a growing sense of something ominous about to happen, but when the violence came it seemed too far away for me to believe it. I sat beside Jessie with my arm over her thin shoulders and watched her face. When we were outside again she and the boys thought it was a good movie. Probably it was. But I couldn't be interested just then in somebody else's unhappiness.

Later that night in bed in the motel room with Bobby and TJ asleep in the room next to ours, I told Jessie some of what I'd been worrying about.

"I know," she said. "But don't you see it'll be all right now? Isn't that what you said? That it was the best thing for him just to leave?"

"That was this morning. When I first heard about it. I felt surer then."

"But nothing's happened to make you change your mind, has it?"

"Not that I know of."

"And there isn't anything we can do about it now, even if there is something?"

"No."

"Then will you please put your arm around me and hold me? It doesn't do any good to worry about it."

"I know."

"And you know I love you."

"I just don't want anything to change."

"Move your arm so I can come closer. There," she said, "isn't that better?"

"Yes. That's much better."

"I thought you'd see reason finally."

We were lying very close together. She felt warm and silky beside me and I began to make love to her then in the dark motel room, with just the dim light showing through the curtains and the sounds of traffic going by outside on the interstate. But everything seemed different now and uncertain. Afterward when we were quiet once more, we lay close together and Jessie went to sleep immediately.

The next morning we got up late and ate breakfast. Then we checked out of the motel. We had decided to spend the day driving over to Boulder and across the mountain to Estes Park. The tourist season was over and skiing hadn't started yet, so it would be quiet and peaceful in the mountains.

When we got to Estes Park in the afternoon we stopped and walked along the streets, looking at Big Thompson River where it went through town and peered in at the shop windows at the pottery and pewter and the expensive brand-name clothes. We bought some locally made chocolate and also some cheese and fruit and sliced ham and dark bread so we could have an evening picnic; then we walked back to the car and drove north out of town along the back way toward Loveland, winding narrowly down to Glen Haven and Drake, and finally pulled off the highway at a place where there were picnic tables beside the creek. It was late in the afternoon then; the canyon was all in shade. We put our coats on and TJ and Bobby climbed among the rocks beside the creek and dropped pebbles into the pools and floated pinecones through the narrow rapids, running alongside to follow the pinecones as they swirled and bobbed on the top of the water. Then we had supper ready, set out on the picnic table. "Do you want to call them?" Jessie said.

I called them but they couldn't hear me because of the noise of the creek. So I walked down to where they were. One of the pinecones had gotten hung up on a snag and they were poking at it with a stick. The stick wasn't long enough and they couldn't quite reach it. "You try," Bobby said.

I took the stick and poked and made a sweeping motion, but couldn't reach it, and leaned farther out and suddenly lost my footing so that I stepped down into the water and filled both shoes. "Jesus," I said. "Christ, that's cold." The boys giggled and pointed at my feet. I was standing in the water with my good shoes on. "You bums," I said. "You lousy bums." I poked the stick again and dislodged the pinecone and it floated away. Then I stepped back onto the bank and, suddenly making a grab, took both boys around the head, wrestling with them against my chest.

"So. You think that's funny, do you? Making a man get his feet wet? You think that's funny?"

"Yes. We do." They were still giggling.

I squeezed them a little bit. "You think so?"

"Yes."

"Still?"

"Yes."

"All right," I said. I squeezed them one more time. "Now what do you think?"

"We still think it's funny."

"Okay," I said, "I guess it is, then." I hugged them both. Then we walked back to the picnic table. I made a play of taking giant steps and sloshing.

"Mom," TJ shouted when we approached the table. "He fell in the creek."

"Who did?"

"Pat."

"Oh my."

"And he got his shoes wet."

"And he cussed too," Bobby said.

"Did you?" Jessie said.

"Hell, no."

"Yes, he did, Mom."

"Maybe," I said. "But they made me."

"What a mess," Jessie said. "Look at you."

"I know it," I said.

"But you should have seen him, Mom," TJ said. They started laughing again and took turns telling her about it while we sat down to eat.

It was cold and almost dark by the time we finished supper. Still it seemed pleasant there, the four of us, sitting at the same table, with the sound of the creek nearby and the smell of pine and blue spruce all around us. Finally we left. The boys had to go to school the next day and Jessie and I had to go back to work.

We drove home out of the mountains in the dark on Highway 34, down through Loveland and Greeley and on through Fort Morgan and Brush onto the High Plains, past Akron and then into Holt County and finally Holt, with its blue streetlights showing from a distance and then closer, and then the streets all quiet and empty when we drove into town. We walked up the steps into their apartment on the edge of town. We put the boys to bed and went to bed ourselves. We were all exhausted. Jessie and I talked very briefly and went to sleep.

Sometime after midnight I woke again, thinking I'd heard a noise. I lay listening for a minute in the dark. Then I heard it again in the front room. I sat up. Now slowly the doorway filled and it was Jack Burdette. In the faint light from the street corner I could see him standing in the door, massive and dark; he smelled of alcohol and there was something across his arm. I started to get up. Then he found the bedroom switch on the wall and turned the light on. Jessie was suddenly awake too. She sat up.

"Hell," he said. "Don't you two never wear clothes? Jesus Christ, look at you."

Jessie pulled the sheet around her. I started to swing out of bed.

"Wait now," Burdette said. "I'm not ready for you to move yet. Just sit there for a minute."

"What do you want?" I said.

"What do you think I want?"

"There's nothing here for you. You know that."

"Yeah," he said. "Yeah, there is something."

He was leaning against the wall, looking at us. He had cleaned up since Friday night, since he had been released. His eyes were bloodshot, but he was clean-shaven now and he was wearing a maroon shirt and a pair of new-looking tan slacks. The shirt was stretched tight over his gut, and lying across his arm was a shotgun. He motioned with it, pointing it at me.

"I told you I had family here. But you never believed me, did you?"

"That's over," I said.

"No, it isn't, goddamn it." He was talking very angrily. "Nothing's over. Is it, Jessie?"

"Yes, it is," she said. "I'm through, Jack. Leave me alone now. Please. I want you to leave me alone."

"Maybe you just think you're through," he said.

"No. I am."

"I'm not, though. You're what I got left. I'm not through."

"But I want you to leave me alone. Can't you just leave? You're good at that."

"I'm taking you with me this time. All three of you."

"No," Jessie said. "No, you're not!" She began to cry, looking fiercely at him. She wrapped the sheet tighter around her.

I stood up. "Goddamn you. Get the hell out of here."

"Shut up," he said. "Shut your mouth."

He stepped away from the wall toward me, leveling the gun at my face.

"And *you* get up," he said to Jessie. "*You* get dressed now." He reached down and jerked the sheet away from her; she was kneeling on the bed with her arms across her breasts. He was still pointing the shotgun at me. "Do what I say. Get dressed and don't say anything."

"Jessie."

"I told you," Burdette said.

"Jessie," I said, "don't."

She was still crying. She looked at me and slowly got out of bed and went over to the closet. She began to get dressed. Burdette stood watching her. And I hated him now; I hated him. While he was watching her I made a sudden grab for the shotgun but he jerked it away and slammed it against my head. Then I was lying on the wood floor beside the bed, naked, sick to my stomach. There was blood running from my ear. I stood up wobbly, bracing myself against the headboard.

"Try that again," he said.

"You son of a bitch. Leave her alone."

"Next time I'll kill you."

Jessie had finished dressing now. She was wearing jeans and a blouse and a warm sweater. He told her to pack some extra things to take with her.

"Where's your suitcase?"

"It's under the bed."

"Get it."

"Jack. Don't do this. Please, don't." Her eyes were red and her hair was tangled. "Please."

"Get your suitcase."

She was still standing in front of the closet. She didn't move. Then he shoved the end of the shotgun barrel against my chest, pushing me against the wall.

"Did you hear me?" he said to her. "Start packing."

She knelt beside the bed and pulled the suitcase out, then she stood and walked around the bed to the dresser and removed some clothes, putting them into the suitcase and closing it.

"Now get me some nylons," Burdette said.

"What?"

"Nylons. Stockings."

"Why?"

"Just do it."

She pulled several pairs of nylons out of the drawer and tossed them to him. One of them fell on the floor and he told her to pick it up and hand it to him. "Now back up," he said. "And face that wall."

"What are you going to do?"

"You'll know in a minute."

"Jack. Don't. Please."

"Shut up. Do what I tell you."

Jessie looked at me once more and then turned, moving to the far wall, and stood facing the wallpaper.

"Okay, lover boy," Burdette said. "It's your turn. Make a slipknot in this." He handed me one of the nylons.

"Go to hell."

He raised the shotgun so that it was against my neck. "Don't you think I'd kill you?"

"Yes. I think you would."

"Then make a knot."

I made a slipknot in the legs of Jessie's nylons and gave it back to him.

He tested it, pulling it tighter. "Now turn around."

"You son of a bitch."

"That's right," he said. "Say good-bye."

The shotgun was still against my neck and I turned around. He pulled my arms behind me and slipped the knot over my wrists, making them burn, and then laid the shotgun on the bed and pulled me down so that I was kneeling and tied my feet and knotted the two ends, stretching me backward on my knees. He wrapped another stocking around my head, across my mouth, gagging me, and then made a loop around the leg of the bedstead. Then he pushed me over. I lay on the floor looking up at him, at his tan pants and maroon-shirted stomach. Against the far wall, Jessie had turned around, facing me. She was crying again.

"All right," Burdette said. "We're done here."

He picked up the shotgun from the bed and lifted her suitcase; he took Jessie by the arm and led her out of the bedroom. That was the last I saw of her. She was wearing a warm sweater and she was crying and her brown hair was tangled.

I didn't see any of the rest of it. I could hear only the frightened sounds coming from the boys' bedroom down the hall. TJ and Bobby were awakened and being forced to dress and I could hear the muffled sound of Jessie's voice trying to reassure them, but the boys were both crying, and then there was the harsh deeper sound of Burdette's voice. When they were finished in the bedroom they walked out through the kitchen toward the back door. The door banged shut and in a moment there was the sound of a car starting up on Hawthorne Street; then there was the sound of it driving away. After that there wasn't anything.

For the rest of that Sunday night and for most of Monday I lay in the bedroom on the floor in the old Fenner house. When he left, Burdette had not bothered to turn the light off and during the night I lay on the floor under the bright overhead light. For some reason that bothered me especially, that no one in Holt noticed it burning. But no one did. So I lay for a long time thinking about that and about other things, and then gradually it began to turn day outside, and now whether or not there was a light on in the bedroom of an apartment house at the west edge of town wouldn't make any difference to anyone. Time passed very slowly. Occasionally I managed to sleep a little. Then I would wake again. My ear had stopped bleeding but my feet and hands felt numb and the edges of my mouth hurt from being stretched.

Meanwhile outside I could hear cars going by and I could hear the sound of kids going to school and the barking of someone's dog. Four or five times during the day the phone rang on the wall out in the kitchen. I lay and listened to it ring. Afterward I learned that one of the calls had been Mrs. Walsh, calling from the *Holt Mercury,* and that another had come from the Holt Cafe, from Jessie's boss, wanting to know why she hadn't returned to work. I never learned who made the other calls.

Finally, late on Monday afternoon, I was released. Mrs. Nyla Waters, Jessie's neighbor, had grown worried about seeing my car parked in front of the house all day so she had called Bud Sealy. And so, about five o'clock, Bud Sealy came over to investigate. He came inside and found me tied up in the bedroom. "What in the hell?" he said. "Jesus Christ."

He had to help me get up. While I got dressed I told him what had happened.

All of that was three months ago. Since then time has passed as usual. It is the middle of January now, the start of another year, and people in Holt are still talking about the events of last fall. In town Joe Don Williams remains particularly upset about things, since it happened to be his shotgun that Burdette had with him that night. Burdette took it from the rack in Williams's unlocked pickup. The pickup was parked in the alley behind Jenny Newcomb's house. So people are talking about that now too.

And in the intervening months the police have begun to send out all-points bulletins again, as they did once before when Burdette disappeared. This time they've charged him with kidnap as well as theft. But they haven't been able to locate him. For as Jessie remarked about him that night in the bedroom: he's good at that. If nothing else, Jack Burdette knows how to disappear.

So I am still in Holt County. I am still publishing the weekly newspaper my father turned over to me years ago. And Wanda Jo Evans is still in Pueblo, living on the Front Range, working for the phone company. And Nora Kramer, that fragile black-haired girl I married out of college a long time ago, is living once more with her father in Denver and they seem to be quite happy.

But Jessie? What about her?

Somewhere in this great world I want to believe that she is all right too. I want to believe that she and TJ and Bobby are still alive, even if it is in California with Jack Burdette. No one has heard anything about them since that night, but I want to believe that much and I hope for more.

Let the game begin!

Barney Northrup was a good salesman. In one day he had rented all of Sunset Towers to the people whose names were already printed on the mailboxes in an alcove off the lobby:

OFFICE	❑	*Dr. Wexler*
LOBBY	❑	*Theodorakis Coffee Shop*
2C	❑	*F. Baumbach*
2D	❑	*Theodorakis*
3C	❑	*S. Pulaski*
3D	❑	*Wexler*
4C	❑	*Hoo*
4D	❑	*J. J. Ford*
5	❑	*Shin Hoo's Restaurant*

Who were these people, these specially selected tenants? They were mothers and fathers and children. A dressmaker, a secretary, an inventor, a doctor, a judge. One was a bookie, one was a burglar, one was a bomber, and one was a mistake. Barney Northrup had rented one of the apartments to the wrong person.

Sunset Towers was a quiet, well-run building. Neighbor greeted neighbor with "Good morning" or a friendly smile, and grappled with small problems behind closed doors. The big problems were yet to come.

■ ■ ■ ■ ■ ■ ■ ■ ■ ■ ■

★"Raskin is an arch storyteller here. . . . Amazingly imaginative, with a cutting edge."   . —*Booklist*, starred review

"A fascinating medley of word games, disguises, multiple aliases, and subterfuges—a demanding but rewarding book."
—*The Horn Book*

"Great fun for those who enjoy illusion, word play, or sleight of hand."   —*The New York Times Book Review*

ALSO BY ELLEN RASKIN

Figgs & Phantoms
The Mysterious Disappearance of Leon (I Mean Noel)
The Tattooed Potato and Other Clues

THE WESTING GAME

E L L E N   R A S K I N

PUFFIN BOOKS

PUFFIN BOOKS
An imprint of Penguin Random House LLC, New York

First published in the United States of America by E.P. Dutton,
a division of Penguin Books USA, Inc., 1978
First paperback edition published by Puffin Books 1992
Reissued 1997
Puffin Modern Classics edition published 2004
This paperback edition published 2021

Visit us online at penguinrandomhouse.com.

THE LIBRARY OF CONGRESS HAS CATALOGED THE PREVIOUS PUFFIN BOOKS EDITION AS FOLLOWS:
Names: Raskin, Ellen, author.
Title: The Westing game / Ellen Raskin
Description: New York : Puffin Books, 2020. | Audience: Ages 8-12. | Audience: Grades 4-6. |
Summary: The mysterious death of an eccentric millionaire brings together an unlikely assortment
of heirs who must uncover the circumstances of his death before they can claim their inheritance.
Identifiers: LCCN 2020006673 | ISBN 9780593118108 (paperback) | ISBN 9780593204504 (ebook)
Subjects: CYAC: Inheritance and succession—Fiction. | Apartment houses—Fiction. |
Chicago (Ill.)—Fiction. | Mystery and detective stories. | Humorous stories.
Classification: LCC PZ7.R1817 We 2020 | DDC [Fic]—dc23
LC record available at https://lccn.loc.gov/2020006673

This edition ISBN 9780593526712

Printed in the United States of America

1 2 3 4 5 6 7 8 9 10

COMR

Text set in Apollo MT

■ **FOR JENNY**
who asked for a puzzle-mystery
■ **AND SUSAN K.**

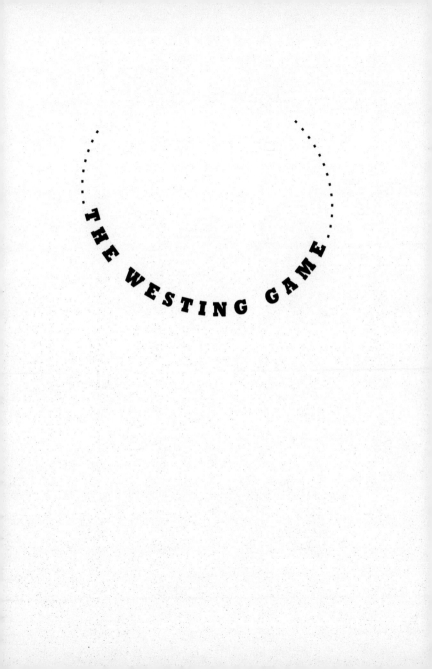

1

THE SUN SETS in the west (just about everyone knows that), but Sunset Towers faced east. Strange!

Sunset Towers faced east and had no towers. This glittery, glassy apartment house stood alone on the Lake Michigan shore five stories high. Five empty stories high.

Then one day (it happened to be the Fourth of July), a most uncommon-looking delivery boy rode around town slipping letters under the doors of the chosen tenants-to-be. The letters were signed *Barney Northrup*.

The delivery boy was sixty-two years old, and there was no such person as Barney Northrup.

■ ■ ■ ■ ■ ■ ■ ■ ■ ■-■

Dear Lucky One:

Here it is—the apartment you've always dreamed of, at a
rent you can afford, in the newest, most luxurious building
on Lake Michigan:

SUNSET TOWERS

- Picture windows in every room
- Uniformed doorman, maid service
- Central air conditioning, hi-speed elevator
- Exclusive neighborhood, near excellent schools
- Etc., etc.

You have to see it to believe it. But these unbelievably elegant apartments will be shown by appointment only. So
hurry, there are only a few left!!! Call me now at 276-7474
for this once-in-a-lifetime offer.

Your servant,
Barney Northrup

P.S. I am also renting ideal space for:

- Doctor's office in lobby
- Coffee shop with entrance from parking lot
- Hi-class restaurant on entire top floor

■ ■ ■ ■ ■ ■ ■ ■ ■ ■ ■

Six letters were delivered, just six. Six appointments were made,
and one by one, family by family, talk, talk, talk, Barney Northrup led the tours around and about Sunset Towers.

"Take a look at all that glass. One-way glass," Barney Northrup said. "You can see out, nobody can see in."

Looking up, the Wexlers (the first appointment of the day)

were blinded by the blast of morning sun that flashed off the face of the building.

"See those chandeliers? Crystal!" Barney Northrup said, slicking his black moustache and straightening his hand-painted tie in the lobby's mirrored wall. "How about this carpeting? Three inches thick!"

"Gorgeous," Mrs. Wexler replied, clutching her husband's arm as her high heels wobbled in the deep plush pile. She, too, managed an approving glance in the mirror before the elevator door opened.

"You're really in luck," Barney Northrup said. "There's only one apartment left, but you'll love it. It was meant for you." He flung open the door to 3D. "Now, is that breathtaking, or is that breathtaking?"

Mrs. Wexler gasped; it was breathtaking, all right. Two walls of the living room were floor-to-ceiling glass. Following Barney Northrup's lead, she ooh-ed and aah-ed her joyous way through the entire apartment.

Her trailing husband was less enthusiastic. "What's this, a bedroom or a closet?" Jake Wexler asked, peering into the last room.

"It's a bedroom, of course," his wife replied.

"It looks like a closet."

"Oh Jake, this apartment is perfect for us, just perfect," Grace Wexler argued in a whining coo. The third bedroom was a trifle small, but it would do just fine for Turtle. "And think what it means having your office in the lobby, Jake; no more driving to and from work, no more mowing the lawn or shoveling snow."

"Let me remind you," Barney Northrup said, "the rent here is cheaper than what your old house costs in upkeep."

How would he know that, Jake wondered.

Grace stood before the front window where, beyond the road, beyond the trees, Lake Michigan lay calm and glistening. A lake view! Just wait until those so-called friends of hers with their classy houses see this place. The furniture would have to be reupholstered; no, she'd buy new furniture—beige velvet. And she'd have stationery made—blue with a deckle edge, her name and fancy address in swirling type across the top: *Grace Windsor Wexler, Sunset Towers on the Lake Shore.*

■ ■ ■ ■ ■ ■ ■ ■ ■ ■ ■

Not every tenant-to-be was quite as overjoyed as Grace Windsor Wexler. Arriving in the late afternoon, Sydelle Pulaski looked up and saw only the dim, warped reflections of treetops and drifting clouds in the glass face of Sunset Towers.

"You're really in luck," Barney Northrup said for the sixth and last time. "There's only one apartment left, but you'll love it. It was meant for you." He flung open the door to a one-bedroom apartment in the rear. "Now, is that breathtaking or is that breathtaking?"

"Not especially," Sydelle Pulaski replied as she blinked into the rays of the summer sun setting behind the parking lot. She had waited all these years for a place of her own, and here it was, in an elegant building where rich people lived. But she wanted a lake view.

"The front apartments are taken," Barney Northrup said. "Besides, the rent's too steep for a secretary's salary. Believe me, you get the same luxuries here at a third of the price."

At least the view from the side window was pleasant. "Are you sure nobody can see in?" Sydelle Pulaski asked.

"Absolutely," Barney Northrup said, following her suspicious stare to the mansion on the north cliff. "That's just the old Westing house up there; it hasn't been lived in for fifteen years."

"Well, I'll have to think it over."

"I have twenty people begging for this apartment," Barney Northrup said, lying through his buckteeth. "Take it or leave it."

"I'll take it."

Whoever, whatever else he was, Barney Northrup was a good salesman. In one day he had rented all of Sunset Towers to the people whose names were already printed on the mailboxes in an alcove off the lobby:

OFFICE	❑	*Dr. Wexler*
LOBBY	❑	*Theodorakis Coffee Shop*
2C	❑	*F. Baumbach*
2D	❑	*Theodorakis*
3C	❑	*S. Pulaski*
3D	❑	*Wexler*
4C	❑	*Hoo*
4D	❑	*J. J. Ford*
5	❑	*Shin Hoo's Restaurant*

Who were these people, these specially selected tenants? They were mothers and fathers and children. A dressmaker, a secretary, an inventor, a doctor, a judge. And, oh yes, one was a bookie, one was a burglar, one was a bomber, and one was a mistake. Barney Northrup had rented one of the apartments to the wrong person.

■ **G H O S T S   O R   W O R S E** ■

ON SEPTEMBER FIRST, the chosen ones (and the mistake) moved in. A wire fence had been erected along the north side of the building; on it a sign warned:

NO TRESPASSING—*Property of the Westing estate.*

The newly paved driveway curved sharply and doubled back on itself rather than breach the city-county line. Sunset Towers stood at the far edge of town.

On September second, Shin Hoo's Restaurant, specializing in authentic Chinese cuisine, held its grand opening. Only three people came. It was, indeed, an exclusive neighborhood; too exclusive for Mr. Hoo. However, the less expensive coffee shop that opened on the parking lot was kept busy serving breakfast, lunch, and dinner to tenants "ordering up" and to workers from nearby Westingtown.

Sunset Towers was a quiet, well-run building, and (except for the grumbling Mr. Hoo) the people who lived there seemed content. Neighbor greeted neighbor with "Good morning" or "Good evening" or a friendly smile, and grappled with small problems behind closed doors.

The big problems were yet to come.

■ ■ ■ ■ ■ ■ ■ ■ ■ ■ ■ ■

Now it was the end of October. A cold, raw wind whipped dead leaves about the ankles of the four people grouped in the Sunset Towers driveway, but not one of them shivered. Not yet.

The stocky, broad-shouldered man in the doorman's uniform, standing with feet spread, fists on hips, was Sandy McSouthers. The two slim, trim high-school seniors, shielding their eyes against the stinging chill, were Theo Theodorakis and Doug Hoo. The small, wiry man pointing to the house on the hill was Otis Amber, the sixty-two-year-old delivery boy.

They faced north, gaping like statues cast in the moment of discovery, until Turtle Wexler, her kite tail of a braid flying behind her, raced her bicycle into the driveway. "Look! Look, there's smoke—there's smoke coming from the chimney of the Westing house."

The others had seen it. What did she think they were looking at anyway?

Turtle leaned on the handlebars, panting for breath. (Sunset Towers was near excellent schools, as Barney Northrup had promised, but the junior high was four miles away.) "Do you think—do you think old man Westing's up there?"

"Naw," Otis Amber, the old delivery boy, answered. "Nobody's seen him for years. Supposed to be living on a private island in the South Seas, he is; but most folks say he's dead.

Long-gone dead. They say his corpse is still up there in that big old house. They say his body is sprawled out on a fancy Oriental rug, and his flesh is rotting off those mean bones, and maggots are creeping in his eye sockets and crawling out his nose holes." The delivery boy added a high-pitched he-he-he to the gruesome details.

Now someone shivered. It was Turtle.

"Serves him right," Sandy said. At other times a cheery fellow, the doorman often complained bitterly about having been fired from his job of twenty years in the Westing paper mill. "But somebody must be up there. Somebody alive, that is." He pushed back the gold-braided cap and squinted at the house through his steel-framed glasses as if expecting the curling smoke to write the answer in the autumn air. "Maybe it's those kids again. No, it couldn't be."

"What kids?" the three kids wanted to know.

"Why, those two unfortunate fellas from Westingtown."

"What unfortunate fellas?" The three heads twisted from the doorman to the delivery boy. Doug Hoo ducked Turtle's whizzing braid. Touch her precious pigtail, even by accident, and she'll kick you in the shins, the brat. He couldn't chance an injury to his legs, not with the big meet coming. The track star began to jog in place.

"Horrible, it was horrible," Otis Amber said with a shudder that sent the loose straps of his leather aviator's helmet swinging about his long, thin face. "Come to think of it, it happened exactly one year ago tonight. On Halloween."

"What happened?" Theo Theodorakis asked impatiently. He was late for work in the coffee shop.

"Tell them, Otis," Sandy urged.

The delivery boy stroked the gray stubble on his pointed chin. "Seems it all started with a bet; somebody bet them a dollar they couldn't stay in that spooky house five minutes. One measly buck! The poor kids hardly got through those French doors on this side of the Westing house when they came tearing

7

out like they was being chased by a ghost. Chased by a ghost—
or worse."

Or worse? Turtle forgot her throbbing toothache. Theo Theodorakis and Doug Hoo, older and more worldly-wise, exchanged
winks but stayed to hear the rest of the story.

"One fella ran out crazy-like, screaming his head off. He never
stopped screaming 'til he hit the rocks at the bottom of the cliff.
The other fella hasn't said but two words since. Something about
purple."

Sandy helped him out. "Purple waves."

Otis Amber nodded sadly. "Yep, that poor fella just sits in the
state asylum saying, 'Purple waves, purple waves' over and over
again, and his scared eyes keep staring at his hands. You see,
when he came running out of the Westing house, his hands was
dripping with warm, red blood."

Now all three shivered.

"Poor kid," the doorman said. "All that pain and suffering for
a dollar bet."

"Make it two dollars for each minute I stay in there, and
you're on," Turtle said.

■ ■ ■ ■ ■ ■ ■ ■ ■ ■ ■ ■

Someone was spying on the group in the driveway.

From the front window of apartment 2D, fifteen-year-old Chris
Theodorakis watched his brother Theo shake hands (it must be a
bet) with the skinny, one-pigtailed girl and rush into the lobby.
The family coffee shop would be busy now; his brother should
have been working the counter half an hour ago. Chris checked
the wall clock. Two more hours before Theo would bring up his
dinner. Then he would tell him about the limper.

Earlier that afternoon Chris had followed the flight of a purple martin (*Progne subis*) across the field of brambles, through
the oaks, up to the red maple on the hill. The bird flew off, but
something else caught his eye. Someone (he could not tell if the

person was a man or a woman) came out of the shadows on the lawn, unlocked the French doors, and disappeared into the Westing house. Someone with a limp. Minutes later smoke began to rise from the chimney.

Once again Chris turned toward the side window and scanned the house on the cliff. The French doors were closed; heavy drapes hung full against the seventeen windows he had counted so many times.

They didn't need drapes on the special glass windows here in Sunset Towers. He could see out, but nobody could see in. Then why did he sometimes feel that someone was watching him? Who could be watching him? God? If God was watching, then why was he like this?

The binoculars fell to the boy's lap. His head jerked, his body coiled, lashed by violent spasms. Relax, Theo will come soon. Relax, soon the geese will be flying south in a V. Canada goose (*Branta canadensis*). Relax. Relax and watch the wind tangle the smoke and blow it toward Westingtown.

■ **TENANTS IN AND OUT** ■

3 UPSTAIRS IN 3D Angela Wexler stood on a hassock as still and blank-faced pretty as a store-window dummy. Her pale blue eyes stared unblinkingly at the lake.

"Turn, dear," said Flora Baumbach, the dressmaker, who lived and worked in a smaller apartment on the second floor.

Angela pivoted in a slow quarter turn. "Oh!"

Startled by the small cry, Flora Baumbach dropped the pin from her pudgy fingers and almost swallowed the three in her mouth.

"Please be careful, Mrs. Baumbach; my Angela has very delicate skin." Grace Windsor Wexler was supervising the fitting of her daughter's wedding dress from the beige velvet couch. Above her hung the two dozen framed flower prints she had selected and arranged with the greatest of taste and care. She could have been an interior decorator, a good one, too, if it wasn't for the pressing demands of so on and so forth.

"Mrs. Baumbach didn't prick me, Mother," Angela said evenly. "I was just surprised to see smoke coming from the Westing house chimney."

Crawling with slow caution on her hands and knees, Flora Baumbach paused in the search for the dropped pin to peer up through her straight gray bangs.

Mrs. Wexler set her coffee cup on the driftwood coffee table and craned her neck for a better view. "We must have new neighbors; I'll have to drive up there with a housewarming gift; they may need some decorating advice."

"Hey, look! There's smoke coming from the Westing house!" Again Turtle was late with the news.

"Oh, it's you." Mrs. Wexler always seemed surprised to see her other daughter, so unlike golden-haired, angel-faced Angela.

Flora Baumbach, about to rise with the found pin, quickly sank down again to protect her sore shin in the shag carpeting. She had pulled Turtle's braid in the lobby yesterday.

"Otis Amber says that old man Westing's stinking corpse is rotting on an Oriental rug."

"My, oh my," Flora Baumbach exclaimed, and Mrs. Wexler clicked her tongue in an irritated "tsk."

Turtle decided not to go on with the horror story. Not that her mother cared if she got killed or ended up a raving lunatic. "Mrs. Baumbach, could you hem my witch's costume? I need it for tonight."

Mrs. Wexler answered. "Can't you see she's busy with Angela's wedding dress? And why must you wear a silly costume like that? Really, Turtle, I don't know why you insist on making yourself ugly."

"It's no sillier than a wedding dress," Turtle snapped back. "Besides, nobody gets married anymore, and if they do, they don't wear silly wedding dresses." She was close to a tantrum. "Besides, who would want to marry that stuck-up-know-it-all-marshmallow-face-doctor-denton . . . ?"

"That's enough of your smart mouth!" Mrs. Wexler leaped up, hand ready to strike; instead she straightened a framed flower print, patted her fashionable honey-blonde hairdo, and sat down again. She had never hit Turtle, but one of these days—besides, a stranger was present. "Doctor Deere is a brilliant young man," she explained for Flora Baumbach's ears. The dressmaker smiled politely. "Angela will soon be Angela Deere; isn't that a precious name?" The dressmaker nodded. "And then we'll have two doctors in the family. Now where do you think you're going?"

Turtle was at the front door. "Downstairs to tell daddy about the smoke coming from the Westing house."

"Come back this instant. You know your father operates in the afternoon; why don't you go to your room and work on stock market reports or whatever you do in there."

"Some room, it's even too small for a closet."

"I'll hem your witch's costume, Turtle," Angela offered.

Mrs. Wexler beamed on her perfect child draped in white. "What an angel."

■ ■ ■ ■ ■ ■ ■ ■ ■ ■ ■

Crow's clothes were black; her skin, dead white. She looked severe. Rigid, in fact. Rigid and righteously severe. No one could have guessed that under that stern facade her stomach was doing flip-flops as Doctor Wexler cut out a corn.

Staring down at the fine lines of pink scalp that showed through the podiatrist's thinning light brown hair did nothing to ease her queasiness; so, softly humming a hymn, she settled her gaze on the north window. "Smoke!"

"Watch it!" Jake Wexler almost cut off her little toe along with the corn.

Unaware of the near amputation, the cleaning woman stared at the Westing house.

"If you will just sit back," Jake began, but his patient did not hear him. She must have been a handsome woman at one time, but life had used her harshly. Her faded hair, knotted in a tight bun on the nape of her gaunt neck, glinted gold-red in the light. Her profile was fine, marred only by the jut of her clenched jaw. Well, let's get on with it, Friday was his busy day, he had phone calls to make. "Please sit back, Mrs. Crow. I'm almost finished."

"What?"

Jake gently replaced her foot on the chair's pedestal. "I see you've hurt your shin."

"What?" For an instant their eyes met; then she looked away. A shy creature (or a guilty one), Crow averted her face when she spoke. "Your daughter Turtle kicked me," she muttered, staring once again at the Westing house. "That's what happens when there is no religion in the home. Sandy says Westing's corpse is up there, rotting away on an Oriental rug, but I don't believe it. If he's truly dead, then he's roasting in hell. We are sinners, all."

■ ■ ■ ■ ■ ■ ■ ■ ■ ■ ■

"What do you mean his corpse is rotting on an Oriental rug, some kind of Persian rug, maybe a Chinese rug." Mr. Hoo joined his son at the glass sidewall of the fifth-floor restaurant. "And why were you wasting precious time listening to an overaged delivery boy with an overactive imagination when you should have been studying." It was not a question; Doug's father never asked questions. "Don't shrug at me, go study."

"Sure, Dad." Doug jogged off through the kitchen; it was no use arguing that there was no school tomorrow, just track practice. He jogged down the back stairs; no matter what excuse he gave, "Go study," his father would say, "go study." He jogged into the Hoos' rear apartment, stretched out on the bare floor and repeated "Go study" to twenty sit-ups.

Only two customers were expected for the dinner hour (Shin Hoo's Restaurant could seat one hundred). Mr. Hoo slammed the reservations book shut, pressed a hand against the pain in his ample stomach, unwrapped a chocolate bar, and devoured it quickly before acid etched another ulcer. Back home again, is he. Well, Westing won't get off so easy this time, not on his life.

A small, delicate woman in a long white apron stood in silence before the restaurant's east window. She stared longingly into the boundless gray distance as if far, far on the other side of Lake Michigan lay China.

■ ■ ■ ■ ■ ■ ■ ■ ■ ■ ■

Sandy McSouthers saluted as the maroon Mercedes swung around the curved driveway and came to a stop at the entrance. He opened the car door with a ceremony reserved only for Judge J. J. Ford. "Look up there, Judge. There's smoke coming from the Westing house."

A tall black woman in a tailored suit, her short-clipped hair touched with gray, slipped out from behind the wheel, handed the car keys to the doorman, and cast a disinterested glance at the house on the hill.

"They say nobody's up there, just the corpse of old man Westing rotting away on an Oriental rug," Sandy reported as he hoisted a full briefcase from the trunk of the car. "Do you believe in ghosts, Judge?"

"There is certain to be a more rational explanation."

"You're right, of course, Judge." Sandy opened the heavy glass door and followed on the judge's heels through the lobby. "I was just repeating what Otis Amber said."

"Otis Amber is a stupid man, if not downright mad." J. J. Ford hurried into the elevator. She should not have said that, not her, not the first black, the first woman, to have been elected to a judgeship in the state. She was tired after a trying day, that was it. Or was it? So Sam Westing has come home at last. Well, she

13

could sell the car, take out a bank loan, pay him back—in cash. But would he take it? "Please don't repeat what I said about Otis Amber, Mr. McSouthers."

"Don't worry, Judge." The doorman escorted her to the door of apartment 4D. "What you tell me is strictly confidential." And it was. J. J. Ford was the biggest tipper in Sunset Towers.

■ ■ ■ ■ ■ ■ ■ ■ ■ ■ ■ ■

"I saw someb-b-b . . ." Chris Theodorakis was too excited to stutter out the news to his brother. One arm shot out and twisted up over his head. Dumb arm.

Theo squatted next to the wheelchair. "Listen, Chris, I'll tell you about that haunted castle on the hill." His voice was soothing and hushed in mystery. "Somebody is up there, Chris, but nobody is there, just rich Mr. Westing, and he's dead. Dead as a squashed June bug and rotting away on a moth-eaten Oriental rug."

Chris relaxed as he always did when his brother told him a story. Theo was good at making up stories.

"And the worms are crawling in and out of the dead man's skull, in and out of his ear holes, his nose holes, his mouth holes, in and out of all his holes."

Chris laughed, then quickly composed his face. He was supposed to look scared.

Theo leaned closer. "And high above the putrid corpse a crystal chandelier is tinkling. It tinkles and twinkles, but not one breath of air stirs in that gloomy tomb of a room."

Gloomy tomb of a room—Theo will make a good writer someday, Chris thought. He wouldn't spoil this wonderful, spooky Halloween story by telling him about the real person up there, the one with the limp.

So Chris sat quietly, his body at ease, and heard about ghosts and ghouls and purple waves, and smiled at his brother with pure delight.

"A smile that could break your heart," Sydelle Pulaski, the

tenant in 3c, always said. But no one paid any attention to Sydelle Pulaski.

■ ■ ■ ■ ■ ■ ■ ■ ■ ■ ■ ■

Sydelle Pulaski struggled out of the taxi, large end first. She was not a heavy woman, just wide-hipped from years of secretarial sitting. If only there was a ladylike way to get out of a cab. Her green rhinestone-studded glasses slipped down her fleshy nose as she grappled with a tall triangular package and a stuffed shopping bag. If only that lazy driver would lend her a hand.

Not for a nickel tip, he wouldn't. The cabbie slammed the back door and sped around the curved driveway, narrowly missing the Mercedes that Sandy was driving to the parking lot.

At least the never-there-when-you-need-him doorman had propped open the front door. Not that he ever helped her, or noticed her, for that matter.

No one ever noticed. Sydelle Pulaski limped through the lobby. She could be carrying a high-powered rifle in that package and no one would notice. She had moved to Sunset Towers hoping to meet elegant people, but no one had invited her in for so much as a cup of tea. No one paid any attention to her, except that poor crippled boy whose smile could break your heart, and that bratty kid with the braid—she'll be sorry she kicked her in the shin.

Juggling her load, earrings jingling and charm bracelet jangling, Sydelle Pulaski unlocked the several locks to apartment 3c and bolted the door behind her. There'd be fewer burglaries around here if people listened to her about putting in dead-bolt locks. But nobody listened. Nobody cared.

On the plastic-covered dining table she set out the contents of the shopping bag: six cans of enamel, paint thinner, and brushes. She unwrapped the long package and leaned four wooden crutches against the wall. The sun was setting over the parking lot, but Sydelle Pulaski did not look out her back window. From the side window smoke could be seen rising from the Westing house, but Sydelle Pulaski did not notice.

"No one ever notices Sydelle Pulaski," she muttered, "but now they will. Now they will."

4 THE HALLOWEEN MOON was full. Except for her receding chin Turtle Wexler looked every inch the witch, her dark unbraided hair streaming wild in the wind from under her peaked hat, a putty wart pasted on her small beaked nose. If only she could fly to the Westing house on a broomstick instead of scrambling over rocks on all fours, what with all she had to carry. Under the long black cape the pockets of her jeans bulged with necessities for the night's dangerous vigil.

Doug Hoo had already reached the top of the cliff and taken his station behind the maple on the lawn. (The track star was chosen timekeeper because he could run faster than anyone in the state of Wisconsin.) Here she comes, it's about time. Shivering knee-deep in damp leaves that couldn't do his leg muscles much good, he readied his thumb on the button of the stopwatch.

Turtle squinted into the blackness that lay within the open French doors. Open, as though someone or some *Thing* was expecting her. There's no such thing as a ghost; besides, all you had to do was speak friendly-like to them. (Ghosts, like dogs, know when a person's scared.) Ghosts or worse, Otis Amber had said. Well, not even the "worse" could hurt Turtle Wexler. She was pure of heart and deed; she only kicked shins in self-defense, so that couldn't count against her. She wasn't scared; she was not scared.

"Hurry up!" That was Doug from behind the tree.

At two dollars a minute, twenty-five minutes would pay for a subscription to *The Wall Street Journal.* She could stay all night.

She was prepared. Turtle checked her pockets: two sandwiches, Sandy's flask filled with orange pop, a flashlight, her mother's silver cross to ward off vampires. The putty wart on her nose (soaked in Angela's perfume in the event she was locked up with the stinking corpse) was clogging her nostrils with sticky sweetness. Turtle took a deep breath of chill night air and flinched with pain. She was afraid of dentists, not ghosts or . . . don't think about purple waves, think about two dollars a minute. Now, one—two—three—three and a half—GO!

Doug checked his stopwatch. Nine minutes.

Ten minutes.

Eleven minutes.

Suddenly a terrified scream—a young girl's scream—pierced the night. Should he go in, or was this one of the brat's tricks? Another scream, closer.

"E-E-E-e-e-e-e-e-e-e!" Clutching the bunched cape around her waist, Turtle came hurtling out of the Westing house. "E-e-e-e-e-e-e-e-e!"

■ ■ ■ ■ ■ ■ ■ ■ ■ ■ ■ ■

Turtle had seen the corpse in the Westing house, but it was not rotting and it was not sprawled on an Oriental rug. The dead man was tucked in a four-poster bed.

A throbbing whisper, "Pur-ple, pur-ple" (or was it "Tur-tle, Tur-tle"—whatever it was, it was scary), had beckoned her to the master bedroom on the second floor, and . . .

Maybe it was a dream. No, it couldn't be; she ached all over from the tumble down the stairs.

The moon was down, the window dark. Turtle lay in the narrow bed in her narrow room, waiting (dark, still dark), waiting. At last slow morning crept up the cliff and raised the Westing house, the house of whispers, the house of death. Two dollars times twelve minutes equals twenty-four dollars.

Thud! The morning newspaper was flung against the front

17

door. Turtle tiptoed through the sleeping apartment to retrieve it and climbed back into bed, the dead man staring at her from the front page. The face was younger; the short beard, darker; but it was he, all right.

SAM WESTING FOUND DEAD

Found? No one else knew about the bedded-down corpse except Doug, and he had not believed her. Then who found the body? The whisperer?

> Samuel W. Westing, the mysterious industrialist who disappeared thirteen years ago, was found dead in his Westingtown mansion last night. He was sixty-five years old.
>
> The only child of immigrant parents, orphaned at the age of twelve, self-educated, hard-working Samuel Westing saved his laborer's wages and bought a small paper mill. From these meager beginnings he built the giant Westing Paper Products Corporation and founded the city of Westingtown to house his thousands of workers and their families. His estate is estimated to be worth over two hundred million dollars.

Turtle read that again: two hundred million dollars. Wow!

> When asked the secret of his success, the industrialist always replied: "Clean living, hard work, and fair play." Westing set his own example; he neither drank nor smoked and never gambled. Yet he was a dedicated gamesman and a master at chess.

Turtle had been in the game room. That's where she picked up the billiard cue she had carried up the stairs as a weapon.

A great patriot, Samuel Westing was famous for his fun-filled Fourth of July celebrations. Whether disguised as Ben Franklin or a lowly drummer boy, he always acted a role in the elaborately staged pageants which he wrote and directed. Perhaps best remembered was his surprise portrayal of Betsy Ross.

Games and feasting followed the pageant, and at sunset Mr. Westing put on his Uncle Sam costume and set off fireworks from his front lawn. The spectacular pyrotechnic display could be viewed thirty miles away.

Fireworks! So that's what was in those boxes stamped *Danger—explosives* stacked in the ground-floor storeroom. What a "pyrotechnic display" that would make if they all went off at the same time.

The paper king's later years were marred by tragedy. His only daughter, Violet, drowned on the eve of her wedding, and two years later his troubled wife deserted their home. Although Mr. Westing obtained a divorce, he never remarried.

Five years later he was sued by an inventor over rights to the disposable paper diaper. On his way to court Samuel Westing and his friend, Dr. Sidney Sikes, were involved in a near-fatal automobile accident. Both men were hospitalized with severe injuries. Sikes resumed his Westingtown medical practice and the post of county coroner, but Westing disappeared from sight.

It was rumored, but never confirmed, that he controlled the vast Westing Paper Products Corporation from a private island in the South Seas. He is still listed as chairman of the board.

"We are as surprised as you are, and deeply saddened," a spokesman for Julian R. Eastman, President and Chief Executive Officer of the corporation, stated when informed that Westing's body was found in his lakeside home. Dr. Sikes' response was: "A tragic end to a tragic life. Sam Westing was a truly great and important man."

The funeral will be private. The executor of the Westing estate said the deceased requested that, in place of flowers, donations be sent to Blind Bowlers of America.

Turtle turned the page of the newspaper, but that was all. That was all?

There was no mention of how the body was found.

There was no mention of the envelope propped on the bedside table on which a shaky hand had scrawled: *If I am found dead in bed*. She had been edging her way against the four-poster, reading the words in the beam of the flashlight, when she felt the hand, the waxy dead hand that lay on the red, white, and blue quilt. Through her scream she had seen the white-bearded face. She remembered running, tripping over the billiard cue, falling down the stairs, denting Sandy's flask, and dropping everything else.

There was no mention of two suspicious peanut butter and jelly sandwiches on the premises, or a flashlight, or a silver cross on a chain.

There was no mention of prowlers; no mention of anyone having seen a witch; no mention of footprints on the lawn: track shoes and sneakers size six.

Oh well, she had nothing to fear (other than losing her mother's cross). Old Mr. Westing probably died of a heart attack—or pneumonia—it was drafty in there. Turtle hid the folded newspaper in her desk drawer, counted her black-and-blue marks in the mirror (seven), dressed, and set out to find the four people who knew she had been in the Westing house last night: Doug Hoo, Theo Theodorakis, Otis Amber, and Sandy. They owed her twenty-four dollars.

■ ■ ■ ■ ■ ■ ■ ■ ■ ■ ■

At noon the sixty-two-year-old delivery boy began his rounds. He had sixteen letters to deliver from E. J. Plum, Attorney-at-Law. Otis Amber knew what the letters said, because one was addressed to him:

> As a named beneficiary in the estate
> of Samuel W. Westing, your attendance
> is required in the south library of the
> Westing house tomorrow at 4 p.m. for
> the reading of the will.

"Means old man Westing left you some money," he explained. "Just sign this receipt here. What do you mean, what does 'position' mean? It means position, like a job. Most receipts have that to make sure the right person gets the right letter."

Grace Windsor Wexler wrote *housewife,* crossed it out, wrote *decorator,* crossed it out, and wrote *heiress.* Then she wanted to know "Who else? How many? How much?"

"I ain't allowed to say nothing."

The other heirs were too stunned by the unexpected legacy to bother him with questions. Madame Hoo marked an *X* and her husband filled in her name and position. Theo wanted to sign the receipt for his brother, but Chris insisted on doing it himself. Slowly, taking great pains, he wrote *Christos Theodorakis, bird-watcher.*

By the time the sun had set behind the Sunset Towers parking lot, Otis Amber, *deliverer,* had completed his rounds.

5 THE MARBLED SKY lay heavy on the gray Great Lake when Grace Windsor Wexler parked her car in the Westing driveway and strode up the walk ahead of her daughters. Her husband had refused to come, but no matter. Recalling family gossip about a rich uncle (maybe it was a great-uncle—anyway, his name was Sam), Grace had convinced herself that she was the rightful heir. (Jake was Jewish, so he could not possibly be related to Samuel W. Westing.)

"I can't imagine what became of my silver cross," she said, fingering the gold-link necklace under her mink stole as she paused to appraise the big house. "You know, Angela, we could have the wedding right here. . . . Turtle, where are you wandering off to now?"

"The letter said— Never mind." Turtle preferred not to explain how she knew the library could be entered from the French doors on the lawn.

The front door was opened by Crow. Although the Sunset Towers cleaning woman always wore black, here it reminded Grace Wexler to dab at her eyes with a lace handkerchief. This was a house of mourning.

The silent Crow helped Angela with her coat and nodded approval of her blue velvet dress with white collar and cuffs.

"I'll keep my furs with me," Grace said. She did not want to be taken for one of the poor relatives. "Seems rather chilly in here."

Turtle, too, complained of the chill, but her mother tugged off her coat to reveal a fluffy, ruffly pink party dress two sizes too large and four inches too long. It was one of Angela's hand-me-downs.

"Please sit anywhere," the lawyer said without glancing from the envelopes he was sorting at the head of the long library table.

Mrs. Wexler took the chair to his right and motioned to her favorite. Angela sat down next to her mother, removed a trousseau towel from her large tapestry shoulder bag, and took up embroidering the monogram D. Slumped in the third chair, Turtle pretended she had never seen this paneled library with its bare and dusty shelves. Suddenly she sat up with a start. An open coffin draped in bunting rested on a raised platform at the far corner of the room; in it lay the dead man, looking exactly as she had found him, except now he was dressed in the costume of Uncle Sam—including the tall hat. Between the waxy hands, folded across his chest, lay her mother's silver cross.

Grace Wexler was too busy greeting the next heir to notice. "Why Doctor D., I had no idea you'd be here; but of course, you'll soon be a member of the family. Come, sit next to your bride-to-be; Turtle, you'll have to move down."

D. Denton Deere, always in a hurry, brushed a quick kiss on Angela's cheek. He was still wearing his hospital whites.

"I didn't know this was a pajama party," Turtle said, relinquishing her chair and stomping to the far end of the table.

■ ■ ■ ■ ■ ■ ■ ■ ■ ■ ■

The next heir, short and round, entered timidly, her lips pressed together in an impish smile that curved up to what must be pointed ears under her straight-cut, steely hair.

"Hello, Mrs. Baumbach," Angela said. "I don't think you've met my fiancé, Denton Deere."

"You're a lucky man, Mr. Deere."

"*Doctor* Deere," Mrs. Wexler corrected her, puzzled by the dressmaker's presence.

"Yes, of course, I'm so sorry." Sensing that she was unwelcome at this end of the room, Flora Baumbach walked on. "Hi, mind if I sit next to you? I promise not to pull your braid."

"That's okay." Turtle was hunched over the table, her small chin resting between her crossed arms. From there she could see everything except the coffin.

Grace Wexler dismissed the next heir with an audible tongue click. That distasteful little man didn't even have the sense to remove his silly aviator's cap. "Tsk." And what in heaven's name was he doing here?

The delivery boy shouted: "Let's give a cheer, Otis Amber is here!" Turtle laughed, Flora Baumbach tittered, and Grace Wexler again clicked her tongue, "Tsk!"

Doug Hoo and his father entered silently, but Sandy gave a hearty "Hi!" and a cheery wave. He wore his doorman's uniform, but unlike Otis Amber, carried his hat in his hand.

Grace Windsor Wexler was no longer surprised at the odd assortment of heirs. Household workers, all, or former employees, she decided. The rich always reward servants in their wills, and her Uncle Sam was a generous man. "Aren't your parents coming?" she asked the older Theodorakis boy as he wheeled his brother into the library.

"They weren't invited," Theo replied.

"Itsss-oo-nn," Chris announced.

"What did he say?"

"He said it's snowing," Theo and Flora Baumbach explained at the same time.

The heirs watched helplessly as the invalid's thin frame was suddenly torn and twisted by convulsions. Only the dressmaker rushed to his side. "I know, I know," she simpered, "you were trying to tell us about the itsy-bitsy snowflings."

Theo moved her away. "My brother is not an infant, and he's not retarded, so please, no more baby talk."

Blinking away tears, Flora Baumbach returned to her seat, the elfin smile still painted on her pained face.

Some stared at the afflicted child with morbid fascination, but most turned away. They didn't want to see.

"Pyramidal tract involvement," Denton Deere whispered, trying to impress Angela with his diagnosis.

Angela, her face a mirror to the boy's suffering, grabbed her tapestry bag and hurried out of the room.

■ ■ ■ ■ ■ ■ ■ ■ ■ ■ ■

"Why hello, Judge Ford." Proud of her liberalism, Grace Windsor Wexler stood and leaned over the table to shake the black woman's hand. She must be here in some legal capacity, or maybe her mother was a household maid, but of one thing Grace was certain: J. J. Ford could no more be related to Samuel W. Westing than Mr. Hoo.

"Can't we get started?" Mr. Hoo asked, hoping to get back in time to watch the football game on television. "I must return to my restaurant," he announced loudly. "Sunday is our busy day, but we are still accepting reservations. Shin Hoo's Restaurant on the fifth floor of Sunset Towers, specializing in . . ."

Doug tugged at his father's sleeve. "Not here, Dad; not in front of the dead."

"What dead?" Mr. Hoo had not noticed the open coffin. Now he did. "Ohhh!"

The lawyer explained that several heirs had not yet arrived. "My wife is not coming," said Mr. Hoo. Grace said, "Doctor Wexler was called away on an emergency operation."

"An emergency Packers game in Green Bay," Turtle confided to Flora Baumbach, who scrunched up her shoulders and tittered behind a plump hand.

"Then we are still waiting for one, no, two more," the lawyer said, fumbling with his papers, his hands shaking under the strict scrutiny of the judge.

Judge Ford had recognized E. J. Plum. Several months ago he had argued before her court, bumbling to the point of incompetence. Why, she wondered, was a young, inexperienced attorney chosen to handle an estate of such importance? Come to think of it, what was *she* doing here? Curiosity? Perhaps, but what about the rest of them, the other tenants of Sunset Towers? Don't anticipate, Josie-Jo, wait for Sam Westing to make the first move.

Light footsteps were heard in the hall. It was only Angela, who blushed and, hugging her tapestry bag close to her body, returned to her seat.

The heirs waited. Some chatted with neighbors, some looked

up at the gilt ceiling, some studied the pattern of the Oriental rug. Judge Ford stared at the table, at Theo Theodorakis's hand. A calloused hand, a healed cut, the shiny slash of a burn on the deep bronze skin. She lowered her hands to her lap. His Greek skin was darker than her "black" skin.

■ ■ ■ ■ ■ ■ ■ ■ ■ ■ ■ ■

Thump, thump, thump. Someone was coming, or were there two of them?

In came Crow. Eyes lowered, without a word, she sat down next to Otis Amber. A dark cloud passed from her face as she eased off a tight shoe under the table.

Thump, thump, thump. The last expected heir arrived.

"Hello, everybody. Sorry I'm late. I haven't quite adjusted to this"—Sydelle Pulaski waved a gaily painted crutch in the air, tottered, and set it down quickly with another thump—"this crutch. Crutch. What a horrible word, but I guess I'll have to get used to it." She pursed her bright red mouth, painted to a fullness beyond the narrow line of her lips, trying to suppress a smile of triumph. Everyone was staring; she knew they would notice.

"What happened, Pulaski?" Otis Amber asked. "Did you pull Turtle's braid again?"

"More likely she visited Wexler the foot butcher," Sandy suggested.

Sydelle was pleased to hear someone come to her defense with a loud click of the tongue. She had not even blinked a false eyelash at those offensive remarks (poise, they call it). "It's really nothing," she reported bravely, "just some sort of wasting disease. But pity me not, I shall live out my remaining time enjoying each precious day to the full." Thump, thump, thump. The secretary kept to the side of the room, avoiding the Oriental rug that might cushion the thump of her purple-striped crutch, as she made her way to the end of the table. Her exaggerated hips were even more exaggerated by the wavy stripes of white on her purple dress.

Purple waves, Turtle thought.

Denton Deere almost fell off his chair, leaning back to follow this most unusual case. First she favored her left leg, then her right leg.

"What is it?" whispered Mrs. Wexler.

The intern did not have the least notion, but he had to say something. "Traveling sporadic myositis," he pronounced quickly and glanced at Angela. Her eyes remained on her embroidery.

The lawyer stood, documents in hand, and cleared his throat several times. Grace Windsor Wexler, her chin tilted in the regal pose of an heiress, gave him her full attention.

"One minute, please." Sydelle Pulaski propped her purple-and-white-striped crutch against the table, then removed a shorthand pad and pencil from her handbag. "Thank you for waiting; you may begin."

■ THE WESTING WILL ■

6 "MY NAME," the young lawyer began, "is Edgar Jennings Plum. Although I never had the honor of meeting Samuel W. Westing, for some reason yet unexplained, I was appointed executor of this will found adjacent to the body of the deceased.

"Let me assure you that I have examined the documents at hand as thoroughly as possible in the short time available. I have verified the signatures to be those of Samuel W. Westing and his two witnesses: Julian R. Eastman, President and Chief Executive Officer of Westing Paper Products Corporation, and Sidney Sikes, M.D., Coroner of Westing County. Although the will you are about to hear may seem eccentric, I pledge my good name and reputation on its legality."

Breathless with suspense, the heirs stared popeyed at Edgar Jennings Plum, who now coughed into his fist, now cleared his throat, now rustled papers, and now, at last, began to read aloud from the Westing will.

I, *SAMUEL W. WESTING, resident of Westing County in the fair state of Wisconsin in the great and glorious United States of America, being of sound mind and memory, do hereby declare this to be my last will and testament.*

FIRST ● *I returned to live among my friends and my enemies. I came home to seek my heir, aware that in doing so I faced death. And so I did.*

Today I have gathered together my nearest and dearest, my sixteen nieces and nephews

"What!"

(Sit down, Grace Windsor Wexler!)

The lawyer stammered an apology to the still-standing woman. "I was only reading; I mean, those are Mr. Westing's words."

"If it's any comfort to you, Mrs. Wexler," Judge Ford remarked with biting dignity, "I am just as appalled by our purported relationship."

"Oh, I didn't mean . . ."

"Hey, Angela," Turtle called the length of the table. "It's against the law to marry that doctor-to-be. He's your cousin."

D. Denton Deere, patting Angela's hand in his best bedside manner, pricked his finger on her embroidery needle.

"I can't tell who said what with this chatter," Sydelle Pulaski complained. "Would you read that again, Mr. Lawyer?"

Today I have gathered together my nearest and dearest, my sixteen nieces and nephews (Sit down, Grace Windsor Wexler!) to view the body of your Uncle Sam for the last time.

Tomorrow its ashes will be scattered to the four winds.

SECOND • *I, Samuel W. Westing, hereby swear that I did not die of natural causes. My life was taken from me—by one of you!*

"O-o-o-uggg." Chris's arm flailed the air, his accusing finger pointed here, no, there; it pointed everywhere. His exaggerated motions acted out the confusion shared by all but one of the heirs as they looked around at the stunned faces of their neighbors to confirm what they heard. Rereading her notes, Sydelle Pulaski now uttered a small shriek. "Eek!"

"Murder? Does that mean Westing was murdered?" Sandy asked the heir on his left.

Crow turned away in silence.

"Does that mean murder?" he asked the heir on his right.

"Murder? Of course it means murder. Sam Westing was murdered," Mr. Hoo replied. "Either that or he ate once too often in that greasy-spoon coffee shop."

Theo resented Hoo's slur on the family business. "It was murder, all right. And the will says the murderer is one of us." He glared at the restaurant owner.

"Have the police been notified of the charge?" Judge Ford asked the lawyer.

Plum shrugged. "I presume they will perform an autopsy."

The judge shook her head in dismay. Autopsy? Westing was already embalmed; tomorrow he would be cremated.

The police are helpless. The culprit is far too cunning to be apprehended for this dastardly deed.

"Oh my!" Flora Baumbach clapped a hand to her mouth on hearing "dastardly." First murder, now a swear word.

> *I, alone, know the name. Now it is up to you. Cast out*
> *the sinner, let the guilty rise and confess.*

"Amen," said Crow.

> **THIRD** • *Who among you is worthy to be the Westing*
> *heir? Help me. My soul shall roam restlessly until that*
> *one is found.*
> *The estate is at the crossroads. The heir who wins*
> *the windfall will be the one who finds the . . .*

"Ashes!" the doorman shouted. Some tittered to relieve the unbearable tension, some cast him a reproachful glance, Grace Wexler clicked her tongue, and Sydelle Pulaski shhh-ed. "It was just a joke," Sandy tried to explain. "You know, ashes scattered to the winds, so the one who wins the windfall gets— Oh, never mind."

> **FOURTH** • *Hail to thee, O land of opportunity! You*
> *have made me, the son of poor immigrants, rich, pow-*
> *erful, and respected.*
> *So take stock in America, my heirs, and sing in*
> *praise of this generous land. You, too, may strike it*
> *rich who dares to play the Westing game.*

"Game? What game?" Turtle wanted to know.

"No matter," Judge Ford said, rising to leave. "This is either a cruel trick or the man was insane."

> **FIFTH** • *Sit down, Your Honor, and read the letter this*
> *brilliant young attorney will now hand over to you.*

It was uncanny. Several heads turned toward the coffin, but Westing's eyes were shut forever.

The brilliant young attorney fumbled through a stack of papers, felt his pockets, and finally found the letter in his briefcase.

"Aren't you going to open it?" Theo asked as the judge resumed her seat and put the sealed envelope in her purse.

"No need. Sam Westing could afford to buy a dozen certificates of sanity."

"The poor are crazy, the rich just eccentric," Mr. Hoo said bitterly.

"Are you implying, sir, that the medical profession is corrupt?" Denton Deere challenged.

"Shhh!"

> SIXTH • *Before you proceed to the game room there will be one minute of silent prayer for your good old Uncle Sam.*

Flora Baumbach was the only heir to cry. Crow was the only one to pray. By the time Sydelle Pulaski could assume a pose of reverence, the minute was up.

■ THE WESTING GAME ■

7

EIGHT CARD TABLES, each with two chairs, were arranged in the center of the game room. Sports equipment lined the walls. Hunting rifles, Ping-Pong paddles, billiard cues (a full rack, Turtle noticed), bows and arrows, darts, bats, racquets—all looked like possible murder weapons to the jittery heirs who were waiting to be told where to sit.

Theo wandered over to the chess table to admire the finely carved pieces. Someone had moved a white pawn. Okay, he'll play along. Theo defended the opening with a black knight.

On hearing Plum's throat-clearing signal, Sydelle Pulaski switched the painted crutch to her left armpit and flipped to a fresh page in her notebook. "Shhh!"

> SEVENTH • *And now, dear friends, relatives, and enemies, the Westing game begins.*
>
> *The rules are simple:*
> * Number of Players: 16, divided into 8 pairs.
> * Each pair will receive $10,000.
> * Each pair will receive one set of clues.
> * Forfeits: If any player drops out, the partner must leave the game. The pair must return the money. Absent pairs forfeit the $10,000; their clues will be held until the next session.
> * Players will be given two days' notice of the next session. Each pair may then give one answer.
> * Object of the game: to win.

"Did you hear that, Crow?" Otis Amber said excitedly. "Ten thousand dollars! Now aren't you glad I made you come, huh?"

"Shhh!" That was Turtle. The object of the game was to win, and she wanted to win.

> EIGHTH • *The heirs will now be paired. When called, go to the assigned table. Your name and position will be read as signed on the receipt.*
>
> *It will be up to the other players to discover who you really are.*

I • MADAME SUN LIN HOO, *cook*
   JAKE WEXLER, *standing or sitting when not lying down*

Grace Wexler did not understand her husband's joke about position. Mr. Hoo did, but he was in no mood for humor; ten thousand

dollars was at stake. Both pleaded for their absent spouses—
"Emergency operation," "My wife doesn't even speak English"—
to no avail. Table one remained empty and moneyless.

2 • TURTLE WEXLER, *witch*
  FLORA BAUMBACH, *dressmaker*

Sighs of relief greeted the naming of Turtle's partner, but Flora
Baumbach seemed pleased to be paired with the kicking witch.
At least, her face was still puckered in that elfin grin. Turtle had
hoped for one of the high-school seniors, especially Doug Hoo.

3 • CHRISTOS THEODORAKIS, *birdwatcher*
  D. DENTON DEERE, *intern, St. Joseph's Hospital, Department
  of Plastic Surgery*

Theo protested: He and his brother should be paired together;
Chris was his responsibility. Mrs. Wexler protested: Doctor D.
should be paired with his bride-to-be. D. Denton Deere protested,
but silently: If this had been arranged for free medical advice,
they (whoever they are) were mistaken. He was a busy man. He
was a doctor, not a nursemaid.

But Chris was delighted to be part of the outside world. He
would tell the intern about the person who limped into the
Westing house; maybe that was the murderer—unless his partner was the murderer! This was really exciting, even better than
television.

4 • ALEXANDER MCSOUTHERS, *doorman*
  J. J. FORD, *judge, Appellate Division of the State Supreme Court*

The heirs watched the jaunty doorman pull out a chair for the
judge. It had never occurred to them that Sandy was a nickname
for Alexander, but that couldn't be what Sam Westing meant by
It will be up to the other players to discover who you really are. Or
could it?

The judge did not return the chip-toothed smile. *Doorman,* he calls himself, and the others had signed simple things, too: *cook, dressmaker.* The podiatrist had even made fun of his "position." She must seem as pompous as that intern, putting on airs with that title. Well, she had worked hard to get where she was, why shouldn't she be proud of it? She was no token; her record was faultless. . . . Watch it, Josie-Jo. Westing's getting to you already and the game has barely begun.

5 • GRACE WINDSOR WEXLER, *heiress*
    JAMES SHIN HOO, *restaurateur*

Grace Windsor Wexler ignored the snickers. If she was not the heiress now, she would be soon, what with her clues, Angela's clues, Turtle's clues, Denton's clues, and the clues of Mr. Hoo's obedient son. Five thousand dollars lost! Oh well, who needs Jake anyway? She'd win on her own. "You'll be happy to know that Mr. Westing was really my Uncle Sam," she whispered to her partner.

So what, thought Mr. Hoo. Five thousand dollars lost! He should have told his wife about this meeting, dragged her along. Sam Westing, the louse, has cheated him again. Whoever killed him deserves a medal.

6 • BERTHE ERICA CROW, *Good Salvation Soup Kitchen*
    OTIS AMBER, *deliverer*

The delivery boy danced a merry jig; but Crow, her sore foot squeezed back into her tight shoe, headed for table six with a grim face. Why were they watching her? Did they think she killed Windy? Could the guilty know her guilt? Repent!

Crow limps, Chris Theodorakis noted.

7 • THEO THEODORAKIS, *brother*
    DOUG HOO, *first in all-state high-school mile run*

They slapped hands, and Doug jogged to table seven. Theo moved more slowly. Passing the chessboard he saw that white had made a second move. He countered with a black pawn. Maybe he should not have written *brother,* but like it or not, that was his position in life. Chris was smiling at him in pure sweetness, which made Theo feel even guiltier about his resentment.

"I guess that makes us partners, Ms. Pulaski," Angela said.

"Pardon me, did you say something?"

8 • SYDELLE PULASKI, *secretary to the president*
  ANGELA WEXLER, *none*

Angela stepped tentatively behind the secretary, not knowing whether to ignore her disability or to take her arm. At least her crippled partner could not be the murderer, but it was embarrassing being paired with such a . . . no, she shouldn't feel that way. It was her mother who was upset (she could feel the indignant anger without having to look at Grace); her perfect daughter was paired with a freak.

What good luck, the hobbling Sydelle Pulaski thought. Now she would really be noticed with such a pretty young thing for a partner. They might even invite her to the wedding. She'd paint a crutch white with little pink nosegays.

Denton Deere was troubled. What in the world did Angela mean by "nun"?

■ ■ ■ ■ ■ ■ ■ ■ ■ ■ ■

Once again Edgar Jennings Plum cleared his throat.

"Nasal drip," Denton Deere whispered, confiding the latest diagnosis to his partner. Chris giggled. What's the crippled kid so happy about, the intern wondered.

NINTH • *Money! Each pair in attendance will now receive a check for the sum of $10,000. The check can-*

not be cashed without the signatures of both partners.
Spend it wisely or go for broke. May God thy gold refine.

A piercing shriek suddenly reminded the Westing heirs of murder. While passing out the checks, the lawyer had stepped on Crow's sore foot.

"Is this legal, Judge?" Sandy asked.

"It is not only legal, Mr. McSouthers," Judge Ford replied, signing her name to the check and handing it to the doorman, "it is a shrewd way to keep everyone playing the game."

> TENTH • *Each pair in attendance will now receive an envelope containing a set of clues. No two sets of clues are alike. It is not what you have, it's what you don't have that counts.*

Placing the last of the envelopes on table eight, the young lawyer smiled at Angela. Sydelle Pulaski smiled back.

"This makes no sense," Denton Deere complained. Four clues typed on cut squares of Westing Superstrength Paper Towels lay on the table before him.

Arms and elbows at odds, with fingers fanned, Chris tried to rearrange the words in some grammatical, if not logical, order.

"Hey, watch it!" the intern shouted, as one clue wafted to the floor.

Flora Baumbach leaped from her chair at the next table, picked up the square of paper, and set it face down before the trembling youngster. "I didn't see it," she announced loudly. "I really didn't see it," she repeated under the questioning gaze of her partner, Turtle Wexler, *witch*.

The word she had seen was *plain*.

The players protected their clues more carefully now. Hunched over the tables, they moved the paper squares this way and that way, mumbling and grumbling. The murderer's name must be there, somewhere.

Only one pair had not yet seen their clues. At table eight Sydelle Pulaski placed one hand on the envelope, raised a finger to her lips, and tilted her head toward the other heirs. Just watch and listen, she meant.

She may be odd, but she's smart, Angela thought. Since each pair had a different set of clues, they would watch and listen for clues to their clues.

■ ■ ■ ■ ■ ■ ■ ■ ■ ■ ■ ■

"He-he-he." The delivery boy slapped his partner on the back. "That's us, old pal: Queen Crow and King Amber."

"What's this: *on* or *no?*" Doug Hoo turned a clue upside down, then right side up again.

Theo jabbed an elbow in his ribs and turned to see if anyone had heard. Angela lowered her eyes in time.

J. J. Ford crumpled the clues in her fist and rose in anger. "I'm sorry, Mr. McSouthers. Playing a pawn in this foolish game is one thing, but to be insulted with minstrel show dialect . . ."

"Please, Judge, please don't quit on me," Sandy pleaded. "I'd have to give back all that money; it would break my wife's heart. And my poor kids. . . ."

Judge Ford regarded the desperate doorman without pity. So many had begged before her bench.

"Please, Judge. I lost my job, my pension. I can't fight no more. Don't quit just because of some nonsensical words."

Sticks and stones can break my bones, but words will never hurt me, she had chanted as a child. Words did hurt, but she was no longer a child. Nor a hanging judge. And there was always the chance . . . "All right, Mr. McSouthers, I'll stay." J. J. Ford sat down, her eyes sparking with wickedness. "And we'll play the game just as Sam Westing would have played it. Mean!"

Flora Baumbach squeezed her eyes together and screwed up her face. She was concentrating.

"Haven't you memorized them yet?" Turtle didn't like the way

Otis Amber's scrawny neck was swiveling high out of his collar. And what was Angela staring at?

"Yes, I think so," the dressmaker replied, "but I can't make heads or tails of them."

"They make perfect sense to me," Turtle said. One by one she put the clues in her mouth, chewed, and swallowed them.

■ ■ ■ ■ ■ ■ ■ ■ ■ ■ ■

"Gibberish," Mr. Hoo muttered.

Grace Windsor Wexler agreed. "Excuse me, Mr. Plum, but what are these clues clues to? I mean, exactly what are we supposed to find?"

"Purple waves," Sandy joked with a wink at Turtle.

Mrs. Wexler uttered a cry of recognition and changed the order of two of her clues.

"It's still gibberish," Mr. Hoo complained.

Other players pressed the lawyer for more information. Ed Plum only shrugged.

"Then could you please give us copies of the will?"

"A copy will be on file . . ." Judge Ford began.

"I'm afraid not, Your Honor," the lawyer said. "The will not, I mean the will will will . . ." He paused and tried again. "The will will not be filed until the first of the year. My instructions specifically state that no heir is allowed to see any of the documents until the game is over."

No copy? That's not fair. But wait, they did have a copy. A shorthand copy!

Sydelle Pulaski had plenty of attention now. She smiled back at the friendly faces, revealing a lipstick stain on her front teeth.

"Isn't there some sort of a last statement?" Sandy asked Plum. "I mean, like the intern says, nothing makes any sense."

ELEVENTH • *Senseless, you say? Death is senseless yet makes way for the living. Life, too, is senseless unless you know who you are, what you want, and which way the wind blows.*

So on with the game. The solution is simple if you know whom you are looking for. But heirs, beware! Be aware!

Some are not who they say they are, and some are not who they seem to be. Whoever you are, it's time to go home.

God bless you all and remember this:
Buy Westing Paper Products!

■ **THE PAIRED HEIRS** ■

8
DURING THE NIGHT Flora Baumbach's itsy-bitsy snowflings raged into a blizzard. The tenants of Sunset Towers awoke from clue-chasing, blood-dripping dreams, bound in twisted sheets and imprisoned by fifteen-foot snowdrifts.

No telephones. No electricity.

Snowbound with a murderer!

The slow procession looked like some ancient, mysterious rite as partner sought out partner on the windowless stairs, and silent pairs threaded through the corridors in the flickering light of crooked, color-striped candles (the product of Turtle's stint at summer camp).

"These handmade candles are both practical and romantic," she said, peddling her wares from apartment door to apartment door to frightened tenants at seven in the morning. (Oh, it's only Turtle.) "And the colored stripes tell time, which is very handy if your electric clock stopped. Each stripe burns exactly one-half hour, more or less. Twelve stripes, six hours."

"How much?"

"Not wishing to take advantage of this emergency, I've reduced the price to only five dollars each."

Outrageous. Even more so when the electricity came on two hours after her last sale. "Sorry, no refunds," Turtle said.

No matter. What was five dollars to heirs of an estate worth two hundred million? Clues, they had to work on those clues. Behind closed doors. Whisper, someone may be listening.

Not all the heirs were huddled in plotting, puzzle-solving pairs. Jake Wexler had retreated to his office after a long and loud argument with his wife. He sure could have used half of that ten thousand dollars, but he wouldn't admit it, not to her. The forfeited money upset her more than the murder of her uncle, if he was her uncle.

Five floors above, Jake's partner stood before the restaurant's front window staring at the froth on the angry lake, and beyond. No one had bothered to tell Madame Hoo about the Westing game.

Other players were snowbound elsewhere: Denton Deere in the hospital, Sandy at home. No one gave a thought to where Otis Amber or Crow might be.

But Sydelle Pulaski was there, thumping her crutch against the baseboards as she limped through the carpeted halls on the arm of her pretty partner. Not one, but seven tenants had invited her to morning coffee or afternoon tea (murderer or not, they had to see Pulaski's copy of that will).

"Three lumps, please. Angela drinks it black." Your health? "Thank the lord I'm still able to hobble about." Your job? "I was private secretary to the president of Schultz Sausages. Poor Mr. Schultz, I don't know how he'll manage without me." Your shorthand notes? "Thank you for the refreshments. I must hurry back for my medication. Come, Angela."

■ ■ ■ ■ ■ ■ ■ ■ ■ ■ ■

One heir had not invited them in, but that didn't stop Sydelle Pulaski from barging into apartment 2D. "Hi, Chris. Just thought we'd pop in to see how you're doing. Don't be scared. I'm not the murderer, Angela is not the murderer, and we don't think you are the murderer. Mind if I sit down?" The secretary toppled into a chair next to the invalid before he could reply. "Here, I stole a macaroon for you. It's so sticky you'll be tasting it all day; I must have six strands of coconut between my upper molars." Chris took the cookie. "Just look at that smile, it could break your heart."

Angela wished her partner had not said that; it seemed so insensitive, so crude. But at least Sydelle was talking to him, which was more than she was able to do. Angela, the fortunate one, standing like a dummy. "Um, I know Denton wants to work on the clues with you. He's snowbound, too."

"You ver-r pred-dy." How did "pretty" come out? He meant to say "nice." Chris bent his curly head over the geography book in his lap. She wasn't laughing at him. It was all right to ask her because she was going to marry his partner. "Wha ar-r g-gra-annz?"

Angela did not understand.

Chris fanned the pages of the book to a picture of a wheat field. "G-gra-annz."

"Oh, grains. You want to know the names of some grains. Let's see, there's wheat, rye, corn, barley, oats."

"O-ohss!" Angela thought the boy was going into a fit, but he was only repeating her last word: oats.

Sydelle was puffing her warm breath on the window and wiping a frosted area clean with her sleeve. "There, now you'll be able to watch the birds again. Anything else we can do for you, young man?"

Chris nodded. "Read m-me short-han n-noos."

The pretty lady and the funny lady moved quickly out the door. One limped, but it was a pretended limp (he could tell), not like the limper on the Westing house lawn.

Oats. Chris closed his eyes to picture the clues:

Grain = oats = Otis Amber. *For* + *d* (from *shed*) = Ford. But neither the delivery boy nor the judge limped, and he still hadn't figured out *she* or *plain*. He'd have to wait for Denton Deere; Denton Deere was smart; he was a doctor.

Chris raised his binoculars to the cliff. Windblown drifts buttressed the house—something moved on the second floor—a hand holding back the edge of a drape. Slowly the heavy drape fell back against the window. The Westing house was snowbound, too, and somebody was snowbound in it.

■ ■ ■ ■ ■ ■ ■ ■ ■ ■ ■ ■

Only one of the players thought the clues told how the ten-thousand-dollar check was to be spent. *Take stock in America,* the will said. *Go for broke,* the will said.

"In the stock market," Turtle said. "And whoever makes the most money wins it all, the whole two hundred million dollars." Their clues:

SEA   MOUNTAIN   AM   O

stood for symbols of three corporations listed on the stock exchange: SEA, MT (the abbreviation for mountain), AMO.

"But *am* and *o* are separate clues," Flora Baumbach said.

"To confuse us."

"But what about the murderer? I thought we were supposed to find the name of the murderer?"

"To put us off the track." If the police suspected murder, she'd be in jail by now. Her fingerprints were over everything in the Westing house, including the corpse. "You don't really think one of us could have killed a living, breathing human being in cold blood, do you, Mrs. Baumbach? Do you?" Turtle did, but the dressmaker was a cream puff.

"Don't you look at me like that, Turtle Wexler! You know very well I could never think such a thing. I must have misunderstood. Oh my, I just wish Miss Pulaski had shown us her copy of the will."

Turtle returned to her calculations, multiplying numbers of shares times price, adding a broker's commission, trying to total the sums to the ten thousand dollars they had to spend.

Flora Baumbach may have been wrong about the murder, but she was not convinced of Turtle's plan. "What about *Buy Westing Paper Products*? I'm sure that was in the will."

"Great!" Turtle exclaimed. "We'll do just that, we'll add WPP to the list of stocks we're going to buy."

Flora Baumbach had watched enough television commercials to know that *Buy Westing Paper Products* meant that as soon as she could get to market, she'd buy all the Westing products on the shelf. Still, it felt good having a child around again. She'd play along, gladly. "You know, Turtle, you may be right about putting our money in the stock market. I remember the will said *May God thy gold refine*. That must be from the Bible."

"Shakespeare," Turtle replied. All quotations were either from the Bible or Shakespeare.

■ ■ ■ ■ ■ ■ ■ ■ ■ ■ ■

Mr. Hoo moved aside a full ashtray with a show of distaste and rearranged the clues. "*Purple fruited* makes more sense."

Grace Wexler looked across the restaurant to the lone figure at the window. "Are you sure your wife doesn't understand English, I mean, after living here so long?"

"That's my second wife. She came over from Hong Kong two years ago."

"She does look young, but it's so hard to tell ages of people of the Oriental persuasion," Grace said. Why was he glaring at her like that? "Your wife is quite lovely, you know, so doll-like and inscrutable."

Hoo bit off half a chocolate bar. He had enough problems with the empty restaurant, a lazy son, and his nagging ulcer; now he had to put up with this bigot.

Grace lit another cigarette and rearranged the clues to read: *purple waves.* "You heard that doorman say 'purple waves'; it must mean something. And that ghastly secretary was wearing a dress with purple waves last night, not to mention her crutch."

"You should not speak unkindly of those less fortunate than you," Hoo said.

"You're quite right," Grace replied. "I thought the poor thing handled her infirmity with great courage—traveling mimosa, my future son-in-law says; he's a doctor, you know. Anyhow, Pulaski couldn't possibly be the murderer, not the way she gimps around. Besides, how could my Uncle Sam know she'd wear purple waves to his funeral?"

Hoo waved the cigarette smoke from his face. "The murderer had to have a motive. How about this: A niece murders her rich uncle to inherit his money?"

Good sport that she was, Grace tossed back her head and uttered an amused "Ha-ha-ha."

"Not that I care," Hoo said. "That cheating moneybags got what he deserved. What's the matter?"

"Look!" Grace pointed to the clues.

FRUITED   PURPLE   WAVES   FOR   SEA

"*For sea!* The murderer lives in apartment 4c!"

"I live in 4c," Hoo barked. "If Sam Westing wanted to say 4c he would have written number 4, letter C. S-e-a means *sea*, like what a turtle swims in."

"Come now, Mr. Hoo, we are both being silly. Have you spoken to your son about his clues?"

"Some son. If you can catch him, you can ask him." Hoo stuffed the rest of the candy bar in his mouth. "And some business I've got here. Everybody orders up, nobody orders down.

That coffee shop is sending me to the poorhouse. And your Angela and that Pulaski woman, they didn't show us the will, they didn't give us their clues, they didn't pay for three cups of jasmine tea and six almond cookies, and you smoke too much."

"And you eat too much." Grace threw her coin purse on the table and stormed out of the restaurant. Change, that's all he'll get from her; he'd have to beg on his knees before she'd sign Grace Windsor Wexler on the ten-thousand-dollar check, that madman. Some pair they made: Attila the Hun and Gracie the useless. Gracie Windkloppel Wexler, heir pretender, pretentious heir.

■ ■ ■ ■ ■ ■ ■ ■ ■ ■ ■

First, the money. They signed their names to the check; half would go into Doug Hoo's savings account; half would go to Theo's parents. Next, the clues:

HIS   N   ON   TO   THEE   FOR

"Maybe they're numbers: one, two, three, four," Theo guessed.

"I still say *on* is *no,*" the bored track star said. He clasped his hands behind his head, leaned back in the coffee shop booth and stretched his long legs under the opposite bench. "And *no* is what we got: *no* real clues, *no* leads, *no* will."

After three cups of coffee, two pastries and a bowl of rice pudding with cream, Sydelle Pulaski had offered nothing in return.

Theo refused to give up. "Are you sure you didn't see anything unusual at the Westing house that night?"

"I didn't kill Westing, if that's what you mean, and the only unusual thing I saw was Turtle Wexler. I think the pest is madly in love with me; how's that for luck?"

"Get serious, Doug. One of the heirs is a murderer; we could all get killed."

"Just because somebody zapped the old man doesn't mean

he's going to kill again. Dad says . . ." Doug paused. His father's comment about awarding a medal to the murderer might be incriminating.

Theo tried another tack. "I was playing chess with somebody in the game room last night."

"Who?"

"That's what's strange; I don't know who. We'll have to find out which one of the heirs plays chess."

"Since when is chess-playing evidence for murder?"

"Well, it's something to go on," Theo replied. "And another thing: The will said no two sets of clues are alike. Maybe all the clues put together make one message, a message that points to the murderer. Somehow or other we'll have to get the heirs to pool the clues."

"Oh, sure. The killer can't wait to hand over the clues that will hang him." Doug rose. Snowbound or not, he had to stay in shape for the track meet. For the rest of the day he jogged through the hallways and up and down stairs, scaring the nervous tenants half out of their wits.

■ ■ ■ ■ ■ ■ ■ ■ ■ ■ ■

Judge J. J. Ford had no doubt that the clues she shared with the doorman were meant for her, but Sam Westing could toss off sharper insults than:

SKIES   AM   SHINING   BROTHER

His choice of words must have been limited; therefore, these clues were part of a longer statement. A statement that named a name. The name of the murderer.

No. Westing could not have been murdered. If his life had been threatened, if he had been in danger of any kind, he would have insisted on police protection. He owned the police; he owned the whole town. Sam Westing was not the type to let himself get killed. Not unless he was insane.

The judge opened the envelope given her by the incompetent Plum. A certificate of sanity, dated last week: "Having thoroughly examined . . . keen mind and memory . . . excellent physical condition . . . (signed) *Sidney Sikes, M.D.*"

Sikes. That sounded familiar. The judge scanned the obituary she had cut from Saturday's newspaper.

> . . . Samuel Westing and his friend, Dr. Sidney Sikes, were involved in a near-fatal automobile accident. Both men were hospitalized with severe injuries. Sikes resumed his Westingtown medical practice and the post of county coroner, but Westing disappeared from sight.

Sikes was Westing's friend (and, she remembered, a witness to the will), but he was also a physician in good standing. She would accept his opinion on Westing's sanity, for the time being at least.

Back to the clues. Look at her, the big-time judge, fussing over scraps of Westing Superstrength Paper Towels. "Forget the clues," she said aloud, rising from her desk to putter about the room.

Nibbling on a macaroon, she stacked the used coffee cups on a tray. If only that Pulaski person had let her study the will. That's where the real clues were buried, among the veiled threats and pompous promises, the slogans and silliness in that hodgepodge of a will.

In his will Sam Westing implied (he did not state, he implied) that (1) he was murdered, (2) the murderer was one of the heirs, (3) he alone knew the name of the murderer, and (4) the name of the murderer was the answer to the game.

The game: a tricky, divisive Westing game. No matter how much fear and suspicion he instilled in the players, Sam Westing knew that greed would keep them playing the game. Until the "murderer" was captured. And punished.

Sam Westing was not murdered, but one of his heirs was guilty—guilty of some offense against a relentless man. And that heir was in danger. From his grave Westing would stalk his enemy, and through his heirs he would wreak his revenge.

Which one? Which heir was the target of Westing's vindictiveness? In the name of justice she would have to find Westing's victim before the others did. She would have to learn everything she could about each one of the heirs. Who are they, and how did their lives touch Westing's, these sixteen strangers whose only connection with one another was Sunset Towers? Sunset Towers—she'd start from there.

Good, the telephones are working again. The number she dialed was answered on the first ring. "Hi there, this is a recording of yours truly, Barney Northrup. I'm at your service—soon as I get back in my office, that is. Just sing out your problem to old Barney here when you hear the beep." Beep.

J. J. Ford hung up without singing out her problem to old Barney. He, too, could be involved in Westing's plot.

The newspaper, she would try the newspaper; surely someone was snowbound there. After eight rings, a live voice answered. "We usually don't supply that kind of information over the phone, but since it's you, Judge Ford, I'll be happy to oblige. Just spell out the names and I'll call back if I find anything."

"Thank you, I'd appreciate that." It was a beginning. Sam Westing was dead, but maybe, just once, she could beat him at his own game. His last game.

■ ■ ■ ■ ■ ■ ■ ■ ■ ■ ■

Having found what she wanted in Turtle's desk, Angela returned to her frilly bedroom where Sydelle Pulaski, glasses low on her nose, was perched on a ruffled stool at the vanity table, smearing blue shadow on her eyelids.

"First we tackle our own clues," the secretary said, frowning at the result in the threefold mirror. Unlucky from the day she was born, she now had a beautiful and well-loved partner. There was always the chance that they alone had been given the answer. She unsealed the envelope and held it out to Angela. "Take one."

Angela removed the first clue: *good*.

Now it was Sydelle's turn. "Glory be!" she exclaimed, thinking she had the name of the murderer. Her thumb was covering the letter *d*. The word was *hood*.

Angela's turn. The third clue was *from*.

Sydelle's turn. The fourth clue was *spacious*.

The fifth and last clue was—Angela uttered a low moan. Her hand shook as she passed the paper to her partner. The fifth and last clue was *grace*.

"Grace, that's your mother's name, isn't it?" Sydelle said. "Well, don't worry, that clue doesn't mean your mother is the murderer. The will says: *It is not what you have, it's what you don't have that counts.*" The secretary had not yet transcribed the shorthand, but she had read it through several times before hiding the notebook in a safe place. "By the way, are you really related to Mr. Westing?"

Angela shrugged. Sydelle assumed that meant no and turned to the clues.

GOOD   GRACE   FROM   HOOD   SPACIOUS

"The only thing I can figure from these clues is: *Good gracious from hood space.* As soon as the parking lot is shoveled out, we'll peek under the hoods of all the cars. A map or more clues may be hidden there. Maybe even the murder weapon. Now, let's hear about the other clues."

Angela reported on the clues gathered in the game room and during the day's comings and goings:

"*King, queen*. Otis Amber said, 'King Otis and Queen Crow.'

"*Purple waves*. Mother switched two clues around when Sandy mentioned those words.

"*On* (or *no*). Doug and Theo could not decide whether that clue was right side up or upside down.

"*Grains*. Chris Theodorakis thinks that clue refers to Otis Amber. You know, grains—oats.

"*MT*." Angela showed her partner the crumpled scrap of paper she had picked up along with Sydelle's dropped crutch during Flora Baumbach's tea party.

$$500 \text{ shares MT at } \$6 = \$3000$$
$$\text{broker's commission} = \underline{+90}$$
$$\$3090$$

"I checked Turtle's diary. She is not following any stock with a symbol like *MT*, so it must be one of her clues. *MT* could stand for either *mountain* or *empty*."

"Excellent," Sydelle Pulaski remarked. Her partner was beautiful, but not dumb. "Read all the clues together now."

> GOOD HOOD FROM SPACIOUS GRACE
> KING QUEEN PURPLE WAVES
> ON (NO) GRAINS MOUNTAIN (EMPTY)

Sydelle was disappointed. "*It is not what you have, it's what you don't have that counts.* And what we don't have is a verb. Nothing makes sense without a verb. What about the judge?"

"Judge Ford thought her clues were an insult, and she said something about playing a pawn in Westing's game. And she had a clipping of the obituary on her desk. This obituary." Angela handed Sydelle the newspaper taken from Turtle's drawer.

"What's that?"

It was a knock on the front door.

It was footsteps in the living room.

It was Theo. "Anyone for a game of chess?" he asked, leaning through the bedroom doorway.

"No, thank you," Sydelle replied, looking very busy.

Theo smiled shyly at Angela and left.

Sydelle read the obituary in Turtle's newspaper. The words *two hundred million dollars* were underlined, but she found a more interesting item. "Sam Westing was a master at chess; no wonder Theo's so interested. Do you know anything about the game, Angela?"

"A little," she replied slowly, putting the pieces in order. "The judge says she's a pawn and Otis Amber says he's the king, Crow's the queen— Oh well, it's probably just a coincidence."

"We can't leave any stone unturned," Sydelle insisted. "As the will says, *Object of the game: to win.*"

"What did you say?"

"Object of the game: to win."

"How about: object of the game: twin. Maybe the murderer is a twin."

"Twin!" Sydelle liked that. The only problem would be getting the murderer to admit that he (or she) is a twin. "Let's get back to my apartment. It's time I transcribed those notes."

Angela helped the invalid to her feet and nervously peered in both directions before stepping into the hallway.

Sydelle chuckled at her timidity. "There's nothing to be scared of, Angela. Westing was murdered for his money, and we're not rich yet. We won't be rich enough to be murdered until we find the name, and by the time we get the money from the estate, the murderer will be locked up in jail."

In spite of the impeccable logic, Angela looked back over her shoulder several times on the way to 3c.

"Strange." Sydelle stood before her open apartment door. She had slammed it shut on leaving, but had not locked the dead bolt; after all, not even a burglar could get into a snowbound building. Unless . . ."

Angela, too frightened to notice that Sydelle ran through the apartment with her crutch in the air, found her partner in the bathroom frantically tossing soiled towels from the hamper.

Sydelle Pulaski stared at the bare wicker bottom, then sank to the rim of the bathtub, shaking her head in disbelief. Someone in Sunset Towers had stolen the shorthand notebook.

EARLY THE NEXT morning a typed index card was tacked to the elevator's back wall:

■ ■ ■ ■ ■ ■ ■ ■ ■ ■ ■

> LOST: Important business papers of no value
> to anyone but the owner. Please return to
> Sydelle Pulaski, 3C. No questions asked.

■ ■ ■ ■ ■ ■ ■ ■ ■ ■

The shorthand notebook was not returned, but the idea of a bulletin board was an instant success. By late afternoon the elevator was papered with notices and filled with tenants facing sideways and backwards, reading as they rode up and down.

■ ■ ■ ■ ■ ■ ■ ■ ■ ■ ■

> *Lost: Silver cross on filigree chain, topaz pin and*
> *earrings, gold-filled cuff links. Return to Grace Windsor*
> *Wexler, 3D. REWARD!*

■ ■ ■ ■ ■ ■ ■ ■ ■ ■ ■

All players willing to discuss sharing their clues come
to the coffee shop tomorrow 10 A.M.

■ ■ ■ ■ ■ ■ ■ ■ ■ ■ ■

*WHOEVER STOLE MY MICKEY MOUSE CLOCK
BETTER GIVE IT BACK. JUST LEAVE IT IN
THE HALL IN FRONT OF APARTMENT 3D
WHEN NO ONE'S LOOKING.*
TURTLE WEXLER

■ ■ ■ ■ ■ ■ ■ ■ ■ ■ ■

ORDER DOWN, NOT UP!
Or come on up to the fifth floor
and dine in elegance
at
<u>SHIN HOO'S RESTAURANT</u>
Specializing in exquisite Chinese cuisine.

■ ■ ■ ■ ■ ■ ■ ■ ■ ■ ■

LOST: STRING OF PEARLS. SENTIMENTAL VALUE. IF
FOUND, PLEASE BRING THEM TO APARTMENT 2C.
THANK YOU. FLORA BAUMBACH (DRESSMAKING
AND ALTERATIONS, REASONABLY PRICED)

■ ■ ■ ■ ■ ■ ■ ■ ■ ■ ■

FOUND: SIX CLUES
The following clues,
printed on squares of Westing Toilet Tissue,
were found in the third-floor hallway:
BRAIDED   KICKING   TORTOISE   'SI   A   BRAT

■ ■ ■ ■ ■ ■ ■ ■ ■ ■ ■

I am having an informal party this evening
from eight o'clock on. You are all invited.
Please come.

                    J. J. Ford, apartment 4D

■ ■ ■ ■ ■ ■ ■ ■ ■ ■ ■

Turtle, wherever you are—
Be home at seven-thirty SHARP!!!
Your loving mother

■ ■ ■ ■ ■ ■ ■ ■ ■ ■ ■

"Mom, I'm home." No one else was.

On reading Mrs. Wexler's note in the elevator, Flora
Baumbach had insisted, "You must do what your mother says."
When Turtle replied, "Like showing her our clues?" Flora
Baumbach's answer was "Perhaps so. After all, she is your mother."

Flora Baumbach was sappy. Always smiling that dumb smile,
always so polite to everybody. And so timid. When they had
finally reached a snowbound broker, Flora Baumbach was so
nervous she dropped the telephone. Turtle had to admit to some
nervousness herself, but it was the first real order she had ever
placed. For a minute there, she thought she might choke on the
thumping heart that had jumped into her throat, but she had
pulled off the transaction like a pro. Now if only the stock market would go up, she'd show Mr. Westing about refining gold.
The next part of the will would read: "Whichsoever pair made
the most money with the ten thousand dollars inherits the whole
estate." She was sure of it.

"Oh, there you are." Grace Wexler acted as if Turtle was the
tardy one, but she quickly sweetened. "Come, dear, let's go to
your room and I'll fix your hair."

Her mother sat behind her on the edge of the narrow bed, loosed the dark brown hair, and brushed it to a gloss. She had not done that with such care in a long, long time.

"Have you eaten?"

"Mrs. Baumbach made me a dinner." Turtle felt the fingers dividing the hair into strands. Her mother was so warm, so close.

"Your poor father's probably starving; he's been so busy on the phone, changing appointments and all."

"Daddy's eating in the coffee shop; I just saw him there." Turtle had dashed in shouting: "The braided tortoise strikes again!" and kicked a surprised Theo in the shin. (It was Doug Hoo, not Theo, who had made the sign.)

Her mother twisted the three strands into a braid. "I think you should wear your party dress tonight; you look so pretty in pink."

Pretty? She had never used that word before, not about her. What's going on?

"You know, sweetheart, I'm rather hurt that you won't tell your own mother about your clues."

So that was it. She should have known. "My lips are sealed," Turtle said defiantly.

"Just one eensy-beensy clue?" Grace wheedled, winding a rubber band around the end of the braid.

"N-n-n," Turtle replied through sealed lips.

Angela came into the small room and tugged Turtle's braid (only her sister could get away with that).

Beaming on her favorite, Grace took her hand, then gasped. "Angela, where's your engagement ring?"

"I have a rash on my finger."

Thump, thump. Sydelle Pulaski appeared in the doorway. "Hi, what's everybody doing in the closet?"

"See, I told you this is a closet," Turtle said.

Grace ignored the complaint. It did no good being nice to that ungrateful child, never satisfied, always whining about something or other. "Oh, hello, Miss Pulaski."

"I've been feeling a bit weakly, thank you, but nothing can

keep me from a party." Sydelle's crutch was painted in black and white squares to match her black and white checkered dress. Her large hoop earrings were also black and white: the white one dangled from her left ear, the black from her right.

"The party is such a lovely idea," Grace said, warming up to the owner of the shorthand notes. "When I saw the invitation in the elevator I suggested to Mr. Hoo that he call the judge to see if she needed hors d'oeuvres; and sure enough, he got an order for six dozen." She turned to Angela. "Hadn't you better get dressed, dear? It's getting late. It's too bad Doctor D. can't escort you to the party, but your father and I will take you."

"Angela and I are going together; we're partners, you know." Sydelle had it all planned. They were to appear in identical costumes; tonight was the night they would discover if one of the heirs was a twin.

"I'm going to the party with Mrs. Baumbach," Turtle remarked. "The sign said everyone's invited."

Again Grace ignored her. "By the way, Miss Pulaski, I do hope you've changed your mind about showing me your notes."

It was the secretary's turn to seal her lips. She wouldn't put it past that uppity Grace Windsor Wexler to steal the notebook from an unfortunate cripple and then rub it in.

Grace tried again, her voice dripping with honey. "You know, of course, that if I do win the inheritance, everything I own goes to Angela."

Turtle bounded up. "Let me out of here: a person can't breathe in this closet." She kicked the bed, kicked the chair, kicked the desk, and elbowed past the disapproving secretary.

"What in the world is wrong with that child?" her mother said.

■ ■ ■ ■ ■ ■ ■ ■ ■ ■

Judge Ford was instructing Theo in the art of bartending when the telephone rang. The snowbound newspaperman had found several items in the files.

"First, the engagement announcement of Angela Wexler to D. Denton Deere. Next, several clippings on a lawsuit brought against Sam Westing by an inventor named . . ."

"Hold on, please." Mr. Hoo waddled in with a large tray of appetizers. The judge pointed him to the serving buffet and apologized to her caller. "I'm sorry, would you repeat that name."

"James Hoo. He claimed Westing stole his idea of the disposable paper diaper."

"One minute, please." The judge cupped her hand over the mouthpiece. "Please don't leave, Mr. Hoo. I was hoping you'd stay for the party, as a guest, of course. Your wife and son, too."

Hoo grunted. He hated parties. He had seen his fill of people eating and drinking and acting like clowns, jabbering like . . . so that's it: jabbering, dropping clues. "I'll be right back."

The receiver hissed with an impatient sigh, then the researcher went on. "I've got a thick file of sports items on another Hoo, a Doug Hoo. Seems he runs a pretty fast mile for a high-school kid. That's all I could find on the names you gave me, but I still have stacks of Westing clippings to go through."

"Thank you so much."

The doorbell rang.

The party was about to begin.

10

"I HOPE WE'RE not too early." Grace Windsor Wexler always arrived at parties fashionably late, but not tonight. She didn't want to miss a thing, or a clue, or wait around in her apartment with a murderer on the loose. "I don't think you've met my husband, Doctor Wexler."

"Call me Jake."

"Hello, Jake," Judge Ford said. A firm handshake, laugh lines around his eyes. He needed a sense of humor with that social-climbing wife.

"What a lovely living room, so practically furnished," Grace commented. "Our apartments are identical in layout, but mine looks so different. You must come see what I've done with it. I'm a decorator, you know. Three bedrooms do seem rather spacious for a single woman."

What does she mean, three bedrooms? This is a one-bedroom apartment. "Would you care for an appetizer, Mrs. Wexler? I'm curious to know exactly how you are related to the Westing family."

The judge had hoped to take the "heiress" by surprise, but Grace gained time by coughing. "Goodness, that ginger is spicy—it's the Szechuan cooking style, you know. How am I related? Let me see, Uncle Sam was my father's oldest brother, or was he the youngest brother of my father's father?"

"Excuse me, I have to greet my other guests." The judge left the prattling pretender. Father's brother or father's father's brother, if the relationship was on the paternal side her maiden name would be Westing.

The party went on and on. No one dared be first to leave. (Safety in numbers, especially with a judge there.) So the guests ate and drank and jabbered; and they watched the other guests eat and drink and jabber. No one laughed.

"I guess murder isn't very funny," Jake Wexler said.

"Neither is money," Mr. Hoo replied glumly.

Deciding that his wife had found the perfect partner, the podiatrist moved on to the two women standing in silence at the front window. "Cheer up, Angie-pie, you'll see your Denton soon enough." His daughter twisted out of his embrace. "Are you all right, Angela?"

"I'm fine." She was not fine. Why did they ask about Denton all the time, as though she was nobody without him? Oh, it wasn't just that. It wasn't even the humiliation of her mother chiding her about the "twin" costume (in front of everybody) and sending her back to their apartment to change clothes. It was more than that, it was everything.

Jake turned to Madame Hoo. "Hi there, partner."

"She doesn't speak English, Dad," Angela said flatly.

"And she never will, Angela, if no one talks to her."

"Snow," said Madame Hoo.

Jake followed her pointing finger. "That's right, snow. Lots and lots of snow. Snow. Trees. Road. Lake Michigan."

"China," said Madame Hoo.

"China? Sure, why not," Jake replied. "China."

Angela left the chatting couple. Why couldn't she have made some sort of friendly gesture? Because she might do the wrong thing and annoy her mother. Angela-the-obedient-daughter did only what her mother told her to do.

"Hello, Angela. One of these tidbits might cheer you up." Judge Ford held the tray before her. "I hear you'll be getting married soon."

"Some people have all the luck," Sydelle Pulaski said, appearing from nowhere to lean over the tray to spear a cube of pork. "Of course, not all us women have opted for marriage, right, Judge Ford? Some of us prefer the professional life, though I must say, if a handsome young doctor like Denton Deere proposed to me, I might just change my mind. Too bad he doesn't happen to be twins."

"Excuse me." The judge moved away.

"I'm not having any luck at all, Angela," Sydelle whined. "If only your mother hadn't made you change clothes someone surely would have mentioned 'twin.' It's much harder to judge reactions when I have to bring up the subject myself. You shouldn't let your mother boss you like that; you're a grown woman, about to be married."

"Excuse me." Angela moved away.

"Yes, thank you, I would like a refill," Sydelle said to nobody and hobbled to the bar. "Something nonalcoholic, please, doctor's orders. Make it a double—twins."

Twins? What's she talking about, Theo wondered, staring at the black and white checkered costume. "Two ginger ales for the chessboard coming right up."

Hidden among her guests, the judge studied the two people standing off in the corner, the only pair in Sunset Towers who were not Westing heirs.

George Theodorakis placed his hand on the shoulder of his invalid son. A large, bronze, hard-working hand. Like Theo's. Theo resembled him in many ways: tall, wide shoulders, slim-waisted, the same thick, straight black hair; but age had chiseled the father's face into sharper planes. His troubled eyes stared across the room at Angela.

Catherine Theodorakis, a slight, careworn woman, gazed down on her younger son with tired, dark-circled eyes.

From his wheelchair Chris watched legs. Other than the funny lady with the shorthand notes, the only limpers were his brother Theo (Turtle had kicked him again) and Mrs. Wexler, who stood on one leg rubbing her stockinged foot against her calf. A high-heeled shoe stood alone on the carpet beneath her. Judge Ford didn't limp; besides, she couldn't be a murderer, in spite of his clues. Nobody here looks like a murderer, they're all nice people, even this fat Chinese man who grumbles all the time.

George Theodorakis greeted Mr. Hoo with "How's business?" Hoo spun around and stomped off from his fellow restaurant owner in a huff of anger.

James Hoo, inventor, that's who the judge wanted to talk to, but there was a problem at the bar. A long line had formed and it wasn't moving.

"There are sixteen white pieces and sixteen black pieces in chess," Theo was explaining to Sydelle Pulaski. "Do you play chess, Judge Ford?"

"A bit, but I haven't played in years." The judge led the secretary away from the crowded bar. Theo must think the Westing game has something to do with chess. He may be right, it certainly is as complicated as a chess game.

"But I did study," Doug was arguing.

The judge interrupted. "I haven't had a chance to thank you for the delicious food, Mr. Hoo. How long have you been in the restaurant business?"

"Running up and down stairs is not studying," Hoo said.

Sydelle Pulaski butted in. "Father and son? You look more like twins."

"You're equal partners with that Theodorakis kid," Hoo continued. "Why didn't you insist on holding the meeting in our restaurant instead of that greasy coffee shop?"

"Because some people don't like chow mein for breakfast," Sydelle Pulaski replied.

"There you are, dear." Grace patted a stray wisp of Angela's hair into place. "We must do something about your coiffure. I'll make an appointment for you with my hairdresser once the snow is cleared; long hair is too youthful for a woman about to be married. I can't understand what got into you, Angela, coming to this party in that old checkered dress and those awful accessories. Just because your partner dresses like a freak . . ."

"She's not a freak, Mother."

"I was just speaking to Mr. Hoo about catering the wedding shower on Saturday; I arranged for little Madame Hoo to serve in one of those slinky Chinese gowns. Where are you going? Angela!"

Angela rushed into Judge Ford's kitchen. She had to get away, she had to be alone, by herself, or she'd burst out crying.

She was not alone. Crow was there. The two women stared at each other in surprise, then turned away.

Poor baby. Crow wanted to reach out to the pretty child; she wanted to take her in her arms and say: "Poor, poor baby, go ahead and cry." But she couldn't. All she could say was "Here."

Angela took the dish towel from the cleaning woman and bunched it against her face to muffle the wrenching sobs.

The guests jabbered on and on about the weather, about food, about football, about chess, about twins. Turtle was slumped on the couch, scornful of dumb grown-up parties. You'd think one of them would know something about the stock market. She missed Sandy. Sandy was the only one in this dumb building she could talk to.

"Remember that quotation: *May God thy gold refine?*" Flora Baumbach asked. "Let's take a poll. I'll bet ten cents it's from the Bible."

"Shakespeare," Turtle argued, "and make it ten dollars."

"Oh my! Well, all right, ten dollars."

Together they made the rounds. Four votes for the Bible, three for Shakespeare, and one abstention (Madame Hoo did not understand the question).

Sydelle Pulaski voted for the Bobbsey twins. "And how do you know those words were in the will?" she asked suspiciously. Too suspiciously.

So that's what "Lost: Important business papers" meant. Somebody stole the shorthand notes. Turtle smiled at the delicious nastiness of it all. "I remember, that's all."

"If you remember so well, tell me what comes before that," Sydelle challenged.

"I don't know, what?"

The secretary had an audience now. "I don't mind telling you, but not if you ask like that."

Theo said, "Please?" not Turtle.

Sydelle turned toward him with what should have been a gracious manner, but she grimaced when the top of the crutch poked her in the chest. "The exact quotation," she announced loudly, hoping she was right, "is *Spend it wisely and may God thy gold refine.*"

Right or wrong, her guess was received with groans of disappointment. The heirs had expected more: a hint, a clue, something. It was time to go home.

11

A PALE SUN rose on the third snowbound morning. Lake Michigan lay calm, violet, now blue, but the tenants of Sunset Towers on waking turned to a different view. Lured by the Westing house, they stood at their side windows scoffing at the danger, daring to dream. Should they or shouldn't they share their clues? Well, they'd go to the meeting in the coffee shop just to see what the others intended to do.

Waiting in her closet of a room Turtle stared at the white-weighted branches of the maple on the hill. A twig snapped in silence, a flurry speckled the crusted snow. Sometimes when her mother was too busy to do her hair she sent Angela in, but today no one came. They had forgotten about her.

Brush and comb clutched in her fists like weapons, she stormed into apartment 2c. "Do you know how to braid hair?"

Flora Baumbach's pudgy fingers, swift with a needle, were clumsy with a comb, but after several tangled attempts she ended up with three equal strands. "My, what thick hair you have. I tried braiding my daughter's hair once, but it was too fine, soft and wispy like a baby's, even in her teens."

That was the last thing Turtle wanted to hear. "Was she pretty, your daughter?"

"All mothers think their children are beautiful. Rosalie was an exceptional child, they said, but she was the lovingest person that ever was."

"My mother doesn't think I'm beautiful."

"Of course, she does."

"My mother says I looked just like a turtle when I was a baby, sticking my head out of the blanket. I still look like a turtle, I guess, but I don't care. Where's your daughter now?"

"Gone." Flora Baumbach cleared the catch in her throat. "There, that braid should hold for the rest of the day. By the way, you've never told me your real name."

"Alice," Turtle replied, swinging her head before the mirror. Not one single hair escaped its tight bind. Mrs. Baumbach would make a good braider if only she'd stop yakking about her exceptional child. Rosalie, what a dumb name. "You'd better get to the meeting now. Remember, don't say a word to anyone about anything. Just listen."

"All right, Alice. I promise."

■ ■ ■ ■ ■ ■ ■ ■ ■ ■ ■

Theo wheeled his brother into the elevator and read the new message on the wall:

$25 REWARD for the return of a gold railroad
watch inscribed: To Ezra Ford in appreciation of
thirty years' service to the Milwaukee Road.
                    J. J. Ford, apartment 4D

"Fod-d-d, fo—de," Chris said.

"That's right, Judge Ford. Must be her father's watch. Probably lost it. I don't think it could have been stolen by anyone at the party last night."

Chris smiled. His brother had not understood him. Good. This might be an important discovery—Judge Ford's name was the same as her apartment number: Ford, 4D.

Theo led the waiting tenants through the kitchen where Mr. and Mrs. Theodorakis handed out cups of tea and coffee. "Sorry, we've run out of cream and lemons. Please help yourself to some homemade pastries."

Walking into the coffee shop was like entering a cave. A wall of snow pressed against the plate-glass window, scaling the door that once opened to the parking lot.

"I've got a car buried out there," Grace Wexler said, slipping into a booth opposite her partner. "Hope I find it before the snowplows do."

"If they ever get here," Mr. Hoo replied. "Good thing this meeting wasn't held in my restaurant, I'd go broke passing out free tea, if you call this tea." He held up a tea bag with contempt, then groaned on seeing his sweat-suited son jog in with a sweet roll between his teeth and vault over his hands onto a stool, "Where's your daughter the turtle?"

Grace Wexler looked around. "I don't know, maybe she's helping her father with his bookkeeping."

"Bookkeeping!" Mr. Hoo let out a whoop. Grace had no idea what was so funny, but she joined him in loud laughter. Nothing stirred people's envy more than a private joke.

Thinking she was being laughed at, Sydelle Pulaski dropped her polka dot crutch and spilled her coffee on Angela's tapestry bag before managing a solid perch on the counter stool.

Clink, clink. Theo tapped a spoon against a glass for attention. "Thank you for coming. When the meeting is over you are all welcome to stay for a chess tournament. Meanwhile, I'd like to explain why my partner and me . . . my partner and I . . . called this meeting. I don't know about your clues, but our clues don't make any sense." The heirs stared at him with blank faces, no one nodded, no one even blinked. "Now then, if no two sets of clues are alike, as the will says, that could mean that each set of clues is only part of one message. The more clues we put together, the better chance we have of finding the murderer and winning the game. Of course, the inheritance will be divided into equal shares."

Sydelle Pulaski raised her hand like a schoolgirl. "What about the clues that are in the will itself?"

"Yes, we'd appreciate having a copy of the will, Ms. Pulaski," Theo replied.

"Well, equal shares doesn't seem quite fair, since I'm the only one here who thought of taking notes." Sydelle turned to the group, one penciled eyebrow arched high over her red sequined spectacles.

Her self-congratulatory pose was too much for Mr. Hoo.

Grunting loudly, he squeezed out of the booth and slapped the shorthand pad on the counter.

"Thief!" the secretary shrieked, nearly toppling off the stool as she grabbed her notebook. "Thief!"

"I did not steal your notebook," the indignant Hoo explained. "I found it on a table in my restaurant this morning. You can believe me or not, I really don't care, because those notes you so selfishly dangled under our noses are completely worthless. My partner knows shorthand and she says your shorthand is nothing but senseless scrawls. Gibberish."

"Pure gibberish," Grace Wexler added. "Those are standard shorthand symbols all right, but they don't translate into words."

"Thief!" Sydelle cried, now accusing Mrs. Wexler. "Thief! Larcenist! Felon!"

"Don't, Sydelle," Angela said softly, her eyes set on the D she was embroidering.

"You wouldn't understand, Angela, you don't know what it's like to be. . . ." Her voice broke. She paused then lashed out at her enemies, all of them. "Who cares a fig about Sydelle Pulaski? Nobody, that's who. I'm no fool, you know. I knew I couldn't trust any one of you. You can't read my shorthand because I wrote in Polish."

Polish?!?!

■ ■ ■ ■ ■ ■ ■ ■ ■ ■ ■ ■

When the meeting was again called to order Mr. Hoo suggested they offer Ms. Pulaski a slightly larger share of the inheritance in exchange for a transcript of the will—in English. "However, I repeat, neither my partner nor I stole the notes. And if anyone here suspects us of murder, forget it, we both have airtight alibis."

Doug choked on his sweet roll. If it got around to alibis, they'd find out where he was the night of the murder. On the Westing house lawn.

Mr. Hoo went on. "And to prove our innocence, my partner and I agree to share our clues."

"One minute, Mr. Hoo." Judge Ford stood. It was time for her to speak before matters got out of hand. "Let me remind you, all of you, that a person is innocent until proven guilty. We are free to choose whether or not to share our clues without any implication of guilt. I suggest we postpone any decision until we have given the matter careful thought, and until the time all of the heirs can attend. However, since we are assembled, I have a question to ask of the group; perhaps others do, too."

They all did. Wary of giving away game plans, the heirs decided the questions would be written out, but no names were to be signed. Doug collected the scraps of paper and handed them to Theo.

"Is anyone here a twin?" he read.

No one answered.

"What is Turtle's real name?" Doug Hoo was planning another nasty sign.

"Tabitha-Ruth," replied Mrs. Wexler with a bewildered look at Flora Baumbach, who said "Alice."

"Well, which is it?"

"Tabitha-Ruth Wexler. I should know, I'm her mother."

Doug changed his mind about the sign. He couldn't spell Tabitha-Ruth.

Theo unfolded the next question. "How many here have actually met Sam Westing?"

Grace Wexler raised her hand, lowered it, raised it halfway, then lowered it again, torn between her claim as Sam Westing's relative and being accused of murder. Mr. Hoo (an honest man) held up his hand and kept it up. His was the only one. Judge Ford did not think it necessary to respond to her own question.

Theo recognized the sprawling handwriting of the next question: "Who got kicked last week?" Chris did not receive an answer. The meeting was adjourned due to panic.

12

IT WAS SO sudden: the earsplitting bangs, the screams, the confusion. Theo and Doug ran into the kitchen; Mrs. Theodorakis ran out. Her hair, her face, her apron were splattered with dark dripping red.

"Blood," Sydelle Pulaski cried, clutching her heart.

"Don't just sit there," Catherine Theodorakis shouted, "somebody call the fire department."

Angela hurried to the pay phone on the wall and stood there trembling, not knowing whether to call or not. They were snowbound, the fire engines could not reach Sunset Towers.

Theo leaned through the kitchen doorway. "Everything's okay. There's no fire."

"Chris, honey, it's all right," Mrs. Theodorakis said, kneeling before the wheelchair. "It's all right, Chris, look! It's just tomato sauce."

Tomato sauce! Mrs. Theodorakis was covered with tomato sauce, not blood. The curious heirs now piled into the kitchen, except for Sydelle Pulaski, who slumped to the counter. She could have a heart attack and no one would notice.

Mr. Hoo surveyed the scene, trying to conceal his delight. "What a mess," he said. "That row of cans must have exploded from the heat of the stove." The entire kitchen was splattered with tomato sauce and soaked in foam from the fire extinguishers. "What a mess."

George Theodorakis regarded him with suspicion. "It was a bomb."

Catherine Theodorakis thought so, too. "There was hissing, then bang, bang, sparks flying all over the kitchen, red sparks, purple sparks."

"Cans of tomato sauce exploded," Doug Hoo said, defending his father. The others agreed. Mrs. Theodorakis was understandably hysterical. A bomb? Ridiculous. Sam Westing certainly did not appear to have been killed by a bomb.

Judge Ford suggested that the accident be reported to the police immediately in order to collect on the insurance.

"You might as well redecorate the entire kitchen," Grace Wexler, decorator, proposed. "It should be functional yet attractive, with lots of copper pots hanging from the ceiling."

"I don't think there's any real damage," Catherine Theodorakis replied, "but we'll have to close for a few days to clean up."

Mr. Hoo smiled. Angela offered to help.

"Angela, dear, you have a fitting this afternoon," Grace reminded her, "and we have so much to do for the wedding shower on Saturday."

In thumped Sydelle Pulaski. "I'm fine now, just a bit woozy. Goodness, what a nasty turn."

■ ■ ■ ■ ■ ■ ■ ■ ■ ■ ■

Having recovered from the nasty turn, Sydelle Pulaski settled down to transcribing her shorthand to Polish, then from Polish to English. Startled by loud banging on her apartment door, she struck the wrong typewriter key.

"Open up!"

Recognizing the voice, Angela unbolted the door to a furious Turtle. "All right, Angela, where is it?"

"What?"

"The newspaper you took from my desk."

Angela carefully dug through the embroidery, personal items, and other paraphernalia in her tapestry bag and pulled out the newspaper folded to the Westing obituary. "I'm sorry, Turtle. I would have asked for it, but you weren't around."

"You don't also happen to have my Mickey Mouse clock in there, too, do you?" Turtle softened on seeing her sister's hurt expression. "I'm only kidding. You left your engagement ring on the sink again. Better go get it before somebody steals that, too."

"Oh, I wouldn't worry about anyone stealing Angela's ring," Sydelle Pulaski remarked. "No mother would stoop that low."

The thought of Grace being the burglar was so funny to Turtle, she plopped down on the sofa and rolled about in laughter. It felt good to laugh; the stock market had fallen five points today.

"Angela, please tell your sister to get her dirty shoes off my couch. Tell her to sit up and act like a lady."

Turtle rose with a tongue click very much like her mother's, but she was not about to leave without striking back. Arms folded, she leaned against the wall and let them have it. "Mom thinks Angela was the one who stole the shorthand notebook." That got them. Look at those open mouths. "Because Mom asked to see it, and Angela does everything she says."

"Anyone could have stolen my notebook; I didn't double-lock my door that day." If Sydelle couldn't trust her own partner, she was alone, all alone.

"Did Mom really say that?" Angela asked.

"No, but I know how she thinks, I know what everybody thinks. Grown-ups are so obvious."

"Ridiculous," scoffed Sydelle.

"For instance, I know that Angela doesn't want to marry that sappy intern."

"Ridiculous. You're just jealous of your sister."

"Maybe," Turtle had to admit, "but I am what I am. I don't need a crutch to get attention." Oh, oh, she had gone too far.

"Turtle didn't mean it that way, Sydelle," Angela said quickly. "She used the word *crutch* as a symbol. She meant, you know, that people are so afraid of revealing their true selves, they have to hide behind some sort of prop."

"Oh, really?" Sydelle replied. "Then Turtle's crutch is her big mouth."

No, Angela thought, hurrying her sister out of the door and back to their apartment, Turtle's crutch is her braid.

■ ■ ■ ■ ■ ■ ■ ■ ■ ■ ■

The newspaperman called again to say he had found some photographs taken at Westingtown parties twenty years ago. "One of those names appears in a caption as Violet Westing's escort: George Theodorakis."

"Go on," the judge said.

"That's all." He promised to send her the clippings in the Westing file as soon as he was shoveled out.

The judge now knew of four heirs with Westing connections: James Hoo, the inventor; Theo's father; her partner, Sandy McSouthers, who had been fired from the Westing paper mill; and herself. But she had to learn more, much more about each one of the heirs if she hoped to protect the victim of Sam Westing's revenge.

She would have to hire a detective, a very private detective, who had not been associated with her in her practice or in the courts. J. J. Ford flipped through the Yellow Pages to *Investigators—Private*.

"Good grief!" Her finger stopped near the top of the list. Was it a coincidence or dumb luck? Or was she playing right into Sam Westing's hand? No choice but to chance it. The judge dialed the number and tapped her foot impatiently, waiting for an answer.

"Hello. If you're looking for a snowbound private investigator, you've got the right number."

Yes, she had the right number. It might be a trick, but it was no coincidence. The voices were one and the same.

13

NO ONE WAS in the kitchen of Shin Hoo's Restaurant when the bomber set a tall can labeled "monosodium glutamate" behind similar cans on a shelf. The color-striped candle would burn down to the fuse at six-thirty;

whoever was working there would be at the other end of the room. No one would be hurt.

> *Due to the unfortunate damage to the coffee shop*
> **SHIN HOO'S RESTAURANT**
> *is prepared to satisfy all dinner accommodations.*
> *Order down, or ride up to the fifth floor.*
> *Treat your taste buds to a scrumptious meal*
> *while feasting your eyes on the stunning snowscape*
> *before it melts away. Reasonable prices, too.*

Grace Wexler tacked her sign to the elevator wall as she rode up to her new job. She was going to be the seating hostess.

"Where's the cook?" Mr. Hoo shouted (meaning his wife). He found Madame Hoo in their rear fourth-floor apartment kneeling before her bamboo trunk, fingering mementoes from her childhood in China. He hurried her up to the kitchen, too harried to find the words that would explain what was happening. Now where was that lazy son of his?

Doug jogged in from a tiring workout on the stairs. How was he supposed to know the restaurant would open early? Nobody bothered telling him.

"Some student you are; anyone with the brain of an anteater could have figured that out: people are short of food, the coffee shop is closed for repairs. Stop arguing, go take a shower, and put on your busboy outfit. Get moving!"

"Don't you think you're rather hard on the boy?" Grace commented.

"Somebody's got to give him a shove. If he had his way, he'd do nothing but run," Hoo replied between bites of chocolate. "You're not so easy on Angela, either."

"Angela? Angela was born good, the perfect child. As for the other one, well . . ."

"It's not easy being a parent," Hoo said woefully.

"You can say that again." Grace held her breath. Her husband would have done just that, said it again, but Mr. Hoo only nodded in shared sympathy. What a gentleman.

Only Mr. and Mrs. Theodorakis ordered down. The other tenants of Sunset Towers lined up at the reservations desk, waiting for Grace Windsor Wexler to lead the way. Oversized menus clutched in her arms, Grace felt the first proud stirrings of power rush up from her pedicured toes to the very top curl on her head. If Uncle Sam could pair off people, so could she.

"You see your brother every day, Chris, how about eating with someone else for a change?" She wheeled the boy to a window table without waiting for an answer. It would have been yes.

The two cripples together, Sydelle Pulaski thought. She'd show that high and mighty hostess, she'd show them all. She and Chris could have private jokes, too, and everybody would be sorry they weren't sitting with them.

"Whas moo g-goo g-gipn?" Chris asked, baffled by the strange words on the menu.

"I think it's boiled grasshopper." Sydelle screwed up her face and Chris laughed. "Or chocolate-covered moose."

"Frenssh-fry m-mouse," Chris offered. Now Sydelle laughed. They both laughed heartily, but no one envied them.

■ ■ ■ ■ ■ ■ ■ ■ ■ ■ ■

"Your brother seems to be enjoying Ms. Pulaski."

Theo nodded, awed by the beautiful Angela, three years older than he, so fair-skinned and blonde, so unattainable. Here he was sitting at the very same table with her, just the two of them, and he couldn't think of a single thing to say that wasn't stupid or childish or childishly stupid.

Usually the quiet one, Angela tried again. "Are you planning to go to college next year?"

Theo nodded, then shook his head. Say something, idiot. "I

73

got a scholarship to Madison, but I'm not going. I'm going to work instead." What big, worried sky-blue eyes. "The operation for Chris will be very expensive." That was worse, now she's feeling sorry for him. "If Chris had been born that way, maybe it wouldn't be so bad, but he was a perfectly normal kid, a great kid. And he's smart, too. About four years ago he started to get clumsy, just little things at first."

"Perhaps my fiancé can help." Angela bit her lip. Theo was not asking for charity. And *fiancé*, what an old-fashioned, silly word. "I went to college for a year. I wanted to be a doctor, but, well, we don't have as much money as my mother pretends. Dad said he could manage if that's what I really wanted, but my mother said it was too difficult for a woman to get into medical school." Why was she gabbing like this?

"I want to be a writer," Theo said. That really sounded like kid stuff. "Would you go back to college if you won the inheritance?"

Angela looked down. It was a question she did not want to answer. Or could not answer.

■ ■ ■ ■ ■ ■ ■ ■ ■ ■ ■

Long before becoming a judge, Josie-Jo Ford had decided to stop smiling. Smiling without good reason was demeaning. A serious face put the smiler on the defensive, a rare smile put a nervous witness at ease. She now bestowed one of her rare smiles on the dressmaker. "I'm so glad we have this chance to become acquainted, Mrs. Baumbach. I had so little time to chat with my guests last night."

"It was a wonderful party."

Flora Baumbach appeared even smaller and rounder than she was as she sat twisting her napkin with hands accustomed to being busy. Was her face permanently creased from years of pleasing customers, or was a tragedy lurking behind that grin? "Have you always specialized in wedding gowns?"

"Mr. Baumbach and I had a shop for many years: Baumbach's for the Bride and Groom. Perhaps you've heard of it?"

"I'm afraid not." The judge would have said no in any case to keep her witness talking.

"Perhaps you've heard of Flora's Bridal Gowns? That's what I called my shop after my husband left. I don't know much about grooms' clothes, they're mostly rentals, anyway." Flora Baumbach lost her timidity; the judge let her chat away. "I'm using heirloom lace on the bodice of Angela's gown; it's been in my family for three generations. I wore it at my wedding, and I dreamed that someday I'd have a daughter who would wear it, too, but Rosalie didn't come along until I was in my forties, and . . ." The dressmaker stopped. Her lips tightened into an even wider grin. "Angela will make such a beautiful bride. Funny how she reminds me of her."

"Angela reminds you of your daughter?" the judge asked.

"Oh my, no. Angela reminds me of another young girl I made a wedding dress for: Violet Westing."

■ ■ ■ ■ ■ ■ ■ ■ ■ ■ ■ ■

The heavy charms on Sydelle Pulaski's bracelet clinked and clunked as she raised a full fork and flourished it in a practiced ritual before aiming it at her open mouth. Chris's movements were even jerkier. *She's a good person,* he thought, *but she thinks too much about herself. Maybe she never had anybody to love.*

"Here, let me help you to some of this delicious sweet and sour ostrich."

Their laughter drowned out the loud groan from another table where Turtle sat alone, a transistor radio plugged in her ear. The stock market had dropped another twelve points.

"I'm starved, let's sit down to eat." Head held high, Grace Wexler led her husband across the restaurant. "All I want is a corned beef sandwich, not a guided tour."

"Would you prefer to sit alone or with that young lady over there?"

"I thought I was going to sit with you."

"Please be seated," Grace replied. "Jimmy, I mean Mr. Hoo, will take your order shortly."

Jake snatched the menu from his wife and watched her glide (gracefully, he had to admit) to the reservations desk and whisper in Hoo's ear. (Jimmy, she calls him.) "That's a fine kettle of fish," he exclaimed, then turned to his dinner companion. "Fine kettle of fish. I'm so hungry even that sounds good, and from the looks of this menu that's probably what I'll get."

"I'm okay," Turtle replied, the final prices of actively traded stocks rumbling in her ear.

Mr. Hoo waddled over. "I recommend the striped bass."

"See, what did I tell you, a kettle of fish."

Turtle switched off the radio. She had heard enough bad news for one day.

"How about spareribs done to a crisp," Hoo suggested; then he lowered his voice. "What's the point spread on the Packers game?"

"See me later," Jake muttered.

"Go ahead and tell him, Daddy," Turtle said. "I know you're a bookie."

■ ■ ■ ■ ■ ■ ■ ■ ■ ■ ■

"Can you stand on your legs?" Sydelle Pulaski asked. "Can you walk at all?"

People never asked Chris those questions; they whispered them to his parents behind his back. "N-n-no. Why?"

"What better disguise for a thief or a murderer than a wheelchair, the perfect alibi."

Chris enjoyed being taken for the criminal type. Now they really were friends. "When you ree m-m-me nos?"

"What? Oh, read you my notes. Soon, very soon." Sydelle

daintily touched the corners of her mouth with the napkin, pushed back her chair, and grabbed her polka-dot crutch. "That was a superb meal, I must give my compliments to the chef." She rose, knocking the chair to the floor, and clumped toward the kitchen door.

"Where is she going?" Angela, starting up to help her partner, was distracted by shouting in the corridor.

"Hello in there, anybody home?" Through the restaurant door came a bundled and booted figure. He danced an elephantine jig, stomping snow on the carpet, flung a long woolen scarf from his neck, and yelled, "Otis Amber is here, the roads are clear!"

That's when the bomb went off.

■ ■ ■ ■ ■ ■ ■ ■ ■ ■ ■

"Nobody move! Everybody stay where you are," Mr. Hoo shouted as he rushed into the sizzling, crackling kitchen.

"Just a little mishap," Grace Wexler explained, taking her command post in the middle of the restaurant. "Nothing to worry about. Eat up before your food gets cold."

A cluster of red sparks hissed through the swinging kitchen door, kissed the ceiling, and rained a shimmering shower down and around the petrified hostess. Fireflies of color faded into her honey-blonde hair and scattered into ash at her feet. "Nothing to worry about," she repeated hoarsely.

"Just celebrating the Chinese New Year," Otis Amber shouted, adding one of his he-he-he cackles.

Mr. Hoo leaned through the kitchen doorway, his shiny straight black hair (even shinier and straighter) plastered to his forehead, water dribbling down his moon-shaped face. "Call an ambulance, there's been a slight accident."

Angela dashed past Mr. Hoo into the kitchen. Jake Wexler made the emergency telephone call and sent Theo to the lobby to direct the ambulance attendants.

"Why are you standing there like a statue," Hoo shouted at his son.

"You told everybody to stay where they were," Doug said.

"You're not everybody!"

Madame Hoo tried to make the injured woman as comfortable as possible on the debris-strewn floor. Angela found the sequined spectacles, wiped off the wet, crystalline mess, and placed them on her partner's nose.

"Don't look so worried, Angela. I'm all right." Sydelle was in pain, but she wanted attention on her own terms, not as a hapless, foolish victim of fate.

"Looks like a fracture," an ambulance attendant said, feeling her right ankle. "Careful how you lift her."

The secretary suppressed a grunt. It was bad enough being drenched by the overhead sprinkler and draped with noodles; now they were carrying her right past them all.

Grace pulled Angela away from the stretcher. "You can visit your friend in a few days."

"Angela, Angela," Sydelle moaned. Pride or not, she wanted her partner at her side.

Angela stood between her determined mother and her distraught partner, paralyzed by the burden of choice.

"Go with your friend, Angie-pie," Jake Wexler said. Other voices chimed in. "Go with Pulaski."

Grace realized she had lost. "Perhaps you should go to the hospital, Angela; it's been so long since you've seen your Doctor D." She winked mischievously, but only Flora Baumbach smiled back.

■ ■ ■ ■ ■ ■ ■ ■ ■ ■ ■

The policeman and the fire inspector visiting the scene agreed that it was nothing more than a gas explosion. Good thing the sprinkler system worked or Mr. Hoo might have had a good fire.

"What kind of a fire is a good fire," Hoo wanted to know.

"And what about the burglaries?" Grace Wexler asked.

"I'm with the bomb squad," the policeman explained. "You'll have to call the robbery detail for that."

"And what about the coffee shop accident?" Theo asked.

"Also a gas explosion."

Jake Wexler asked about the odds of having two explosions in two days in the same building.

"Nothing unusual," the fireman replied, "especially in weather like this, no ventilation, snow packed over the ducts." He instructed the tenants to air out their kitchens before lighting ovens.

Mrs. Wexler turned up the heat in her apartment and kept the windows open for the next three days. She did not want anything blowing up during Angela's party.

But the Wexler apartment was exactly where the bomber planned to set the next bomb.

■ PAIRS REPAIRED ■

14
THE SNOWPLOWS PLOWED and a warm sun finished the job of freeing the tenants of Sunset Towers (and the figure in the Westing house) from their wintry prisons.

Angela, disguised in her mother's old beaver coat and hat and in Turtle's red boots, was the first one out. Following Sydelle's instructions she hastily searched under the hood of every car in the parking lot. Nothing was there (nothing, that is, that didn't seem to belong to an automobile engine). So much for *Good gracious from hood space.*

Next came Flora Baumbach. Behind her a bootless Turtle tiptoed through puddles. Miracle of miracles: the rusty and battered Chevy started, but the dressmaker's luck went downhill from there. First, the hood of her car flew up in the middle of traffic. Then, after two hours of watching mysterious symbols move across the lighted panel high on the wall of the broker's office, her eyes began to cross. After three hours the grin faded from her face. "I'm getting dizzy," she said, shifting her position on the hard wooden folding chair, "and worse yet, I think I've got a splinter in my fanny."

"Look, there goes one of our stocks," Turtle replied.

SEA	GM	LVI	MGC	T		AMI	I
5$8½	5000$67	32¼		2$14	1000$65¼	3$19¼	8$22½

Flora Baumbach caught a glimpse of SEA 5$8½ as it was about to magically disappear off the left edge of the moving screen. "Oh my, I've forgotten what that means."

Turtle sighed. "It means five hundred shares of SEA was traded at $8.50 a share."

"What did we pay?"

"Never mind, just write down the prices of our stocks as they cross the tape like I'm doing. Once school opens it's all up to you." Turtle did not tell her partner that they had bought two hundred shares of SEA at $15.25 a share. On that stock alone they had a loss of $1,350, not counting commissions. It took nerves of steel to play the stock market.

■ ■ ■ ■ ■ ■ ■ ■ ■ ■ ■ ■

"The Mercedes is wiped clean and shiny like new," the doorman boasted. His face reddened around old scars as he rejected a folded five-dollar bill. "No tips, Judge, please, not after all you've done for the wife and me." The judge had given him the entire ten thousand dollars.

J. J. Ford pocketed the bill and, to make amends for her thoughtless gesture, asked the doorman about his family.

Sandy perched on the edge of a straight-backed chair, adjusted his round wire-framed glasses, repaired at the bridge with adhesive tape, across his broken nose, and told about his children. "Two boys still in high school, one daughter married and expecting my third grandchild (her husband just lost his job so they all moved in with us), another daughter who works part-time as a typist (she plays the piano real good), and two sons who work in a brewery."

"It must have been difficult supporting such a large family," the judge said.

"Not so bad. I picked up odd jobs here and there after I got fired from the Westing plant for trying to organize the union, but mostly I boxed. I wasn't no middleweight contender, but I wasn't bad, either. Got my face smashed up a few times too many, though; still get some pretty bad headaches and my brain gets sort of fuzzy. Some dummy of a partner you got stuck with, huh, Judge?"

"We'll do just fine, partner." Judge Ford's attempt at familiarity fell flat. "I did try to phone you, but your name was not listed."

"We don't have a phone no more; couldn't afford it with the kids making so many calls. But I did make some headway on our clues. Want to see?" Sandy removed a paper from the inside of his cap and placed it on the desk. Judge Ford noticed a flask protruding from the back pocket of his uniform, but his breath smelled of peppermint.

The clues as figured out by Alexander McSouthers:

SKIES AM SHINING BROTHER

SKIES—*Sikes* (Dr. Sikes witnessed the will)
AM BrothER—*Amber* (Otis Amber)
SHINing—*Shin* (the middle name of James Shin Hoo
or what Turtle kicks)
BROTHER—*Theo or Chris Theodorakis*

"Remarkable," the judge commented to Sandy's delight. "However, we are looking for one name, not six."

"Gee, Judge, I forgot," Sandy said dejectedly.

Judge Ford told him about Theo's proposal, but Sandy refused to go along. "It seems too easy, the clues adding up to one message, especially for a shrewd guy like Westing. Let's stick it out together, just the two of us. After all, I got me the smartest partner of them all."

Shallow flattery for the big tipper, the judge thought. McSouthers was not a stupid man; if only he was less obsequious—and less of a gossip.

The doorman scratched his head. "What I can't figure out, Judge, is why I'm one of the heirs. Unless Sam Westing just up and died, and there is no murderer. Unless Sam Westing is out to get somebody from his grave."

"I agree with you entirely, Mr. McSouthers. What we have to find out is who these sixteen heirs are, and which one, as you say, was Westing 'out to get.'"

Sandy beamed. They were going to play it his way.

■ ■ ■ ■ ■ ■ ■ ■ ■ ■ ■

"What you need is an advertising campaign."

"What I need is my half of the ten thousand dollars."

"Five thousand dollars is what I estimate the redecorating and the newspaper ads will cost."

"Get out of here, get out!"

Grace stared at Hoo's smooth, broad face, at the devilish tufts of eyebrow so high above those flashing eyes, then she turned her back and walked out. Sometimes she wondered about that man—no, he couldn't be the murderer, he couldn't even kill the waterbug in the sink this morning. Grace spun around to see if she was being followed on the footstep-hushing carpet in the third-floor hall. No one was there, but she heard voices. They were coming from her kitchen. It was nothing, just Otis Amber shouting at Crow, something about losing their clues.

"I remember them, Otis," Crow replied in a soft voice. She felt strangely at peace. Just this morning she had been given the chance to hide her love in Angela's bag, the big tapestry shoulder bag she carries next to her heart. Now she must pray that the boy comes back.

"I remember them, too, that's not the point," Otis Amber argued. "What if somebody else finds them? Crow? Are you listening to me, Crow?"

No, but Grace Wexler was listening. "Really, Mr. Amber, can't you find another time to discuss your affairs with my cleaning woman. And where are you going, Crow?"

Crow was buttoned up in a black moth-eaten winter coat; a black shawl covered her head.

"It's freezing in here." Otis Amber shut the window.

Grace opened the window. "The last thing I need is a gas explosion," she said peevishly.

"Boom!" he replied. The two women were so startled that the delivery boy sneaked up on the unsuspecting for the rest of the week, shouting "Boom!"

Besides shouting "Boom!" Otis Amber delivered groceries from the shopping center to Sunset Towers, back and forth, to and fro. Not only did the tenants have to restock their bare shelves, they had to add Westing Paper Products by the gross to their orders. "Idiots, just because the will said *Buy Westing Paper Products*," he muttered, hefting a bulky bag from the compartment attached to his bike. Even Crow was using Westing Disposable Diapers to polish the silver and Westing Paper Towels to scrub the floors. (Is that what happened to their clues?) Poor Crow, she's taking this game harder than he had expected. She's been acting strange again.

"Boom!" Otis Amber shouted as the intern hurried by.

"Idiot," muttered Denton Deere.

Denton Deere paced the floor. "Listen, kid, I'd like to help you, but I'm only an intern specializing in plastic surgery. It would be different if you wanted a nose job or a face-lift." He had meant to be amusing; it sounded cruel.

Chris had not asked for charity. All he wanted was to play the game with the intern.

All the intern wanted was half of the ten thousand dollars. "I hear your brother suggested sharing clues. Sounds like a fine idea." No response. *Maybe the kid thinks I'm the murderer. The tenants must think so, the way they peered over their shoulders; and that delivery boy shouting like that. Why me? I'm a doctor; I took an oath to save lives, not take them.* "I'm a very busy man, Chris, I have lots of sick people depending on me. Oh well." Plowing his fingers through his stringy mouse-brown hair to keep it out of his eyes (*when would he find time for a haircut?*), he seated himself next to the wheelchair. "The clues are in my locker. What were they? 'The rain in Spain falls mainly on the plain'?"

"*F-for p-plain g-g-grain shed.*" Chris spoke slowly. He had practiced his recitation over and over, hour after lonely hour. "*G-grain*—oats—Otis Amber. *F-for, shed*—she, F-Ford. F-Ford lives in f-four D."

"Ford, apartment 4D, good thinking, Chris," The intern rose. "Is that all?"

Chris decided not to tell him about the limper on the lawn, not until the next time. His partner would have to visit him a next time, and a next time, as long as he didn't sign the check.

"Now, about signing the check," Denton Deere said.

Chris shook his head. No.

On a bench in the lobby Angela embroidered her trousseau, waiting for Denton. Dad had tried to teach her to drive, but she was too timid; he, too impatient. Why bother with driving lessons, her mother said, anyone as pretty as you can always find a handsome young man to chauffeur you. She should have insisted. She should have said no just once to her mother, just once. It was too late now.

Theo came in with an armload of books. "Hi, Angela. Hey, I found that quotation, or rather, the librarian found it. You know: *May God thy gold refine.*"

"Really?" Angela thought it unnecessary to remind him that it was Flora Baumbach and Turtle who had asked about the quotation, not she.

What lush lips, what white teeth, what fine and shiny hair. Theo fumbled between the pages of a chemistry book for the index card. On it was written the third verse of "America, the Beautiful":

> America! America!
> May God thy gold refine
> Till all success be nobleness
> And every gain divine.

Theo had begun reading the refrain and ended up singing. He shyly laughed off his foolishness. "I guess it doesn't have anything to do with money or the will, just Uncle Sam's patriotism popping up again."

"Thank you, Theo." Angela stuffed her embroidery in the tapestry bag on seeing Denton Deere rush off the elevator.

"Hello, Doctor Deere, how about a game of chess?"

"Let's go," the intern said, ignoring Theo.

Sandy opened the front door for the couple, whistling "America, the Beautiful." The doorman was a good whistler, thanks to his chipped front tooth.

"I can't drive you home; I'm on duty tonight."

"I'll take a cab."

"Why must you go back to the hospital? Your crazy partner isn't dying, you know."

"She's not crazy."

"She made up her so-called wasting disease, I call that crazy. Nothing was wrong with her legs until the explosion in the Chinese restaurant."

"You're wrong."

"First you ask me to look in on her, now you don't want my opinion. Anyhow, I called in a psychiatrist. Maybe you should talk to him, too. I've never seen you so troubled. What's wrong, the wedding dress isn't ready, the guest list is too long? You'll have to cope with more important matters than that once we're married. Unless you don't want to get married. Is that it?"

Angela twisted the engagement ring her mother made her wear in spite of the rash. No, she did not want to get married, not right away, but she couldn't say it, she couldn't tell him—them, not like that. Denton would be so hurt, her mother . . . the engagement was announced in the newspaper, the wedding gown, the shower . . . but once they found out she wasn't their perfect Angela . . .

How long has she been sitting here in the hospital corridor? A man in a business suit (the psychiatrist?) came out of Sydelle's room. "You must be Angela," he said. How had Sydelle described her—a pretty young thing? "I hear you're going to marry one of our interns." She was going to get married, her one claim to fame.

"How is Ms. Pulaski, Doctor?"

"Do you mean is she crazy? No. No more or less than anybody else in town."

"But the crippling disease, she made that up?"

"So what? The woman was lonely and wanted some attention, so she did something about it. And quite creatively, too. Those painted crutches are a touch of genius."

"Is that normal? I mean, it's not insane to shock people into noticing who you are?"

The doctor patted Angela's cheek as though she were a child. "No one was hurt by her little deception. Now, go in and say hello to your friend."

"Hello, Sydelle."

Without makeup, without jewelry, clothed only in a white hospital gown, she looked older, softer. She looked like a sad and homely human being. "You talk to the doctors?"

"It's a simple fracture," Angela replied.

"What else?" Sydelle turned her face to the wall.

"The doctor says your disease is incurable, but you could have a remission lasting five years, even more, if you take good care of yourself and don't overdo it."

"The doctor said that?" Maybe a few people could be trusted. "Did you bring my makeup? I must look a mess."

In the overstuffed tapestry bag, under Sydelle's cosmetic case, Angela found a letter. It was a strange letter, written in a tense and rigid hand:

> *Forgive me, my daughter. God bless you, my child.*
> *Delight in your love and the devil take doctor dear. Hast*
> *thou found me, O mine enemy? The time draws near.*

Taped at the bottom were two clues:

THY   BEAUTIFUL

■ **FACT AND GOSSIP** ■

15

FRIDAY WAS BACK to normal, if the actions of suspicious would-be heirs competing for a two-hundred-million-dollar prize could be considered normal.

At school, Theo studied, Doug Hoo ran, and Turtle was twice

sent to the principal's office for having been caught with a transistor radio plugged in her ear.

The coffee shop was full of diners.

Shin Hoo's restaurant had reopened, too, but no one came.

J. J. Ford presided at the bench, and Sandy McSouthers presided at the front door, whistling, chatting, collecting tidbits of gossip, and adding some of his own.

Flora Baumbach, her strained eyes shielded by dark glasses, drove Turtle to school on her way to the broker's office and picked her up in the late afternoon with a sheet of prices copied from the moving tape. They had lost $3,000 in five days.

"Paper losses," Turtle said. "Doesn't mean a thing. Besides, I didn't pick these stocks. Mr. Westing did."

Did he? The dressmaker thought of the clue Chris had dropped; no stock symbol had five letters or even resembled the word *plain*. But Flora Baumbach played fair and kept the secret to herself.

■ ■ ■ ■ ■ ■ ■ ■ ■ ■ ■

Four people stood in the driveway's melting snow, shivering as the sun dropped behind Sunset Towers. The fifth jogged in place. No smoke had risen from the chimney since that fateful Halloween; still they stared up at the Westing house, murder on their minds.

"He looked too peaceful to have been murdered," Turtle said. She sneezed and Sandy handed her a Westing tissue.

"How would you know?" Doug replied. "How many people have you seen murdered?"

"Turtle's right," her friend Sandy said. "If Westing expected it, he'd have seen it coming. His face would have looked scared."

"Maybe he didn't see it coming," Theo argued. "The killer was very cunning, Westing said. I read a mystery once where the victim was allergic to bee stings and the murderer let a bee in through an open window."

"The window wasn't open," Turtle said, wiping her nose. "Besides, Westing would have heard the buzzing and jumped out of bed."

Doug had an idea. "Maybe the murderer injected bee venom in his veins."

Otis Amber flung his arms in the air. "Whoever said Sam Westing was allergic to bees?"

Doug tried again. "How about snake venom? Or poison? Doctors know lots of poisons that make it look like heart attacks."

Turtle almost kicked Doug, track meet or not. Her father was a doctor. She would not have minded if he had said "interns."

"I once heard about a murderer who stabbed his victim with an icicle," the doorman said. "It melted, leaving no trace of a murder weapon."

"That's a good one," Turtle exclaimed appreciatively.

Sandy had more. "Then there was a Roman who choked on a single goat hair someone put in his milk. And there was the Greek poet who was killed when an eagle dropped a tortoise on his bald head."

"Maybe Westing was just sleeping until Turtle stumbled and fell on his head," Doug suggested.

"That's not funny, Doug Hoo." How could she ever have had a crush on that disgusting jerk?

Doug would not let up. "And who was that suspicious person in red boots I saw opening the hoods of cars in the parking lot the other morning?" He looked at Turtle's booted feet.

"The thief stole my boots and put them back again. They leak."

"A likely story, Tabitha-Ruth." Doug pulled her braid and ran into the lobby at full speed.

Sandy placed a large hand on Turtle's shoulder, a comforting hand, and a restraining one.

Otis Amber hopped on his bike. "Can't stand around chit-chatting about a murder that never happened. Sam Westing was a madman. Insane. Crazy as a bedbug." He pedaled off, shouting back, "We ain't murderers, none of us."

Theo could not agree. If there was no murderer, there was no answer; and without an answer, no one could win. "Sandy, did anybody leave Sunset Towers on Halloween night, before Turtle and Doug?"

The doorman scratched his head under his hat, thinking. "One day seems like the next, people coming and going. I can't remember."

"Try."

Sandy scratched harder. "Only ones I recall are Otis Amber and Crow. They left together about five o'clock."

"Thanks." Theo hurried into the building to check his clues.

Turtle had no reason to suspect Otis Amber or Crow or any of the heirs. Money was the answer. Her only problem was that dumb stock market; it didn't want to play the game. "Sandy, tell me another story."

"Okay, let's see. Once, long ago in the olden days, there was this soothsayer who predicted the day of his own death. That day came, and the soothsayer waited to die and waited some more, but nothing happened. He was so surprised and so happy to be alive that he laughed and laughed. Then, at one minute to midnight, he suddenly died. He died laughing."

"He died laughing," Turtle repeated thoughtfully. "That's profound, Sandy. That's very profound."

■ ■ ■ ■ ■ ■ ■ ■ ■ ■ ■

"Where's everybody?" The apartment was empty, as usual. Jake Wexler decided that Shin Hoo's was going to have a paying customer.

"I'd like a table, if you're not too crowded."

"I think I can squeeze you in," Hoo said, leading the podiatrist through the empty restaurant. "You must have liked those spareribs."

"Yeah, sure." Jake watched his wife slowly stack her papers at the reservations desk. At last, seeming to recognize him, she walked over. Jake returned his unlit cigar to his pocket (Grace hated the smell).

"I've already eaten," Grace said, sitting down.

"Hello to you, too," Jake replied.

He probably thinks that's funny. Since when do people go around saying hello to their husbands?

"What's new with you, Grace? Where are the kids? And what are all those presents doing on the coffee table? It's not your birthday and it's not our anniversary." What was she so upset about? "Or is it?"

"No, it isn't. Those are gifts for Angela, the wedding shower is tomorrow. Don't worry, you're not supposed to be there, just girls. The doorbell was ringing all morning, I couldn't leave the apartment for an instant; one at a time he delivered them, the smirking fool, and each time he shouted 'Boom!'"

She looked especially attractive today, Jake thought. Between the ringing doorbell and the booms, she had managed time for the beauty parlor and the sunlamp.

Mr. Hoo set the spareribs on the table and lowered himself to a chair.

Grace lost her scowl. "Since you're here, Jake, I'd like your opinion on the advertising campaign I'm planning. Jimmy and I are having a slight disagreement. I say that Shin Hoo's sounds like every other Chinese restaurant to English-speaking ears."

English-speaking ears? Jake bit his lip in an effort to keep silent.

"I say the restaurant needs a name people won't forget," Grace continued. "A name like Hoo's On First."

Jake could not help himself. He tried to cover a loud guffaw with louder coughing. Hoo pounded him on the back and apologized for the ginger.

"You remember that old baseball routine, Jake," Grace prompted.

Yes, he did. "Who's on second? No, What's on second; Who's on first."

"It's an idiotic name," Hoo argued. "Hoo's On First sounds like my restaurant is on First Street, or worse yet, on the first floor. Customers will end up in the coffee shop drinking dishwater tea."

"Not the way I'll promote it, they won't," Grace insisted. "Well, what's your opinion, Jake?"

The podiatrist put down the sparerib he was about to bite into. "Hoo's On First is a dandy name."

Before he could pick up the rib again, Hoo whisked the plate off the table. "Who elected you judge, anyhow?"

■ ■ ■ ■ ■ ■ ■ ■ ■ ■ ■

The judge returned to Sunset Towers with clippings from the newspaper's files. Faithful Sandy was waiting.

Hoping to interrogate both George Theodorakis and James Shin Hoo, they alternated their dinner orders. One night they would order up, the next night they would order down. To their disappointment Theo delivered up. They had no questions to ask him, but he had one for the doorman.

"Chess?" Sandy replied. "Sorry, don't know the game. I'm a whiz at hearts, though. 'Shooter,' they call me."

Theo left them to their sandwiches and their work.

The private detective the judge had hired was still investigating the heirs, so tonight's project would be the Westing family.

Judge Ford opened the thin folder on Mrs. Westing. Mrs. Westing—no first name, no maiden name. In the few newspaper photographs in which she appeared, always with her husband, the captions read: Mr. and Mrs. Samuel W. Westing. A shadowy figure, a shy woman, she seemed to slip behind her husband before the camera clicked, or had her face masked by a floppy hat brim. A slim woman dressed in the fashion of the time: long, loose chemise, narrow shoes with sharply pointed toes and high spiked heels. A nervous woman, her hands, especially in the later pictures, were blurred. In the final photograph a black veil covered her face. She seemed to lean unsteadily against the stocky frame of her husband as they left the cemetery.

Sandy reported his findings. "Jimmy Hoo never met Mrs. Westing. Neither did Flora Baumbach. She says Violet's fiancé brought her to the shop for fittings. She says it's bad luck for a groom to see the bride in the wedding gown before the wedding; I guess she's right. Well, that's it. Nobody else admits to having known Mrs. Westing, except me."

"You knew her, Mr. McSouthers?" the judge asked.

"Well, not exactly, but I saw her once or twice." The doorman described Mrs. Westing as blonde, full-lipped, a good figure though on the skinny side. "Mostly I recall those full lips because she had a mole right here." He pointed to the right corner of his mouth.

Judge Ford did not remember a mole; she remembered copper-colored hair and thin lips, but it was so long ago, and well—Mrs. Westing was white. Very white.

Next, Westing's daughter. The judge studied the photograph under the headline:

VIOLET WESTING TO MARRY SENATOR

The senator turned out to be a state senator, a hack politician, now serving a five-year jail term for bribery. But Flora Baumbach was right about the resemblance. Violet Westing did look like Angela Wexler. And that was George Theodorakis, all right, dancing with her in the society page clippings.

"What does it all mean, Judge?" Sandy asked, squinting at the pictures through his smeared glasses. "Angela looks like Westing's daughter, and Theo looks like his father, the man Violet Westing really wanted to marry."

"How did you know that?"

Sandy shrugged. "It was common gossip at the time, that

93

Westing's daughter killed herself rather than have to marry that crooked politician. . . ."

Now the judge remembered; her mother had written her about the tragedy. "Tell me, Mr. McSouthers, you seem to know what's going on in this building: Is Angela Wexler involved with Theo in any way?"

"Oh no." Sandy was certain of that. "Angela and her intern seem happy enough with each other. At least, I hope so. I mean, if Sam Westing wanted to replay that terrible drama, Angela Wexler would have to die."

■ THE THIRD BOMB ■

16 "BOOM!"

Grace Wexler slammed the door on the delivery boy's silly face and returned to her party with a pink-ribboned gift. The gossiping guests were sipping jasmine tea from Westing Paper Party Cups, nibbling on tidbits from Westing Paper Party Plates, and wiping their fingers on Westing Paper Party Napkins. Madame Hoo served in a tight-fitting silk gown slit high up her thigh, a costume as old-fashioned and impractical as bound feet. Women in China wore blouses and pants and jackets. That's what she would wear when she got home.

Grace clapped her hands for attention. "Girls, girls! It's time for the bride-to-be to open her presents. Angela, you sit here and everybody gather round."

Angela did as her mother said. She lowered herself to a cushion on the floor, ringed by gift boxes and surrounded by vaguely familiar faces. She had not invited her few friends from college; they were bent on careers, this wasn't their thing. These were her mother's friends and the newly married daughters of her mother's friends—and Turtle, who was leaning against the wall, arms folded, smirking. Lucky Turtle, the neglected child.

"Read it out loud, dear," Grace ordered, as Angela opened the card tied to the yellow-ribboned box.

> *To the bride-to-be in the kitchen stuck,*
> *An asparagus cooker and lots of luck.*
>> *from Cookie Barfspringer*

"Thank you," Angela said, wondering which one was the Barfspringer.

The next gift was an egg poacher.

The box in pink ribbons contained another asparagus cooker.

"I sure hope Doctor Deere likes asparagus," someone remarked. The giver said she could return it for something else, although two might come in handy. "A doctor's wife has so much entertaining to do."

Angela glanced at her watch and reached for the tall, thin carton wrapped in gold foil.

"Look how Angela's hands are shaking; she's as nervous as a groom." Giggles. "Bride-to-be jitters." More giggles.

Slowly, Angela unknotted the gold ribbon. Carefully, she unfolded the gold foil. How neatly she did everything, the perfect child; not like Turtle, who ripped off wrappings, impatient to see what was inside.

"Hurry up, Angela, you're such a poke," Turtle complained. Suddenly there she was, kneeling down to peek under the lid.

"Get away!" Angela cried, jerking the gift up and away from her sister as the lid blasted off with a shattering bang. Bang! Bang! A rapid rat-a-tat-tat. Rockets shooting, fireballs bursting, comets shrieking, sparks sizzling. Two dozen framed flower prints falling off the wall.

Then it was over. Screams hushed to whimpers and the trembling guests crawled out from under tables and peered out of closets.

"Is anyone hurt?" Grace Wexler asked nervously. Other than

being scared out of ten years of their lives, thank you, they were fine. "Where's Angela?"

Angela was still seated on the cushion in the middle of the floor. Fragments of the scorched box lay in her burned hands. Blood oozed from an angry gash on her cheek and trickled down her beautiful face.

■ ■ ■ ■ ■ ■ ■ ■ ■ ■ ■ ■

Heirs, beware, Sam Westing had warned. They should have listened. Now it was too late.

The suspicious heirs gathered in the lobby around the police captain called in by Judge Ford. One of them was a murderer, they thought, and one of them was a bomber, and one of them was a thief. But which was which and who was who? Or could it be one and the same?

"Some game," Mr. Hoo grumbled, unwrapping a chocolate bar. One ulcer wasn't enough, Sam Westing had to give him three more. "Some game. The last one alive wins."

(Now, there's a likely suspect, Otis Amber thought. Hoo, the inventor; Hoo, the angry man, the madman.)

"The last one alive wins," Flora Baumbach repeated. "Oh my, what a terrible thing to say."

(Can't trust that dressmaker, Mr. Hoo thought. How come she's grinning at a time like this?)

The captain offered no help at all. "Neither the bomb squad nor the burglary detail has enough evidence to search the apartments," he explained.

"You call that justice?" Sandy asked.

(Good-natured Sandy couldn't be the one. He wasn't in the building when the first two bombs went off, or when the judge's watch was stolen, Jake Wexler thought. On the other hand, he sure did hate Sam Westing.)

"Yes, Mr. McSouthers, justice is exactly what I call it."

(Not her, not the judge, in spite of the clues, Chris thought. Unless she's one of those Black Panthers in disguise.)

"Those weren't gas explosions, those were bombs. Right?" Theo pressed the captain.

(A nice kid, that Theo. Doug, too, Flora Baumbach thought. But how often had she seen television interviews of next-door neighbors saying: Can't believe he killed thirteen people, he was such a nice kid. Oh my, oh my, what's gotten into me, thinking such a thing?)

The captain would not call them bombs. "More like childish pranks," he said.

(Childish pranks! That brat's capable of anything.)

Turtle stuck out her tongue at the sneering Doug Hoo.

"Evil pranks of the devil," Crow muttered. Her blessed Angela was almost killed.

"Crow could be the one. Bring hellfire down on all of us," Theo whispered to Chris, "but she wasn't in the building when the first two bombs went off."

"Yes, s-she was."

"No, she wasn't."

The captain described the so-called bombs. "Just a few fireworks triggered by a squat striped candle set in a tall open jar; the ribbon probably hid the air holes in the box. No one would have been hurt if the young lady had not tilted the box toward herself."

"A time bomb," Grace Wexler said, glaring at the person who delivered the gifts.

(An unhappy woman, that self-appointed heiress, the judge thought. Unfulfilled, possibly disturbed. Capable of the burglaries, perhaps, but not the bombings. She wouldn't have hurt her own daughter—at least, not Angela.)

"Don't look at me like that," Otis Amber shouted at Mrs. Wexler. "I don't own no striped candles, or no fireworks, neither."

(That idiot is the likeliest of all, Grace thought. But he wasn't around when the coffee shop blew up.)

"O-o-o-ggg a-a-ahh." The excitement was too much for Chris Theodorakis.

(That was one heir no one suspected. And Angela, of course, no one could suspect her.)

Otis Amber was not even sure of that. "Still waters run deep," he said. "He-he-he."

Turtle could not let him get away with that, even if it was true.

"Otis Amber limps," Chris noted the next day.

■ ■ ■ ■ ■ ■ ■ ■ ■ ■ ■ ■

Her family kept reassuring her. "You're going to be fine, Angela, just fine."

The loud snore that erupted from the next hospital bed was Sydelle Pulaski pretending to be asleep.

"I still don't remember," Angela mumbled. Her bandaged cheek made speaking difficult. Her face hurt, her hands hurt—hurt very much.

"Traumatic amnesia," Jake Wexler said. "It happens after sudden accidents. Don't worry, Angie-pie, you're going to be fine."

"You're going to be fine, Angela, just fine," Grace said despondently. "I'll be back tomorrow. Come, Turtle."

"In a minute." Turtle waited for the door to close. She touched her sister's bandaged hand. "Thanks."

"For what?"

Another snore from Sydelle.

"Just thanks. The fireworks would have gone off in my face if you hadn't pulled the box toward you. Here, I brought your tapestry bag; I didn't look at your notes or clues, honest." But she had removed the incriminating evidence.

"Turtle, tell me the truth. How bad is it?"

"The doctor had to take some glass out of your hands, but no stitches. The burns will heal okay."

"And my face?"

"Some scarring, not bad really, Angela. Besides, you always said being pretty wasn't important, it's who you really are that counts."

Angela wondered about that. Maybe she was wrong. Maybe pretty was important. Maybe she was crazy, she must have been crazy.

"Don't worry, you'll still be pretty," Turtle said. "But, wow, that sure was a dumb thing to do."

Sydelle Pulaski's eyes popped open in surprise. Quickly she squeezed them shut and uttered another loud snore. Well, what do you know? Her sweet, saintly partner was the bomber. Good for her!

■ SOME SOLUTIONS ■

17 MONDAY WAS A gray, rainy day. Depressing. So was the stock market, which fell another six points. Turtle was jittery.

All the heirs were jittery. The bomb squad was called in several times to examine suspicious parcels. One turned out to be a sealed vacuum cleaner bag full of dust that Crow had set behind the incinerator door. Another was a box delivered to Mrs. Wexler. In it were bonbons (her favorite) and a note: *Love and kisses, Jake.*

"What do you mean, how come? Can't I send candy to my wife without getting the third degree? I thought you were looking on the thin side, okay?"

Grace made him eat the first piece.

The next day Grace received a larger box. In it the bomb squad found one dozen long-stemmed roses and a note: *For no reason at all, just love, Jake.*

The bomb squad was called again when Turtle ran after her partner through the lobby shouting "Mrs. BAUM-bach, Mrs. BAUM-bach!" Someone thought she had shouted "Bomb! Bomb!"

A hollow wind wailed through damp Tuesday. In the morning the stock market rose three points. "Bullish," said Flora Baumbach. In the afternoon the market dropped five points. "Bearish," said Flora Baumbach. Those were the only two trading terms she had learned.

Madame Hoo, a quicker student than the dressmaker, had learned more words: partner, money, house, tree, road, pots, pans, okay, football, good, rain, spareribs. Her teacher, Jake Wexler, visited her in the kitchen before he sat down to his daily lunch in the Chinese restaurant. Today his wife and Jimmy Hoo agreed to eat with their only customer on the promise that he would help them with their clues and not take a share of the inheritance if they won.

Grace laid their five words on the table.

"These are clues?" Jake looked down on *purple waves for fruited sea*. He switched two squares of Westing Superstrength Towels. "*Purple fruited* makes more sense. How about grapes or plums?"

Grace was about to insist on *purple waves,* but plums reminded her of something. "Plum," she said aloud. "Plum. Wasn't the lawyer's name Plum?"

"You're right, Grace," Mr. Hoo said excitedly. "You're absolutely right." He tore one of the clues in two: *fruit/ed.* "Ed Purple-fruit. Ed Plum!"

"We got it, we got it," Grace cried, leaping up to embrace her partner.

"I never did trust lawyers," Mr. Hoo shouted gleefully.

"What about the other clues: *for sea waves*?" Jake asked, but the happy, hugging and dancing, celebrating pair did not hear him.

"Boom!" said Madame Hoo, placing a plate of spareribs on the table. That word she had learned from Otis Amber.

■ ■ ■ ■ ■ ■ ■ ■ ■ ■ ■

Sandy was proud of the notebook he bought, with its glossy cover photograph of a bald eagle in flight (sort of appropriate, he explained to the judge; fits in with Uncle Sam and all that). In it he painstakingly entered the information culled from reports the private detective delivered each day to Judge Ford's office: photostats of birth certificates, death notices, marriage licenses, drivers' licenses, vehicular accident reports, criminal records, hospital records, school records. To these the doorman added the results of his own snooping.

"My investigator is having a difficult time getting into the not-so-public records of Westingtown," the judge said. "We'll have to put the Westings aside and begin with the heirs."

"Since we're feasting on chicken with water chestnuts," Sandy said, "I'll start off with the Hoos." (Doug had delivered down.) He read aloud from his entry:

● HOO

JAMES SHIN HOO. Born: James Hoo in Chicago. Age: 50. Added Shin to his name when he went into the restaurant business because it sounded more Chinese. First wife died of cancer five years ago. Married again last year. Has one son: Douglas.

SUN LIN HOO. Age: 28. Born in China. Immigrated from Hong Kong two years ago. Gossip: James Hoo married her for her 100-year-old sauce.

DOUGLAS HOO (called Doug). Age: 18. High-school track star. Is competing in Saturday's track meet against college milers.

Westing connection: Hoo sued Sara Westing over the invention of the disposable paper diaper. Case never came to court (Westing disappeared). Settled with the company last year for $25,000. Thinks he was cheated. Latest invention: paper innersoles.

"I can take some credit for those paper innersoles," Sandy bragged. "My feet were killing me, standing at the door all day, so I said to Jimmy: 'Jimmy, if only somebody would invent a good innersole that didn't take up so much room like those foam-rubber things.' And sure enough, he did it. They're great, I got a pair in my shoes now, wanna see?"

"No, thank you." The judge was eating.

■ ■ ■ ■ ■ ■ ■ ■ ■ ■ ■ ■

It was past midnight when Theo finished his homework in the dim light of the study lamp. The wind was still howling, and something (a word? a phrase?) was still eluding him. He had been studying solutions in chemistry. Solutions—that was it! The solution is simple, the will said. He was sure of it.

By changing *for* and *thee* to the numbers *four* and *three,* Theo was able to arrange the clues into a formula (whether or not it was a chemical solution, let alone the Westing solution, was another matter).

$$N \quad H(IS) \quad FOR \quad NO \quad THEE \quad (TO) = NH^4NO^3$$

But four clue letters were left out: *isto, osit, itso, otis.* OTIS! He had it: a formula for an explosive, and the name of the murderer! He had to tell Doug.

"Where g-g-gogin?"

"Shhh!" Theo smoothed the blanket over his sleepy brother in the next bed, struggled into his bathrobe, and stumbled over the wheelchair as he tiptoed out of the room.

The elevator made too much noise, use the stairs. The cement was cold, he had forgotten his slippers. Two unmarked doors, which one? Tap, tap. Tap. A grunting voice, dragging footsteps. Please, let it be Doug, not Mr. Hoo or Judge Ford.

It was Crow. Clutching a robe about her gaunt frame, her unknotted hair hanging long and limp, she tried to focus her dulled eyes on the shocked face of her visitor. "Theo! Theo! The wind, I heard the wind. I knew you would come."

"Me?"

Grasping his hand, she pulled him into the maid's apartment between 4C and 4D and shut the door. "We are sinners, yet shall we be saved. Let us pray for deliverance, then you must go to your angel, take her away."

Theo found himself kneeling on the bare floor next to the praying Crow. He must be dreaming.

"Amen."

18

IT WAS FLORA Baumbach who braided Turtle's hair now, sometimes in three strands, sometimes four, sometimes twined with ribbons, while Turtle read *The Wall Street Journal*.

"Listen to this: 'The newly elected chairman of the board of Westing Paper Products Corporation, Julian R. Eastman, announced from London where he is conferring with European management that earnings from all divisions are expected to double in the next quarter.'"

"That's nice," Flora Baumbach said, not understanding a word of it.

Turtle gave the order for the day. "Listen carefully. As soon as you get to the broker's office I want you to sell AMO, sell SEA, sell MT, and put all the money into WPP. Okay?"

Oh my! That meant selling every stock mentioned in their clues and buying more shares of Westing Paper Products—at a loss of some thousands of dollars. "Whatever you say, Alice, you're the smart one."

Flora Baumbach's hands were gentle, they never hurried or pulled a stray hair. Flora Baumbach loved her, she could tell. "I like when you call me Alice," Turtle said, "but I better not call you Mrs. Baumbach anymore, because of the bomb scare, you know." Calling her Flora would spoil everything. "Maybe I could call you Mrs. Baba?"

"Why not just Baba?"

That's exactly what Turtle (Alice) wanted to hear. "Was your daughter, Rosalie, very smart, Baba?"

"My, no. You're the smartest child I ever met, a real business-woman."

Turtle glowed behind *The Wall Street Journal*. "I bet Rosalie baked bread and patched quilts and dumb stuff like that."

The dressmaker's sure fingers fumbled over the red ribbons she was weaving into a four-strand braid. "Rosalie was an exceptional child. The friendliest, lovingest . . ."

Turtle crumpled the newspaper. "Let's go. I'm late for school and you've got that big trade to make."

"But I haven't finished tying the ribbons."

"Never mind, I like them hanging." Turtle felt like kicking somebody, anybody, good and hard.

■ ■ ■ ■ ■ ■ ■ ■ ■ ■ ■

Sandy was not at the door when they left. He was in apartment 4D neatly writing in his patriotic notebook information gathered on the next heir.

● BAUMBACH

> FLORA BAUMBACH. Maiden name: Flora Miller. Age: 60. Dressmaker. Husband left her years ago, sends no money. She had a disabled child, Rosalie. Sold bridal shop last year after Rosalie died of pneumonia, age 19. Spends most of her time at the stockbrokers.
>
> *Westing connection:* Made wedding gown for Violet Westing, which she never got to wear.

Sandy turned to a fresh page, propped his feet on the judge's desk, and began to read the data supplied by the private investigator on Otis Amber. He laughed so hard he nearly fell off the tilting chair.

■ ■ ■ ■ ■ ■ ■ ■ ■ ■

Haunted by last night's dream, Theo jogged behind his partner
halfway to the high school before he uttered a breathless "Stop!"

Doug Hoo stopped.

"Who lives in the apartment next to yours?"

"Crow. Why?"

"Nothing." How come he didn't know that? Because no one
ever wonders where a cleaning woman lives, that's why. But he
wasn't like that, was he? Still, it must have been a dream. In the
dream, the nightmare, Crow had given him a letter, but the only
thing he found in his bathrobe pocket this morning was a
Westing Paper Hankie. "Hey, wait!" Doug had started off again.
"I figured out our clues. Ammonium nitrate. It's used in fertilizers, explosives, and rocket propellants."

"I knew those clues were a pile of fertilizer," Doug replied,
jogging easily. Only one thing mattered: Saturday's big track
meet. If he won or came in a fast second he'd have his pick of athletic scholarships. He didn't need the inheritance.

"Stand still and listen." Theo grabbed Doug by the shoulders
and held him flat-footed to the ground. "Like it or not we're partners, and you've got to do your share."

"Sure," Doug replied. His father was angry, his partner was
angry, and a bomber was blowing up Sunset Towers floor by
floor. Some game! "What do you want me to do?"

"Follow Otis Amber."

■ ■ ■ ■ ■ ■ ■ ■ ■ ■

Head tilted back, Flora Baumbach squirted drops in her eyes,
blinked, and stared again at the moving tape.

HR	WPP	BRY	TA	Z	WPP
· 1000$42½	5000$39¼	27	5$17¼	5000$27¼	5000$39½

"Oh my!" Westing Paper Products had jumped four and a quarter, no, four and a half points. Her eyes must be blurry from the medicine. The dressmaker sat on the edge of her chair, biting her fingernails, waiting for WPP to cross the board again. There: WPP $40. Oh my, oh my! This morning she had paid thirty-five dollars a share. There it goes again: WPP $40¼. Oh my, oh my, oh my!

■ ■ ■ ■ ■ ■ ■ ■ ■ ■ ■ ■

After classes, instead of running around the indoor track, Doug Hoo jogged out of the gym to the shopping center six blocks away. There was Otis Amber, placing two cake boxes in the compartment of his bike. He picked up a package from the butcher shop, and pedaled off, unaware of the sweat-suited figure trotting half a block behind him, and went into Sunset Towers to make his deliveries.

"Hi, Doug. Gonna run the mile under four minutes on Saturday?" the doorman asked.

"Sure hope so. Do me a favor, Sandy, give a loud whistle when Otis Amber comes out. Okay?"

Chip-toothed Sandy gave such a loud whistle that Otis Amber would have been deafened if the flaps of the aviator's helmet had not been snug against his ears.

Leaving his bicycle in the parking lot, Otis Amber boarded a bus. Doug ran the five uphill miles to a house with the placard: E. J. Plum, Attorney. He ran another three uphill miles after the bus that took the delivery boy to the hospital entrance.

Doug sank down in a waiting-room chair, wiped his face on his sweatshirt and picked up a magazine. Fascinated by the centerfold picture, he almost missed Otis Amber, who dashed out of the hospital as though fleeing for his life.

Hiding behind parked cars, Doug followed the delivery boy to another bus, ran four steep miles to a stockbroker's office (how is it that all roads go uphill?), from the broker to the high school, from the high school (downhill, at last) back to Sunset Towers.

The exhausted track star leaned against the side of the building, thankful he was not a long-distance runner.

"I gotcha!" Otis Amber poked a skinny finger into Doug's ribs. "He-he-he," he cackled, handing the startled runner a letter. "It's from that lawyer Plum. Says all the heirs gotta be at the Westing house this Saturday night. Sign here."

With his last ounce of energy he wrote *Doug Hoo, miler* on the receipt, then slid down the wall to a weary squat. Some miler. His feet were blistered; his muscles, sore; he could barely breathe, he might never run another step in his life.

■ ■ ■ ■ ■ ■ ■ ■ ■ ■ ■ ■

On receiving the notice of the Westing house meeting, Judge Ford canceled her remaining appointments and hurried home. Time was running out.

Sandy read to her from his notebook:

● AMBER

OTIS JOSEPH AMBER. Age: 62. Delivery boy. Fourth-grade dropout. IQ: 50. Lives in the basement of Green's Grocery. A bachelor. No living relatives.
Westing connection: Delivered letters from E. J. Plum, Attorney, both times.

"I would've guessed Otis had an IQ of minus ten," Sandy said with a smile.

"Go on to the next heir," the judge replied.

● DEERE

D. DENTON DEERE. Age: 25. Graduate of UW Medical School. First-year intern, plastic surgery. Parents live in Racine (not heirs).

Westing connection: Engaged to Angela Wexler (see Wexlers), who looks like Sam Westing's daughter, Violet, who was also engaged to be married, but to a politician, not an intern.

"That's awful complicated, I know," the doorman apologized, "but it's the best I could do."

● PULASKI

SYDELLE PULASKI. Age: 50. Education: high school, one year secretarial school. Secretary to the president of Schultz Sausages. Is taking her first vacation in 25 years (six months' saved-up time). Lived with widowed mother and two aunts until she moved to Sunset Towers. Walked with a crutch even before she broke her ankle in the second bombing. Now needs two crutches (she paints them!).
Westing connection: ?

"We don't have any medical reports on her muscular ailment," Sandy reported. "The nurse at Schultz Sausages said she was in perfect health when she left on vacation."

"Strange," the judge remarked. A suspicious malady, no apparent Westing connection, somehow Sydelle Pulaski did not seem to fit in.

■ ■ ■ ■ ■ ■ ■ ■ ■ ■ ■

Sydelle Pulaski clasped the translated notes to her bosom. "My little secret, mustn't peek," she said coyly, but the doctors had come to see Angela.

The plastic surgeon loosed the tape from her check and peered under the gauze. "One graft should do it, but we can't operate until the tissue heals," he said to the intern, then spoke to the patient. "Call my secretary for an appointment in two months."

He strode out of the room, leaving Denton Deere to replace the bandage.

"I don't want plastic surgery," Angela mumbled. It still hurt to talk.

"Nothing to be frightened of. He's the best when it comes to facial repairs, that's why I brought him in."

"We'll have to postpone the wedding."

"We can have a small informal wedding."

"Mother wouldn't like that."

"How about you, Angela, what do you want?" He knew her unspoken answer was "I don't know."

The door flew open and slammed against the adjacent wall. "Where do you think you're going?" Denton pulled Turtle to a halt by one of the streaming ribbons twisted in her braid. "The sign says No Visitors."

"I'm not a visitor, I'm a sister. And get your germy hands off my hair."

Denton Deere hurried to seek first aid for his bleeding shin and sent the biggest male nurse on the floor to take care of Turtle, the same male nurse who chased Otis Amber out of the hospital for sneaking up on a nurse's aide carrying a specimen tray and shouting, "Boom!"

Turtle had time for one question. "Angela, what did you sign on the receipt this time after 'position'?"

"*Person.*"

"I changed mine to *victim*," Sydelle said.

Turtle paid no attention to the victim. She was more interested in the two men entering the room: the burly male nurse and that creep of a lawyer, Plum. "I gotta go. Don't say anything to anybody about anything, Angela, no matter what happens. Not even to a lawyer. You know nothing, you hear? Nothing!" She skirted Ed Plum, ducked under the outstretched hairy hands of the male nurse, slid down the hall, scampered down the stairs and out of the hospital.

"Hi, how are you?" Ed Plum smiled at Angela, ignoring the

patient in the other bed. He didn't recognize Ms. Pulaski without her painted crutch. "I'm sorry to hear about your accident. Otis Amber told me about it. Just thought I'd drop in for a chat." The young lawyer, who had admired the pretty heiress from the minute he first laid eyes on her, did not have a chance to chat.

Grace Wexler entered the room, saw the answer to the clues: Ed Purple-fruit, the murderer, standing over her daughter, and uttered a blood-curdling shriek.

■ ■ ■ ■ ■ ■ ■ ■ ■ ■ ■ ■

Three visitors in one day! The first was Otis Amber with a letter and another receipt to sign. Chris had pretended to be scared by the "Boom!" but he wasn't really. He had twitched because he was excited about going to the Westing house again, even if he hadn't figured out the clues.

Then Flora Baumbach came to see him. He wasn't nervous at all with that nice lady. She smiles that funny smile because she's sad inside. She once had a daughter named Rosalie. She told him how Rosalie would sit in the shop and say hello to the customers, and how she would feel the fabrics. Mrs. Baumbach made wedding dresses, which are mostly white, so she bought samples of materials with bright colors and patterns because Rosalie loved colors best. Rosalie had 573 different swatches in her collection before she died. Mrs. Baumbach said her daughter might have been an artist if things had turned out differently.

What would I have been if things had turned out differently?

The third visitor entered. Limping! His partner was limping! Too much excitement, his stupid body was jerking all over the place.

Denton Deere sat down next to the wheelchair. "Take it easy, Chris. Calm down, kid, I'm not the creature from the black lagoon, you know."

His partner, a doctor, watched horror movies on television, too. Slowly arms untangled, legs unsnarled. Slowly Chris stuttered out his news: Flora Baumbach felt so guilty about seeing their dropped clue that she told him one of her clues: *mountain.* "But we m-mus-n t-tell T-Turtle."

"Don't worry," the intern said, displaying a bruised shin.

Chris laughed, then stopped. "I s-sorry."

"*Mountain,* hmmm." Denton Deere thought about the new clue. "If a treasure is hidden in a grain shed on a mountain plain, I sure don't have time to look for it. Do you?"

"N-n-n."

"Let's forget the clues, I have something more important to tell you. Don't get excited, okay?"

Chris nodded. His partner was going to ask for the money.

Denton Deere stood. "I'll get your toothbrush and pajamas, then we'll go to the hospital. Don't get excited."

Chris got excited. How could he explain that what he wanted from his partner was companionship, not more probing, pricking doctors with their bad news that made his mother cry?

"Listen, Chris, can you hear me? Just overnight. I found a neurologist, a nerve doctor, who works on problems like yours."

"Op-p-pra-shn?"

"No operation. Did you hear me, Chris? No operation. The doctor thinks a new medicine may help, but he has to examine you, make some tests. I have your parents' permission, but no one will touch you unless we talk it over first, you and me, together. I promise."

Chris grimaced trying to smile. His partner said talk it over, the two of them, together. They were really partners now. "You c-c-cn have m-money."

"What? Oh, the money. Later. Here, let me take those, you won't need them in the hospital." Chris clung to his binoculars. "Well, I guess you do need them. Ready? Here we go!"

All of a sudden he was leaving Sunset Towers, pushed by his limping partner. Maybe Doctor Deere is not who and what he says he is. Maybe he is being kidnapped for ransom. Maybe he's being held hostage. Oh boy, he hasn't had so much fun in years.

19

THURSDAY WAS A sunny day, a glorious day; the autumn air was crisp and clear. None of the heirs noticed.

WPP crossed the tape at $44 . . . $44½ . . . $46. Forty-six dollars a share! Oh my! ("Don't sell until I give the word, Baba," Alice-Turtle had said.) Baba. The dressmaker smiled at her new name and eased back in the chair, but not for long. WPP $48¼. Oh my, oh my! Flora Baumbach bit her thumbnail to the quick. If only the child was here.

The child was being examined by the school nurse, having been caught again with a radio plugged in her ear. Turtle blamed her misbehavior on a toothache. "The only thing that soothes the horrendous pain is listening to music."

"You should see a dentist," the nurse said.

"I have an appointment next week," Turtle lied. "Can I go home now? The pain is truly unbearable."

"No." The nurse packed the tooth with foul-tasting cotton and sent her back to class. So every half hour Turtle had to ask permission to go to the lavatory in order to keep up with the latest stock market reports. "Bladder infection," she explained.

■ ■ ■ ■ ■ ■ ■ ■ ■ ■ ■ ■

Crow polished Mrs. Wexler's silver teapot with a Westing Disposable Diaper for the third time. Two more days, the day after next. It was too painful, going back to that house, but Otis said she must, to collect her due. It was her penance to go back, not her due. Blessed is he who expects nothing.

"Boom! Just a warning to keep doors locked," the delivery boy said, dumping a carton of Westing Paper Products on the kitchen floor. "You know, Crow old pal, I think I figured out who the bomber is."

Crow stiffened as she stared at her distorted reflection in the shining silver. "Who?"

"That's right," Otis Amber said. "James Shin Hoo. He wanted to put the coffee shop out of business, right? Then he had to bomb his own restaurant so nobody would suspect him, right? And he catered the Wexler party. Nobody would notice if the caterer brought in an extra box along with the food, right?"

James Shin Hoo was the bomber. Crow's hands trembled, her face blotched with hate. That beautiful, innocent angel reborn; Sandy said her face will be scarred for life. James Shin Hoo, beware! Vengeance shall be mine.

■ ■ ■ ■ ■ ■ ■ ■ ■ ■ ■ ■

The judge rearranged her docket in order to have these last days free. (Leave it to Sam Westing to interfere with her work.)

Sandy turned to his next entry. "It's an interesting one."

● **CROW**

BERTHE ERICA CROW. Age: 57. Mother died at childbirth, raised by father (deceased). Education: 1 year of high school. Married at 16, divorced at 40. Ex-husband's name: Windy Windkloppel. Hospital records: problems related to chronic alcoholism. Police record: 3 arrests for vagrancy. Gave up drinking when she took up religion. Started the Good Salvation Soup Kitchen on Skid Row. Works as cleaning woman in Sunset Towers, lives in maid's apartment on fourth floor. *Westing connection:* ?

"Yes, it is interesting," Judge Ford replied, "but it hardly tells us what we want to know."

■ ■ ■ ■ ■ ■ ■ ■ ■ ■ ■ ■

"You've got a customer." Jake Wexler pointed a sparerib at the black-clad figure standing at the restaurant door.

"Must be a bill collector," Hoo said, frowning over his account book.

Grace looked up, saw it was only the cleaning woman, and returned to the sports photographs she was sorting. A dozen or more superstars would be framed and hung on one wall of Hoo's On First.

"Come on over and join us," Jake shouted.

Limping to their table, Crow heard Mrs. Wexler click her tongue. Sinful woman, she'll go to hell with her pride and her covetousness, and take that foot-butcher of a husband with her. And that one, the fat one, the glutton, the bomber, the mutilator of innocent children.

Maybe she is a customer, Hoo thought, recognizing the face clenched in righteous anger as that of a diner not being served fast enough. He rose and pulled out a chair for Crow. "My wife will be serving a Chinese tea lunch shortly."

Madame Hoo placed a variety of dumplings on the table, giggled at Jake, and ran back to the kitchen.

That tittering Madame Hoo was a beautiful woman. And quite young. Grace, casting a suspicious eye on her husband, was suddenly seized by a surge of gnawing jealousy (maybe it was just the fried dumpling).

Madame Hoo returned to pour the tea. Jake patted her hand. Good, Grace noticed, she's clutching her stomach, about time she felt jealous. The podiatrist turned his smile to Crow. "Nothing wrong with your appetite, I'm happy to see."

"Nothing is wrong with my mouth," the cleaning woman replied, looking down at her plate, "it's my feet that hurt. That corn you cut out didn't heal yet, I got a callus on the sole of my left foot, and my ingrown toenail is growing in again."

Grace clasped a hand over her mouth and ran out of the restaurant. Mr. Hoo headed for the kitchen.

"Your trouble comes from years of wearing the wrong kind of shoes," Jake lectured.

Crow wasn't listening. James Shin Hoo, the bomber, was coming back. He had something in his hand.

"Here, Crow, try these. I invented them myself. Paper innersoles. They'll make you feel like you're floating on air. It's tough standing on your feet all day. Here, take them."

Crow examined the two pads of spongy folded paper. "How much?"

"Nothing, compliments of the house."

Still suspicious, Crow slipped the innersoles into her shoes and tried walking. What a blessed relief. Otis Amber was wrong. James Shin Hoo was a charitable man, he couldn't be the bomber. Crow floated out of the restaurant without paying for her lunch.

■ ■ ■ ■ ■ ■ ■ ■ ■ ■ ■ ■

"Oh no, not another victim," Sydelle Pulaski cried, stuffing her notes under the mattress.

The nurse wheeled Chris next to Angela's bed and explained that the boy was being tested for a new medication. "Are you all right?" she asked, bending over the squirming patient.

Chris was trying to remove a blank, sealed envelope from his bathrobe pocket. He knew his brother had a crush on Angela. He figured Theo must have sneaked upstairs in the wrong bathrobe to slip this letter under Angela's door, then remembered she was in the hospital and was too shy to give it to her in person.

"Look at that smile," Sydelle exclaimed.

"F-from Theo," he said. Chris hoped to watch Angela read the love letter, but the nurse insisted he return to his room.

"Bye-bye, good luck," Sydelle called. Angela waved a bandaged hand.

"*M-moun-t-tain,*" Chris replied. "From T-turtle." Serves her right for kicking his partner.

Mountain, Angela thought. Turtle's MT stood for *mountain,* not *empty.* And the letter was not from Theo.

> *Your love has 2, here are 2 for you.*
> *Take her away from this sin and hate*
> *NOW! Before it is too late.*

Again two clues were taped at the bottom:

WITH   MAJESTIES

"Crow and Otis Amber's clues are not *king* and *queen,*" she told Sydelle. "They are *with thy beautiful majesties.*"

■ ■ ■ ■ ■ ■ ■ ■ ■ ■ ■

Sandy and the judge were still at work on the heirs.

● WEXLER

JAKE WEXLER. Age: 45. Podiatrist. Graduated from Marquette. Married 22 years, has two daughters (see below).

GRACE WINDSOR WEXLER. Born Gracie Windkloppel. Age: 42. Married to above. Claims to be an interior decorator. Spends most of her time in the Chinese restaurant or the beauty parlor. She and Jake (see above) have two daughters (see below).

ANGELA WEXLER. Age: 20. Engaged to marry D. Denton Deere (also an heir). One year college (high grades). Victim of third bombing. Embroiders a lot.

TURTLE WEXLER. Real name: Tabitha-Ruth Wexler. Age: 13. Junior-high-school student. Plays the stock market. Smart kid, but kicks people. Flora Baumbach calls her Alice.

Westing connection: Grace Windsor Wexler claims that Sam Westing is her real uncle. Angela looks like Violet Westing, so does Grace in a way, except she's older.

Sandy fidgeted with his pen. "There's something I didn't write down. Maybe I shouldn't tell you, you being a judge and all, but, well, Jake Wexler . . . he's a bookie."

No, he should not have told her. "A small-time operator, I'm sure, Mr. McSouthers," the judge replied coldly. "It can have no bearing on the matter before us. Sam Westing manipulated people, cheated workers, bribed officials, stole ideas, but Sam Westing never smoked or drank or placed a bet. Give me a bookie any day over such a fine, upstanding, clean-living man."

The doorman's face reddened. He pulled the dented flask from his hip pocket and downed several swigs.

She had been too harsh. "Would you like me to fix you a drink, Mr. McSouthers?"

"No thanks, Judge. I prefer my good old Scotch."

"Windkloppel!" The judge's outburst was so unexpected, Sandy had a hard time keeping down the last swig.

"Grace Wexler's maiden name is not Windsor, it's Windkloppel," the judge exclaimed, riffling through the pages of Sandy's notebook. "Here it is: 'Berthe Erica Crow. Ex-husband's name: Windy Windkloppel.'"

Sandy stopped coughing, started laughing. "Grace Windsor Wexler is related to somebody all right; she's related to the cleaning woman. Think she knows, Judge?"

"I doubt it. Besides, we cannot be certain of the relationship. I'd like to see the documents in Crow's folder again."

"I'm sure it's Windkloppel, Judge, I checked all my spellings three times over."

Judge Ford reread the private investigator's reports. "Mr. McSouthers, it is Windkloppel, but look carefully at the name of the woman in this interview."

Berthe Erica Crow? Sure I knew her. She and her pa lived in the upstairs flat. We were best friends, almost like sisters, but she was the pretty one with her beautiful complexion and long gold-red hair. She left school to marry a guy named Windkloppel. Haven't seen or heard from her since. She's not in any trouble, is she?

Transcript of a taped interview with Sybil Pulaski, November 12.

"Pulaski!" the doorman said.

"Not just Pulaski," the judge pointed out. "*Sybil* Pulaski. Sam Westing wanted Crow's childhood friend, Sybil Pulaski, to be one of his heirs. He got Sydelle Pulaski instead."

"Gee, Judge, I never noticed that; boy, am I dumb. But what does it mean?"

"What it means, Mr. McSouthers, is that Sam Westing made his first mistake."

■ CONFESSIONS ■

20

FRIDAY CAME QUICKLY to the Westing heirs. Too quickly. Time was running out.

Turtle skipped school. She was in trouble enough, but she could build her own school and hire her own kind of teachers once she became a millionaire.

In spite of having Turtle at her side, Flora Baumbach still stared at the ever-changing, endless tape from the edge of the chair, chewed what remained of her fingernails, and uttered an "Oh my!" each time WPP went by. At two o'clock Westing Paper Products sold at fifty-two dollars a share, its highest price in fifteen years.

"Now, Baba. SELL!"

Doug Hoo had a legitimate excuse from classes: tomorrow was the big track meet. He jogged, he sprinted, he ran at full speed—not on the track, but on the trail of Otis Amber. Back and forth from the shopping center to Sunset Towers, again and again and again and . . . hey, this is a new direction.

Otis Amber parked his delivery bike in front of a rooming house and went inside. Doug waited, hidden in a doorway across the street. And waited. People came and went, but no Otis Amber. Doug jogged up and down the block for two hours. Still no sign of Otis Amber.

Doug was cold and hungry, but at least his feet didn't hurt anymore. Last night when he asked Doc Wexler about the blisters, the podiatrist told him to see his father—his father, of all people. But those paper innersoles really worked.

At five o'clock Otis Amber skipped out of the rooming house, hopped on his bicycle, and returned to Sunset Towers empty-handed. Doug's assignment was over, well, almost over. Where was Theo?

■ ■ ■ ■ ■ ■ ■ ■ ■ ■ ■

Theo was being patched up in the hospital emergency room after a slight miscalculation in his "solution" experiment. Fortunately, no one else was around when the lab blew up.

"You like playing with explosives, kid?" the bomb squad detective asked. Accidents in high-school chemistry were not unusual, but this student lived in Sunset Towers.

"I was experimenting on chemical fertilizers," Theo replied, wincing as the doctor probed his shoulder for a glass shard.

"The first bomb went off in your folks' coffee shop, right? Your mother and father work you pretty hard, don't they?"

"They work harder than I do. Why all the questions? Your captain said the Sunset Towers explosions were just fireworks."

"Sure they were, but bombers have a funny habit of going in for bigger and bigger bangs. Until they get caught."

Theo had an alibi. He was nowhere near the Wexler apartment the day the third bomb went off. The detective grunted a warning about careless chemistry, but Theo had already learned his lesson. "Ouch!"

■ ■ ■ ■ ■ ■ ■ ■ ■ ■ ■ ■

At last the coffee shop owner himself delivered the up order. The judge came right to the point. "Mr. Theodorakis, tell me about your relationship with Violet Westing. I have reason to believe a life is in danger or I would not ask."

It was a question he had expected. "I grew up in Westingtown where my father was a factory foreman. Violet Westing and I were, what you'd call, childhood sweethearts. We planned to get married someday, when I could afford it, but her mother broke us up. She wanted Violet to marry somebody important."

The judge had to interrupt. "Her mother? Are you saying it was Mrs. Westing who arranged the marriage, not Sam Westing?"

George Theodorakis nodded. "That's right. Sam Westing tried to involve Violet in his business. I guess he hoped she'd take over the paper company one day; but she had her heart set on being a teacher. Besides, Violet didn't have much of a business sense. After that her father never paid her much attention."

"Go on." The judge held the witness in her stare.

The subject was becoming painful, and Mr. Theodorakis faltered several times in the telling. "Mrs. Westing handpicked that politician—probably figured the guy would end up in the White House and her daughter would be First Lady. But Violet thought he was nothing but a cheap political hack, a cheap crook. Violet was a gentle person, an only child. She couldn't turn against her mother, she couldn't face marrying that guy. . . . I guess she couldn't find any way out, except . . . Mrs. Westing sort of went off her rocker after Violet's death, and I . . . well, it was a long time ago."

"Thank you, Mr. Theodorakis," the judge said, ending the interrogation. The man had a different life now, different loves, different problems. "Thank you, you have been a big help."

Sandy was now able to complete the entry:

● THEODORAKIS

THEO THEODORAKIS. Age: 17. High-school senior. Works in family coffee shop. Wants to be a writer. Seems lonely; can't find anyone to play chess with.

CHRISTOS THEODORAKIS. Age: 15. Younger brother of above. Confined to wheelchair; disease struck about four years ago. Knows a lot about birds. *Westing connection:* Father was childhood sweetheart of Sam Westing's daughter (who looked like Angela Wexler). Mrs. Westing broke up the affair. She wanted daughter to marry somebody else, but Violet Westing killed herself before the wedding. Neither parents of above are heirs.

"I hear the new medicine they're trying out on Chris is doing some good," Sandy reported. "But the poor kid needs more help than medicine. He's real smart, you know. Chris could have a real future, be a scientist or a professor, even; but it will take a pile of money, more money than his folks could ever make, to put him through college with a handicap like that."

"The parents interest me more," the judge said. "Why are they not heirs?"

Sandy had some thought on that, too. "Maybe Sam Westing didn't want to embarrass George Theodorakis, him being married and all. Or maybe Westing figured he'd be too busy with his coffee shop to stay in the game. Or maybe Westing blamed him for his daughter's death, figuring they should have eloped."

"No, if Sam Westing blamed Mr. Theodorakis, he would have made him an heir in this miserable game," the judge replied. "There are too many maybe's here, which is what Sam Westing planned. We must not allow ourselves to be distracted from the real issue: Which heir did Sam Westing want punished?"

"The person who hurt him most?" Sandy guessed.

"And who would that be?"

"The person who caused his daughter's death?"

"Exactly, Mr. McSouthers. Sam Westing plotted against the person he held responsible for his daughter's suicide, the person who forced Violet Westing to marry a man she loathed."

"Mrs. Westing? But that's not possible, Judge. Mrs. Westing is not one of the heirs."

"I think she is, Mr. McSouthers. The former wife of Sam Westing *must* be one of the heirs. Mrs. Westing is the answer, and whoever she is, she is the one we have to protect."

■ THE FOURTH BOMB ■

21

THE DOOR TO apartment 2c opened. Flora Baumbach screamed, and Turtle flung herself on the pile of money they had been counting.

It was Theo, not the thief. "Can I borrow your bike for a few hours? It's very important." Theo was not a runner like Doug, who was fuming about his being so late. He needed the bicycle to follow Otis Amber, right now.

Turtle stared at him in stony silence.

"I didn't make that sign in the elevator; besides, you already kicked me for it. Please, Turtle." She still wouldn't answer, punk kid. "I had a long talk with the police today, but I refused to tell them who the bomber was."

"What's that supposed to mean?"

What does she think it means? It means that he and everybody else knows that Turtle is the bomber. "Never mind. Can I have your bike or not?"

"Why do you want it?"

Theo ground his teeth. Take it easy; anger won't help any more than blackmail did. Try being a good guy. "I saw Angela in the hospital today. She sends her regards."

"What's that supposed to mean?"

"You let me have that bike, Turtle Wexler, or—or else!"

Turtle did not have to ask what "or else" meant: police—bomber—Angela, but how did Theo find out? "Here!" She threw the padlock key across the room and waited for him to rush out before she let go of the money.

"He's such a nice boy," Flora Baumbach remarked.

"Sure," Turtle replied, dialing the telephone number of the hospital. "Angela Wexler, room 325."

"Room 325 is not accepting any calls."

Turtle hung up the phone. If Theo knew, others knew. Angela had set off those fireworks wanting to get caught, but it was different now. Now she was confused, now she was just plain scared. They could force a confession out of her in no time, the guilt was right there staring out of those big blue eyes. Maybe they're questioning her now. "Baba, I'm not feeling so good; I think I'll go home to bed."

■ ■ ■ ■ ■ ■ ■ ■ ■ ■ ■ ■

Weaving through rush-hour traffic on Turtle's bike, Theo trailed the bus to a seamy downtown district across the railroad tracks where Crow and Otis got off. Skid Row. The pair wandered through the dimly lit, littered, and stinking street, bending over grimy bums asleep in doorways, raising them to their unsteady feet, and leading the ragtag procession into a decaying storefront. Paint was peeling off the letters on the window: Good Salvation Soup Kitchen.

A drunken wreck of a man lurched into Theo, who put a quarter into the filthy outstretched hand, more out of fright than charity.

Snatches of hymn-singing drifted toward him as the last of the stragglers staggered through the door. Theo crossed the narrow street and pressed his nose against the steamy soup-kitchen window. Rows of wretched souls sat hunched on wooden benches. Crow stood before them in her neat black dress, her hands raised toward the crumbling ceiling. Behind her Otis Amber stirred a boiling mess in a big iron pot.

Theo pedaled back to Sunset Towers at a furious pace. Whatever brought Crow and Otis Amber to these lower depths was none of his business. He hated himself for spying. He hated Sam Westing and his dirty money and his dirty game. Theo felt as dirty as the derelicts he spied on. Dirtier.

■ ■ ■ ■ ■ ■ ■ ■ ■ ■ ■ ■

The judge thought they had finished with the heirs.

"Not quite," the doorman said.

● McSOUTHERS

ALEXANDER MCSOUTHERS. Called Sandy. Age: 65. Born: Edinburgh, Scotland. Immigrated to Wisconsin, age 3. Education: eighth grade. Jobs: mill worker, union organizer, prizefighter, doorman. Married, six children, two grandchildren.
Westing connection: Worked in Westing Paper plant 20 years. Fired by Sam Westing himself for trying to organize the workers. No pension.

Sandy turned to a blank page, pushed his taped glasses up the broken bridge of his nose, and looked at the judge. "Name?"

It had not seemed sporting to investigate one's own partner, but McSouthers was right, this was a Westing game. Of course, she had kept some facts from him about the other heirs, but only because she did not trust his blabbering. "Josie-Jo Ford, with a hyphen between Josie and Jo."

"Age?"

"Forty-two. Education: Columbia; law degree, Harvard." The judge waited for the doorman to enter the information in his slow, cramped lettering. He had to be meticulous in order to prove he was better than his eighth-grade education. It's a pity he had not gone further, he was quite a clever man.

"Jobs?"

"Assistant district attorney. Judge: family court, state supreme court, appellate division. *Appellate* has two *p*'s and two *l*'s. Never married, no children."

"Westing connection?"

The judge paused, then spoke so rapidly Sandy had to stop taking notes. "My mother was a servant in the Westing household, my father worked for the railroad and was the gardener on his days off."

"You mean you lived in the Westing house?" Sandy asked with obvious surprise. "You knew the Westings?"

"I barely saw Mrs. Westing. Violet was a few years younger than I, doll-like and delicate. She was not allowed to play with other children. Especially the skinny, long-legged, black daughter of the servants."

"Gee, you must have been lonely, Judge, having nobody to play with."

"I played with Sam Westing—chess. Hour after hour I sat staring down at that chessboard. He lectured me, he insulted me, and he won every game." The judge thought of their last game: She had been so excited about taking his queen, only to have the master checkmate her in the next move. Sam Westing had deliberately sacrificed his queen and she had fallen for it. "Stupid child, you can't have a brain in that frizzy head to make a move like that." Those were the last words he ever said to her.

The judge continued: "I was sent to boarding school when I was twelve. My parents visited me at school when they could, but I never set foot in the Westing house again, not until two weeks ago."

"Your folks must have really worked hard," Sandy said. "An education like that costs a fortune."

"Sam Westing paid for my education. He saw that I was accepted into the best schools, probably arranged for my first job, perhaps more, I don't know."

"That's the first decent thing I've heard about the old man."

"Hardly decent, Mr. McSouthers. It was to Sam Westing's advantage to have a judge in his debt. Needless to say, I have excused myself from every case remotely connected with Westing affairs."

"You're awfully hard on yourself, Judge. And on him. Maybe Westing paid for your education 'cause you were smart and needy, and you did all the rest by yourself."

"This is getting us nowhere, Mr. McSouthers. Just write: Westing connection: Education financed by Sam Westing. Debt never repaid."

■ ■ ■ ■ ■ ■ ■ ■ ■ ■ ■ ■

Theo, upset over his Skid Row snooping, took out his anger on the up button, poking it, jabbing it, until the elevator finally made its way down to the lobby. Slowly the door slid open. He stared down at the sparking, sputtering arsenal, yelled and belly-flopped to the carpet as rockets whizzed out of the elevator, inches above his head. Boom! Boom! A blinding flash of white fire streaked through the lobby, through the open entrance door, and burst into a chrysanthemum of color in the night sky. Then the elevator door closed.

The bomber had made one mistake. The last rocket blasted off when the elevator returned to the third floor. Boom!

By the time the bomb squad reached the scene (by way of the

stairs), the smoke had cleared, but the young girl was still huddled on the hallway floor, tears streaming down her turtle-like face.

"For heaven's sake, say something," her mother said. "Tell me where it hurts."

The pain was too great to be put into words. Five inches of Turtle's braid were badly singed.

Grace Wexler attacked the policeman. "Nothing but a childish prank, you said. Some childish prank; both my children cruelly injured, almost killed. Maybe now you'll do something, now that it's too late."

Unshaken by the mother's anger, the policeman held up the sign that had been taped to the elevator wall:

THE BOMBER STRIKES AGAIN!!!

On the reverse side was a handwritten composition: "How I Spent My Summer Vacation" by Turtle Wexler.

Grace grabbed the theme and shook it at her daughter, who was being rocked in Flora Baumbach's arms. "Somebody stole this from you, didn't they, Turtle? You couldn't have done such an awful thing, not to Angela, not to your own sister, could you Turtle? Could you?"

"I want to see a lawyer," Turtle replied.

■ ■ ■ ■ ■ ■ ■ ■ ■ ■ ■

The bomb squad, faced with six hours' overtime filling out forms and delivering the delinquent to a juvenile detention facility, decided it was best for all concerned to escort the prisoner to apartment 4D and place her in the custody of Judge Ford.

Judge Ford put on her black robe and seated herself behind the desk. Before her stood a downcast child looking very sad and very sorry. Not at all like the Turtle she knew. "You surprise me,

Turtle Wexler. I thought you were too smart to commit such a dangerous, destructive, and stupid act."

"Yes, ma'am."

"Why did you do it, Turtle? To hurt someone, to get even with someone?"

"No, ma'am."

Of course not. Turtle kicked shins, she was not the type to bottle up her anger. "You do understand that a child would not receive as harsh a penalty as an adult would? That there would be no permanent criminal record?"

"Yes, ma'am. I mean, no, ma'am."

She was protecting someone. She had set off the fireworks in the elevator to divert suspicion from the real bomber. But who was the real bomber? Nothing to do but drag it out of her, name by name, starting with the least likely. "Are you protecting Angela?"

"No!"

The judge was astounded by the excited response. Angela could not be the bomber, not that sweet, pretty thing. Thing? Is that how she regarded that young woman, as a thing? And what had she ever said to her except 'I hear you're getting married, Angela' or 'How pretty you look, Angela.' Had anyone asked about her ideas, her hopes, her plans? If I had been treated like that I'd have used dynamite, not fireworks; no, I would have just walked out and kept right on going. But Angela was different. "What a senseless thing to do," the judge said aloud.

"Yes, ma'am." Turtle stared down at the carpet, wondering if she had given Angela away.

Judge Ford rose and placed an arm around Turtle's bony shoulders. She had never wished for a sister until this moment. "Turtle, will you give me your word that you will never play with fireworks again?"

"Yes, ma'am."

"While we're at it, do you have anything else to confess?"

"Yes, ma'am. I was in the Westing house the night Mr. Westing died."

"Good lord, child, sit down and tell me."

Turtle began with the purple-waves story, went on to the whisperings, the bedded-down corpse, the dropped peanut butter and jelly sandwiches and her mother's cross, and ended with the twenty-four dollars she had won.

"Did either you or Doug Hoo call the police?"

"No, ma'am, we were too scared, we just ran. Is that a crime?"

The judge said it was a criminal offense to conceal a murder.

"But Mr. Westing didn't look murdered," Turtle argued. "He looked asleep, like he did in the coffin. He looked like a wax dummy."

"A wax dummy?"

Now Turtle was the one surprised by the excited response. The judge thinks it might have been a real wax dummy, not a corpse at all. Then what happened to Sam Westing?

The judge regained her composure. "Not reporting a dead body is a violation of the health code, but I wouldn't worry about it. Is there anything else, Turtle?"

"Yes, ma'am," Turtle replied, glancing at the portable bar. "Could I have a little bourbon?"

"What?"

"Just a little. On a piece of cotton to put in my cavity. My tooth hurts something awful."

Relieved at not having a juvenile alcoholic on her hands, Judge Ford prepared the home remedy. "Is that better? Good. You may go home now."

Home meant going to Baba. Baba loved her no matter what, and Turtle didn't care if the others thought she was the bomber—except Sandy. He was walking toward her right now, walking his bouncy walk, but not smiling. Sandy is disappointed in her, he thinks she hurt her own sister, he doesn't want to be friends anymore.

"How's my girl?" Sandy said, cupping his hand under her chin and lifting her head. "Whew! Hitting the bottle again?"

"It's just bourbon on cotton for my toothache."

"Yeah, I've heard that one before."

"Honest, Saaan-eee." Turtle was pointing inside her wide-open mouth.

The doorman peered in. "Wow, that's some cavity, it looks like the Grand Canyon. Tomorrow morning you're going to see my dentist—no back talk. He's very gentle, you won't feel a thing. Promise you'll go?"

Turtle nodded.

Sandy smiled. "Good, then down to business. My wife's having a birthday tomorrow. I thought one of your gorgeous striped candles would make a swell present."

"There's only one candle left," Turtle replied. "It's the best of the lot. Six super colors. I spent a lot of time making it; that's why I wouldn't part with it. But since it's for your wife's birthday, Sandy, I'll let you have it for only five dollars. And I won't charge you sales tax."

■ ■ ■ ■ ■ ■ ■ ■ ■ ■ ■

"Try not to stick your fanny out so far," Angela said from her chair. Now that Sydelle Pulaski depended on crutches, she lurched clumsily, hobbled by old habits.

"Just keep reading those clues." The secretary straightened, shoulders back, stomach in, until her next step.

With their telephone switched off and Contagious Disease added to the No Visitors sign, the bomb victims had privacy at last. Sydelle had twice read the entire will aloud. Now Angela, her hands unbandaged, was reshuffling the collected clues.

GRAINS   SPACIOUS   GRACE   GOOD   HOOD
WITH   BEAUTIFUL   MAJESTIES   FROM   THY   PURPLE
WAVES   ON(NO)   MOUNTAIN

"Again," Sydelle ordered. "Change them around and read either the word *on* or the word *no;* both together are confusing."

GOOD   SPACIOUS   GRAINS   WITH   GRACE
ON   THY   PURPLE   MOUNTAIN   HOOD   WAVES
FROM   MAJESTIES   BEAUTIFUL

"Shh!" Someone was at the door. Angela picked up the note that was slipped underneath.

> *My darling Angela: I guess the sign on the door*
> *means I should stay away, too. I understand. We*
> *both need time to think things over. I'll wait. I love*
> *you—Denton*

"What does it say, what does it say?" Sydelle pressed, but Angela read only the postscript aloud:

> P.S. *You have another admirer. Chris wants to give*
> *you and Ms. Pulaski one of our clues. (Flora*
> *Baumbach has seen it, too.) The word is* plain.

"Like an airplane?" Sydelle asked.
"No, plain, like ordinary. Like the wide open plains."
"Plains, grains. Quick, Angela, read the clues again."

GOOD   HOOD   FROM   SPACIOUS   PLAIN
GRAINS   ON   WITH   BEAUTIFUL   WAVES
GRACE   THY   PURPLE   MOUNTAIN   MAJESTIES

"That's it, Angela. We got it, we got it!" Sydelle could barely control her excitement. "The will said, *Sing in praise of this gen-*

erous land. The will said, *May God thy gold refine.* America, Angela, America! *Purple mountain majesties,* Angela. Whoopee!"

Fortunately Sydelle Pulaski was close to the bed when she threw her crutches in the air.

■ LOSERS, WINNERS ■

22

SATURDAY MORNING, a new message was posted in the elevator:

> I, TURTLE WEXLER, CONFESS TO THOSE
> FOUR BOMBS. I'M SORRY, IT WAS A DUMB
> THING TO DO AND I WON'T DO IT AGAIN.
> BUT! I AM NOT THE BURGLAR AND I NEVER
> MURDERED ANYBODY, EVER.
>   YOUR FRIEND, TURTLE
> P.S. TO MAKE UP FOR SCARING YOU, I WILL
> TREAT EVERYBODY HERE TO AN EXQUISITE
> CHINESE CUISINE DINNER WHEN I WIN THE
> INHERITANCE.

"Poor Grace," Mr. Hoo said. "One daughter almost killed, the other one a bomber. Smart-aleck kid, first she blows up my kitchen, then she advertises my cuisine. Win the inheritance—ha! Maybe I'm lucky my son is a dumb jock."

"Boom," Madame Hoo said happily. She knew where they were going. Always on the day when Doug ate six eggs for breakfast, he ran around and around a big track and people clapped and gave him a shiny medal. Doug was so proud of his medals. She would never take them, not even the gold one, not even if it took her two more years to pay to go back to China. No, she would never take Doug's medals, and she would never sell that wonderful clock with the mouse who wears gloves and points to the time.

"You must be out of your mind, Jake Wexler. Go to a track meet with all those people pointing at me, snickering, saying: 'Look, there she is, the mother of Cain and Abel.' I'm not even sure I have the nerve to show my face at the Westing house tonight."

"Come on, Grace, it'll do you good." The podiatrist urged his reluctant wife down the third-floor hall. "Stop thinking about yourself for a change, think how poor Turtle must feel."

"Don't ever mention that child to me again, not after what she did to Angela. I never told you this, Jake, but I've always had a sinking sensation that the hospital mixed up the babies when Turtle was born."

"It's no wonder she wanted to blow us all up."

Grace's despair exploded in anger. "Oh, I get it, you're putting the blame on me. If you had given her a good talking to about kicking people when I asked, she might not have ended up a common criminal."

"Whatever became of that fun-loving woman I married, what was her name—Gracie Windkloppel?"

Grace quickly looked around to see if anyone had overheard that ugly name, but they were in the elevator, alone. "Oh, I know what people think," she complained. "Poor Jake Wexler, good guy, everybody's friend, married to that uppity would-be decorator. Well, Angela's not going to have to scrimp and save to make ends meet; she's going to marry a real doctor. I'll see to that."

"Sure you will, Grace, you'll see that Angela doesn't marry a loser like her father." A real doctor, she says. A podiatrist is a "real" doctor—well, it is these days, but when he went to school it was different. He could have gone back, taken more courses, but he was married by then, a father—oh, who's he kidding. Gracie's right, he is a loser. Next she'll mention having to give up her family because she married a Jew—no, she never brings that up, Grace with all her faults would never do that.

The elevator door opened to the lobby. Grace turned to her silent, sad-eyed husband, the loser. "Oh, Jake, what's happening to us? What's happening to me? Maybe they're right, maybe I'm not a nice person."

Jake pressed the CLOSE DOOR button and took his sobbing wife into his arms. "It's all right, Gracie, we're going home."

The doors opened on the second floor. "Mom! What's the matter with her, Daddy, she's crying? Gee, Mom, I'm sorry, it was just a few fireworks." If her mother ever found out who the real bomber was, she'd really go to pieces.

Turtle looked even more like a turtle today with her sad little face peering out of the kerchief tied under her small chin. "Let go of the door, Turtle," Jake said. "And have a good time at the track meet. You, too, Mrs. Baumbach."

Track meet? They weren't going to a track meet. And they sure were not going to have a good time.

Grace was still sobbing on Jake's shoulder as he led her into their apartment.

"Mother, what's the matter? What's wrong with her, Dad?"

"Nothing, Angela, your mother's just having a good cry. Why don't you and Ms. Pulaski leave us alone for a while."

"Come, Angela," Sydelle said, prodding her with the tip of one of her mismatched crutches. "We have some painting to do."

Angela looked back at the embracing couple; her father's face was buried in her weeping mother's tousled hair. They had not asked how she got home from the hospital (by taxi), they had not asked if she was still in pain (not much), they had not even peeked under the bandage to see if a scar was forming on her cheek (there was). Angela was on her own. Well, that's what she wanted, wasn't it? Yes, yes it was! She uttered a short laugh, and her hand flew up to the pain in her face.

"Do I look funny or something?"

"No, I wasn't laughing at you, Sydelle, I'd never laugh at you. It's just that suddenly everything seemed all right."

"It's all right, all right," her partner replied, unlocking the four locks on her apartment door. "Tonight's the night we're going to win it all."

Were they? The will said look for a name. They had a song, not a name.

"'O beautiful for spacious skies,'" Sydelle began to sing, "'For purple waves of grain.'"

"Not purple," Angela corrected her, "amber. 'For amber waves of grain.'"

Amber!

■ ■ ■ ■ ■ ■ ■ ■ ■ ■ ■

Judge Ford paced the floor. Tonight Sam Westing would wreak his revenge unless she could prevent it. If she was right, the person in danger was the former Mrs. Westing. And if Turtle was right about the wax dummy, Sam Westing himself might be there to watch the fun.

There was a knock on her door. The judge was surprised to see Denton Deere, even more surprised when he wheeled Chris Theodorakis into her apartment. "Hello, Judge. Everybody else in the building is going to the track meet, it seems. I passed Sandy on the way out and he said you wouldn't mind having Chris for part of the afternoon. I've got to get back to the hospital."

"Hello, Judge F-Ford." Chris held out a steady hand which the judge shook.

"You're looking well, Chris."

"The m-medicine helped a lot."

"It's a big step forward," the intern said. Wrong word, the kid may never leave that wheelchair. "An even more effective medication is now in the developmental stage." That really sounded pompous. "Well, so long, Chris. See you tonight. Thanks, Judge."

"He knows lots of b-big words," Chris said.

"Yes, he certainly does," Judge Ford replied. What was she going to do with this boy here? She had so much to think about, so much to plan.

"You c-can work. I'll birdwatch," Chris offered, wheeling to the window, his binoculars banging against his thin chest.

"Good idea." The judge returned to her desk to study the newspaper clippings. Mrs. Westing: a tall, thin woman. She may no longer be thin, but she would still be tall. About sixty years old. If Sam Westing's former wife was one of the heirs, she had to be Crow.

"Look!" Chris shouted, startling the judge into dropping her files to the floor. She rushed to his side, thinking he needed help. "Look up there, Judge. Isn't it b-beautiful?"

High in the fall sky a V of geese was flying south. Yes, it was a beautiful sight. "Those are geese," the judge explained.

"C-canada goose (*Branta c-canadensis*)," Chris replied.

The judge was impressed, but she had work to do. Stooping to gather the dropped clippings, she was confronted by the face of Sam Westing. The photograph had been taken fifteen years ago. Those piercing eyes, the Vandyke beard, that short beaked nose (like a turtle's). The wax dummy in the coffin had been molded in the former image of Sam Westing as he had looked fifteen years ago—not as he looked now. She searched the folder. No recent photographs, no hospital records, no death certificate, just the accident report from the state highway police: Dr. Sidney Sikes suffered a crushed leg and Samuel W. Westing had severe facial injuries. Facial injuries! It was the face that had disappeared fifteen years ago, not the man. Westing had a different face, a face remodeled by plastic surgery. A different face and a different name.

Now what? Her gaze rested on her charge at the window. Feeling her eyes, Chris turned around. The boy has a nice smile.

■ ■ ■ ■ ■ ■ ■ ■ ■ ■ ■ ■

"I hope you are better at filling cavities than making false teeth," Turtle said, gripping the arms of the dentist's chair. In a glass cabinet against the wall three rows of dentures grinned at her with crooked teeth, overlapping teeth, notched teeth.

"Those faults are what makes the dentures look real," the dentist explained. "Nothing in nature is quite perfect, you know. Now, open your mouth wide. Wider."

"Ow!" Turtle screamed before the probe touched tooth.

"Just relax, young lady, I'll tell you when to say 'Ow!'"

Turtle tried to think about other things. False teeth, buck-teeth—that rotten bucktoothed Barney Northrup stopped by this morning to tell the Wexlers they would have to pay for all the damage done by the bombs. Barney Northrup had called her parents "irresponsible" and had called her something worse, much worse. He sure was surprised by that kick; it was her hardest one ever.

"Now you can say 'Ow!'" The dentist unclipped the towel from her shoulder.

Turtle passed her tongue over the drilled tooth. She had not felt a thing, but the real pain was yet to come. Flora Baumbach was taking her to the beauty parlor to have her singed hair cut off.

■ ■ ■ ■ ■ ■ ■ ■ ■ ■ ■ ■

College teams from five states competed in the first indoor track meet of the season, but the big event, the mile run, was won by a high-school senior.

"That's my boy, that's my Doug," Mr. Hoo shouted, one voice among thousands cheering the youngster on his victory lap.

Cameras flashed as Doug posed, smiling broadly, index fingers high in the air. "I owe it all to my dad," he told reporters, and cameras flashed again as Doug flung an arm around the proud Mr. Hoo. Just wait until the next Olympics, the inventor thought. With Doug's feet and my innersoles, he'll run them all to the ground.

Later that evening Madame Hoo, chattering in unintelligible Chinese, made it known that she wanted Doug to wear his prize to the Westing house. Standing on tiptoe she placed the ribbon over his bent head and patted the shiny gold medal in place on his chest. "Good boy," she said in English.

■ ■ ■ ■ ■ ■ ■ ■ ■ ■ ■

A saddened Sandy returned to apartment 4D. "Hi, Chris. Did you talk to him, Judge?"

"Talk to whom?"

"Barney Northrup. He was waiting at the front door when I got back from the track meet, mad as a wet cat. Said he had lots of complaints about me—never being on duty, drinking on the job—lies like that. He fired me right on the spot. I told him you wanted to see him, figuring you might put in a good word so he'd let me stay on."

"No, Mr. McSouthers, I'm sorry, but I haven't seen Barney Northrup since I rented this apartment." Barney Northrup, was that Westing's disguise: false buckteeth, slick black wig, pasted-on moustache?

"Well, it's not the first time I got fired for no cause." The dejected doorman blew his nose loudly in a Westing Man-Sized Hankie. "Hey Chris, bet you don't know the Latin name of the red-headed woodpecker."

That was a hard one. Chris had to say *Melanerpes erythro-cephalus* very slowly.

"Some smart kid, hey, Judge? Chris, the judge and I have a little business to discuss. Excuse us for a minute."

Judge Ford joined the doorman in the kitchen. "Our game plan is this, Mr. McSouthers. We give no answer. No answer at all. Our duty is to protect Westing's ex-wife."

"Crow?" Sandy guessed.

"That's right."

"There's something else that's been bothering me, Judge. I know it sounds crazy, but, well, I found out Otis Amber doesn't live in the grocer's basement, and he's not as dumb as he pretends. He's a snoop and a troublemaker and I don't think he is who he says he is."

"And who do you think Otis Amber is?" the judge asked.

"Sam Westing!"

Judge Ford leaned against the sink and pressed her head against the cabinet. If Sandy was correct, she had played right into the man's hands—Sam Westing's hands.

■ ■ ■ ■ ■ ■ ■ ■ ■ ■ ■ ■

"C'mon, Crow, you always like to get there early to open the door for people."

Crow had stopped in the middle of the steep road to stare up at the Westing house. "I've got a funny feeling that something evil is waiting for me up there, Otis. It's a bad house, full of misery and sin. He's still there, you know."

"Sam Westing is dead and buried. Come on, if we don't go we gotta give the money back, and we already spent it on the soup kitchen."

"I feel his presence, Otis. He's looking for a murderer, Violet's murderer."

"Stop scaring yourself with crazy notions, you sound like you're on the bottle again."

Crow strode ahead.

"I didn't mean that, Crow, honest. Look up there at that moon. Isn't it romantic?"

"Somebody's in real danger, Otis, and I think it's me."

23

LAWYER PLUM WAS there and one pair of heirs when Otis Amber danced into the game room. "He-he-he, the Turtle's lost its tail, I see."

Turtle slumped low in her chair. Flora Baumbach thought the short, sleek haircut was adorable, especially the way it swept forward over her little chin, but Turtle did not want to look adorable. She wanted to look mean.

The dressmaker fumbled past the wad of money in her handbag. "Here, Alice, I thought you might like to see this."

Turtle glanced at the old snapshot. It's Baba, all right, except younger. Same dumb smile. Suddenly she sat upright.

"That's my daughter, Rosalie," Flora Baumbach said. "She must have been nine or ten when that picture was taken."

Rosalie was squat and square and squinty, her protruding tongue was too large for her mouth, her head lolled to one side. "I think I would have liked her, Baba," Turtle said. "Rosalie looks like she was a very happy person. She must have been nice to have around."

Thump-thump, thump-thump. "Here come the victims," Sydelle Pulaski announced.

Angela greeted her sister with a wave of her crimson-streaked, healing hand. Turtle had convinced her not to confess: It would mean a criminal record, it would kill their mother, and no one would believe her anyhow. "I like your haircut."

"Thanks," Turtle replied. Now Angela had to love her forever.

Most of the heirs had to comment on Turtle's hair. "You look like a real businesswoman," Sandy said. "Well, that's an improvement," Denton Deere said. "You look n-nice," Chris said. Only Theo, bent over the chessboard, said nothing. White had moved the king's bishop since the last meeting. It was his move.

At last the stares turned from Turtle's hair to a more surprising sight. Judge Ford strode in as regally as an African princess, her noble head swathed in a turban, her tall body draped in yards of handprinted cloth. She slipped a note to Denton Deere then sailed to her place at table four. Goggle-eyed Otis Amber was speechless; they all were, except for Sandy. "Gee, that's a nifty outfit, Judge. Is that what you call ethnic?"

The judge did not reply.

Applaud, the local hero has arrived! Doug raised his arms, pointing his index fingers to the flaking gilt ceiling in the I'm-number-one sign, and acknowledged the clapping with a victory lap around the room.

"Here come the Wexlers," Mr. Hoo remarked, seating his puzzled wife at table one.

Turtle exchanged an anxious glance with Angela. The last time they saw their mother she was crying her head off; now the tears were gone from her bleary eyes, but she was staggering, giggling, her hair was a mess.

"Sorry we're late," Jake apologized. "We lost track of time." They had been clinking wineglasses in a small cafe (the cafe they used to go to before they were married), toasting good times. They had had many good times together, many good memories shared, it seems—three big wine bottles full.

Happy Grace waved at the heirs. She felt so wonderful, so overflowing with love for Jake, for everybody.

"Hi, Mom," Turtle called.

Grace blinked at a young short-haired girl. "Who's that?"

Jake greeted his partner with a "How are you this fine day?"

"Doug win," replied Madame Hoo.

Having opened the door to the last of the heirs, a tense and troubled Crow took her seat next to Otis Amber. Ghost-threatened, she waited for the unseen.

"Hey, lawyer, can we open these?" Otis Amber shouted, waving an envelope. A similar envelope lay on each table.

His forehead creased with uncertainty, Ed Plum fumbled through his papers. "I guess so" was his opinion.

Cheers erupted as the heirs withdrew the checks.

Again Judge Ford signed her name to the ten-thousand-dollar check and handed it to the doorman. "Here you are, Mr. McSouthers, this should tide you over until you find another job."

Sandy's heartfelt thanks were muffled by Sydelle Pulaski's loud "Shhhh!"

"Shhhhhhhh!" Grace Wexler mimicked, then she dropped her head into her crossed arms on the table and fell asleep to the sound of the lawyer's throat-clearing coughs.

> TWELFTH • *Welcome again to the Westing house. By now you have received a second check for ten thousand dollars. Before the day is done you may have won more, much more.*
>
> *Table by table, each pair will be called to give one, and only one, answer. The lawyer will record your response in case of a dispute. He does not know the answer. It is up to you.*

1 • MADAME SUN LIN HOO, *cook*
   JAKE WEXLER, *bookie*

Bookie? He really must have been distracted when he signed that receipt. Jake studied the five clues on the table:

OF   AMERICA   AND   GOD   ABOVE

Even knowing his wife's clues didn't help; he'd have to gamble on a long shot. "Say something," he said to his partner.

"Boom!" said Madame Hoo.

Ed Plum wrote *Table One: Boom.*

2 • FLORA BAUMBACH, *dressmaker*
   TURTLE WEXLER, *financier*

Turtle read a prepared statement: "In spite of the fact that the stock market dropped thirty points since we received our ten thousand dollars, we have increased our capital to $11,587.50, an appreciation of twenty-seven point eight percent calculated on an annual basis."

Flora Baumbach slapped a wad of bills on the table and two clinking quarters. "In cash," she said.

Ed Plum asked them to repeat their answer.

"Table two's answer is $11,587.50."

Sandy applauded. Turtle took a bow.

3 • CHRISTOS THEODORAKIS, *ornithologist*
    D. DENTON DEERE, *intern*

Ornithologist? His brother must have given him that fancy title when he filled in the receipt. Maybe he would become an ornithologist someday. He was a lucky person, getting that medicine and all. He didn't want to accuse anybody, not Judge Ford (apartment 4D), not Otis (grain) Amber, not the limper (just about everybody limped at one time or other—today Sandy was limping). "I think Mr. Westing is a g-good man," Chris said aloud. "I think his last wish was to do g-good deeds. He g-gave me a p-partner who helped me. He g-gave everybody the p-perfect p-partner to m-make friends."

"What is table three's answer?" the lawyer asked.

Denton Deere replied. "Our answer is: Mr. Westing was a good man."

4 • J. J. FORD, *judge*
    ALEXANDER MCSOUTHERS, *fired*

"We don't have an answer," the ex-doorman responded as planned.

The judge looked at table three. Denton Deere, her note in his hand, shook his head, which meant: No, Otis Amber has not had plastic surgery done on his face. The judge turned to table six. Otis Amber could not be Sam Westing (she was right to have trusted him). But Crow is expecting something to happen. Crow knows she is the answer, she knows she is the one.

5 ● GRACE WINDKLOPPEL WEXLER, *restaurateur*
   JAMES HOO, *inventor*

Grace raised her head. "Did someone say Windkloppel?"

"Never mind Windkloppel, it's our turn," Hoo snarled. The lawyer got names and positions all fouled up, and I've got a drunk for a partner. He prodded Grace to her feet.

Faces were swirling, the floor was swaying. Grace grabbed the edge of the floating table and gave her answer in a thick, slurred voice. "The newly decorated restaurant, Hoo's On First, the eatery of athletes, will hold its grand reopening on Sunday. Specialty of the day: fruited sea bass on purple waves."

Grace sat down where the chair wasn't. Turtle gasped, Angela looked away, the heirs tittered as Jake helped his wife up from the floor.

"What is table five's answer, please?" the lawyer pressed.

"Ed Plum," said Mr. Hoo.

"Yes, sir?"

"That's our answer: Ed Plum."

"Oh."

6 ● BERTHE ERICA CROW, *mother*
   OTIS AMBER, *deliverer*

"Mother? Did I write *mother*?" Crow mumbled.

"Is that your answer?" Ed Plum asked.

"I don't know," Otis Amber replied. "Is 'mother' our answer,

Crow?" He could have sworn she had again signed the receipt *Good Salvation Soup Kitchen*.

Crow repeated "mother," and that's what the lawyer wrote down.

7 ● DOUG HOO, *champ*
   THEO THEODORAKIS, *writer*

Their clues: a chemical formula for an explosive and the letters *o-t-i-s*. Doug, basking in glory, didn't care. Theo stood, turned to the man he was about to accuse, and saw the scene in the soup kitchen, saw Otis Amber cooking soup for the dirty, hungry men. "No answer," Theo said sitting down.

8 ● SYDELLE PULASKI, *victim*
   ANGELA WEXLER, *person*

Sydelle was dressed for the occasion in red and white stripes. Leaning on crutches decorated with white stars on a field of blue to match the cast on her ankle, she hummed into a pitch pipe and began to sing one note above the pitch she played.

> O beautiful for spacious skies,
> For amber waves of grain,
> For purple mountain majesties
> Above the fruited plain.

What a spectacle she made, her wide rear end sticking out, singing in that tuneless, nasal voice. The derisive smiles soon faded as, pair by pair, the heirs heard their code words sung.

> America! America!
> God shed His grace on thee,
> And crown thy good with brotherhood
> From sea to shining sea.

"Such a beautiful song," Grace Wexler slurred, but the others sat in somber silence. Even Turtle thought table eight had won.

"What is your answer?" Ed Plum asked.

"Our answer," Sydelle Pulaski announced with certainty, "is Otis Amber."

The heirs listened to the lawyer read the next document, but their eyes stayed fixed on table eight's answer: Otis Amber.

> **THIRTEENTH** • *Okay, folks, there will be a short break before the big winner is announced. Berthe Erica Crow, please rise and go to the kitchen for the refreshments.*

Dazed with fear, Crow rose. The thirteenth section. Thirteen was an unlucky number.

Judge Ford told Sandy to follow her. "Hey, Crow, old pal, do me a favor and fill this for me," he said, handing her his flask as they left through the door. "I'll go on the wagon starting tomorrow. Promise."

Angela left the room, too, concerned over Crow's trance-like state. Turtle followed Angela to make sure she didn't end up in the fireworks room again. The judge remained seated, watching the remaining heirs, who were watching Otis Amber. The delivery boy had had enough of their suspicions; he swept a pointed finger across their range, imitating the sound of a machine gun: "Rat-a-tat-tat-tat-tat."

Crow and Angela came back with two large trays; Turtle returned empty-handed, puzzled but much relieved.

The judge joined Denton Deere and Chris at table three, bringing a plate of small cakes with her. "None of the heirs have had plastic surgery as far as I can tell," the intern remarked. "But your partner sure could have used some."

The judge studied Sandy McSouthers' prizefighter's face as he leaned against the open doorway. Their eyes met and he lifted his flask in salute. "Anybody want a drink?"

"Sure," Grace Wexler replied with a giggle, but Jake gave her a cup of strong black coffee instead.

"We must keep our wits about us, Mr. McSouthers," Judge Ford said, walking toward him. "Sam Westing has not made his final move."

"Nothing like Scotch to clear the head," he replied. He took a long swig, coughed, wiped his mouth on the sleeve of his uniform, and glared at Crow with narrowed, watery eyes.

Theo grinned down at the chess table. White had made another move, a careless move. He licked the cake crumbs from his fingers, wiped his hand on a Westing Paper Tea Napkin, and took his opponent's queen from the board. At least he had won the chess game.

Perched on a corner of table eight, the young lawyer tried to start a conversation with Angela, ignoring Sydelle Pulaski, who twice asked, "Surely *you* must have the answer, Mr. Plum?" She nudged her partner.

"Surely you must have the answer, Mr. Plum," Angela repeated sweetly.

"Oh, of course; at least, I assume I do," he replied. "My instructions are to open the documents one by one at the scheduled time." He checked his watch. "Oops!" He was one minute late.

Ed Plum hurried to the billiard table, tore open the next envelope, and pulled out the document, cutting his finger on the paper's edge.

> FOURTEENTH • *Go directly to the library. Do not pass Go.*

■ **WRONG ALL WRONG** ■

24

GRACE WEXLER CLUNG unsteadily to Mr. Hoo's arm. "Where are we going?"

"Who knows," Hoo replied. "We didn't even pass Go."

Partner sat with partner at the long library table, moaning

with impatience as Ed Plum opened another envelope, removed a tagged key, tried to unlock the top right-hand desk drawer, reread the tag, unlocked the upper left-hand drawer, and found the next document:

FIFTEENTH • *Wrong! All answers are wrong!*

"What!" Sydelle Pulaski cried.

> *I repeat: Wrong! All answers are wrong! Partnerships are canceled; you are on your own. Alone.*
> *The lawyer will leave and return with the authorities at the appointed time. And time is running out. Hurry, find the name before the one who took my life takes another.*
> *Remember: It is not what you have, it's what you don't have that counts.*

Madame Hoo knew from the shifting eyes that a bad person was in the room. She was the bad person. They would find out soon. The crutch lady had her writing-book back, but all those pretty things she was going to sell, they wanted them back, too. She would be punished. Soon.

"How much time do we have?" Turtle asked.

Ed Plum left the library without answering. And locked the door!

"Oh my!" Flora Baumbach ran to the French doors. They opened.

Sydelle Pulaski complained of a chill, and the dressmaker had to shut the doors, but she left them unlatched, just in case.

Mr. Hoo said the tea tasted funny, maybe they had all been poisoned. Denton Deere diagnosed paranoia.

The doorman, who was pacing the room, replied that anyone who was not paranoid, after being told that the murderer would kill again, was really crazy. He stopped to pat Turtle's slumped shoulders. "Cheer up, my friend, the game's not over yet," Sandy whispered. "You still can win. I hope you do."

Otis Amber told everyone to sit where he could watch them.

Theo rose. "I think it's about time we played as a team and shared our clues and shared the inheritance."

With the murderer? Well, all right. Agreed.

Sydelle Pulaski still thought the answer had something to do with "America, the Beautiful." "Does anybody have a clue word that is not in the song?"

"I'm not sure," Doug said mischievously. "Sing it again."

No one cared for that idea. "*It is not what you have, it's what you don't have that counts,*" Jake Wexler reminded them. "Maybe some words in the song are missing from the clues."

That makes sense. "Does anyone have the word *amber*?" Mr. Hoo asked.

"Not again," Otis Amber groaned. "You heard the will, it said all answers were wrong. Well, I was one of the wrong answers."

"But Mr. Westing wrote the will before the game began." Sydelle argued. "Perhaps he assumed we weren't smart enough to find you out so soon."

Judge Ford did not interfere (Otis Amber could take care of himself). She had to be prepared to defend Crow when the time came.

Crow sat with her head bowed, waiting.

No one had the word *amber,* but two pairs had *am* in their clues. "Two *ams* do not an *amber* make," Sydelle declared. "Two *ams* stand for *America, America.*"

"I've got *America,*" Jake Wexler shouted. "I've got *America.*"

Ravings of a madman, Mr. Hoo thought. The podiatrist, could he be the one?

Jake explained in a calmer voice. "The two *ams* could not stand for *America, America,* because one of my clues is *America.*"

Sandy stood, took a long swig from his flask, coughed, then spoke in a hoarse voice. "We're getting nowhere. Why doesn't everybody hand in their clues so Ms. Pulaski can arrange them in order and we can see what's missing?"

Her eyes narrowed with suspicion, the judge watched Sandy collect the clues. "Just write them out again," he said to Turtle, who had eaten the originals. Then he placed the paper squares before the secretary and resumed his seat. What was her partner doing? Why was he playing into Westing's hands? He knows the answer, he knows he's leading the heirs to Crow. Again the judge studied the doorman's battered face: the scars; the bashed-in nose; the hard, blue eyes under those taped spectacles. The baggy uniform. Everyone was given the perfect partner, Chris said. Chris was right. She was paired with the one person who could confound her plans, manipulate her moves, keep her from the truth. Her partner, Sandy McSouthers, was the only heir she had not investigated. Her partner, Sandy McSouthers, was Sam Westing.

■ ■ ■ ■ ■ ■ ■ ■ ■ ■ ■ ■

The secretary quickly arranged the clues in order:

> O BEAUTIFUL FOR SPACIOUS SKIES
> FOR AM   WAVES OF GRAIN
> FOR PURPLE MOUNTAIN MAJESTIES
> ABOVE   FRUITED PLAIN
> AMERICA AM
> GOD SHED HIS GRACE ON THEE
> AND   N THY GOOD WITH BROTHERHOOD
> FROM SEA TO SHINING SEA

"The missing words," Sydelle Pulaski announced, "are *ber, the, erica,* and *crow.* Berthe Erica Crow!"

Crow paled.

Judge Ford stood. "May I have everyone's attention? Thank you. Please listen very carefully to what I have to say.

"We found the answer to Sam Westing's puzzle, now what are we going to do? Remember: We have no evidence of any kind against this unfortunate woman. We don't even have proof that Sam Westing was murdered.

"Can we accuse an innocent woman of a murder that has never been proved? Crow is our neighbor and our helper. Can we condemn her to a life imprisonment just to satisfy our own greed? For money promised in an improbable and illegal will? If so, we are guilty of a far greater crime than the accused. Berthe Erica Crow's only crime is that her name appears in a song. Our crime would be selling—yes, I said selling, selling for profit—the life of an innocent, helpless human being."

The judge paused to let her words sink in, then she turned to her partner. Her voice hardened. "As for the master of this vicious game . . ." She paused. What's happening to him?

"Uh—uh——UHHH!" Sandy's hand flew to his throat. He struggled to his feet, red-faced and gasping, and crashed to the floor in eye-bulging agony.

Jake Wexler and Denton Deere hurried to his aid. Theo pounded on the door, shouting for help. Ed Plum unlocked the door and two strange men rushed past him. One, carrying a doctor's bag, quickly limped on crooked legs to the side of the writhing doorman. "I'm Doctor Sikes. Everyone, please move away."

The heirs heard a low groan, then a rasping rattle . . . then nothing.

"Sandy! Sandy!" Turtle screamed, pushing through the restraining hands. She looked down on the doorman sprawled at her feet. His face was twisted in rigid pain; his mouth gaped over the chipped front tooth. The taped glasses had fallen from his blue eyes that were locked in an unseeing stare. Suddenly his body straightened in one last violent twitch. His right eye closed, then opened again, and Sandy moved no more.

"He's dead," Doctor Sikes said, gently turning her away.

"Dead?" Judge Ford repeated numbly. How could she have been so wrong? So very wrong?

A sob tore through Turtle's soul as she ran to Baba's comforting arms. "Baba, Baba, I don't want to play anymore."

■ ■ ■ ■ ■ ■ ■ ■ ■ ■ ■ ■

The second stranger, the sheriff of Westing county, herded them back to the game room. Without thinking, the heirs seated themselves at the assigned tables.

Turtle sat quietly; it was Flora Baumbach's turn to weep. Crow waited. Only the throbbing veins in her tightly clasped hands told of her torment.

"Excuse me, sir," Ed Plum said. "I realize this may seem inappropriate, but according to Samuel W. Westing's will, I must read another document on the hour."

The sheriff checked his watch. What kind of a madhouse is this? And there's something mighty fishy about this cocky kid-lawyer calling in the middle of dinner, insisting that I hurry right over. That was half an hour before anybody died. "Go ahead," he grumbled.

Plum cleared his throat three times under the sheriff's suspicious glare.

> SIXTEENTH ● *I, Samuel W. Westing of Westingtown, born Sam "Windy" Windkloppel of Watertown (I had to change my name for business purposes. After all, who would buy a product called Windkloppel's Toilet Tissues? Would you?) do hereby declare that if no one wins, this will is null and void.*
>
> *So hurry, hurry, hurry, step right up and collect your prize. The lawyer will count off five minutes. Good luck and a happy Fourth of July.*

"Windkloppel, did someone say Windkloppel?" Grace Wexler slurred.

"I knew Westing wasn't an immigrant's name," Sydelle Pulaski said. "I knew it."

"The man was insane," Denton Deere diagnosed.

Shhh! They were struggling with their conscience. Millions and millions of dollars just for naming her name.

One minute is up!

The heirs stared at the answer: Berthe Erica Crow. A religious fanatic, maybe even crazy, but a murderer? They had no evidence that Westing was murdered, the judge said so.

Crow waited. She had not suffered enough for her sins, her penance was yet to begin.

Two minutes are up!

Two hundred million dollars, Turtle thought, but who gets it? The last part the lawyer read wasn't very businesslike. Besides, she could never peach on anybody, not even Crow. Who cares about anything anyhow—Sandy is dead, Sandy was her friend, now she'll never see him again—ever.

Judge Ford tried not to look at the empty chair at her table, McSouthers' chair. Her one concern was the safety of Crow. The judge watched the heirs and waited. Crow waited.

Three minutes are up!

Westing wasn't murdered, the judge said so, but what about Sandy? He was drinking from the flask Crow filled and he died choking. Poison?

Crow felt the eyes on her. The hating eyes. They scoffed at her beliefs, they joked about her soup kitchen. Only two people here mattered to her. She was so tired, so tired of waiting. Of waiting.

Four minutes are up!

"The answer is Berthe Erica Crow."

"No," Angela cried. "No, no!"

"She's crazy," Otis Amber shouted. "She don't know what she's saying."

"Yes I do, Otis," Crow said flatly and repeated her statement: "The answer is Berthe Erica Crow." She rose and turned to the confused lawyer. "I am Berthe Erica Crow. I am the answer and I am the winner. I give half of my inheritance to Otis Amber, to be used for the Good Salvation Soup Kitchen. I give the rest of the money to Angela."

■ **WESTING'S WAKE** ■

25

SANDY WAS DEAD. Crow had been arrested. The fourteen remaining heirs of Samuel W. Westing sat in Judge Ford's living room wondering what had happened.

"At least the guilt is not on our hands," Mr. Hoo said, trying to convince himself that a clear conscience was worth two hundred million dollars.

"Crow's going to jail," Otis Amber wailed, "and all you do is pat yourself on the back for not being a stoolie."

"Let me remind you that Crow confessed," Sydelle Pulaski reminded him.

"Crow only confessed to being the answer, nothing more," Angela said, pressing her hand against the tearing pain in her cheek.

"Even if Sam Westing wasn't murdered, like the judge said," Doug Hoo argued, "there was nothing wrong with Sandy until he drank from the flask Crow filled."

"If Crow is innocent," Theo said, "that means the murderer is still here in this room."

Flora Baumbach tightened her grip on Turtle, who was nestled in her arms.

"Poor Crow," Otis Amber muttered, "poor Crow."

"Poor Sandy, you should say," Turtle responded angrily. "Sandy's the one who's dead. Sandy was my friend."

"You should have remembered that before you kicked him," Denton Deere remarked.

"I never kicked Sandy, never."

The intern turned sideways in his chair in case of attack, but the kicker stayed slumped in sadness. "Well, someone kicked him today. That was one mean bruise he had on his shin."

"That's a lie, that's a disgusting lie," Turtle shouted. "The only person I kicked today was Barney Northrup and he deserved it. I didn't even see Sandy until tonight at the Westing house. Right, Baba?"

"That's right," Flora Baumbach said, handing Turtle a Westing Facial Tissue.

But Turtle was not about to cry again in front of everybody, like a baby. If only she could forget how he looked, suffering, dying: the twisted body, the chipped tooth, that horrible twitch, that one eye (that was the worst) that one eye blinking. Sandy used to wink at her like that when he was alive. When he was alive. Turtle blew her nose loudly to keep from sobbing.

"Sandy was my friend, too," Theo said. "I was playing chess with him in the game room, but he didn't know I knew."

"Why is everybody lying?" Turtle slumped further into Flora Baumbach's arm. Sandy was her friend, not Theo's. And Sandy didn't know how to play chess.

The judge, too, was surprised. "How can you be certain it was Mr. McSouthers you were playing with, Theo?"

"That's what partners are for. Doug watched the chess table to see who was moving the white pieces," Theo replied.

Again the track star thrust his I'm-number-one fingers high in the air.

Dumb jock, thought Mr. Hoo. Doesn't he realize this is a wake? But he is the champ. My son's the champ.

"Doug win," said Madame Hoo. They did not suspect her anymore. Good, very good. But it was so sad about the door guard.

Theo went on in a mournful voice. "I'm sort of glad Sandy didn't go back to the chessboard after my last move. He never knew he lost the game."

"Did you checkmate him?" the judge asked. Could she have been right about McSouthers after all? No. A disguise was one thing, but Sam Westing lose a game of chess? Never.

"Well, not exactly checkmate," Theo replied, "but Sandy would have had to resign. I took his queen."

The queen's sacrifice! The famous Westing trap. Judge Ford was certain now, but there were still too many unanswered questions. "I'm afraid greed got the best of you, Theo. By taking white's queen you were tricked into opening your defense. I know, I've lost a few games that way myself."

Theo recalled the position of the chessmen, thankful that his skin was too dark to reveal his blushing.

Turtle almost smiled. That Theo thinks he's so smart; well, Sandy showed him, Sandy beat him at chess. But Sandy didn't play chess. And she never kicked him either. Bucktoothed Barney Northrup was the one she kicked, not Sandy. But Sandy had the sore shin. Bucktoothed, chip-toothed, the crooked false teeth in the dentist's office (Sandy's dentist). "Cheer up, my friend, the game's not over. You still can win. I hope you do." Those were the last words Sandy said to her. He winked when he said that. Winked! One eye winked! Dead Sandy had winked at her!

Sandy had winked!

"Oh my," Flora Baumbach exclaimed as Turtle suddenly bolted from her arms.

"Angela, could I see your copy of the will?"

Angela handed it over (she could not refuse her sister anything, now).

■ ■ ■ ■ ■ ■ ■ ■ ■ ■ ■ ■

Turtle leaned against the dark window, poring over Sydelle Pulaski's transcript of the will:

> FIRST. I returned to live among my
> friends and my enemies. I came home to

> seek my heir, aware that in doing so I
> faced death. And so I did.

"To seek my heir," Turtle repeated to herself.

> Today I have gathered together my
> nearest and dearest, my sixteen nieces
> and nephews (Sit down, Grace Windsor
> Wexler!) to view the body of your Uncle
> Sam for the last time.
>   Tomorrow its ashes will be scattered
> to the four winds.

Winds? "Windkloppel," Turtle said aloud. Her mother had been right all along about being related to Sam Westing.

"Windkloppel," Grace mumbled. Jake patted her head.

"Windkloppel," the judge repeated. At least she could explain that. "Crow married a man named Windkloppel, who then changed his name to Westing. Berthe Erica Crow is the former wife of Samuel W. Westing. They had one child, a daughter, who drowned the night before her wedding. It was rumored that she killed herself rather than marry the man her mother had chosen for her. If Sam Westing blamed his wife for their daughter's death, then the sole purpose of this game was to punish Crow."

Crow was Sam Westing's ex-wife? The heirs found that hard to believe. "Then why would Mr. Westing give her a chance to inherit the estate?" Theo asked.

"M-maybe he wanted his enemies to for-g-give him," Chris said.

"Ha!" said Mr. Hoo, one of the enemies.

Turtle read on:

> SECOND. I, Samuel W. Westing, hereby swear
> that I did not die of natural causes. My life
> was taken from me—by one of you!

> The police are helpless. The culprit is far
> too cunning to be apprehended for this
> dastardly deed.

"What does dastardly mean?"

"Oh my!" Flora Baumbach was relieved to hear Jake Wexler define the word as "cowardly."

> I, alone, know the name. Now it is up to
> you. Cast out the sinner, let the guilty
> rise and confess.

> THIRD. Who among you is worthy to be
> the Westing heir? Help me. My soul shall
> roam restlessly until that one is found.

For the first time since Sandy died, Turtle smiled.

Judge Ford sat in glassy-eyed thought, elbows propped on the desk top, her chin resting on her folded hands. Why, indeed, was Crow an heir? Sam Westing could have pointed his clues at the Sunset Towers cleaning woman without naming her an heir.

"Crow's not going to inherit anything, not if she's in jail for murder," Otis Amber complained bitterly. "All your talk about chess and sacrificing queens. Crow's the one who's been sacrificed."

"What did you say?" the judge asked.

"I said Crow's the one who's been sacrificed."

Uttering a low groan, Judge Ford sank her head in her hands. The queen's sacrifice! She had fallen for it again. Westing had sacrificed his queen (Crow), distracting the players from the real game. Sam Westing was dead, but somehow or other he would make his last move. She knew it; she felt it deep in her bones. Sam Westing had won the game. "Stupid, stupid, stupid!"

The heirs stared in amazement. First they are told that Samuel W. Westing was married to their cleaning woman, now a judge is calling herself stupid. It couldn't be true.

"Sam Westing wasn't stupid," Denton Deere declared. "He was insane. The last part of the will was sheer lunacy. *Happy Fourth of July,* it said. This is November."

"It's November fifteenth," Otis Amber cried. "It's poor Crow's birthday."

Turtle looked up from the will. Crow's birthday? Sandy had bought a striped candle for his wife's birthday, a three-hour candle. The game is still on! Sam Westing came back to seek his heir. "You can still win. I hope you do," he said. How? How? *It is not what you have, it's what you don't have that counts.* Whatever it was she didn't have, she'd have to find it soon. Without letting the others know what she was looking for. "Judge Ford, I'd like to call my first witness."

■ **TURTLE'S TRIAL** ■

26

HOO WAS FURIOUS. "Haven't we had enough game-playing," he complained. "And led by a confessed bomber, no less."

Judge Ford rapped for silence with the walnut gavel presented to her by associates on her appointment to a higher court. Higher court? This was the lowest court she had ever presided at: a thirteen-year-old lawyer, a court stenographer who records in Polish, and the judge in African robes. Oh well, she had played Sam Westing's game, now she would play Turtle's game. The similarity was astounding; Turtle not only looked like her Uncle Sam, she acted like him.

"Ladies and gentlemen," Turtle began, "I stand before this court to prove that Samuel W. Westing is dead and that Sandy McSouthers is dead, but Crow didn't do it."

159

Pacing the floor, hands behind her back, she confronted each of the heirs in turn with a hard stare. The heirs stared back, not knowing if they were the jury or the accused.

Grace Wexler blinked up at her daughter. "Who's that?"

"The district attorney," Jake replied. "Go back to sleep."

Now frowning, now smiling a secret smile, Turtle acted the part of every brilliant lawyer she had seen on television who was about to win an impossible case. The only flaw in her imitation was an occasional rapid twist of her head. (She liked the grown-up feeling of shorter hair swishing around her face.)

"Let me begin at the beginning," she began. "On September first we moved into Sunset Towers. Two months later, on Halloween, smoke was seen rising from the chimney of the deserted Westing house." Her first witness would be the person most likely to have watched the house that day. "I call Chris Theodorakis to the stand."

Chris lay a calm hand on the Bible and swore to tell the truth, the whole truth, and nothing but the truth. What fun!

"You are a birdwatcher, Mr. Theodorakis, are you not?"

"Yes."

"Were you birdwatching on October thirty-first?"

"Yes."

"Did you see anyone enter the Westing house?"

"I s-saw s-somebody who limped."

Good, now she was getting somewhere. "Who was that limping person?"

"It was D-doctor Sikes."

"Thank you, you are excused." Turtle turned to her audience. "Doctor Sikes was Sam Westing's friend, a witness to the will, and his accomplice in this game. On the day in question he limped into the Westing house to build a fire in the fireplace. Why?" Her next witness might answer that.

■ ■ ■ ■ ■ ■ ■ ■ ■ ■ ■

Judge Ford instructed the witness to remove his aviator's helmet. His gray hair was tousled but barbered. "And place your gun in the custody of the court."

"Oh my!" Flora Baumbach gasped as Otis Amber unzipped his plastic jacket, pulled a revolver from his shoulder holster, and handed it to the judge, who locked the gun in her desk drawer.

Turtle was as startled as the other tenants. "Mr. Amber," she began bravely, "it seems that we are not all who we say we are. In other words, who exactly are you?"

"I am a licensed private investigator."

"Then why were you disguised as an idiot delivery boy?"

"It was my disguise."

Turtle was dealing with a practiced witness. "Mr. Amber, who employed you?"

"That's privileged information."

The judge interceded. "It would be best to cooperate, Mr. Amber. For Crow's sake."

"I had three clients: Samuel W. Westing, Barney Northrup, and Judge J. J. Ford."

Turtle stumbled over her next question. "What were you hired to do and when and what did you find out? Tell us everything you know." It was unsettling to see Otis Amber act like a normal human being.

"Twenty years ago, after his wife left him, Samuel W. Westing hired me to find Crow, keep her out of trouble, and make sure she never used the Westing name. I assumed this disguise for that purpose. I mailed in my reports and received a monthly check from the Westingtown bank until last week, when I was notified that my services were no longer needed. But Crow still needs me, and I'll stick by her, no matter what. I've grown fond of the woman; we've been together such a long time."

"How and why did Barney Northrup hire you?"

"Amber is second in the phone book under *Private Investigators;* maybe Joe Aaron's phone was busy that day. Anyhow, Barney Northrup wanted me to investigate six people."

"What six?"

"Judge J. J. Ford, George Theodorakis, James Hoo, Gracie Windkloppel, Flora Baumbach, and Sybil Pulaski. I made a mistake on the last one; I wasn't aware of the mix-up until I looked into Crow's early life for the judge. It seems I confused a Sybil Pulaski with a Sydelle Pulaski."

"Would you please repeat that," the court stenographer asked.

"Sydelle Pulaski," Otis Amber repeated, then turned to the judge. "I couldn't tell you about Crow's relationship to Sam Westing—conflict of interest, you understand."

Judge Ford understood very well. Sam Westing had predicted every move she would make. That's why Otis Amber, with his privileged information, was one of the heirs; that and to convince Crow (the queen) to play the game.

Turtle had more questions. "Are you saying that Barney Northrup didn't ask you to investigate Denton Deere or Crow or Sandy?"

"That's right. Denton Deere turned up in my report on Gracie Windkloppel—the Wexlers. Barney Northrup said he was looking to hire a cleaning woman for Sunset Towers, good pay and a small apartment, so I recommended Crow. I don't know how Sandy got the doorman's job."

"Mr. Amber, you were also hired by Judge Ford, I assume to find out who everybody really was. Did you investigate all sixteen heirs for the judge?"

"I didn't investigate the judge or her partner."

The judge bristled at the reminder of her stupidity.

"Therefore," Turtle continued, "you have never investigated the man we knew as Sandy McSouthers for any of your clients?"

"Never."

"One more question." It was the question she had planned to ask before learning that Otis Amber was not who he seemed to be. "On the afternoon of Halloween, when we were watching the smoke in the Westing house chimney, you told a story about a corpse on an Oriental rug."

"I saw it," Grace Wexler cried, "I saw him."

Turtle forgot the rules of the court and hurried to her mother. "Who did you see, Mom? Who? Who?"

(Terrified by the who's, Madame Hoo slipped away.)

"The doorman," Grace replied, lifting her dazed face to her husband. "He was dead. On an Oriental rug, Jake. It was awful."

Jake stroked his wife's hair. "I know, Gracie, I know."

Turtle returned to her witness. "Mr. Amber, did you tell that spooky story to dare one of us to go to the Westing house that night?"

"Not really. Sandy told me the story that morning, and we decided to scare you kids with it, being Halloween."

"Thank you, Mr. Amber, you may step down." (*Step down* was a term used in court; the floor was level here.) Turtle turned to her baffled audience. "A fire was started in the fireplace to call attention to the deserted house. Then a spooky story was told to dare someone to go into the house. That someone was me. I sneaked in the house, followed Dr. Sikes' whispers, and found the corpse of Samuel W. Westing in bed. I now call D. Denton Deere to the stand."

■ ■ ■ ■ ■ ■ ■ ■ ■ ■ ■

Turtle stared at her most unfavorite heir. "Intern Deere, you saw the body of Samuel W. Westing in the coffin. Did he appear to have been poisoned?"

"I could not say; he was embalmed."

"You are under oath, Intern Deere. Do you swear that the body of Samuel W. Westing was embalmed?"

What kind of a trick question was that? "I cannot swear to it, no. I did not examine the body in the coffin."

"Could the body in the coffin, which you did not examine, have been no body at all? Could it have been a wax dummy dressed in the costume of Uncle Sam?"

"I am not an expert on wax dummies."

"Yes or no?"

"Yes, it's possible, anything is possible." What's the brat driving at? Or is she just trying to make a fool of me?

"Intern Deere, you may not be an expert in wax dummies, but you are an expert in medical diagnosis, and you did examine the body of Sandy McSouthers. Correct?"

"Yes to the first question, no to the second. I did not examine Sandy; I tried to make him comfortable until help arrived. He was still alive when Doctor Sikes took over."

Turtle turned quickly to conceal her smile. "But surely you saw enough symptoms to make one of your famous diagnosises." She peered at the judge from the corner of her eye. That last word didn't sound right.

"Coronary thrombosis," the intern diagnosed, "but that's just an educated guess. In simple language: heart attack."

"Then Sandy could not have died of an overdose of lemon juice, which is what I saw Crow put in his flask?" Turtle could have called on Angela to testify to that, but she didn't want her screwy sister confessing all over the place.

"I never heard of anyone dying as a result of lemon juice consumption," the expert replied.

"One more question, Intern Deere. Do you swear that Sandy had a bruise on his shin resulting from a kick?"

"Absolutely. I should know, having been the recipient of such a kick myself."

"You may step down."

■ ■ ■ ■ ■ ■ ■ ■ ■ ■ ■

"I call Sydelle Pulaski to the stand. SYDELLE PULASKI!"

Overcome with excitement, the secretary had to be helped to her feet for the oath-taking.

"Ms. Pulaski, I must compliment you on your good thinking in taking down the will in shorthand."

"Professional habit."

"This looks professional, all right. The typing is perfect— well, almost perfect. It seems you left out the last word in section three:

> The estate is at the crossroads. The heir
> who wins the windfall will be the one
> who finds the

"Finds the what, Ms. Pulaski? Finds the what?"

Sydelle squirmed under Turtle's hard stare. Leave it to the brat to discover my one error. "There was so much talking I couldn't hear the last word."

"Come now, Ms. Pulaski, you claim to be a professional."

Hounding the witness and doing it quite well, Judge Ford thought, coming to the secretary's defense. "I don't think anyone heard the word, Turtle. Mr. McSouthers made a joke about ashes at that point."

"You are excused, Ms. Pulaski," Turtle said offhandedly, her eyes on the will. The judge was right. Sandy had joked about ashes scattered to the winds. Winds, Windy Windkloppel, no, it still didn't make sense. *It is not what you have, it's what you don't have that counts*—maybe no word was ever there. She read on:

> FOURTH. Hail to thee, O land of
> opportunity! You have made me, the
> son of poor immigrants, rich, powerful,
> and respected.
>   So take stock in America, my heirs,
> and sing in praise of this generous
> land. You, too, may strike it rich who
> dares play the Westing game.

<u>FIFTH</u>. Sit down, Your Honor, and read
the letter this brilliant young attorney
will now hand over to you.

"Judge Ford, could you introduce as evidence the letter that brilliant young attorney handed over to you?"

"It is just the usual certification of sanity, signed by Doctor
Sikes," the judge replied as she removed the envelope from her files.
But the letter was gone; the envelope now contained a receipt:

Check received, November 1	$ 5,000
Check received, November 15	+5,000
Total amount paid by Judge Ford	$10,000
Cost of educating Josie-Jo Ford	-10,000
Amount owed to Sam Westing	0

"I'm afraid the original letter has been replaced by a personal
message. It has no bearing on this case, and . . ."

"Yes, please." A trembling Madame Hoo stood before the judge.
"For to go to China," she said timidly, setting a scarf-tied bundle
on the desk. Weeping softly, the thief shuffled back to her seat.

The judge unknotted the scarf and let the flowered silk float
down around the booty: her father's railroad watch, a pearl
necklace, cuff links, a pin and earrings set, a clock. (Grace Wexler's silver cross never did turn up.)

"My pearls," Flora Baumbach exclaimed with delight.
"Wherever did you find them, Madame Hoo? I'm so grateful."

Madame Hoo did not understand why the round little lady
was smiling at her. Cautiously she peered through her fingers.
Oh! The other people did not smile. They know she is bad. And
Mr. Hoo, his anger is drowned in shame.

"Perhaps stealing is not considered stealing in China," Sydelle
Pulaski said in a clumsy gesture of kindness.

The judge rapped her gavel. "Let us continue with the case on hand. Are you ready, counselor?"

"Yes, Your Honor, in a minute." Turtle approached the frightened thief. "Here, you can keep it."

With shaking hands Madame Hoo took the Mickey Mouse clock from Turtle and clutched the priceless treasure to her bosom. "Thank you, good girl, thank you, thank you."

"That's okay."

The heirs were anxious for the trial to continue. They pitied the poor woman, but the scene was embarrassing.

■ ■ ■ ■ ■ ■ ■ ■ ■ ■ ■

One half hour to go. Turtle was so close to winning she could feel it, taste it, but still the answer eluded her. "Ladies and gentlemen, who was Sam Westing?" she began. "He was poor Windy Windkloppel, the son of immigrants. He was rich Sam Westing, the head of a huge paper company. He was a happy man who played games. He was a sad man whose daughter killed herself. He was a lonely man who moved to a faraway island. He was a sick man who returned home to see his friends and relatives before he died. And he did die, but not when we thought he did. Sam Westing was still alive when the will was read."

The judge rapped for order.

Turtle continued. "The obituary, probably phoned in to the newspaper by Westing himself, mentioned two interesting facts. One: Sam Westing was never seen after his car crashed. Two: Sam Westing acted in Fourth of July pageants, fooling everybody with his clever disguises. Therefore I submit that Sam Westing was not only alive, Sam Westing was disguised as one of his own heirs.

"No one would recognize him. With that face bashed in from the car crash, his disguise could be simple: a baggy uniform, a chipped front tooth, broken eyeglasses."

Sandy?

Does she mean Sandy?

The judge had to pound her gavel several times.

"Yes, ladies and gentlemen," Turtle went on, "Sam Westing was none other than our dear friend Sandy, the doorman. But Sam Westing did not drink, you say. Neither did Sandy. I used his flask on Halloween and there was a funny aftertaste in my pop, but not of whiskey; I know how whiskey tastes, because I use it for toothaches. It was medicine. Sandy was a sick man, and the flask was part of his disguise, but it also contained the medicine that kept him alive."

Turtle surveyed her stupefied audience. Good, they bought her little fib. "As I said earlier, I saw Crow fill the flask with lemon juice in the kitchen, but I saw something even more interesting on my way back to the game room: I saw Sandy coming out of the library. Sam Westing, as Sandy, wrote the last part of the will *after* the answers were given, then locked it in the library desk with a duplicate key.

"But what about the murder, you ask," Turtle said, even though no one had asked. "There was no murder. The word murder was first mentioned by Sandy, to put us off the track. *I did not die of natural causes,* the will says. *My life was taken from me—by one of you!* Sam Westing's life was taken from him when he became Sandy McSouthers. And Sandy died when his medicine ran out." Turtle paused in a pretense of letting the heirs mull over her last words, trying to figure out what to do next.

Why did Turtle leave out Barney Northrup, the judge wondered. She knows Northrup and McSouthers were the same man because of the bruised shin. Either she doesn't want to confound the jury, or she has no more idea than I have why Sam Westing had to play two roles.

Why did Sam Westing have to play *two* roles, Turtle wondered. He had a big enough part as the doorman without playing the real-estate man as well. Why *two* roles? No, not two, three. Windy Windkloppel took three names; one: Samuel W. Westing; two: Barney Northrup; three: Sandy McSouthers.

The judge had a question. "Surely Mr. McSouthers could have had his prescription refilled, or are you implying he committed suicide?"

"Pardon me?" Turtle was searching the will.

> The estate is at the crossroads. The heir
> who wins the windfall will be the one
> who finds the
>
> FOURTH.

That's it, that has to be it: *The heir who wins the windfall will be the one who finds the fourth!* Windy Windkloppel took four names, and she knew who the fourth one was! Keep calm, Turtle Alice Tabitha-Ruth Wexler. Slowly, very slowly, turn toward the judge, act dumb, and ask her to repeat the question. "I'm sorry, Your Honor, would you repeat the question?"

Turtle knows something. The judge had seen that expression before. Sam Westing used to look like that just before he won a game. "I asked if you consider Sandy's death a suicide."

"No, ma'am," Turtle said sadly. Very sadly. "Sandy McSouthers–Sam Westing suffered terribly from a fatal disease. He was a dying man who chose his time to die. Let me read from the will:

> SIXTH. Before you proceed to the game
> room there will be one minute of silent
> prayer for your good old Uncle Sam.

"Ladies and gentlemen, heirs (for we all inherited something), let us bow our heads in silent prayer for our benefactor Sam Westing, alias Sandy the doorman."

"Crow!" Otis Amber leaped to his feet as Ed Plum led the cleaning woman through the door.

27

HIS AVIATOR'S HELMET again flapping over his ears, Otis Amber danced up to his soup-kitchen companion, flung his arms around the taut body, and squeezed her tightly. "Hey Crow old pal, old pal, old pal."

"They said I was innocent, Otis. They said I was innocent," she replied vaguely.

Angela, too, wanted to hug her in welcome, but closeness was not possible for either of them. Instead, Angela offered a crooked smile. Crow nodded and lowered her eyes, only to raise them to Madame Hoo, clutching a Mickey Mouse clock. "Things very good," Madame Hoo said, extending her free hand and shaking Crow's hand up and down.

"It was all a regrettable mistake," Ed Plum explained to the judge. "Can you imagine, that sheriff wanted to arrest me, not Crow—me, Edgar Jennings Plum—he wanted to arrest the attorney! Fortunately, the coroner determined that Mr. McSouthers died of a heart attack, as did Samuel W. Westing."

"Then Turtle's right," Theo said. "There was no murder. The coroner was part of the plot."

Ed Plum had no idea what Theo was talking about. Masking his ignorance with arrogance, he continued. "I had my suspicions about this entire affair from the start. I came here for one reason only: to announce my resignation from all matters regarding the Westing estate, with sincere apologies to all concerned."

"Wasn't there a last document?" Judge Ford asked, knowing that Sam Westing had to make his last move.

"Yes, but as I no longer take a legal interest . . ."

"Please turn it over to the court."

Baffled by the word "court," the lawyer set the envelope on the desk and found his way out of Sunset Towers.

Without once clearing her throat, Judge Ford proceeded to read the final page of the will of Samuel W. Westing.

SEVENTEENTH • *Good-bye, my heirs. Thanks for the fun and games. I can rest in peace knowing I was loved as your jolly doorman.*

EIGHTEENTH • *I, Samuel W. Westing, otherwise known as Sandy McSouthers and others, do hereby give and bequeath all the property and possessions in my name as follows:*

To all of you, in equal shares, the deed to Sunset Towers;

And to my former wife, Berthe Erica Crow, the ten-thousand-dollar check forfeited by table one, and two ten-thousand-dollar checks endorsed by J. J. Ford and Alexander McSouthers.

NINETEENTH • *The sun has set on your Uncle Sam. Happy birthday, Crow. And to all of my heirs, a very happy Fourth of July.*

Judge Ford set the document down. "That's it."

That's it? What about the two hundred million dollars, the heirs wanted to know.

"We lost the game," the judge explained, staring at Turtle, her face a mask of sad, childlike innocence as she nestled once again in Flora Baumbach's arms. "I think."

Turtle rose and walked to the side window, seeking the Westing house, which stood invisible in the moon-clouded night. (Hurry up, Uncle Sam, I can't keep up this act much longer. The candle must have burned through the last stripe by now.)

Behind her the discontented heirs grumbled: He made fools of us all. He played us like puppets. He was a g-good m-man. He was a vengeful man, a hateful man. Windkloppel? He tricked us, the cheat. A madman, stark raving mad.

"Oh my, oh my, just listen to you," Flora Baumbach said. "You each have ten thousand dollars more than you started with and an apartment building to boot. The man is dead, so why not think the best?"

BOOM!

BOOM!

BOOM!

"Happy Fourth of July," Turtle shouted as the first rockets lit up the Westing house, lit up the sky.

BOOM-BOOM-BOOM-BOOM.

BOOM!!!

The heirs gathered around Turtle at the window.

BOOM! Stars of all colors bursting into the night, silver pinwheels spinning, golden lances up-up-BOOM! crimson flashes flashing blasting, scarlet showers BOOM! emerald rain BOOM! BOOM! orange flames, red flames leaping from the windows, sparking the turrets, firing the trees. . . .

"BOOM!" cried Madame Hoo, clapping her hands with delight.

The great winter fireworks extravaganza, as it came to be called, lasted only fifteen minutes. Twenty minutes later the Westing house had burned to the ground.

"Happy birthday, Crow," Otis Amber said, reaching for her hand.

■ ■ ■ ■ ■ ■ ■ ■ ■ ■ ■ ■

The orange glow of the morning sun had just begun its climb up the glass front of Sunset Towers when Turtle set out to collect the prize. She pedaled north past the cliff, still smoldering with the charred remains of the Westing house. Reaching the crossroads, she turned into the narrow lane whose twisting curves mimicked the shoreline.

The heir who wins the windfall will be the one who finds the fourth. It was so simple once you knew what you were looking for. Sam *West*ing, Barney *North*rup, Sandy Mc*South*ers (west, north, south). Now she was on her way to meet the fourth identity of Windy Windkloppel. She could probably have figured out the address, too, instead of looking it up in the Westingtown phone book—there it was, number four Sunrise Lane.

A long driveway, its privacy guarded by tall spruce, led to the modern mansion of the newly elected chairman of the board of Westing Paper Products Corporation. Turtle climbed the stairs, rang the bell, and waited. The door opened.

Turtle felt her first grip of panic as she confronted the crippled doctor. Could she have been wrong? "I'd like to see Mr. Eastman, please," she said nervously. "Tell him Turtle Wexler is here."

"Mr. Eastman is expecting you," Doctor Sikes said. "Go straight down the hall."

The hall had an inlaid marble floor (no Oriental rugs). Reaching its end, she entered a paneled library (this one filled with books). There he was, sitting at the desk.

Julian R. Eastman rose. He looked stern. And very proper. He wore a gray business suit with a vest, a striped tie. His shoes were shined. He limped as he walked toward her, not the crooked limp of Doctor Sikes, just a small limp, a painful limp. Again Turtle was gripped by panic. He seemed so different, so important. She shouldn't have kicked him (the Barney Northrup him). He was coming closer. His watery-blue eyes stared at her over his rimless half-glasses. Hard eyes. His teeth were white, not quite even (no one would ever guess they were false). He was smiling. He wasn't angry with her, he was smiling.

"Hi, Sandy," Turtle said. "I won!"

■ AND THEN . . . ■

28

TURTLE NEVER TOLD. She went to the library every Saturday afternoon, she explained (which was partly true). "Make your move, Turtle, you don't want to be late for the wedding."

The ceremony was held in Shin Hoo's restaurant. Grace Wexler, recovered from a world-record hangover, draped a white cloth over the liquor bottles and set a spray of roses on the bar. No drinks would be served today.

Radiant in her wedding gown of white heirloom lace, the bride walked down the aisle, past the tables of well-wishers, on the arm of Jake Wexler. Mr. Hoo, the best man, beamed with pride at her light footsteps as he supported the knee-knocking, nervous groom.

A fine red line of a scar marked Angela's check, but she looked content and lovely as ever in her pale blue bridesmaid's gown. The other bridesmaid wore pink and yellow with matching crutches.

The guests cried during the wedding and laughed during the reception. Flora Baumbach smiled and cried at the same time. "You did a good job altering the wedding dress, Baba," Turtle said, which made the dressmaker cry even harder.

"A toast to the bride and groom," Jake announced, raising his glass of ginger ale. "To Crow and Otis Amber!"

The heirs of Uncle Sam Westing clinked glasses with the members of the Good Salvation Soup Kitchen, sobered up for this happy occasion. "To Crow and Otis Amber!"

■ ■ ■ ■ ■ ■ ■ ■ ■ ■ ■ ■

Apartment 4D was bare. For the last time Judge Ford stared out the side window to the cliff where the Westing house once stood. She would never solve the Westing puzzle; perhaps it was just as well. Her debt would finally be repaid—with interest; the money she received from the sale of her share of Sunset Towers would pay for the education of another youngster, just as Sam Westing had paid for hers.

"Hi, Judge Ford, I c-came to say g-good-bye," Chris said, wheeling himself through the door.

"Oh hello, Chris, that was nice of you, but why aren't you studying? Where's your tutor?" She looked at the binoculars hanging from his neck. "You haven't been birdwatching again, have you? There will be plenty of time for birds later; first you must catch up on your studies if you want to get into a good school." Good heavens, she was beginning to sound like Mr. Hoo.

"Will you c-come to see m-me?" Chris asked. "It g-gets sort of lonely with Theo away at c-college."

The judge gave him one of her rare smiles. He was a bright youngster ("Real smart," Sandy had said), he had a good future (Sandy had said that, too), he needed her influence and the extra money, but she might smother him with her demands. "I'll see you when I can, and I'll write to you, Chris. I promise."

■ ■ ■ ■ ■ ■ ■ ■ ■ ■ ■ ■

Hoo's Little Foot-Eze (patent pending) was selling well in drugstores and shoe repair shops.

"Once we capture the Milwaukee market I'll take you to China," James Hoo promised his business partner.

"Okay," Madame Hoo replied, toting up accounts on her abacus. No hurry. She had many friends in Sunset Towers now. And no more cooking, no more tight dresses slit up her thigh. Her husband had bought her a nice pantsuit to wear when they called on customers, and for her birthday Doug had given her one of his medals to wear around her neck.

■ ■ ■ ■ ■ ■ ■ ■ ■ ■ ■ ■

The secretary to the president of Schultz Sausages was back on the job. Her ankle mended, Sydelle Pulaski had discarded her crutches. She had all the attention she could handle without them; after all, she was an heiress now. (It wasn't polite to ask how much, but everyone knew Sam Westing had millions.) Of course she could retire to Florida, she said, but what would poor

Mr. Schultz do without her? And then one unforgettable Friday Mr. Schultz, himself, took her to lunch.

■ ■ ■ ■ ■ ■ ■ ■ ■ ■ ■ ■

Jake Wexler had given up his private practice (both private practices) now that he had been appointed consultant to the governor's inquiry panel for a state lottery (thanks to a recommendation by Judge Ford). Grace was proud of him, and his daughters were doing well. In fact everything was fine, just fine.

Hoo's On First was a great success. Grace Wexler, the new owner, offered free meals to the sports figures who came to town, and everyone wanted to eat where the athletes ate. The restaurant's one windowless wall was covered with autographed photographs of Brewers, Packers, and Bucks. Grace straightened the framed picture of a smiling champion, signed: *To Grace W. Wexler, who serves the number-one food in town—Doug Hoo.* She certainly was a lucky woman: a respected restaurateur, wife of a state official, and mother of the cleverest kid who ever lived. Turtle was going to be somebody someday.

A narrow scar remained, and would always remain, on Angela's cheek. It was slightly raised, and she had developed a habit of running her fingers along it as she pored over her books. Enrolled in college again, she lived at home to save money for the years of medical school ahead. She had returned the engagement ring to Denton Deere; she had not seen him since Crow's wedding. Ed Plum had stopped calling after ten refusals. Angela had neither the time nor the desire for a social life what with studying, her weekly shopping date with Sydelle, and Sundays spent helping Crow and Otis in the soup kitchen.

"Study, study, study," Turtle said.

Angela saw little of her sister, who was either at school, in Flora Baumbach's apartment, or at the library. "Hi, Turtle, how come you're so happy today?"

"The stock market jumped twenty-five points."

The newlyweds, Crow and Otis Amber, moved into the apartment above the Good Salvation Soup Kitchen. The storefront mission had been renovated and expanded with the money from the inheritance. Grace Wexler had supervised the decorations: copper pots hung from the ceiling; the pews were padded with flowered cushions and fitted with hymnbook pockets and drop-leaf trays. There was meat in the soup and fresh bread every day.

■ FIVE YEARS PASS ■

29

THE FORMER DELIVERY boy danced into the Hoos' new lakefront home. "Let's give a cheer, the Ambers are here!" Otis came to celebrate Doug's victory, wearing the old zippered jacket and aviator's helmet. He had even let a stubble grow on his chin. The only thing missing was his delivery bike (they had come in the soup-kitchen van).

"Thank you for the generous donation, Mr. Hoo. God bless you," Crow said. "Otis and I distributed the innersoles among our people. It helped their suffering greatly." She looked worn, her skin pulled tight against the fragile bones, and she still wore black.

Mr. Hoo, on the other hand, was stouter and less angry. In fact, he was almost happy. Business was booming. Milwaukee loved Hoo's Little Foot-Eze, and so did Chicago and New York and Los Angeles, but he still had not taken his wife to China.

Theo Theodorakis, graduate of journalism school, cub reporter, held up the newspaper, hot off the press:

OLYMPIC HERO COMES HOME

Four columns were devoted to the history and achievement of the gold medal winner who had set a new record for the 1500-

meter run. Theo had not actually written the article on the local hero, but he had sharpened pencils for the reporter who did.

"Take a bow, Doug," Mr. Hoo said, beaming.

Doug leaped on a table and thrust his index fingers high in the air. "I'm number one!" he shouted. The Olympic gold medal hung from his neck, confetti from the parade dotted his hair. The Westing heirs cheered.

■ ■ ■ ■ ■ ■ ■ ■ ■ ■ ■

"Hello, Jake, I'm so glad you could come," Sunny (as Madame Hoo was now called) said, shaking the hand of the chairman of the State Gambling Commission.

"Boom!" Jake Wexler replied.

■ ■ ■ ■ ■ ■ ■ ■ ■ ■ ■

"Hello, Angela." Denton Deere had grown a thick moustache. He was a neurologist. He had never married.

"Hello, Denton." Angela's golden hair was tied in a knot on the nape of her neck. She wore no makeup. She was completing her third year of medical school. "It's been a long time."

"Remember me?" Sydelle Pulaski wore a red and white polka-dot dress and leaned on a red and white polka-dot crutch. She had sprained her knee dancing a tango at the office party.

"How could I ever forget you, Ms. Pulaski?" Denton said.

"I'd like you to meet my fiancé, Conrad Schultz, president of Schultz Sausages."

"How do you do."

■ ■ ■ ■ ■ ■ ■ ■ ■ ■ ■

"Judge Ford, I'd like you to meet my friend, Shirley Staver." Chris Theodorakis was in his junior year at college. A medication, recently discovered, kept his limbs steady and his speech well controlled. He sat in a wheelchair, as he always would.

"Hello, Shirley," the judge said. "Chris has written so much about you. I'm sorry I'm such a poor correspondent, Chris; I found myself in a tangle of cases this past month." She was a judge on the United States Circuit Court of Appeals.

"Chris and I were both chosen to go on a birdwatching tour to Central America this summer," Shirley said.

"Yes, I know."

■ ■ ■ ■ ■ ■ ■ ■ ■ ■ ■

For old times' sake Grace Wexler catered the party herself and passed among the guests with a tray of appetizers. She owned a chain of five restaurants now: Hoo's On First, Hoo's On Second, Hoo's On Third, Hoo's On Fourth, Hoo's On Fifth.

"Who's that attractive young woman talking with Flora Baumbach?" Theo asked.

"Why, that's my daughter Turtle. She's really grown up, hasn't she? Second year of college and she's only eighteen. Calls herself T. R. Wexler now."

T. R. Wexler was radiant. Earlier that day she had won her first chess game from the master.

■ THE END? ■

30 TURTLE SPENT THE night at the bedside of eighty-five-year-old Julian R. Eastman. T. R. Wexler had a master's degree in business administration, an advanced degree in corporate law, and had served two years as legal counsel to the Westing Paper Products Corporation. She had made one million dollars in the stock market, lost it all, then made five million more.

"This is it, Turtle." His voice was weak.

"You can die before my very eyes, Sandy, and I wouldn't believe it."

"Show some respect. I can still change my will."

"No you can't. I'm your lawyer."

"That's the thanks I get for that expensive education. How's the judge?"

"Judge Ford has just been appointed to the United States Supreme Court."

"What do you know, honest Josie-Jo on the Supreme Court. She was a smart kid, too, but she never once beat me at chess. Tell me about the others, Turtle. How's poor, saintly Crow?"

"Crow and Otis are still slopping soup," Turtle fibbed. Crow and Otis Amber had died two years ago, within a week of each other.

"And that funny woman with the painted crutches, what's her name?"

"Sydelle Pulaski Schultz. She and her husband moved to Hawaii. Angela keeps in touch."

"Angela. And how is your pretty sister, the bomber?"

Turtle never knew he knew. "Angela is an orthopedic surgeon." Julian R. Eastman was an old man, but suddenly his mind, too, was old. For the first time since the Westing game he was wearing the dentures with the chipped front tooth. He had turned back to his happiest times. Sandy was dying, he was really dying. Turtle held back her tears. "Angela and Denton Deere are married. They have a daughter named Alice."

"Alice. Doesn't Flora Baumbach call you Alice?"

"She used to, she calls me T. R. as everyone does."

"How is the dressmaker, Turtle? Tell me about them, tell me about all of them."

Flora Baumbach had given up dressmaking when she moved in with Turtle years ago. "Baba is well, everyone is well. Mr. and Mrs. Theodorakis (remember, they had the coffee shop in Sunset

Towers), they retired to Florida. Chris and his wife Shirley teach ornithology at the university. They're both professors. Chris discovered a new subspecies on his last trip to South America; it's named after him: the something-Christos parrot."

"The something-Christos parrot, I like that. And the track star? Has he won any more medals?"

"Two Olympic golds in a row. Doug is a sports announcer on television."

"And how is Jimmy Hoo's invention going? I gave him the idea, you know."

"It looks like a real winner, Sandy." Mr. Hoo, too, was dead. Sunny Hoo finally made her trip to China, but returned to carry on the business.

"And tell me about my niece, Gracie Windkloppel. Does she still think she's a decorator?"

"Mom went into the restaurant business, has a chain of ten. Nine are quite successful. I keep telling her to give up on Hoo's On Tenth, to cut her losses, but she's stubborn as ever. I guess she hangs on to it because it's in Madison, to be near Dad. He's now the state crime commissioner."

"He's well qualified for the job. And your husband, how's his writing coming along?"

He had remembered. "Theo's doing fine. The first novel sold about six copies, but it got great reviews. He's just about finished with his second book."

"And when are you two going to have children?"

"Some day." Turtle and Theo had decided against having children because of the possibility of inheriting Chris's disease. "If it's a boy we'll name him Sandy, and if it's a girl, well, I guess we can name her Sandy, too."

The old man's voice was barely audible now. "Did you say Angela had a little girl?"

"Yes, Alice, she's ten years old."

"Is she pretty like her mother?"

"I'm afraid not, she looks a lot like you and me."

"Turtle?"

"Yes, Sandy."

"Turtle?"

"I'm right here, Sandy." She took his hand.

"Turtle, tell Crow to pray for me."

His hand turned cold, not smooth, not waxy, just very, very cold.

Turtle turned to the window. The sun was rising out of Lake Michigan. It was tomorrow. It was the Fourth of July.

■ ■ ■ ■ ■ ■ ■ ■ ■ ■ ■ ■

Julian R. Eastman was dead; and with him died Windy Windkloppel, Samuel W. Westing, Barney Northrup, and Sandy McSouthers. And with him died a little of Turtle.

No one, not even Theo, knew her secret. T. R. Wexler was understandably sad over the death of the chairman of the board of the Westing Paper Products Corporation. She had been his legal adviser; she would inherit his stock and serve as a director of the company until the day she, too, would be elected chairman of the board.

Veiled in black, she hurried from the funeral services. It was Saturday and she had an important engagement. Angela brought her daughter, Alice, to the Wexler-Theodorakis mansion to spend Saturday afternoons with her aunt.

There she was, waiting for her in the library. Baba had tied red ribbons in the one long pigtail down her back.

"Hi there, Alice," T. R. Wexler said. "Ready for a game of chess?"